JOYCE CAROL OATES is a recipient of the National Book Critics Circle Lifetime Achievement Award, the National Book Award and the PEN/Malamud Award, and has been nominated for the Pulitzer Prize. Her books include *We Were the Mulvaneys*, *The Falls* and, most recently, *The Sacrifice* and *The Lost Landscape*. Her memoir *A Widow's Story* was a critically acclaimed bestse
of Humanities at Princeton U

NOVELS BY JOYCE CAROL OATES

With Shuddering Fall (1964)

A Garden of Earthly Delights (1967)

Expensive People (1968)

them (1969)

Wonderland (1971)

Do with Me What You Will (1973)

The Assassins (1975)

Childwold (1976)

Son of the Morning (1978)

Unholy Loves (1979)

Bellefleur (1980)

Angel of Light (1981)

A Bloodsmoor Romance (1982)

Mysteries of Winterthurn (1984)

Solstice (1985)

Marya: A Life (1986)

You Must Remember This (1987)

American Appetites (1989)

Because It Is Bitter, and Because It Is My Heart (1990)

Black Water (1992)

Foxfire: Confessions of a Girl Gang (1993)

What I Lived For (1994)

Zombie (1995)

We Were the Mulvaneys (1996)

Man Crazy (1997)

My Heart Laid Bare (1998)

Broke Heart Blues (1999)

Blonde (2000)

Middle Age: A Romance (2001)

I'll Take You There (2002)

The Tattooed Girl (2003)

The Falls (2004)

Missing Mom (2005)

Black Girl / White Girl (2006)

The Gravedigger's Daughter (2007)

My Sister, My Love (2008)

Little Bird of Heaven (2009)

Mudwoman (2012)

The Accursed (2013)

Carthage (2014)

The Sacrifice (2015)

THE MAN WITHOUT A SHADOW

JOYCE CAROL OATES

FOURTH ESTATE • *London*

Fourth Estate
An imprint of HarperCollins*Publishers*
1 London Bridge Street
London SE1 9GF

www.4thestate.co.uk

First published in Great Britain by Fourth Estate in 2016

First published in the United States by Ecco in 2016

1

A catalogue record for this book is
available from the British Library

ISBN 978-0-00-816538-3

Designed by Shannon Nicole Plunkett

Printed and bound in Great Britain by
Clays Ltd, St Ives plc

MIX
Paper from
responsible sources
FSC® C007454

FSC™ is a non-profit international organisation established to promote
the responsible management of the world's forests. Products carrying the
FSC label are independently certified to assure consumers that they come
from forests that are managed to meet the social, economic and
ecological needs of present and future generations,
and other controlled sources.

Find out more about HarperCollins and the environment at
www.harpercollins.co.uk/green

TO MY HUSBAND CHARLIE GROSS,
MY FIRST READER

The annihilation is not the terror.
The journey is the terror.

—ELIHU HOOPES

THE MAN WITHOUT A SHADOW

CHAPTER ONE

NOTES ON AMNESIA: PROJECT "E.H." (1965–1996)

She meets him, she falls in love. He forgets her.

She meets him, she falls in love. He forgets her.

She meets him, she falls in love. He forgets her.

At last she says good-bye to him, thirty-one years after they've first met. On his deathbed, he has forgotten her.

HE IS STANDING on a plank bridge in a low-lying marshy place with his feet just slightly apart and firmly on his heels to brace himself against a sudden gust of wind.

He is standing on a plank bridge in this place that is new to him and wondrous in beauty. He knows he must brace himself, he grips the railing with both hands, tight.

In this place new to him and wondrous in beauty yet he is fearful of turning to see, in the shallow stream flowing beneath the bridge, behind his back, the drowned girl.

. . . naked, about eleven years old, a child. Eyes open and sightless, shimmering in water. Rippling-water, that makes it seem that the

girl's face is shuddering. Her slender white body, long white tremulous legs and bare feet. Splotches of sunshine, "water-skaters" magnified in shadow on the girl's face.

SHE WILL CONFIDE in no one: "On his deathbed, he didn't recognize me."

She will confide in no one: "On his deathbed, he didn't recognize me but he spoke eagerly to me as he'd always done, as if I were the one bringing him hope—'Hel-*lo?*' "

BRAVELY AND VERY publicly she will acknowledge—*He is my life. Without E.H., my life would have been to no purpose.*

All that I have achieved as a scientist, the reason you have summoned me here to honor me this evening, is a consequence of E.H. in my life.

I am speaking the frankest truth as a scientist and as a woman.

She speaks passionately, yet haltingly. She seems to be catching at her breath, no longer reading from her prepared speech but staring out into the audience with moist eyes—blinded by lights, puzzled and blinking, she can't see individual faces and so might imagine his face among them.

In his name, I accept this great honor. In memory of Elihu Hoopes.

At last to the vast relief of the audience the speech given by this year's recipient of the Lifetime Achievement Award of the American Psychological Association has ended. Applause is quick and scattered through the large amphitheater like small flags flapping in a weak, wayward wind. And then, as the recipient turns from the podium, uncertain, confused—in belated sympathy the applause gathers and builds into a wave, very loud, thunderous.

She is startled. Almost for a moment she is frightened.

Are they mocking her? Do they—*know*?

Stepping blindly away from the podium she stumbles. She has left behind the heavy and unwieldy eighteen-inch cut-crystal trophy in the shape of a pyramid, engraved with her name. Quickly a young person comes to take the trophy for her, and to steady her.

"Professor Sharpe! Watch that step."

"Hel-*lo!*"

Here is the first surprise: Elihu Hoopes greets Margot Sharpe with such eager warmth, it's as if he has known her for years. As if there is a profound emotional attachment between them.

The second surprise: Elihu Hoopes himself, who is nothing like Margot Sharpe has expected.

It is 9:07 A.M., October 17, 1965. The single defining moment of Margot Sharpe's life as it will be the single defining moment of Margot Sharpe's career.

Purely coincidentally it is the eve of Margot Sharpe's twenty-fourth birthday—(about which no one here in Darven Park, Pennsylvania, knows, for Margot has uprooted her midwestern life and cast it among strangers)—when she is introduced by Professor Milton Ferris to the amnesiac patient Elihu Hoopes as a student in Professor Ferris's neuropsychology laboratory at the university. Margot is the youngest and most recent addition to the renowned "memory" laboratory; she has been accepted by Ferris as a first-year graduate student, out of numerous applicants, and she is dry-mouthed with anticipation. For weeks, she has been reading material pertinent to *Project E.H.*

Yet, the amnesiac E.H. is so friendly, and so gentlemanly, Margot feels comforted at once.

The man is unexpectedly tall—at least six feet two. He is

straight-backed, vigorous. His skin exudes a warm glow and his eyes appear to be normal though Margot knows that the vision in his left eye is very poor. He is not at all the impaired individual Margot has expected to meet, who had to relearn a number of basic physical skills since the devastating injury to his brain just fifteen months before, when he was thirty-seven.

Margot thinks that E.H. emanates an air of manly *charisma*—that mysterious quality to which we respond instinctively without being able to explain. He is even well dressed, preppy-style, in clean khakis, a long-sleeved linen shirt, oxblood moccasins with patterned cotton socks—in contrast to other patients at the Institute whom Margot has glimpsed lolling about in hospital gowns or rumpled civilian wear. She has been told that E.H. is a descendant of an old, distinguished Philadelphia family named Hoopes, onetime Quakers who were central to the Underground Railway in the years preceding the Civil War; E.H. has a large, extended family in the area, but no wife, children, parents.

Elihu Hoopes is something of an artist, Margot has learned. He has sketchbooks, he keeps a journal. In his former lifetime he'd been a partner in a family-owned investment firm in Philadelphia but before that he'd been a student at Union Theological Seminary and a civil rights activist and supporter. Is it strange that Elihu Hoopes is unmarried, at nearly forty? Margot wonders if this somewhat patrician individual has had a history of relationships with women in which the women were found wanting, and cast aside—never guessing that his time for love, marriage, fathering children would come so abruptly to an end.

Camping alone on an island in Lake George, New York, the previous summer, E.H. was infected by a particularly virulent strain of herpes simplex encephalitis, that usually manifests itself as a cold sore on a lip, and fades within a few days; in E.H.'s case, the viral infection traveled along his optic nerve and into his brain, resulting in a prolonged high fever that ravaged his memory.

Unfortunately E.H. lingered too long before calling for help. Like a morbidly curious scientist he'd recorded his temperature in a notebook, in pencil—(the highest recorded reading was 103.1 degrees F)—before he'd collapsed.

This was ironic: a macho self-destructiveness. Like the premature death of the painter George Bellows who'd been reluctant to leave his studio to get help, though stricken by appendicitis.

In the vast Adirondack region there'd been no first-rate hospital, no adequate medical treatment for such a rare and catastrophic infection. By the time the delirious and convulsing man had been brought by ambulance to the Albany Medical Center Hospital where emergency surgery was performed to reduce the swelling in his brain it was already too late. Something essential had been destroyed in his brain, and the damage appears to be irreversible. (It is Milton Ferris's hypothesis that the damaged region is the small seahorse-shaped structure called the hippocampus, located just above the brain stem and contiguous with the cerebral cortex, about which not much is yet known, but which seems to be essential for the consolidation and storage of memory.) And so, E.H. can form no new memories, and his memories of the past are erratic and uncertain; in clinical terms E.H. suffers from partial retrograde amnesia, and total anterograde amnesia. Though he continues to test high on standardized I.Q. tests, and despite his seemingly normal appearance and manner, E.H. is incapable of "remembering" new information for more than seventy seconds; often, it is less than seventy seconds.

Seventy seconds! A nightmare to contemplate.

The only consolation, Margot thinks, is that E.H. is a highly congenial person, and seems to thrive upon the attentions of strangers. The nature of his affliction at least precludes mental anguish—(so Margot thinks). His memories of the distant past are sometimes vividly detailed and oneiric; more recent memories (for approximately eighteen months preceding his illness) are likely to be cloudy and indistinct; both have been described as "mildly dissociative"—as if belonging to another person, not E.H. The subject is susceptible to moods, but a very limited range of moods; his affect has flattened, as a caricature is a flattened portrait of the complexity of human personality.

(Uncannily, E.H. will always recall events out of his past in the same way, using the same vocabulary; but he is never altogether certain if he is remembering correctly, even when external verification confirms that he is remembering correctly.)

Though E.H. doesn't consistently remember certain of his relatives (whose faces are altering with time), he can identify the faces of famous people in photographs (if they predate his illness). At times, he demonstrates a remarkable, *savant*-like memory for recitations: statistics, historical dates, song lyrics, comic-strip characters and film dialogue (he is said to have memorized the entirety of the silent film *Potemkin*), passages from poems memorized in school (Whitman's "When Lilacs Last in the Dooryard Bloom'd" is his favorite) and from revered American speeches (Abraham Lincoln's *Gettysburg Address,* Franklin Delano Roosevelt's *The Only Thing We Have to Fear Is Fear Itself* and *Four Freedoms,* Martin Luther King, Jr.'s *I Have a Dream*). He retains curiosity for "news"—watches TV news, each day reads at least two newspapers including the *New York Times* and the *Philadelphia Inquirer*—without the ability to remember any of it. Each day he completes the *New York Times* crossword puzzle as (his family has attested) he'd only occasionally taken time to complete the puzzle before his illness. ("Eli didn't have that kind of time to waste.")

Without seeming to think at all E.H. can recite multiplication tables, solve algebra problems without using a pencil, add up lengthy columns of numbers. It isn't a surprise to learn that "Elihu Hoopes" had been a successful businessman in a highly competitive field.

Margot thinks that it is difficult to feel for this healthy-seeming man the visceral pity one might feel for a (visibly) handicapped person, for E.H.'s loss is far more subtle. In fact, though E.H. has been told repeatedly that he has a severe neurological deficit, it doesn't seem that he quite understands that there is anything significant wrong with him—why he feels compelled to keep a notebook, for instance, as he'd begun to do after his illness.

Already Margot Sharpe has begun to keep a notebook herself. This will be a quasi-private document, primarily scientific, but partially a diary and journal, stimulated by her participation in Milton Ferris's memory lab; through her career she will draw upon the material of the notebook, or rather notebooks, for her scientific papers and publications. "Notes on Amnesia: Project E.H." will run into many notebooks to be eventually transcribed into a computer file to be continued to the very day of E.H.'s death (November 26, 1996) and beyond charting the fate of the amnesiac's posthumous brain after it has been removed—very carefully!—from its skull.

But on this morning in October 1965 in the University Neurological Institute at Darven Park, Pennsylvania, all of Margot Sharpe's life as a scientist lies before her. Introduced to "E.H." she is dry-mouthed and tremulous as one who has been brought to the edge of a precipice to see a sight that dazzles her eyes.

Will my life begin, at last? My true life.

IN SCIENCE IT is understood that there are *significant* matters, and there are *trivial* matters.

So too in the matter of lives.

For it is a fact not generally, not publicly acknowledged: we have lives that are *true lives,* and we have lives that are *accidental lives.*

Perhaps it is rare that an individual discovers his *true life* at any age. Perhaps it is usually the case that an individual lives *accidentally* through an entire life. In terms of its consequence to what is called society or posterity, the *accidental life* is scarcely more than an addition of zeroes.

This is not to suggest that an *accidental life* is equivalent to a *trivial life.* Such lives may be enjoyable, and fulfilling: we all want to love and to be loved and within our families, and within a small circle of friends, we may feel ourselves cherished, thus exalted. But such lives pass away leaving the larger world untouched. There is scarcely a ripple, there is no shadow. There will be no memory of the merely *accidental.*

Margot Sharpe has come from a family of *accidental lives.* This family, in semi-rural north-central Ojibway County, Michigan, in a region of *accidental lives.* Yet already as a child of twelve she'd determined that she would not live so uncalculated a life as the lives of those who surrounded her and her way of discovering her *true life* would be through leaving her hometown Orion Falls, and her family, as soon as that was possible.

In Orion Falls young people may go away—to enlist in the armed forces, to branches of the state university, to nursing school, and so forth; but they all return. Margot Sharpe knows that she *will not return.*

Margot has always been curious, highly inquisitive. Her first, favorite book was the illustrated *Darwin for Beginners* which she'd discovered on a library shelf, aged eleven. Here was a book with a magical story—"evolution." Another favorite book of her childhood was *Marie Curie: A Woman in Physics.* In high school she'd happened to read an article on B. F. Skinner and "behaviorism" that had intrigued and excited her. She has always asked questions for which there are not ready answers. To be a scientist, Margot thinks, is to know which questions to ask.

From the great Darwin she learned that the visible world is an accumulation of facts, conditions: results. To understand the world you must reverse course, to discover the processes by which these results come into being.

By reversing the course of time (so to speak) you acquire mastery over time (so to speak). You learn that "laws" of nature are not mysteries but knowable as the exits on Interstate 75 traversing the State of Michigan north and south.

Is it unjust, ironic?—that catastrophe in one life (the ruin of E.H.) precipitates hope and anticipation in others (Milton Ferris's "memory" lab)? The possibility of career advancement, success?

It is the way of science, Margot thinks. A scientist searches for her subject as a predator searches for her prey.

At least, no one had introduced the encephalitis virus into Elihu Hoopes's brain with the intention of studying its terrible consequences, as Nazi doctors might have done; or performed radical psychosurgery on him for some presumably beneficial purpose. Chimps and dogs, cats and rats have been so experimented upon, in great numbers, and for a while in the 1940s and 1950s there'd been a vogue of prefrontal lobotomies on hapless human beings, with frequently catastrophic (if not very accurately recorded) results.

Sometimes the radical changes caused by lobotomies were perceived, by the families of the patients at least, to be "beneficial." A rebellious adolescent becomes abruptly tractable. A sexually adventurous adolescent (usually female) becomes passive, pliant, asexual. An individual prone to outbursts of temper and obstinacy becomes childlike, docile. "Beneficial" for family and for society is not always so for the individual.

In the case of Elihu Hoopes it seems likely that a personality change of a radical sort had been precipitated by his illness, for no adult male of E.H.'s achievement and stature would be so trusting and childlike, so touchingly and naively *hopeful*. You have the uneasy feeling, in E.H.'s presence, that here is a man desperate to *sell himself*—to be *liked*. The change in E.H. is allegedly so extreme that his fiancée broke off their engagement within a few months of his illness, and E.H.'s family, relatives, friends visit him ever less frequently. He lives in the affluent Philadelphia suburb Gladwyne with an aunt, the younger sister of his (deceased) father, herself a "rich" widow.

From personal experience Margot knows that it is far easier to accept a person ravaged by physical illness than one ravaged by memory loss. Far easier to continue to love the one than the other.

Even Margot who'd loved her "great-grannie" so much as a little girl had balked at being taken to visit the elderly woman in a nursing home. This is not something of which Margot is particularly proud, and so she has begun a process of forgetting.

But E.H. is very different from her elderly relative suffering from (it would be diagnosed after her death) Alzheimer's. If you didn't know the condition of E.H. you would not immediately guess the severity of his neural deficit.

Margot wonders: Was E.H.'s encephalitis caused by a mosquito bite? Was it a particular species of mosquito? Or—is it a common mosquito, itself infected? In what other ways is herpes simplex encephalitis transmitted? Have there been other instances of such infections in the Lake George, New York, region? In the Adirondacks? She supposes that research scientists in the Albany area are investigating the case.

"How horrible! The poor man . . ."

It is the first thing you say, regarding E.H. When you are safely out of his earshot.

Or rather, it is the first thing Margot Sharpe says. Her lab colleagues are more adjusted to E.H. for they have been working with him for some time.

Nervously Margot smiles at the stricken man, who does not behave as if he understands that he is *stricken.* She smiles at him, which inspires him to smile at her, with a flash of something like familiarity. (She thinks: He isn't sure if he should know me. He is looking for cues from me. I must not send him misleading cues.)

Margot is new to such a situation. She has never been in the presence of a living "subject." She can't help but feel pity for E.H., and horror at his predicament: how abruptly Elihu Hoopes was transformed from being an attractive, vigorous, healthy man in the prime of life to a man near death, losing more than twenty pounds, white blood count plummeting, extreme anemia, delirium. A herpes simplex infection resulting in encephalitis is so rare, E.H. might more readily have been struck by lightning.

Yet E.H.'s manner isn't at all guarded, wary, or stiff; he might be a host welcoming guests to his home, whose names he doesn't quite recall. Indeed he seems at home in the Institute setting—at least, he doesn't seem disoriented. For these sessions at the Institute E.H. is brought from his aunt's suburban home near Philadelphia by an attendant, in a private car; originally E.H. was a patient at the Institute, and then an outpatient; he is still under the medical care of Institute staff. Though E.H. recognizes no one, yet it is flattering to him, how so many people recognize *him.*

He seems to have little capacity for brooding, as he has lost his capacity for self-reflection. Margot is touched by the way he pronounces her name—"Mar-*go*"—as if it were a beautiful and unique name and not a harsh spondee that has always somewhat embarrassed her.

Though Milton Ferris hasn't intended for the introduction of his youngest lab member to be anything more than a fleeting *pro forma* gesture, E.H. takes pleasure in drawing out the ritual. He shakes her hand in a way both courtly and caressing. And unmistakably he leans close to Margot as if inhaling her.

"Welcome—'Margot Sharpe.' You are a—new doctor?"

"No, Mr. Hoopes. I'm a graduate student in Professor Ferris's lab."

Quickly E.H. amends: " 'Graduate student—Professor Ferris's lab.' Yes. I knew that."

In an enthusiastic voice E.H. repeats Margot's words precisely, as if they were a riddle to be decoded.

Individuals who are memory-challenged can contend with the handicap by repeating facts or strings of words—"rehearsing." But Margot wonders if E.H.'s repetitions carry with them comprehension, or only rote mimicry.

To the brain-damaged man, much in ordinary life must be fraught with mystery at all times—where is he? What is this place? Who are the people who surround him? Beyond these perplexities is the larger, greater mystery of his very existence, his survival after near-death, which is (Margot supposes) too profound for him to consider. The amnesiac with a very limited short-term memory is like one who stands so close to a mirror that his face is virtually pressed against it—he cannot "see" himself.

Margot wonders what E.H. sees, looking into a mirror. Is his face a surprise to him, each time? *Whose face?*

It is touching, too—(though this might be attributable to the man's neurological deficit and not his gentlemanly nature)—that, in his attitude toward his visitors, E.H. makes no distinction between the least consequential person in the room (Margot Sharpe) and the most consequential (Milton Ferris); he has lost his instinctive capacity for *ranking.* It isn't clear what he makes of Ferris's other assistants, or rather "associates" (as Ferris would call them: *de facto* they are "assistants") whom he has met before: another, older female graduate student, several postdoctoral fellows, and an allegedly brilliant young assistant professor who is Ferris's protégé at the Institute and has published several important papers with him in neuroscience journals.

E.H. is slow to surrender Margot Sharpe's hand. He continues to stand close beside Margot as if surreptitiously sniffing her hair, her body. Margot is uneasy, for she doesn't want to annoy Milton Ferris; she knows that her supervisor is waiting for an opportunity to initiate the morning's testing, which will require several hours in the Institute testing-room, even as E.H. in his concentration upon the young, black-haired, attractive woman seems to have forgotten the reason for his guests' visit.

(It occurs to Margot to wonder if a brain-damaged person might be likely to compensate for memory loss with a heightened olfactory sense? A plausible and exciting possibility which she might one day explore, Margot thinks.)

(The amnesiac subject is clearly far more interested in Margot than in the others—she hopes that his interest isn't just frankly sexual. It occurs to her to wonder if the subject's sexuality has been affected by his amnesia, and in what way . . .)

But E.H. speaks to her in a kindly manner, as if she were a young girl.

" 'Mar-*go*.' I think you were in my grade school class at Gladwyne Day—'Mar-go Madden'—unless it was 'Margaret Madden' . . ."

"I'm afraid not, Mr. Hoopes."

"No? Really? Are you sure? This would have been in the late 1930s. In Mrs. Scharlatt's sixth-grade class you sat at the front, far left by the window. You had silver barrettes in your hair. *Margie Madden*."

Margot feels her face heat. It is just not the flirtation that makes her uneasy but a kind of complicity of hers, as of the others who are listening, in their reluctance to tell E.H. frankly of his condition.

It would be Dr. Ferris's obligation to tell him this; or rather, to tell him again. (For E.H. has been told many times.)

"I—I'm afraid not . . ."

"Well! Will you call me 'Eli'? Please."

" 'Eli.' "

"Thank you! That's very kind."

E.H. consults a little notebook he keeps in a pocket of his khakis, and jots down a note. He holds the notebook at a slight, subtle angle so that no one can see what he is writing; yet not so emphatically an angle that the gesture is insulting to Margot.

Margot has been told that the amnesiac has been keeping notebooks since he'd recovered from his illness and was strong enough to hold a pen in his hand. So far he has accumulated many dozens of these small notebooks as well as sketchbooks measuring forty-eight inches by thirty-six inches; he never arrives at the Institute without both of these. Apparently the notebook and the sketchbook serve different functions. In the notebooks E.H. jots down stray facts, names, times and dates; he inserts columns torn from magazines and newspapers from the fourth-floor lounge. (Male staffers who use the fourth-floor men's restroom report finding such detritus there each day that E.H. is on the premises—that is how they know, they say, that "your fancy amnesiac" has been there.) The sketchbooks are for drawings.

The complex neurological skills needed for reading, writing, and mathematical calculation seem not to have been much affected by E.H.'s illness, as they were acquired before the infection. So E.H. reads brightly from the notebook: " 'Elihu Hoopes attended Amherst College and graduated summa cum laude with a double major in economics and mathematics . . . Elihu Hoopes has attended Union Theological Seminary and has a degree from the Wharton School of Business.' " E.H. reads this statement as if he has been asked to identify himself. Seeing his visitors' carefully neutral expressions he regards them with a little tic of a smile as if, for just this moment, he understands the folly and pathos of his predicament, and is begging their indulgence. *Forgive me!* The amnesiac has learned to gauge the mood of his visitors, eager to engage and entertain them: "I know this. I know who I am. But it seems reasonable to check one's identity frequently, to see if it is still there." E.H. laughs as he snaps the little notebook shut and slips it back into his pocket, and the others laugh with him.

Only Margot can barely bring herself to laugh. It seems to her cruel somehow.

There is laughter, and there is laughter. Not all laughter is equal.

Laughter too depends upon memory—a memory of previous laughter.

Dr. Ferris has told his young associates that their subject "E.H." will possibly be one of the most famous amnesiacs in the history of neuroscience; potentially he is another Phineas Gage, but in an era of advanced neuropsychological experimentation. In fact E.H. is far more interesting neurologically than Gage whose memory had not been severely affected by his famous head injury—the penetration of his left frontal lobe by an iron rod.

Dr. Ferris has cautioned them against too freely discussing

E.H. outside their laboratory, at least initially; they should be aware of their "enormous good fortune" in being part of this research team.

Though she is only a first-year graduate student Margot Sharpe doesn't have to be told that she is fortunate. Nor does Margot Sharpe need to be told not to discuss this remarkable amnesiac case with anyone. She does not intend to disappoint Milton Ferris.

Ferris and his assistants are preparing batteries of tests for E.H., of a kind that have never before been administered. The subject is to remain pseudonymous—"E.H." will be his identity both inside and outside the Institute; and all who work with him at the Institute and care for him are pledged to confidentiality. The Hoopes family, which has donated millions of dollars to the University of Pennsylvania's School of Medicine, has given permission exclusively to the University Neurological Institute at Darven Park for such testing so long as E.H. is willing and cooperative—as indeed, he appears to be. Margot doesn't like to think that a kicked dog, yearning for human approval and love, desperate for a connection with the "normal," could not be more eagerly cooperative than the dignified Elihu Hoopes, son of a wealthy and socially prominent Philadelphia family.

Elihu Hoopes is trapped in a perpetual present, Margot thinks. Like a man wandering in circles in a twilit woods—a man without a shadow.

And so he is thrilled to be saved from such a twilight and made the center of attention even if he doesn't know quite why. How otherwise does the amnesiac know that he exists? Alone, without the stimulation of attentive strangers asking him questions, even the twilight would fade, and he would be utterly lost.

" 'MARGO NOT-MADDEN'?—THAT is your name?"

At first Margot can't comprehend this. Then, she sees that E.H. is attempting a sort of joke. He has taken out his little notebook again, and has painstakingly inscribed in it what appears to be a diagram in logic. One category, represented by a circle, is M M and a second category, also represented by a circle, is M Not-M. Between the two circles, which might also be balloons, since strings dangle from them, is a broken line.

"My days of mastering symbolic logic seem to have abandoned me," E.H. says pleasantly, "but I think the situation is something like this."

"Oh—yes . . ."

How readily one humors the impaired. Margot will come to see how, within the amnesiac's orbit, as within the orbit of the blind or the deaf, there is a powerful sort of pull, depending upon the strength of will of the afflicted.

Still, Margot is uncertain how to respond. It is a feeble and somehow gallant attempt at humor but she doesn't want to encourage the amnesiac subject in prevarication—she knows, without needing to be told, that her older colleagues, and Milton Ferris, will disapprove.

Also, an awkward social situation has evolved which involves caste: the (subordinate) Margot Sharpe has supplanted, in E.H.'s limited field of attention, the (predominant) Milton Ferris. It is even possible that the brain-damaged man (deliberately, craftily) has contrived to "neglect" Dr. Ferris who stands just at his elbow waiting to interrupt—("neglect" is a neurological term referring to a pathological blindness caused by brain damage); and so it is imperative that Margot ease away from E.H. so that Ferris can reassert himself as the (obvious) person in authority. Margot hopes to execute this maneuver as inconspicuously as possible without either the impaired man or the distinguished neuropsychologist seeing what she is doing.

Margot doesn't want to hurt E.H.'s feelings, even if his feelings are fleeting, and Margot doesn't want to offend Milton Ferris, the most distinguished neuroscientist of his generation, for her scientific career depends upon this fiercely white-bearded individual in his late fifties about whom she has heard "conflicting" things. (Milton Ferris is the most brilliant of brilliant scientists at the Institute but Milton Ferris is also an individual whom "you don't want to cross in any way, even inadvertently. Especially inadvertently.") As a young woman scientist, one of very few in the Psychology Department at the University, Margot knows instinctively to efface herself in such circumstances; as an undergraduate at the University of Michigan with a particular interest in experimental cognitive psychology, she absorbed such wisdom through her pores.

Also, it was abundantly clear: there were virtually no women professors in the Psychology Department, and none at all in Neuroscience at U-M.

Margot is not a beautiful young woman, she is sure. She has a distrust of conventional "beauty"—her more attractive girl-classmates in school were distracted by the attention of boys, in several cases their lives altered (young love, early pregnancies, hasty marriages). But Margot considers herself a canny young woman, and she is determined not to make mistakes out of naïveté. If E.H. is a kind of dog in his eagerness to please, Margot is not unlike a dog rescued from a shelter by a magnanimous master—one who must be assured, at all times, in the most subtle ways possible, that he is indeed *master*.

In his steely jovial way Milton Ferris is explaining to E.H.

that Margot is "too young" to have been a classmate of his in the late 1930s—"This young woman from Michigan is new to the university and new to our team at the Institute where she will be assisting us in our 'memory project.' "

E.H. frowns thoughtfully as if he is absorbing the information packed into this sentence. Affably he concurs: " 'Michigan.' Yes—that makes it unlikely that we were classmates at Gladwyne."

In the same way E.H. is trying to behave as if the term "memory project" is familiar to him. (Margot wonders if this persuasive and congenial persona has been a nonconscious acquisition in the amnesiac. She wonders whether testing has been done in the acquisition of such "memory" by individuals as brain-damaged as E.H.)

As Milton Ferris speaks expansively of "testing," E.H. exhibits eagerness and enthusiasm. Over the course of the past eighteen months he has been tested countless times by neurologists and psychologists but it isn't likely that he can remember individual sessions or tests. From before his injury he retains a general knowledge of what a "test" is—he knows what an "I.Q. test" is. From before his injury he might know that his I.Q. was once tested at 153, when he was eighteen years old; but he can't know that, after his injury, his I.Q. has been tested several times, and has been measured in the range of 149 to 157. Still of superior intelligence, at least theoretically.

This is fascinating to Margot: E.H.'s pre-injury vocabulary, language skills, and mathematical abilities have survived more or less intact but (it is said) he can't retain new words, concepts, or facts even if they are embedded in familiar information. He has been observed taking notes on the financial section of his favorite newspapers but when asked about what he has been inscribing a few minutes later he shrugs disdainfully—"*Homo sapiens* is the species that 'makes' and 'loses' money. What else is new?" He has forgotten what had so engrossed him but he can readily invent a substitute with which to disguise his memory loss.

At times E.H. seems to know that John F. Kennedy was assassinated recently—(two years ago)—while at other times E.H. speaks of "President Kennedy" as if the man were still alive—"Kennedy will need to revise his position on Cuba. He will need to lead the country *out of the quagmire of Vietnam*."

And, grandiloquently: "Some of us are hoping to get to Washington, to meet with the president. The situation is getting more and more urgent."

It would seem delusional except, as Ferris has noted, the Hoopes family of Philadelphia has long had ties with state and federal politicians.

Like many brain-afflicted individuals E.H. carries with him dictionaries and other word-books; he keeps long lists of words in his notebooks alphabetically arranged—that is, there are pages of A's, B's, C's, and so forth. (E.H. takes pleasure in consulting these when he does the *Times* crossword puzzle as, his family has attested, he'd never consulted a dictionary when doing the puzzle before his illness.) His proficiency in math is impressive. His knowledge of world geography is impressive. He can discuss rival economic theories—Keynesian, classical, Marxist; he likes to expound upon von Neumann's *Theory of Games and Economic Behavior,* key lines of which he has memorized. But if questioned he can only repeat more or less what he has already said; his ideas are fixed, like his vocabulary. No new ideas or revisions of the past can penetrate. And if he is challenged his affable nature vanishes and he becomes irritable, ironic. He is adept at board games and puzzles of a kind he'd mastered when he was a boy but he can't easily learn new games.

Margot supposes that if E.H. could reason more clearly he would assume that the repeated tests he undergoes constitute a kind of treatment or therapy that might allay his condition; but he can't know his "condition" though it has been explained to him repeatedly; and he can't know that the tests are in fact "repeated" or that they are for the sake of experimental research—that's to say for the sake of neuroscience and not for the sake of the subject.

Ferris is speaking carefully to E.H.: "Mr. Hoopes—Eli—let me explain again that I am a neuropsychologist who teaches at the University of Pennsylvania and these are members of my lab. We've been working with you for the past fifteen weeks here at the Institute at Darven Park, each Wednesday, and we have made some exciting preliminary discoveries. You have met me before, and we have gotten along splendidly! I am 'Milton Ferris'—"

E.H. nods vehemently, even a little impatiently, as if he knows all this: " 'Mil-ton Fer-ris'—yes. 'Dr. Ferris.' "

"I am not a 'doctor'—I am a professor. I have a Ph.D. of course but that is not essential! Please just call me—"

" 'Professor Fer-ris.' Yes."

"And I have explained—I am not a clinician."

This is a way of telling the subject *I am not a medical doctor. You are not my patient.*

But E.H. seems to purposefully misunderstand, awkwardly joking: "Well, Professor—that makes two of us. *I am not a clinician, either.*"

E.H. has spoken a little too loudly. Is this a way of signaling irritation with Professor Ferris? Since his attention has been forcibly removed from black-haired Margot Sharpe?

(Margot wonders too if E.H. is speaking quickly as if to signal, subliminally, that he isn't much interested in the information that Milton Ferris is providing him; despite his severe amnesia E.H. "remembers" enough from previous exchanges to know that he won't remember this information, either, thus resents being given it.)

While his visitors look on E.H. leafs through his little notebook until he comes to a crucial page. He smiles, showing the page to Margot rather than to Ferris—a drawing of two tennis players, one of them wildly flailing with his racket as a ball sails over his head. (Is this player meant to be E.H.? The player's hair and features suggest that this is so. And the other player, with a blurred face and exaggerated grin, is meant to be—Death?)

"This—'tennis'—I used to play. Pretty damned good on the Amherst team. Are we going to play 'tennis' now?"

"Eli, you're an excellent tennis player. You can play tennis another day. But right now, if you'd like to take a seat, and . . ."

" 'Excellent'? Is that so? But I have not played tennis in a long time, I think."

"In fact, Eli, you played tennis just last week."

Eli stares at Ferris. This is not what Eli has expected to hear and he seems incapable of absorbing it but without missing a beat Ferris says in a warm and uplifting voice, "Now, Eli, you've always trounced *me*. And it has been reported to me not only that you'd played with one of the best players on the staff but you'd won each game."

" 'Reported'—really!"

E.H. laughs, faintly incredulous.

Margot sees: the poor man is feeling the unease of one being made to understand that the most complete knowledge of himself can come only from the outside—from strangers.

A melancholy conviction, Margot thinks, to realize that you can't know yourself as reliably as strangers can know you!

Patiently Milton Ferris explains to E.H. why he has been brought to the Institute that morning, and why Ferris and his laboratory are going to be "testing" him—as they'd done in the past; E.H. listens politely at first, then becomes bemused and beguiled by Margot whom he has rediscovered: she is wearing a black wraparound skirt with black tights beneath, a black jersey pullover that fits her petite frame tightly, and black ballerina flats—the clothes of a schoolgirl dancer and not the crisp white lab coats of the medical staff or the dull-green uniforms of the nursing staff. There is no laminated ID on her lapel to inform him of her name.

Annoyed, Ferris says: "Whenever you'd like to begin, Mr. Hoopes—Eli. That's why we're here."

"Why you are here, Doctor. But why am I here?"

"You've enjoyed our tests in the past, Eli, and I think you will again."

"That's why I am here—to 'enjoy' myself?"

"We are hoping to establish some facts concerning memory. We are hoping to explore the question of whether memory is 'global' in the brain—not localized; or whether it is localized. And you have been helping us, Eli."

"Have they kicked me out of the office?—has someone taken my place? My brother Averill, and my uncle—" E.H. pauses as if, for a vexed moment, he can't recall the name of one of his Hoopes relatives, an executive at Hoopes & Associates, Inc.; then he rallies, with one of his enigmatic remarks: "Where else would I be, if I could be somewhere else?"

Milton Ferris assures E.H. that he is in "just the right place, at just the right time to make history."

"Did I tell you? I've heard Reverend King speak. Several times. That is 'history.'"

"Yes. An extraordinary man, Reverend King . . ."

"He spoke in Philadelphia on the steps of the Free Library, and he spoke in Birmingham, Alabama, at a Negro church that was subsequently burnt to the ground by white racists. He is a very brave man, a saint. He is a saint of *courage.* I intend to march with him again when my condition improves—as I've been promised."

"Of course, Eli. Maybe we can help arrange that."

"It's because I was clubbed on the head—billy clubbed—in Alabama. Did I show you? The scar, where my hair doesn't grow . . ."

E.H. lowers his head, flattens his thick dark hair to show them a faint zigzag line in his scalp. Margot feels an impulse to reach out and touch it—to stroke the poor man's head.

She understands—*It's loneliness he feels most.*

"Yes, you did show us your scar, Eli. You're a very lucky man to have escaped with your life."

"Am I! You think that's what I managed, Doctor—to 'escape with my life.' " E.H. laughs sadly.

Milton Ferris continues to speak with E.H., humoring him even as he soothes him. Margot can imagine Ferris calming an excited laboratory animal, a monkey for instance, as it is about to be "sacrificed."

For such is the euphemism in experimental science. The lab animals are not *killed,* certainly not *murdered:* they are *sacrificed.*

Shortly, in E.H.'s presence, you come to see that the amnesiac's smiling is less childlike and eager than desperate, and piteous. His is the eagerness of a drowning person hoping to be rescued by someone, anyone, with no idea what rescue might be, or from what.

In me he sees—something. A hope of rescue.

In profound neural impairments there may yet be isolated islands of memory that emerge unpredictably; Margot wonders if her face, her voice, her very scent might trigger dim memories in E.H.'s ruin of a brain, so that he feels an emotion for her that is as inexplicable to him as it might be to anyone else. Even as he tries to listen to Dr. Ferris's crisp speech he is looking longingly at Margot.

Margot has seen laboratory animals rendered helpless, though still living and sensate, after the surgical removal of parts of their brains. And she has read everything she could get her hands on, about amnesia in human beings. Still it is unnerving for her to witness such a condition firsthand, in a man who might pass, at a little distance, as normal-seeming—indeed, *charismatic.*

"Very good, Eli! Would you like to sit down at this table?"

E.H. smiles wryly. Clearly, he doesn't want to *sit down;* he is most at ease on his feet, so that he can move freely about the room. Margot can imagine this able-bodied man on the tennis court, fluid in motion, not wanting to be fixed in place and so at a disadvantage.

"Here. At this table, please. Just take a seat . . ."

" 'Take a seat'—where take it?" E.H. smiles and winks. He makes a gesture as if about to lift a chair; his fingers flutter and flex. Ferris laughs extravagantly.

"I'd meant to suggest that you might *sit in a chair. This chair.*"

E.H. sighs. He has hoped to humor this stranger with the fiercely white short-trimmed beard and winking eyeglasses who speaks to him so familiarly.

"Heil yes—I mean, hell yes—Doctor!"

E.H.'s smile is so affable, he can't have meant any insult.

As they prepare to begin the morning's initial test E.H.'s attention is drawn away from Margot who plays no role at all except as observer. And Margot has eased into the periphery of the subject's vision where probably he can't see her except as a wraith. She assumes that he has forgotten the names of others in the room to whom he'd been introduced—Kaplan, Meltzer, Rubin, Schultz. It is a relief to her not to be competing with Milton Ferris for the amnesiac's precarious attention.

After his illness E.H.'s performance on memory tests showed severe short-term loss. Asked by his testers to remember strings of digits, he wavered between five and seven. Now, months later, he can recall and recite nine numbers in succession, when required; sometimes, ten or eleven. Such a performance is within the normal range and one would think that E.H. is "normal"—his manner is calm, methodical, even rather robotic; then as complications are introduced, as lists become longer, and there are interruptions, E.H. becomes quickly confused.

The experiment becomes excruciating when lists of digits are interrupted by increasing intervals of silence, during which the subject is required to "remember"—not to allow the digits to slip out of consciousness. Margot imagines that she can feel the poor man straining not to lose hold—the effort of "rehearsing." She would like to clasp his hand, to comfort and encourage him. *I will help you. You will improve. This will not be your entire life!*

Impairment is the great leveler, Margot thinks. Eighteen months ago, before his illness, Elihu Hoopes would scarcely have glanced twice at Margot Sharpe. She is moved to feel protective toward him, even pitying, and she senses that he would be grateful for her touch.

Forty intense minutes, then a break of ten minutes before tests continue at an ever-increasing pace. E.H. is eager and hopeful and cooperative but as the tests become more complicated, and accelerated, E.H. is thrown into confusion ever more quickly (though he tries, with extraordinary valor, to maintain his affable "gentlemanly" manner). As intervals grow longer, he seems to be flailing about like a drowning man. His short-term memory is terribly reduced—as short as forty seconds.

After two hours of tests Ferris declares a longer break. The examiners are as exhausted as the amnesiac subject.

E.H. is given a glass of orange juice, which is his favorite drink. He hasn't been aware until now that he's thirsty—he drinks the juice in several swallows.

It is Margot Sharpe who brings E.H. the orange juice. This female role of nurturer-server is deeply satisfying to her for E.H. smiles with particular warmth at her.

She feels a mild sensation of vertigo. Surely, the amnesiac subject is perceiving *her*.

Restless, exhausted without knowing (recalling) why, E.H. stands at a window and stares outside. Is he trying to determine where he is? Is he trying to determine who these strangers are, "testing" him? He is a proud man, he will not ask questions.

Like an athlete too long restrained in a cramped space or like a rebellious teenager E.H. begins to circle the room. This behavior is just short of annoying—perhaps it is indeed annoying. E.H. ignores the strangers in the room. E.H. flexes his fingers, shakes his arms. He stretches the tendons in his calves. He reaches for the ceiling—stretching his vertebrae. He mutters to himself—(is he cursing?)—yet his expression remains affable.

"Mr. Hoopes? Would you like your sketchbook?"—one of the Institute staff asks, handing the book to him.

E.H. is pleased to see the sketchbook. E.H. is (perhaps) surprised to see the sketchbook. He pages through it frowning, holding the book in such a way to prevent anyone else seeing its contents.

Then, he discovers his little notebook in a shirt pocket. This he opens eagerly, and peruses. He records something in the notebook, and slips it back into his pocket. He looks into the sketchbook again, discovers something he doesn't like and tears it out, and crumples it in his hand. Margot is fascinated by the amnesiac's behavior: Is it coherent, to him? Is there a purpose to it? She wonders if, before his illness, he'd kept a little notebook like this one, and carried an oversized sketchbook around with him; possibly he had. And so the effort of remembering these now is not unusual.

If he believes himself alone, with no one close to observe him, E.H. ceases smiling. He's frowning and somber like one engrossed in the heart-straining effort of *trying to figure things out.*

Margot thinks how sad, how exhausting, the amnesiac can't remember that he has been involved in this effort for any sustained period of time. He might have been in this place for a few minutes, or a few hours. He seems to know that he doesn't live here, but he has no clear idea that he is living with a relative in Gladwyne and not by himself in Philadelphia as he'd been at the time of his illness.

No matter how many times a test involving rote memory is repeated, E.H. never improves. No matter how many times E.H. is given instructions, he has to be given the instructions yet another time.

The amnesiac's brain resembles a colander through which water sifts continually, and never accumulates; those years before his illness, which constitute most of the man's life of thirty-eight years, resemble a still, distant water glimpsed through dense foliage as in a hallucinatory landscape by Cézanne.

Margot wonders if there can be some residual, unfathomable memory in the part of E.H.'s brain that has been damaged? Whether, at the periphery of the damage, in adjoining tissue, some sort of neurogenesis, or brain repair, might take place? And could such neurogenesis be *stimulated*?

So relatively little is known of the human brain, after so many millennia! The brain is the only organ whose functions must be theorized from observed behavior, and whose basic physiology is scarcely comprehended at the present time—that is, 1965. Only animal brains can be examined "live"—primarily monkey brains. Invasive exploration of the (living, normal) human brain is forbidden. Margot wonders: Are complex memories distributed throughout the cerebral cortex, or localized?—and if localized, how? From what is known of E.H.'s brain, the hippocampus and adjacent tissue had been devastated by the viral infection—but have other parts of the brain remained unimpaired? Unless E.H. undergoes brain surgery, Margot thinks, or sophisticated scanning machines are developed to "X-ray" the brain, it isn't likely that the precise anatomy of E.H.'s brain will be known until after his death when the brain can be autopsied.

In that instant Margot feels a glimmer of horror, and excitement. She sees E.H. on a marble slab in a morgue: a corpse, skull sawed open. The pathologist will remove the brain that will be fixed, sectioned, stained, examined and analyzed by the neuroscientist.

She will be the neuroscientist.

E.H. glances worriedly at her as if he can read her thoughts. Margot feels her face burn like one who has dared to touch another intimately, and has been detected.

But I will be your friend, Mr. Hoopes!—Eli.

I will be the one you can trust.

"Unlocking the mystery of memory"—Margot Sharpe will be among the first.

With an uplifted forefinger, to retain Margot's attention, E.H. leafs through his little notebook in search of something significant. In his bright affable voice he reads:

"'There is no journey, and there is no path. There is no wisdom, there is emptiness. There is no emptiness.'" He pauses to add, "This is the wisdom of the Buddha. But there is no wisdom, and there is no Buddha." He laughs, with inexplicable good humor.

His examiners stare at him, unable to join in.

TESTING RESUMES. E.H. appears eager again, hopeful.

It is hard to comprehend: to the subject, the morning's adventure is only now beginning. He has forgotten that he is "tired."

Like appetite, "tiredness" depends much upon memory. Margot would not have believed this could be so—it seems unnatural!

A scientist soon learns: much in Nature is "unnatural."

At this midpoint Milton Ferris departs. He has an appointment—a luncheon perhaps. The principal investigator entrusts his assistants to run the tests he has designed without his supervision.

Margot follows instructions diligently: even when she knows what to do next she waits for Alvin Kaplan, Ferris's protégé, to instruct her. Testing E.H. is laborious, repetitive, yet fascinating—memory tests of various kinds, auditory and visual, of gradually increasing complexity.

One of the tests seems purposefully designed to frustrate and discourage the subject. E.H. is instructed by Kaplan to count "as high as you can without stopping." E.H. begins counting and continues for an impressively long time, beyond seventy seconds; his counting is methodical, by rote. Then, at numeral eighty-nine, Kaplan interrupts, distracting E.H. by showing him a card with an elaborate geometrical design E.H. is asked to describe—"Looks like three pyramids upside down or maybe—pineapples?"

And now when Kaplan asks E.H. to continue with his counting, E.H. is utterly baffled. He has no idea how to proceed.

"'Counting'—what? What was I 'counting'?"

"You were counting numbers 'as high as you can'—then you stopped to describe this card. But now, Eli, you can continue."

" 'Continue'—what?"

"You don't remember the count?"

" 'Count'—? No. I don't remember."

E.H. stares at the illustrated card that has distracted him, registering now that it is a trick.

"I played cards when I was a little boy. I played checkers and chess, too." E.H. glances about as if looking for more cards, or game boards.

E.H.'s fingers twitch. His usually affable eyes glare with fury. How he would like to tear into bits the stupid card with a picture of pyramids, or pineapples!

Seeing the look in E.H.'s face Margot feels a twinge of guilt. She wonders if the test isn't cruel after all—mental cruelty. Though E.H. has clearly enjoyed being the epicenter of attention until now.

Margot thinks—*But he won't remember! He will forget.*

She thinks of those laboratory animals of decades past whose vocal cords were sometimes cut—monkeys, dogs, cats. So that their cries of pain and terror could not be expressed; their torturers were spared hearing, and did not need to register their suffering. Before a new and more humane era of animal experimentation but well within the memory of Milton Ferris, she is sure.

Ferris has often joked of the new "humane" era—its restrictions on animal research, the zealotry of "animal terrorists" protesting experiments of the kind he'd done himself not long ago with splendid results.

Margot does not like to speculate how she would have behaved in such laboratories, in the past. Would she have protested the suffering of animals? Or would she have silently, shamefully concurred?—for to have objected would have been tantamount to being expelled from the great man's lab, and from a career in neuroscience itself.

Margot tells herself it is all science: a quest for the truth that is elusive, deep-lying.

For truth is not lying on the surface of the earth, scattered bits of fossil you might fit together like a jigsaw puzzle. Truth is buried, hidden, labyrinthine. What others see is likely to be surface—superficial. The scientist is one who *delves deeper*.

E.H. is looking blankly about the examining room, which has become an unknown place to him. It's as if a stage set has been dismantled and all that remains are barren walls. The bright eager smile has faded from his lips. Elihu Hoopes is a marooned man who has suffered a grievous loss; his manner exudes, not charisma, but desperation. "You were at eighty-nine, Mr. Hoopes," Margot says gently, to comfort the forlorn man. "You were doing very well when you were interrupted." She ignores the stares of Kaplan and the others which are an indication to her that she has misspoken.

Hearing Margot's soft but insistent voice behind him E.H. turns to her in surprise. He has been focusing his attention upon Kaplan and he has totally forgotten Margot—he registers surprise that there are several others in the room, and Margot behind him, sitting in a corner like a schoolgirl, observing and taking notes.

"Hel-lo!—hel-*lo!*"

It is clear that E.H. has never seen Margot Sharpe before: she is a diminutive young woman with unusually pale skin, black eyebrows and lashes, glossy black bangs hiding much of her forehead; her almond-shaped eyes would be beautiful if not so narrowed in thought.

She is eccentrically dressed in black, layers of black like a dancer. Notebook on her lap, pen in hand, frowning, yet smiling, she is—very likely—a young doctor? medical student? (Not a nurse. He knows that she is not a nurse.) Yet, she isn't wearing a white lab coat. There is no ID on her lapel which vexes and intrigues E.H.

Ignoring Kaplan and the others E.H. extends his hand to shake the young woman's hand. "Hel-*lo!* I think we know each other—we went to school together—did we? In Gladwyne?"

The black-haired young woman hesitates. Then gracefully rises from her seat and comes to him, to slip her hand into his, with a smile.

"Hello, Mr. Hoopes—'Eli.' I am Margot Sharpe—whom you have never met before today."

ACROSS THE GIRL'S white face beneath the rippling water are shadows of dragonflies and "skaters." It is strange to see, the shadows of the insects are larger than the living insects.

He has discovered her, in the stream. No one else knows—he is alone in this place.

But he doesn't look, he has not (yet) seen the drowned girl. He was not there, so he cannot see. He cannot remember what he has not seen.

On the plank bridge in this strange place so many years later he does not turn his head. He does not glance around. He grips the railing tight in both his hands, bravely he steels himself against the anticipated wind.

CHAPTER TWO

"Mr. Hoopes? Eli?"

"Hel-lo!"

"My name is Margot Sharpe. I'm Professor Ferris's associate. We've met before. We've come to take up a little of your time this morning . . ."

"Yes! Wel-come."

Light coming up in his eyes. That leap of hope in his eyes.

"Wel-come, Margot!"

Her hand gripped in his, a clasp of recognition.

He does remember me. Not consciously—but he remembers.

She can't write about this, yet. She has no scientific proof, yet.

The amnesiac will discover ways of "remembering." It is a non-declarative memory, it bypasses the conscious mind altogether.

For there is emotional memory, as there is declarative memory.

There is a memory deep-embedded in the body—a memory generated by passion.

Suffused with happiness, Margot Sharpe feels like a balloon rapidly, giddily filling with helium.

"MR. HOOPES? ELI?"

"Hel-lo! Hel-*lo.*"

He has not ever seen her before. Eagerly he smiles at her, leans close to her, to shake her hand.

In his large, strong hand, Margot Sharpe's small hand.

"You may not recall, we've met before—'Margot Sharpe.' I'm one of Professor Ferris's research associates. We've been working together for—well, some time."

"'Mar-got Sharpe.' Yes. We've been working together for—some time." E.H. smiles gallantly as if he knows very well how long they've been working together, but it is a secret between them.

Today E.H. has the larger of his sketchbooks with him. He has finished the *New York Times* crossword puzzle—the newspaper page is discarded as usual, on the floor.

E.H. has been sketching with a stick of charcoal, seated beside a window in the anterior of the fourth-floor testing-room. He appears to be oblivious of the plate glass window that is dramatically lashed with rain, as he is oblivious of his clinical surroundings; the objects of E.H.'s art, which excite his fierce attention, are almost exclusively interior, and he does not care to share them with others.

(Except sometimes, Margot Sharpe.)

(Though Margot knows not to ask E.H. to see his drawings but to wait for E.H. to offer to show her. The offer, if it comes, will come spontaneously.)

"Do you have any idea how long we've been working together, Eli?"—Margot always asks.

E.H.'s smile wavers. He speaks thoughtfully, gravely.

"Well—I think—maybe—six weeks."

"Six weeks?"

"Maybe more, or maybe less. You know, I have some problem with what is called 'memory.'"

"How long have you had this problem, Eli?"

"How long have I had this problem? Well—I think—maybe—six weeks." E.H. smiles at Margot, with a pleading expression. He is still gripping Margot's hand; gently, she has to detach it.

"Do you know what has caused this problem, Eli?"

"Well, it's 'neurological.' I suppose they've done X-rays. I think I remember my head shaved. My skull was fractured in Birmingham, Alabama—no one knew at the time. A 'hairline' fracture. But then, at the lake back in July, a few months ago, there was a fire. I think that's what they told me—a fire. Hard to believe that I was careless leaving burning embers in the fireplace but—something happened." E.H. pauses, frowning like one who is struggling to pull up, from the depths of a well, something unwieldy, very heavy that is straining every muscle in his body. "A fire, that burnt up my damned brain."

"A fever, maybe?"

"A fever is a fire. In the damned brain."

It is a wet windy overcast morning in March 1969.

SHE THINKS, HIS name has been eerily prescient—*Hoopes.*

For Elihu Hoopes has lived, for the past four and a half years, in an indefinable present-tense. A kind of time-hoop, a Möbius strip that turns upon itself, to infinity.

Except "infinity" is less than seventy seconds.

There is no *was* in Elihu Hoopes's life, there is only *is.*

Forever he will be thirty-seven years old. Forever, he will be confused about where he is, and what has happened to him.

A fire? I think it was a fire. Or, Granddaddy's two-passenger single-prop plane crash-landed on the island, and burst into flames.

And later in the hospital, I think there was a fire, too. My clothes and hair were wet, but smoldering. I could smell my hair singed. I may have breathed in some of the fire, and burnt my lungs.

They said that I had a high fever but—it was a fire, I could see and smell.

The girl was not found. There were rescue parties searching for her. In the woods around Lake George. On the islands.

If someone had taken her, it was believed he might've taken her to one of the islands. If he had a boat. If no one saw.

In his little, light Beechcraft aircraft painted bright chrome yellow like a giant bird Granddaddy flew above the lake. Many times Granddaddy flew above the lake, you would hear the prop-plane engine passing low over the roof of the house.

Granddaddy said, Come with me, Eli! We will search together for your lost cousin.

Not the first time the little boy had flown in the plane with his grandfather but it would be the last.

IN HIS BRIGHT affable voice E.H. begins to read from his notebook.

" 'There is no journey, and there is no path. There is no wisdom, there is emptiness. There is no emptiness.' "

Pausing to add, "This is the wisdom of the Buddha. But there is no wisdom, and there is no Buddha."

He laughs, sadly.

"There is no test, and there is no 'testes.' "

And he laughs again. Sadly.

SHE HAS BEEN instructed: to discover, you have to destroy.

To locate the source of behavior in the brain, you have to destroy much of the brain.

Monkey-, cat- and rat-brains. In search of elusive and mysterious memory. Years, decades, thousands of animal-brains, hundreds of thousands of hours of surgery. Systematically, methodically. Meticulous lab records. Unyielding cruelty of the research scientist to whom no (living) specimen is an end in itself but a (possible) means to a greater end. Hundreds of thousands of animals sacrificed in the pursuit of the "engram"—the brain's ostensible record of memory.

A principle of experimental neuroscience.

No one can surgically explore a (living, normal) human brain, only just animal-brains. And all these decades, results have been inconclusive. Margot Sharpe notes in her amnesia logbook the (famous/infamous) conclusion of the great experimental psychologist Karl Lashley:

This series of experiments has yielded a good bit of information about what and where the memory trace is not. I sometimes feel . . . the necessary conclusion is that (memory) is just not possible.

THE CHASTE DAUGHTER. How lucky Margot Sharpe has been! And she wants to think—*My career—my life—lies all before me.*

By 1969 the phenomenon of the amnesiac "E.H." is beginning to be known in scientific circles.

An extraordinary case of total anterograde amnesia! And the subject otherwise in good health, intelligent, cooperative, sane—a rarity in brain pathology research where living patients are likely to be psychotic, moribund, or brain-rotted alcoholics.

Articles by Milton Ferris of the University Neurological Institute at Darven Park on "E.H." have begun to appear in the most prestigious neuroscience journals; usually these articles list Ferris's research associates as co-authors, and Margot Sharpe is among them. Seeing her name in print, in such company, has been deeply gratifying to Margot, and it has happened with surprising swiftness.

Rich with data, graphs, statistics, and citations, the articles bear such titles as "Losses in Recent Memory Following Infectious Encephalitis"—"Retention of 'Declarative' and 'Non-declarative' Memory in Amnesia: A History of 'E.H.' "—"Short-Term Retention of Verbal, Visual, Auditory and Olfactory Items in Amnesia"—"Encoding, Storing, and Retrieval of Information in Anterograde Amnesia." Their preparation is a lengthy, collaborative effort of months, or even years, with Milton Ferris overseeing the process. No paper can be submitted to any journal, of course, without Ferris's imprimatur, no matter who has actually designed and executed the experiments, and who has done most of the research and writing. Recently, Margot has been given permission by Ferris to design experiments of her own involving sensory modality, and the possibility of "non-declarative" learning and memory. In the prestigious *Journal of American Experimental Psychology* a paper will soon appear with just the names of Milton Ferris and Margot Sharpe as authors; this is a forty-page extract from Margot's dissertation titled "Short-Term and Consolidated Memory in Retrograde and Anterograde Amnesia: A Brief History of 'E.H.' " It is, Milton Ferris has told Margot, the most ambitious and thoroughly researched paper of its kind he has ever received from a female graduate student—"Or any female colleague, for that matter."

(Ferris's praise is sincere. No irony is intended. It is 1969—it is not an age of gender irony in scientific circles, where few women, and virtually no feminists, have penetrated. To her shame, Margot has been thrilled to hear Milton Ferris spread the word of her to his colleagues, who've made a show of being impressed. Margot doesn't want to think that her mentor's praise is somewhat mitigated by the fact that there are only two women professors in the Psychology Department at the university, both "social psychologists" whom the experimental psychologists and neuroscientists treat with barely concealed scorn.)

That the lengthy article has been accepted so relatively quickly after Margot submitted it to the *Journal of American Experimental Psychology* must have something to do with Ferris's intervention, Margot thinks. It has not escaped her notice that one of the editors of the journal is a protégé of Ferris of the late 1940s; Ferris himself is listed among numerous names on the masthead, as an "advisory editor."

In any case, she has thanked Ferris.

She has thanked Ferris more than once.

Margot is conscious of her very, very good luck. Margot is anxious to sustain this luck.

It isn't enough to be brilliant, if you are a woman. You must be demonstrably more brilliant than your male rivals—your "brilliance" is your masculine attribute. And so, to balance this, you must be suitably feminine—which isn't to say emotionally unstable, volatile, "soft" in any way, only just quiet, watchful, quick to absorb information, nonoppositional, self-effacing.

Margot thinks—*It is not difficult to be self-effacing, if you have a face at which no one looks.*

"HEL-*LO!*"

"Hello, Mr. Hoopes—'Eli.' How are you?"

"Very good, thanks. How are *you*?"

In the vicinity of E.H. you feel the gravitational tug of the present tense.

In the vicinity of E.H., you glance about anxiously for your own shadow, as if you might have lost it.

Margot is very lonely except—Margot is not lonely when she is with E.H. Others in Ferris's lab would be astonished to learn that Margot Sharpe who is so stiffly quiet in their presence speaks impulsively at times to the amnesiac subject E.H.; she has confided in him, as to a close and trusted friend, when they are alone together and no one else can hear.

She has volunteered to take E.H. for walks in the parkland behind the Institute. She has volunteered to take E.H. downstairs to the first-floor cafeteria, for lunch. If E.H. is scheduled for medical tests she volunteers to take him.

She is cheerful in E.H.'s company, as E.H. is cheerful in hers. She has boasted to E.H. of her academic successes, as one might boast to an older relative, a father perhaps. (Though Margot doesn't think of Elihu Hoopes as *fatherly:* she is too much attracted to him as a man.) She has admitted to him that she is, at times, very lonely here in eastern Pennsylvania, where she knows no one—"Except you, Eli. You are my only friend." E.H. smiles at this revelation as if their exchange was a part of a test and he is expected to speak on cue: "Yes—'my only friend.' You are, too."

Margot knows that E.H. lives with an aunt, and assumes that he must see family members from time to time. She knows that his engagement was broken off a few months after E.H.'s recovery from surgery, and that his fiancée never visits him. What of his other friends? Have they all abandoned him? Has E.H. abandoned *them*? The impaired subject will wish to retreat, to avoid situations that exacerbate stress and anxiety; E.H. is safest and most secure at the Institute perhaps, where he can't fail to be, almost continuously, the center of attention.

Margot thinks how for the amnesiac subject, are not all exchanges part of a test? *Is not life itself a vast, continuous test?*

It isn't clear during their intimate exchanges if E.H. remembers Margot's name—(frequently, he confuses her with his childhood classmate)—but unmistakably, he remembers *her.*

He understands that she is a person of some authority: a "doctor" or a "scientist." He respects her, and relates to her in a way he doesn't relate to the nursing staff, so far as Margot has observed.

Of course, you can say anything to E.H. He will be certain to forget it within seventy seconds.

And how difficult this is to comprehend, even for the "scientist": what Margot has confided in E.H. is inextricably part of her memory of him, but it is not part of his memory of her.

Margot confides in E.H.: her imagination is so aflame she has trouble sleeping through the night. She wakes every two or three hours, excited and anxious. New ideas! New ideas for tests! New theories about the human brain!

She tells E.H. how badly she wants to please Milton Ferris; how fearful she is of disappointing the man—(who is frequently disappointed with young colleagues and associates, and has a reputation for running through them, and dismissing them); she wants to think that Ferris's assessment of her "brain for science" is accurate, and not exaggerated. It's her fear that Ferris has made her one of his protégées because she is a young woman of extreme docility and subservience to *him.*

Margot confesses to E.H. how sometimes she falls into bed without removing her clothing—"Without showering. Sleeping in my own *smell.*"

(So that E.H. is moved to say, "But your *smell* is very nice, my dear!")

She confesses how exhausted she makes herself working late at the lab as if in some way unknown to her she disapproves of and dislikes herself—can't bear herself except as a vessel of work;

for she will not be loved if she doesn't excel, and there is no way for her to excel except by working and pleasing her elders, like Milton Ferris. She recalls from a literature class at the University of Michigan a nightmarish short story in which the body of a condemned man is tattooed with the law he'd broken, which he is supposed to "read"—she doesn't recall the author's name but has never forgotten the story.

E.H. says, with an air of affectionate rebuke, "No one forgets Franz Kafka's 'In the Penal Colony.' "

He too had read it as an undergraduate—at Amherst.

Margot is surprised, and touched. "You remember it, Eli? That's—of course, that's . . ." It is utterly normal and natural for E.H. to remember a story he'd read years before his illness. Yet, Margot who'd read the story not nearly so long ago, could not recall the title.

E.H. begins to recite: " ' "It's a peculiar apparatus," said the Officer to the Traveler, gazing with a certain admiration at the device . . . It appeared that the Traveler had responded to the invitation of the Commandant only out of politeness, when he'd been invited to witness the execution of a soldier condemned to death for disobeying and insulting his superior . . . Guilt is always beyond doubt.' "

E.H. laughs, strangely. Margot has no idea why.

Something about the man without a shadow reciting these lines makes her fearful—*I don't want to know. Oh please!—I don't want to know.*

THEY HAVE NEVER told him—*Your cousin is dead. Your cousin was dead as soon as she disappeared.*

No one saw. No one knows.

Wake up, Eli! Silly Eli, it's only a dream.

So much Eli has seen that summer, only a dream.

SHE RENTS A single-bedroom unit in dreary university graduate housing, overlooking a rock-filled ravine at the edge of the sprawling campus. (The University Neurological Institute at Darven Park is several miles away in an upscale Philadelphia suburb.) She avoids her neighbors, who seem so much less serious than she, given to playing music loudly, and talking and laughing loudly; especially, she avoids married couples—the thought of marital intimacy, the pettiness of domestic life and sheer waste of time required for such a life, makes her feel faint. She has no time for friends—she has ceased writing to her friends from college; they seem diminished to her now, like pygmies. One or two of the men in Ferris's lab have—(she thinks, she isn't absolutely sure)—have made sexual advances to her, awkwardly and obliquely; with similar awkwardness, and much embarrassment, she has discouraged them—*No I don't think so. I—I don't think—it's a good idea to see each other outside the lab . . .* Seeing her fellow researchers in such relentless intimacy, day following day, for hours each day, it is not possible for Margot to harbor romantic feelings toward the men, or feelings of friendship for the other women; like rivalrous siblings they are easily irritated by one another, and easily provoked to jealousy, for each is vying with the others continuously—(how fatiguing this is!)—for admiration, approval, affection from Milton Ferris.

Work has become her addiction, as work has become her salvation. In human relations you never know where you stand; in your work you can mark progress clearly, and your progress will be noted by others—your distinguished elders.

It is slightly shameful to Margot, how she lives for Milton Ferris's praise—*Good work, Margot!*—a murmur like a caress along the length of her body.

At times she is sure that there is an (implicit, unstated) promise between her and Ferris, like a match not yet struck.

At other times, seeing how Ferris's interest waxes, wanes, waxes, she is sure of nothing.

He, Ferris, with his wiry white beard, bristling manner and sharp-glinting eyeglasses, his flashes of wit, sarcasm, insight, and frequent brilliance—(all who work with the man are convinced of his genius)—has become a figure of considerable (if forbidden) romance to Margot Sharpe. He is fifty-seven years old, he has become famous in the field of neuropsychology; he has long been a member of the National Academy of Science. He is (said to be) happily married, or in any case stolidly married. Yet—*We are special to each other.*

Margot feels a sensation of weakness, faintness—when Ferris singles her out for praise in the lab. Her face flushes with blood, her heart beats with great happiness. It has often been so, for Margot has been, through her life, the exemplary good-girl student: the Daughter.

She is the Chaste Daughter. She is the one who, if you believe in her, will never betray you.

Yet Margot thinks—*I am not in love with Milton Ferris.*

Then—*I must never allow him to know.*

In the night in her bed. In this strange darkness, in her bed. Sometimes she slides her arm around her waist, in mimicry of an embrace. Sometimes she caresses her ribs through her skin, taking a kind of mournful pleasure in so intimate (and unthreatening) a touch. Shuts her eyes tight to summon sleep. And there is

Elihu Hoopes standing before her with his eager, hopeful smile and stricken eyes—*Margot?* Hel-*lo.*

E.H. says—*Margot? I am so lonely.*

(IN LIFE, MARGOT knows that E.H. will never say these words. For E.H. will never remember Margot from one encounter to another.)

"He is our 'amnesiac'—his identity must be kept absolutely confidential."

Milton Ferris speaks lightly—there is something meant to be playful about the words *our amnesiac*—but of course he is utterly serious. Everyone at the Institute who comes into contact with Elihu Hoopes, who knows his identity, is sworn to secrecy; others are not told his name—"For legal reasons."

Since Ferris has begun to publish his "exciting" and "controversial" research on E.H., scientists at other universities have contacted him with requests for interviews with the amnesiac subject. Ferris has refused most of these requests as impractical, since, as he says, he and his researchers are currently studying E.H., and it is not possible to subject E.H. to further testing.

"He is our subject, *exclusively.* That is the agreement."

Milton Ferris has become vehement on the subject. *Exclusively* is an unmistakable claim.

PROFESSOR SHARPE, DID you ever consider at any time that you and your fellow researchers were exploiting the individual known in scientific literature as "E.H."?

No. I did not.

Really? At no time, Professor Sharpe, during the thirty-one years you studied him, did it occur to you that you might be behaving unethically, in exploiting his handicap? His "amnesia"?

I said no. I did not.

And do you speak for your fellow researchers, as well? Do you speak for the neuroscientific community?

I speak for myself. The others can speak for themselves.

But "E.H." could not speak for himself—could he? Did "E.H." ever comprehend the nature of his affliction?

I've told you, I speak for myself. That is all.

"That is all"—Professor Sharpe? After thirty-one years?

HE IS NOT being exploited, he is being protected from exploitation!

Margot Sharpe wants to protest. In time, Margot Sharpe will protest publicly.

For E.H. is a neurological wonder, capable of odd, unpredictable feats of memory while incapable of remembering "familiar" faces or what he has just eaten for lunch, or whether he has eaten at all. He has astonished observers by interrupting a rote-memory test to recite the names of his grade school classmates at Gladwyne Elementary School in 1935, desk by desk. On other occasions E.H. has recited Major League Baseball statistics, dialogue from favored comic strips Dick Tracy, Terry and the Pirates, Little Orphan Annie, and song lyrics of Oscar Hammerstein. He can recite passages from speeches by Lincoln, Roosevelt, John F. Kennedy, Martin Luther King, Jr. By heart he knows the entirety of the American *Declaration of Independence* and portions of John Locke's *The Rights of Man.* He knows passages from Thoreau's *Walden,* Whitman's *Leaves of Grass,* Jean Toomer's *Cane.* On the

Institute court he plays tennis with zest and cunning; he can play piano by "sight" reading—some classics, some American popular songs, and Czerny exercises to grade eight. He is remarkably gifted at jigsaw puzzles, crossword puzzles, plastic puzzles of the kind that fit in the palm of the hand and involve moving numbered squares about in a specific pattern. (How Margot hates those damned plastic puzzles!—she'd never been able to do these with the skill of her brothers, whose grades in school were always inferior to hers; when E.H. offers his puzzle for her to try she pushes it away.) If journalists hear of E.H., Margot can imagine sensational TV coverage, articles in *People, Time,* and *Newsweek,* the *Philadelphia Inquirer* and other local publications. Neighbors, acquaintances, medical workers and researchers who know E.H. would be plied with interview requests. Fortunately the Hoopes family isn't in need of money, so there is little likelihood of E.H. being exploited by his own relatives.

Margot thinks—*I vow, I will protect Elihu Hoopes from exploitation.*

"'Elihu Hoopes.'"

These syllables, he hears murmured aloud. The sounds seem to come out of the air about his head.

The strangeness of the proposition—(he cannot think it is a *fact*)—that these syllables, these sounds, four stresses, constitute a "name"—and the name is "his."

His body, his brain. His name. Yet, where is *he*?

It is a peculiar way of speaking, he'd thought long ago as a child—before the fever burnt up his brain. Why would anyone say—*I am Elihu Hoopes.*

Again he hears the syllables, in a hoarse, slightly derisive voice. "'Elihu Hoopes'—who *was*."

IS HE AT Lake George? But where? Not on one of the islands, which have no trails so clearly defined as the trail he sees here, leading through a pinewoods, and out of sight.

Nor is there a plank bridge at the lake quite like this bridge, so far as he can recall.

How lost he feels! No idea how old he is, or where the others are. No idea if he is hungry, if he has eaten recently or not for a very long time.

The others. Scarcely knows what this means: parents, grandparents, adult relatives, young and elder cousins. A child has but a vague sense of *others*. Apart from relatives, many adults seem interchangeable—faces, names. Ages.

So many adults, in a child's life! Children nearer his age, for instance young cousins, are more vividly delineated and named.

Where is Gretchen?—she has gone away.

When will you see Gretchen again?—maybe not for a while.

He is trying to recall if this is before the "search party"—(but why would there be a "party"—in the woods? Why a "party" when the girl is gone away somewhere, and the adults are sad?)—or after; if this is before Granddaddy insisted upon taking up the Beechcraft, and had to make an emergency landing on one of the islands.

Trying to recall if the fever in his brain is the fire from the crash, or the fire in the hospital.

Beyond the plank railing is a shallow stream. He has been hearing the murmurous sound of the flowing water for some time, without realizing. Only when he sees the stream, and identifies the flowing water, does he hear it.

Gripping the railing tightly in both hands. Standing with his feet apart, to brace himself against a sudden wind. (Though there is no wind.) Facing a marshy area dense with swamp grasses, tall reeds, pussy willows and cattails. Trees denuded of bark, hunched over like elderly figures, choked with vines. A smell of wet, rotted things. And everywhere, strips of shimmering water like strips of phosphorescence that glow in the dark as warnings.

Below the plank bridge—so loosely fitted, you can see between the boards—is the shallow stream that flows so slowly you can scarcely determine in which direction water is flowing.

And on the water's surface he sees something curious, that makes him smile: small antic winged insects—"dragonflies."

He has not seen these glittery insects until now, leaning over the railing. And there are others—"skaters." (How does he know these names? Effortless as the meandering stream, and as near-imperceptible, "skaters" and "dragonflies" float into his thoughts.)

He has heard of "dragon"—and he has heard of "fly." It is a novel thing, to put them together: "dragonfly." *He* did not do this, he thinks. But someone did.

He has been leaning over the plank railing, staring down. His mouth is slightly open, he breathes quickly and anxiously. For he is in the presence of something profoundly significant whose meaning is hidden to him—which causes him to think that he must be very young. He is not the other, older Elihu—that has not happened yet.

This is a relief! (Is this a relief? For whatever will happen, will happen.)

He sees: what is arresting about the insects is that their shadows are magnified in the streambed a few inches below the surface of the water upon which they swim. If you observe the shadows that are rounded and soft-seeming you could not deduce that they have been cast by the insects with their sharply-delineated wings.

If you observe the shadows below, you can't observe the insects. If you observe the insects, you can't observe the shadows.

He is beginning to feel a mild anxiety in the region of his chest—he does not know why.

He sees, beyond the marsh are low-lying shapes—"hills." Though these could be stage sets, painted to resemble "hills."

He has not turned to look around, to see what is behind him. It is crucial, he must not look behind him. That is why he is gripping the plank railing so tightly, and why he stands with his feet apart, to steady himself.

Will not look. *Has not (yet) seen the girl's body in the shallow stream.*

"ELI, THANK YOU!"

Carefully, Margot spreads E.H.'s most recent drawings and charcoal sketches on a table.

Dozens of pages from E.H.'s oversized sketchbook.

Dark, shadowed scenes—it isn't clear what their subjects are—interiors? forests? caves? Here and there, a barely recognizable human figure, crouching in darkness.

In admiring silence Margot stares at the pages from E.H.'s sketchbook. The pencil drawings are meticulously drawn, the charcoal sketches light and feathery. Margot has learned to be cautious in her response to E.H.'s art—the man's affable manner can alter swiftly at such times. (There is a side to E.H. few have seen: sudden fury, unexpressed except by a tightening of facial muscles, a clenching of fists.) In fact, Margot Sharpe is the only person she knows, including Milton Ferris himself, who has been allowed by E.H. to see his art. This is flattering—E.H. trusts *her.*

Unlike her fellow researchers, who've become accustomed to their eccentric amnesiac subject over the months and years, Margot often discovers something about E.H. that deepens her respect for him, even as it's likely to heighten her sense of the distance between them. She wants to think that she is the man's friend, not just the amnesiac's researcher. She wants to think that there is a special rapport between them—from their very first meeting, this has been evident. If others humor him, or scarcely listen to his meandering remarks, Margot makes a point of listening, and replying; often, she lingers to talk with E.H. after the testing session is over for the day, and her lab partners have left. She never becomes impatient with the amnesiac subject, and she never becomes bored with administering tests though some of the tests are needlessly repetitive.

Experimental psychology is in itself repetitive, and overall not so very inspired as Margot had thought at the outset of graduate school. Scientific "truth" is more likely to be discovered by slow increments than by sudden lightning-flashes. Experimenting—assembling data—"evidence." This is the collaborative effort of the lab assistants who prepare reports for the principal investigator Milton Ferris to analyze, assess, and consolidate.

Margot has discovered that E.H.'s art before his amnesia had been executed with a degree of skill and assurance that he seems to have lost, as he has certainly lost a wide range of subjects. Before the encephalitis, Elihu Hoopes had been a good enough amateur photographer to have exhibited his work in Philadelphia, including once in a group show titled "Young Philadelphia Photographers 1954" at the Philadelphia Museum of Art. His subjects were various—portraits and close-ups, street scenes, river scenes, civil rights marches and demonstrations, uniformed policemen in riot gear. He'd never been a full-time artist but had developed a distinctive style of drawing, sketching, painting. Post-amnesia, E.H. was said to have lost interest in photography, as if he has forgotten entirely that he'd ever been a photographer or (Margot thinks) has repudiated an art that demands technical precision, and an ongoing interest in the outside world. (In an experiment of her own devising about which she hasn't told Milton Ferris, Margot has shown E.H. reproductions of his photographs from the 1950s and early 1960s, and E.H. replied flippantly—"What's this? Not bad." He'd seemed to think that the portraits might be a trick—"Nobody I know, anymore." He'd shown more interest in photography books Margot brought for him—black-and-white plates by Ansel Adams, Walker Evans, Imogen Cunningham—though even this interest was fleeting: Margot was likely to discover the expensive books left behind in the testing-room.)

Since his illness, E.H.'s talent for art seems much diminished. The post-amnesiac pencil drawings are fervid but amateurish: the artist compulsively fills in every square inch of the paper, leaving little that is blank or empty, to be filled in by the viewer's imagination; the effort of studying a typical drawing of E.H.'s is considerable. You can see that the artist has taken time with the pencil drawings—too much time. Where Elihu Hoopes's drawings were once lightly, deftly and minimally executed, now he meticulously shades in degrees of darkness, as if to suggest shadows within shadows; he is partial to cross-hatching, a visual cliché. Some of the drawings are so detailed and the pencil lines so faint, Margot can scarcely make out what they are supposed to represent. (Margot has given E.H. sets of pencils, and a pencil sharpener, as well as spray to preserve the charcoal, but it isn't clear if he uses these.) The charcoal sketches are more accomplished, not so labored over and more resembling E.H.'s pre-amnesiac work, but have been carelessly preserved, smeared with fingerprints. As if, Margot thinks, the artist executes his work in a kind of trance and then, upon waking, forgets it.

Margot's response is always enthusiastic—"Eli, so much fascinating work! You've been busy this week. You've been inspired."

Inspired is not the right word. *Haunted,* more likely.

As Margot shifts the drawings slowly along the table from left to right, E.H. peers at them with a kind of perplexed pride. She understands that he doesn't remember most of what he has done even as he tries to give no sign of surprise.

The charcoal drawings depict a marshland beneath a low, ominous sky. There are misshapen trees, fallen limbs, tall grasses and a shallow stream with a rippling surface. In one of the drawings you can see what appears to be a figure in the stream—a pale, naked figure, a child perhaps, with long flowing hair and opened and sightless eyes. (Margot feels her mouth go dry, seeing this.) E.H. makes a sound of impatience or disdain—he fumbles to take hold of the drawing, and jerks it along, replacing it with another. Margot can see that the charcoal is smearing, E.H. hasn't sprayed fixative on it. As if nothing is wrong Margot continues as she'd been doing, shifting the drawings along the table . . . (E.H. is breathing quickly and shallowly. Margot is not sure what she has seen. The figure on its back in the stream was very impressionistic.) The last drawings in the group resemble the first drawings almost identically—more marshland scenes, and the stream; insects on the water's surface casting small soft shadows below. And finally there is a vast lake or inland sea ringed with pine trees. The sky here is massive, like a canyon. The water's surface here is rippling, tremulous. There is an atmosphere of tranquility that, the more closely you look, becomes an atmosphere of dread.

"Eli? Is this Lake George?"

"Maybe."

"Such a beautiful lake, I know! I've never seen it."

Margot always speaks brightly to E.H. It is her professional manner, worn like a shield.

"I've only seen pictures of Lake George—photographs. Some of these, Eli, you'd taken yourself, years ago . . ." Margot speaks carefully, but Eli does not respond.

"Eli, what has happened here at the lake? Has something happened here?"

E.H. stoops over the drawings, to stare at them. As if trying to recall them. He seems to be feeling pain, behind his eyes. Impulsively he says, "It did not happen yet."

"What 'did not happen yet'?"

E.H. shakes his head. How can he know, he seems to be pleading, when it hasn't happened yet?

Margot has come to the end of the drawings. She'd like very much to turn back, to examine the (pale, naked?) figure in the stream. She isn't even sure that this is what she saw—she is feeling uneasy, for E.H. is standing very close to her, his breath on the side of her face.

Apart from his firm and caressing handshake each time they meet, E.H. has never touched Margot Sharpe. He does not—(she has noticed)—touch anyone except to shake hands, and he is sensitive to being touched by medical staff. Yet, Margot has imagined that E.H. would often like to touch *her.*

She seems to recall that he has. He has touched *her.*

In a dream, possibly. One of her many dreams of Darven Park, that grip her intensely by night but fade upon waking, like pale smoke streaming upward.

It is déjà vu she feels, at such times. The most mysterious of quasi-memories.

E.H. is saying, "It did not happen—yet. It is the 'safe time'—before."

"Before what, Eli?"

E.H.'s face is shutting up. Like a grating being pulled down over a store window. Rudely abrupt, and Margot Sharpe is being excluded.

"Eli? Before—what?"

E.H. snatches up the drawings and sketches—shuffles them crudely together—returns them to their folder. He is hurried, harried—doesn't seem to care if some of the pages are torn. Margot cries, "Oh! Eli. Let me help . . ." She would like to take the folder from him, to reassemble his art more carefully. She will bring waxed paper to insert between the charcoal drawings. But E.H. is finished with his art for the day.

Crudely he laughs—"Poor bastard whoever did this, his future is all used up."

Alone with E.H. in the testing-room. In the corridor outside there are voices, but the door is shut.

Margot thinks—*He could hurt me. Swiftly, his hands. His hands are so strong.*

Margot thinks—*What a ridiculous thought! Eli Hoopes is my friend, he would never hurt me.*

She is ashamed of herself, thinking such a thing. She is utterly baffled and dismayed at having thought it.

"THE ARTIST PRE- and Post-Amnesia: A Study of 'E.H.'"

This is the title of a slide presentation—(subject to Milton Ferris's approval)—Margot Sharpe hopes to give at an upcoming meeting of the American Psychological Association in San Francisco, December 1970. Milton Ferris has read an early draft of the paper and has been guardedly enthusiastic—his concern is that Margot Sharpe, his Ph.D. student, may be "getting ahead of herself."

Margot wants to protest, this is ridiculous! She has heard the cautionary expression more than once, applied to other young scientists who assist Ferris—"Getting ahead of himself."

Though obviously it is more reprehensible for a woman—"Getting ahead of *herself*."

What a long time it is taking Margot Sharpe, to complete requirements for her Ph.D.! Nearly five years.

Each time she has thought she might have finished, her advisor has further criticisms and suggestions. He is always (guardedly) enthusiastic about her work, it is clear that he likes and trusts her, appreciating (perhaps) her taciturnity in the lab, her somber and diligent way of implementing experiments, rarely questioning his judgment as others might—(Kaplan, for instance. There is a volatile paternal-filial relationship between Ferris and Kaplan, which Margot Sharpe envies; she knows that Kaplan is devoted to Ferris, with whom he has been working for nearly eight years). As Ferris is the chair of her Ph.D. committee, and has taken an avuncular, if not a paternal, interest in her since her arrival in his lab, Margot knows that she must placate him in every way—more than placate, she must *please*.

When she thinks of it, five years isn't such a long time to acquire a Ph.D. with Milton Ferris who is known for helping his (hand-picked, elite) former students throughout their professional careers.

THE SPECIAL CASE. "We'll be famous one day, Eli! You and me."

"Will we!"—E.H. smiles at Margot Sharpe affably if perplexedly.

"You are a 'special case'—you must know. This is why we've

been studying you for years. We are challenging the belief that complex memories are distributed throughout the cerebral cortex—not localized in a small area. We think that you suggest otherwise, Eli!"

"'Memory'—'cere-bral cor-tex.'" E.H. pronounces these words as if he has never heard them before. As if they are words in a foreign language, incomprehensible to him. He laughs at Margot with a kind of childlike delight which is troubling to Margot, who knows that the *essential E.H.* is a much more intelligent person, given to irony.

Is it a game he is playing with us, continuously inventing a personality like a shield?

A personality that does not offend. Inspires sympathy, not cruelty.

As if he can read Margot's thoughts E.H. says, with a frown and a wink, "Well—if you think so, Doctor—I am happy for you. I am happy for the future of neuroscience."

Of course—it is not advised to speak with subjects about the nature of the experiments in which they are involved. Such exchanges remind Margot uneasily of brain surgery: the skull sawed open, the living brain exposed, but since there is no pain (*why no pain?*—one has to marvel) the patient is kept conscious and the surgeon can speak to him during the operation.

Margot wonders: What is the protocol for such brain surgery? Do the surgeon and his assistants *chat* with the immobilized patient, or is the exchange elevated, grave? A patient so self-aware as Elihu Hoopes might wish to entertain with comical monologues, impersonations of Jimmy Durante, Jack Benny and Rochester, Sid Caesar and Imogene Coca—(as he has been doing lately at the Institute in the interstices of test-taking) . . .

Margot chooses to laugh at E.H.'s enigmatic remark. She is moved to touch E.H.'s striped-cotton dress-shirt sleeve, lightly.

The most gossamer of touches, it is very possible to pass unnoticed by the amnesiac subject, as by anyone who happens to be observing.

"Eli, you are so very witty!"

Gentlemanly Elihu Hoopes certainly notices this touch, though he doesn't respond—this, too, a gentlemanly gesture.

And Margot knows that, within seventy seconds, and long before he has been returned to his residence in suburban Philadelphia where he lives with a widowed aunt, E.H. will have totally forgotten their exchange and this lightest of touches.

LATE-WINTER/EARLY-SPRING 1974, A new battery of tests.

In these, E.H. is given varying lists of nonsense-terms to memorize. By degrees, the lists are lengthened. On the whole E.H. performs within the "normal" range—for this, he's given a good deal of praise by the testers.

Until now, the test is more or less routine. E.H. is told that he is performing well, as he is frequently told. With a wink he asks, "Is there a test for 'testes'? Is it a little weeny *test-ie*?"

Margot and others laugh, awkwardly. Is E.H. simulating a kind of dementia, as a (controlled) parody of his brain-damage?

As a man with a limp might exaggerate his limp, to arouse laughter and dispel pity.

The testing resumes. E.H. performs well.

Then in the midst of one of E.H.'s recitations there is an interruption, and another set of lists is introduced. This is a short list of only three items but when E.H. is instructed to return to the first list he is hopelessly lost. Within a few seconds his frail memory has been overturned—it isn't just that E.H. can't recall the items, he is unable even to recall that there was a test preceding the current test.

Margot thinks—It's as if a shaky cart heaped with an unwieldy cargo has been pulled by an intrepid donkey up a steep and uneven hill—the cart topples over, the cargo falls to the ground.

"Eli, let's try again. Take a deep breath. Relax . . ."

The test-with-interruptions is repeated several times. Each time E.H. performs very poorly. Though he has no memory beyond seventy seconds it seems clear that, with each test, he is becoming ever more frustrated and discouraged. It is noted by examiners that the amnesiac subject is "remembering" an upsetting emotion if not its precise origin.

By the end of the battery of tests E.H. is ashen-faced, sober. His smile has long since faded.

The test is a model of sadistic ingenuity. Margot Sharpe, a co-designer, feels a flush of shame.

"Eli? Mr. Hoopes?"

"Yes? Hel-*lo* . . ."

"Your work today has been very, very good. Outstanding, in fact. Thank you!"

Uncomprehendingly E.H. gazes at Margot Sharpe who has been designated to tell the amnesiac subject that, despite hours of a demonstration of *severe memory loss,* he has in fact done very well.

Weakly smiling E.H. rubs his jaw which is not quite so smooth-shaven as it had been when he'd first arrived at the Institute. "Well—thank *you.*" He gazes at Margot imploringly as if he has more to say to her—something to ask of her—but has lost heart, and does not ask.

THE CRUEL HANDSHAKE. Promptly at 10:30 A.M. Alvin Kaplan enters the testing-room. Margot Sharpe who has been working with the amnesiac subject on a series of tests involving visual cues for much of the morning introduces him to E.H. (Close by, unobtrusively with a small camera, a graduate student is filming the encounter.)

"Eli, I'd like you to meet my colleague Alvin Kaplan. He's a professor of neuropsychology at the university and a member of Professor Ferris's lab."

E.H. rises to his feet. E.H. smiles brightly. That look of hope in the man's eyes!—Margot never ceases to be moved.

Boldly E.H. extends his hand: "Hello, Professor!"

"Hello, Mr. Hoopes."

E.H. has met Alvin Kaplan many times of course—(Margot might hazard a guess: approximately fifty times?)—but E.H. has no memory of the man.

It would be an ordinary exchange except as Kaplan shakes E.H.'s hand he squeezes the fingers, hard. E.H. reacts with surprise and pain, and disengages his hand.

Yet, Kaplan doesn't betray any social cue that he has deliberately caused E.H. pain, nor even that he notices E.H.'s reaction. So far as you would guess, Kaplan has shaken E.H.'s hand "normally"—but E.H. has reacted "abnormally."

Poor E.H. is so socialized, so eager to pass for normal, he disguises and minimizes his own pain. Taking his cues from Kaplan and Margot Sharpe (who is his "friend" in the testing-room, he thinks)—he "understands"—(mistakenly)—that the aggressive young Kaplan hasn't intended any harm, nor is he aware of having afflicted harm. Post-handshake, Kaplan behaves entirely normally, speaking to E.H. as if nothing at all were amiss; nor does Margot Sharpe, smiling at both men, indicate that she has noticed—anything.

How can I do this to Eli! This is a terrible betrayal.

Fairly quickly, E.H. recovers from the surprise of the cruel handshake. If his fingers ache, after a few seconds he has no idea why; since he has no idea why, his fingers soon cease to ache.

In the original, classic experiment the French neuroscientist Édouard Claparède shook hands with his amnesiac subject with a pin between his fingers—so that there could have been no mistaking the intention of the experimenter to inflict pain. But Margot and Kaplan have devised a more subtle, possibly more cruel variant that involves, as well, a degree of social interaction as interesting in itself as the "memory" of pain.

After scarcely more than a minute E.H. is laughing and joking with his testers—Margot Sharpe, Alvin Kaplan. So long as both are in his presence E.H. is consciously aware of them. (Fascinating to Margot that the amnesiac's seventy-second limit of short-term memory can be so extended, like water flowing into water—seamless, indivisible.) But then, a few minutes later, after the arrival of another member of the lab to distract the subject, Kaplan slips away unobtrusively—and "vanishes" from E.H.'s consciousness.

Warmly Margot says: "Shall we continue, Eli? You've been doing exceptionally well."

"Have I! Thank you for saying so—is it 'Mar-gr't'?"

"Margot. My name is Margot."

"'Marr-*got*.' Gotcha!"

E.H. winks at Margot. Sometimes, peering at Margot with a look of sly intimacy, if no one else is near E.H. draws his tongue along the surface of his lips in a way that is startling to Margot, and disturbing.

Sexual innuendo—is it? Or just—E.H.'s awkward humor?

It is believed that the injury to E.H.'s brain has radically reduced his sexual drive. In general there has been observed in the amnesiac subject a "flattening" of affect—as if the afflicted man, by nature sensitive and quick-witted, were forced to perceive the world through a bulky, swaddling scrim of some kind, or through a mask with raddled eye-holes. He tries to play a role of normalcy, but not always very skillfully. E.H. has been observed behaving in a way that might be described as warmly emotional—"affectionate and paternal"—with younger women medical workers and attendants, but no one has reported him behaving in an overtly sexual manner. Still less, in a way that might be described as sexually aggressive.

There is an essential restraint, a kind of emotional *goodness* in the man, Margot has thought.

This is nothing Margot Sharpe can ever "record"—unfortunately!

One hour and ten minutes later, at the conclusion of a battery of tests, when E.H. is resting in a chair by a window, carefully hand-printing in his little notebook, there is a knock at the door, and Margot Sharpe goes to open it—and Alvin Kaplan steps inside.

"Eli, I'd like you to meet my colleague Alvin Kaplan. He's a professor of neuropsychology at the university and a member of Professor Ferris's lab."

E.H. rises to his feet. E.H. smiles brightly and puts away his little notebook. That look of hope in the man's eyes!—Margot feels a pang of apprehension.

Boldly E.H. extends his hand: "Hello, Professor!"

"Hello, Mr. Hoopes."

When Margot first met Alvin Kaplan in 1965, as a first-year graduate student, he'd been an assistant professor in the Department of Psychology at the university; young, without tenure, yet one of Milton Ferris's "anointed"—already the recipient of a coveted research grant from the National Science Endowment. In the intervening years Kaplan has been promoted in the department, with tenure; he is still wiry-limbed and inclined to irony, though he has gained about fifteen pounds, and seems less uncertain of himself now that he has married, has become a father, and has begun to publish extensively. Margot never challenges Alvin Kaplan, whom she recognizes as very smart, and very shrewd; she guesses that he feels rivalrous toward her, as another of Milton Ferris's protégés, his only serious competitor in the lab for the elder scientist's admiration, favoritism, and affection. Yet Margot is self-effacing in Kaplan's presence, and finds it easy to admire him—to praise him. For Kaplan does have very good ideas. She knows that it would be a terrible blunder to offend him.

Though E.H. has met Kaplan many times, he appears to have no memory of him, as usual.

Or does he? As Kaplan reaches out to shake E.H.'s hand, E.H. hesitates, as he has never hesitated previously; clearly, he is wary about shaking this stranger's hand, assesses the situation and seems to make a stoic decision yes, he will shake Kaplan's hand—and again, Kaplan squeezes his hand unnaturally hard, and E.H. reacts with surprise and pain, in wincing silence; and quickly disengages his hand.

Yet—once again—Kaplan doesn't betray any social cue that he has deliberately caused E.H. pain, nor even that he notices E.H.'s reaction. So far as you would guess Kaplan has shaken E.H.'s hand "normally"—but E.H. has reacted "abnormally."

After just a few minutes the encounter ends with a remark of Kaplan's—a signal to the graduate student who has been filming.

"Very nice to meet you, Mr. Hoopes! I've heard much about you."

E.H. smiles, guardedly. But doesn't ask what the visitor has heard.

Kaplan and Margot exchange a glance—it is a fact, the amnesiac hasn't reacted identically each time, with each handshake. His behavior has been modified by the "cruel handshake"—even as he has forgotten the specific circumstances of the handshake.

In the women's restroom to which she flees as soon as she can, Margot trembles with excitement over this discovery. It is a profound discovery!

The amnesiac subject is "remembering"—in some way.

As a seemingly blind person may "see"—in some way.

Some part of the brain is functioning like memory. This is not supposed to be happening, *yet it is happening.*

Suddenly Margot is feeling nauseated. The very excitement she feels over her discovery is making her sick.

At the sink she bends double, and gags. Yet she does not vomit.

The sensation returns several times. She gags, but does not vomit. To the mirror-face she says, "Oh God. What are we doing to him. What am I doing to him. Eli! God forgive me."

AS PLANNED KAPLAN enters the testing-room. It is 11:08 A.M. of the following Wednesday—a week after the most recent confrontation.

Margot Sharpe and two other researchers have been working with E.H. for much of the morning. The tests they've been administering to the amnesiac are variants of the "distraction" test, with visual, auditory, and olfactory cues and interruptions. Margot has remained in the room with E.H. more or less continuously through the morning, and he has not seemed to "forget" her; though, when she slips away to use a restroom, and returns, she half-suspects that the amnesiac is only just pretending he isn't surprised to see her, a stranger close beside him, smiling at him as if she knows him.

He has learned to compensate for the mystery that surrounds him. Surprise to the amnesiac no longer registers as "surprise."

Such observations and epiphanies, Margot Sharpe records in her log, still in notebook form. One day, these will be included in the appendix of her most acclaimed book—*The Biology of Memory.*

"Have we met before, Mr. Hoopes?" Kaplan asks.

E.H. shakes his head *no.* He looks to Margot Sharpe, his "friend" in the lab, who says, with a pause, "I don't think so, Professor. I don't think that you and Mr. Hoopes have met."

Kaplan glances sidelong at Margot Sharpe. "Mr. Hoopes and I have *not met*—it isn't a matter of what you think, Miss Sharpe, but of what I know."

It's as if Kaplan has struck Margot with the back of his hand, to discipline her. Margot feels a stab of rage. *Tell your own lies, you bastard. Cold heartless unfeeling son of a bitch.*

Of course, they have rehearsed *the cruel handshake.* It is not a very difficult experiment, if it's even an "experiment"—Margot knows how she should behave.

Yet, what does it matter? E.H. will begin to forget within seconds.

"Eli, I'd like you to meet my colleague Professor Alvin Kaplan . . ."

But this time, as Kaplan approaches E.H. with his usual smile, the amnesiac stands very still, and visibly stiffens. E.H. is smiling a wide, forced smile even as his eyes glare.

Then, he extends his hand bravely to be shaken—but before

Kaplan can squeeze his hand, E.H. squeezes Kaplan's hand, very hard.

Kaplan winces, and jerks his hand away. For a moment he is too surprised to speak.

Then, red-faced and teary-eyed, he manages to laugh. He glances sidelong at Margot Sharpe, who is astonished as well.

"Mr. Hoopes, you've got a strong handshake! Man, that *hurt.*"

Kaplan is so stunned by the amnesiac's unexpected reaction, he has reverted to a way of speaking that isn't his own but copied from undergraduate speech. Margot laughs nervously, yet with relief.

Coolly, E.H. gives no sign that he has behaved out of character. His smile is less forced, you might say it is a triumphant smile, though much restrained.

And restrained too, E.H.'s ironic remark: "One of us is a tennis player, I guess—'Professor.' That's how you get a 'strong handshake.' "

MARGOT AND KAPLAN are impressed with E.H.'s most recent response to the handshake. The amnesiac seems to have learned without conscious memory; he has acted reflexively. *Subject "remembers" pain. Behavior indicates non-declarative memory.*

Their joint paper will be "Non-declarative Memory in Amnesia: The Case of E.H." (1973–74). But the experiment is far from complete.

Next time the "visitor" returns to shake E.H.'s hand, a week later, the amnesiac subject behaves as if he is "trusting"—somewhat stoically, he extends his hand to be shaken, and endures the painful handshake without wincing.

Margot thinks that this is evidence of E.H. having retained some memory; Kaplan does not.

To Margot's surprise Kaplan is dismissive of E.H. He has seen in the amnesiac virtually nothing of the subtlety of response Margot is certain she has seen and recorded in her meticulously kept notebook. (To Margot's dismay this subtlety isn't clear in the grainy video a graduate student provides.)

Kaplan says flatly, "The subject behaves mechanically. His reactions are programmed. He is almost exactly the same each time. Only if we shorten the interval to twenty-four hours does he 'remember' something. Otherwise, the neurons in his brain must be firing in precisely the same way each time. He's a zombie—worse, a robot. He can't change."

Margot is dismayed to hear this and moved to protest. "Eli might be tempering his response because of his respect for the situation. His sense of what the Institute is—the fact that you are a 'professor.' He'd like to swear at you, strike you—at least, squeeze your hand in retaliation as he'd done last time—but he doesn't dare. He suffers the squeezed hand in silence because he's a socialized being. He has been schooled in non-violence, in the civil rights movement. He has been conditioned to be polite."

"Bullshit! Poor bastard is a robot. There's a key in his back we have to wind. He can't 'remember' being hurt beyond a day or two. Even then, he doesn't really 'remember.' "

"He feels something like a premonition. That's a kind of memory."

" 'Premonition'—what is that? There is no neurological basis for 'premonition.' "

"I don't mean 'premonition' *literally*. You know that."

Margot raises her hand as if to strike Kaplan in the face. Instantaneously Kaplan shrinks back, lifting an arm to protect himself. Margot cries in triumph, "You see? What you did just now? You protected yourself—it's a reflex. That's what E.H. has been doing—protecting himself against *you*."

Kaplan is mildly shocked by Margot Sharpe. Indeed, it will not ever be quite forgotten by Kaplan that the subordinate Margot Sharpe actually "raised" her hand against him even to demonstrate the phenomenon of involuntary reflexive action.

"Look, the subject is brain-damaged. We're experimenting to determine if there's another avenue of 'memory' in amnesia. Why are you so protective of this poor guy? Are you in love with him?"

Kaplan laughs as if nothing can be more ridiculous, and more unlikely.

But Margot Sharpe has already turned, and is walking away.

Go to hell. We hate you. We wish you would die.

MARGOT DOWNS A shot of whiskey her lover has poured for her.

Fire-swift, her throat illuminated like a flare. Her chest, that seems to swell with elation—the thrill of despair.

I have abased myself before this man. My shame can go no further.

Yet, she is smiling. She sees in her lover's eyes that he wants her, still—she is a young woman, in the eyes of this man who is thirty-two years her senior.

Their time together is hurried, like a watch running fast. He tells her of his early, combative life in science: his impatience with the limitations of behaviorism, his feuds with colleagues at Harvard (including the great B. F. Skinner himself), his eventual triumphs. The several men who were his mentors, and those who were his detractors and who tried to sabotage his career (again, the "tyrannical" Skinner). His first great discoveries in neuropsychology. His academic appointments, his research grants, his awards and election to the National Academy at the age of thirty-two—one of the youngest psychologists ever elected to the Academy. He tells her of his children's accomplishments, and he tells her that his wife is a good, kind, decent woman, an "exemplary" woman whom he has nonetheless hurt, and continues to hurt. He tells Margot that he loves her, and does not intend to hurt *her.*

Is this a pledge? A vow? It is even true?

Another shot of whiskey?—her zealous lover pours her a drink without asking her, and Margot does not say no.

CHAPTER THREE

Hel-*lo!*"

"Eli, hello."

(Does he remember her? Margot is beginning to believe yes, the amnesiac definitely remembers *her.*)

"We have some very interesting tests for today, Eli. I think you will like them."

" 'Tests'—yes. I am good at tests—it seems."

E.H. rubs his hands together. His smile is both anxious-to-please and hopeful.

It is true, E.H. is very good at tests! And when E.H. fails a test, it is sometimes nearly as significant (in terms of the test) as if he had not failed.

Before they begin, however, E.H. insists that Margot try his favorite "brainteaser" puzzle, which fits in the palm of a hand, and consists of numbered, varicolored squares of plastic which you move around with a thumb until there is an ideal conjunction of numerals and colors. E.H. is something of a marvel at the Institute where no one on the staff, not even the younger, male attendants, can come near his speed in solving the puzzle; others, including most of the women, and certainly Margot Sharpe, are totally confused by the little puzzle, and made to feel like idiots desperately shoving squares about with their thumbs until E.H. takes it from them with a bemused chuckle—"Excuse me! Like this."

And within seconds, E.H. has lined up the squares, to perfection.

Margot pleads with E.H., please no, she doesn't want to try the maddening little thing, she knows there is a trick to it—(obviously: but what is the "trick"?)—and she doesn't have time for such a silly game; but E.H. presses it on her like an eager boy, and so with a sigh Margot takes the palm-sized plastic puzzle from him and moves the little squares about with her thumb—tries, tries and *tries*—and fails, and *fails*—until her eyes fill with tears of vexation at the damned thing and E.H. takes it from her with a bemused chuckle—"Excuse me! Like this."

And within seconds, E.H. has lined up the squares, to perfection.

His smile is that of the triumphant, just slightly mocking pubescent boy.

"HEL-*LO!*"

"Eli, hello."

Does he remember her? Margot is certain that he does—in some way.

He doesn't understand that he is an experimental subject. He is data. He thinks—

(But what does E.H. think? Even to herself Margot is reluctant to concede—*The poor man thinks he is one like us.*)

E.H. has been told many times that he is an "important" person. He believes that this fact—(if it is a fact)—both predates his illness (when he'd had a position of much responsibility in his family's investment firm and had been a civil rights activist) and has something to do with his illness (if it is an "illness" and not rather a "condition")—but he isn't certain what it entails.

The "old" Elihu Hoopes—a man of considerably higher than average intelligence, achievement, and self-awareness—cohabits uneasily with the "new" Elihu Hoopes who feels keenly his disabilities without being able to comprehend them.

"Good that our hunting rifles and shotguns are kept at the lake," E.H. has said to Margot Sharpe, with a sly wink. "And good that such weapons are not kept *loaded*."

What does this mean? Margot feels a frisson of dread.

More than once the amnesiac subject has made this enigmatic remark to Margot Sharpe but when she asks him to explain it, E.H. simply smiles and shakes his head—"You're the doctor, Doctor. You tell me."

MARGOT REPORTS TO Milton Ferris: "I think that—sometimes—unpredictably—E.H. is 'remembering' things in little clusters that, so far as we know, he shouldn't be able to remember. For instance, last week we watched a short film on Spain, and while E.H. has forgotten having seen the film, and has forgotten me, he seems to be remembering some fragments from the film. He's been 'thinking of Spain,' he told me, out of nowhere. And I think he remembers some of the Spanish music from the film, I've heard him begin to hum when we're working together. And he's been making sketches that are different from his usual sketches—'They just come to me, Doctor. Do you know what they are?'—and they are scenes that look vaguely Spanish. An exotic building or temple that resembles the Alhambra, for instance . . ."

It is like a tightrope performance, speaking to Milton Ferris.

There is the content of Margot's words, and there is the tension of speaking to *him*.

"Very good, Margot. Good work. Keep records, we'll see what develops."

Laying his hand on Margot's shoulder lightly, to thank her, and also to dismiss her. For Milton Ferris is a busy man, and has many distractions.

Margot pauses feeling a sensation like an electric current coursing through her body. Margot swallows hard, her mouth has gone dry.

Between them, a moment's rapport—sexual, and covert.

But soon then, disappointingly, E.H. seems to forget Spain. He stops humming Spanish-sounding music when Margot is near, and he returns to his familiar sketch-subjects. When Margot carefully pronounces "Spain"—"Spanish"—"Alhambra"—E.H. regards her with a polite, quizzical smile and no particular recognition; when she shows him photographs of Spanish settings, he says, "Either Spain or a South American country—though I guess that must be the Alhambra."

"Did you ever visit the Alhambra, Eli, that you can remember?"

"Well! I can hardly say that I've visited the Alhambra that I *don't remember*."

Pleasantly E.H. laughs. Margot sees the unease in his eyes.

In fact, Margot knows that E.H. has not visited Spain. Surprisingly for a man of his education, social class, and artistic interests, E.H. has not traveled extensively abroad; the energies of his young manhood were focused upon American settings.

"Were you there, with me? Are these photographs we took together?"—E.H.'s remark is startling, and difficult to interpret: flirtatious, belligerent, ironic, playful.

Margot understands that the amnesiac subject tries to determine the plausible answer to a question by questioning his interrogator. At such times his voice takes on an almost childlike mock-innocence as if (so Margot speculates) he knows that you are onto his ruse but, if you liked him, you might play along with it.

"Yes, Eli. We were there together, you and me. For three weeks in Spain, when . . ."

It is wrong of Margot Sharpe to speak in such a way, and she knows it. But the words leap from her, and cannot be retrieved.

"Were we! And were other travelers with us, or—"

E.H. gazes at her plaintively, yearningly.

Margot regrets her impulsive remark, and is grateful that no one is close by to overhear.

"—were you my 'fiancée'—is that why we were together?"

"Yes, Eli. That is why."

"Or was it our honeymoon? Was that it?"

"Yes. Our honeymoon."

"Were we happy?"

"Oh, very happy!"—Margot feels tears flooding her eyes.

"And are we married now? Have you come to take me home?"

"Soon, Eli! When you're discharged from this—clinic . . . Of course, I will take you home."

"Do you love me? Do I love *you*?"

Margot is trembling with excitement, audacity. She has gone too far. She has no idea why she has said such things.

It is a Skinnerian experiment, Margot thinks: stimulus/response. Behavior/reward/reinforcement.

A Skinnerian experiment in which Margot Sharpe is the subject.

It is clear, and she should prevent it: when E.H. smiles at her in a way that suggests sexual craving, Margot feels a surge of visceral excitement, a thrill of happiness, and can barely restrain herself from smiling at him in turn.

Instinctively—unconsciously—the amnesiac subject is conditioning her, the neuropsychologist, to respond to his feeling for her; and as Margot responds, she is further conditioning him.

She has begun to notice a twinge of excitement, yearning, in the region of her heart when she enters the perimeter of E.H.'s awareness. He does not see Margot Sharpe, whose name he can't remember, but he sees *her:* a young woman whose face he finds attractive partly or wholly because it reminds him of a face out of his childhood, a comfort to him in the terrible isolation of amnesia. He is looking at Margot with such yearning you would certainly think that he is, or has once been, her lover.

"Do you love me? Do I love *you*?"—it is a genuine question.

Margot feels a wave of guilt. And anxiety—for what if Milton Ferris were to know of her unprofessional behavior, her weakness!

She must break the transference—the "spell." Quickly she calls over a nurse's aide to watch over E.H. while she goes to use a restroom; and when she returns she sees E.H. in an animated conversation with the young female aide, who laughs at the handsome amnesiac's witty remarks as if she has never heard anything quite so funny.

He has totally forgotten Margot Sharpe of course.

When Margot approaches he turns to her, with a quick courteous smile, like one who has become accustomed to being the center of attention without questioning why, only perceptibly annoyed at being interrupted—"Hello! Hel-*lo!*"

"Hel-*lo!*"

"Eli, hello."

Does he remember *her*? It is very tempting for Margot Sharpe to think yes, he remembers *her*.

Though she knows better of course. As a scientist of the brain she knows that this terribly damaged man cannot truly remember her.

This is a day when Margot Sharpe has come to the Institute alone. She has driven alone in her own vehicle, a Volvo sedan; she has not ridden with the other lab colleagues, as usual; she is feeling somewhat agitated, after a night of disturbing dreams, and is grateful not to have to talk and relate to anyone else.

She is particularly grateful that she has been scheduled to work with the amnesiac subject alone that day. For being with the amnesiac subject as he takes his interminable tests is not like being with another person, even as it is not like being alone with oneself.

(It is not a very happy day in Margot Sharpe's life. It has not been a very happy week in Margot Sharpe's life, nor has it been a happy month in Margot Sharpe's life. But Margot Sharpe is not one to acknowledge personal problems when she is performing professionally.)

More frequently in recent years, Milton Ferris has designated Margot Sharpe his surrogate in *Project E.H.* Ferris trusts Margot Sharpe "without qualification"—(he has told her, and this is greatly flattering to her)—and behaves as if she were now his favored protégée at the university; he has been responsible for Margot being hired in a tenure-track position in the Psychology Department, and at a good salary. Of his numerous younger colleagues, Margot Sharpe seems to be the one Milton Ferris trusts most in the wake of the departure of Alvin Kaplan.

There has been some good news for the university memory lab—a renewal and an expansion of their federal grant, the elaborate proposal for which Margot did much of the work. And now

Milton Ferris has become a consultant for a popular PBS science program and is often in Washington, D.C., at the National Institutes of Health; and he is often traveling abroad, with a need for someone like Margot in the lab whom he can trust as his protégée, his emissary, his representative. At the present time, Milton Ferris has embarked upon an ambitious lecture tour in China under the auspices of the USIA.

Alvin Kaplan, Ferris's male protégé, has recently left the university. He has been promoted to professor of experimental psychology at Rockefeller University—a remarkable position for one so young. Like Margot Sharpe, now assistant professor of psychology and neuroscience at the university, Kaplan has co-published numerous papers with Milton Ferris.

Both Alvin Kaplan and Margot Sharpe delivered papers on their groundbreaking research in amnesia at the most recent American Association of Experimental Psychology conference in San Francisco.

Saw your name in the newspaper!—occasionally someone will call Margot Sharpe. Family member, relative, old friend from the University of Michigan. *Sounds just fascinating, the work you are doing.*

Sometimes, Margot will receive a call or a letter—*Why don't we ever hear from you any longer, Margot? Do I have the wrong address?*

Once, Margot couldn't resist showing E.H. a copy of the prestigious *Journal of American Experimental Psychology* in which the major article appeared under her name—"Distraction, Working Memory, and Memory Retention in the Amnesiac 'E.H.'" Her heart beat rapidly as E.H. perused it with a small wondering smile.

(Was she behaving unprofessionally? She would have been devastated if a colleague found out.)

Gentlemanly E.H. reacted with bemusement, not resentment—

"Is 'E.H.' meant to be me? Never knew I was so important." He asked if he might take the journal home with him so that he could read it carefully—to try to "understand what the hell is going on inside my 'scrambled brains' "—and Margot said of course. And so Margot placed the journal on a table in the testing-room for E.H. to take home with him.

(Confident that the amnesiac would forget the journal within seventy seconds and she could easily slip it back into her bag without him noticing.)

Since then Margot has several times showed E.H. journals with articles about "E.H."—some of them co-authored by Milton Ferris and his team of a half-dozen associates including Margot Sharpe, others by just Milton Ferris and Margot Sharpe.

By degrees, they have become associated with each other as scientists. Collaborators.

It has been years. Has it been years?

In the memory lab, time passes strangely.

It was only the other day (it seems) when Margot was first introduced to "Elihu Hoopes"—who'd stared at her with a kind of recognition, hungry, yearning, and squeezed her small pliant hand in his.

I know you. We know each other. Don't we?

We were in grade school together . . .

E.H. squeezes Margot's hand in his strong dry fingers. She has been anticipating this—she doesn't pull her hand away from his grasp so quickly as she does when others are in the room with them.

"Mr. Hoopes—'Eli.' I'm so happy to see you."

"I'm so happy to see *you*."

There is something different about this morning, Margot thinks.

Margot thinks—*But I can't. It would be wrong.*

Still they are clasping hands. With no one else in the testing-room to observe they are free of social restraint. Between them, there is but the residue of instinct.

"Do you remember me, Eli? 'Margot.' "

"Oh yes—'Margot.' "

"Your friend."

"Yes, my friend—'Mar-got.' "

Conscientiously, E.H. pronounces her name *Mar-go.* So quick at mimicry is E.H., one would think his skill a kind of memory.

"I think I knew you in—was it school? Grade school?"

"Yes. Gladwyne."

We were close friends through school. Then you went to Amherst, and I went to Ann Arbor.

We were in love, but—something happened to part us . . .

(Wouldn't Eli realize, Margot Sharpe is much younger than he is? At least seventeen years?)

(Yet: E.H. is a perpetual thirty-seven and Margot Sharpe is now thirty-four. If E.H. were capable of thinking in such terms he would be thinking that, magically, the young woman psychologist has caught up with him in age.)

"I've been looking forward to today since—last Wednesday. We're doing such important work, Eli . . ."

"Yes. Yes we are, Mar-*go.*"

It is very exciting, their proximity. Their privacy. Margot can feel the man's breath on her face as he leans over her.

E.H. seems to be inhaling Margot. She wants to think that her scent has become familiar to him. (She has conducted olfactory memory tests with him of her own invention indicating that yes, E.H. is more likely to remember smells than other sensory cues; his memory for smells of decades ago is more or less undiminished.)

E.H. is taller than Margot by at least five inches, so that she is forced to look up at him and this is pleasurable to her, as to him.

Is E.H. nearly forty-seven now? How quickly the years have passed! (For E.H. no time at all has passed.)

His hairline is receding from his high forehead, and his russet-brown hair is fading to a beautiful shade of pewter-gray, yet E.H. remains youthful, straight-backed. His forehead is lightly creased with bewilderment or worry that quickly eases away when he smiles at a visitor.

"Eli, how have you been?"

"Very good, thank you. And you?"

The question is genuine. E.H. is anxious to *know*.

All of the world is clues to the amnesiac. Like a box of jigsaw puzzle pieces that has been overturned, scattered. Through some effort—(a superhuman effort beyond the capacity of any normal individual)—these countless pieces might be fitted together again into a coherent and illuminating whole.

Is E.H. "very good"? Margot knows that the poor man had bronchitis for several weeks that winter. Terrible fits of coughing, that made testing impossible at times. Not only were short-term memories slipping out of the amnesiac's brain as through a large-holed colander but the severe coughing seemed to exacerbate loss of memory.

(Margot has been concerned about E.H.'s health in recent years. She is assured that the amnesiac receives physical examinations at the Institute, that his blood, blood pressure, and other vital signs are routinely tested. In her own case, Margot often forgets to schedule dental appointments, gynecological appointments, eye examinations—and how much more likely to neglect himself is a man with memory deficits.)

E.H. has forgotten the bronchitis and its discomforts. E.H. has forgotten his original, devastating illness. E.H. quickly forgets all physical distress, maladies. He may be susceptible to moods—but E.H. quickly forgets all moods.

He has lost weight, Margot estimates about five to eight pounds. His face is the face of a handsome ascetic. He retains the alert and agile air of an ex-athlete but he has become an ex-athlete who anticipates pain.

Today he is wearing neatly pressed khakis, an English-looking striped shirt, and a dark green cashmere sweater. His socks are a very dark purple patterned in small yellow checks. All of his clothing is purchased at expensive men's stores like J. Press, Ralph Lauren, Armani. Margot has seen these clothes before, she thinks, but not for some time. (Who assists E.H. with his wardrobe? Sees that his things are laundered, dry-cleaned? Margot supposes it must be the watchful and loving guardian-aunt with whom he lives.) Even in the throes of amnesia E.H. exhibits a touching masculine vanity. Margot always compliments him on his clothing, and E.H. always says, "Thank you!"—and pauses as if he has more to say, but can't remember what it is.

Margot Sharpe has done what few of her science colleagues would do, or would consider it proper for a scientist to be doing: daringly, like an investigative reporter, or indeed a detective, she has looked into the background of the amnesiac subject E.H. In all she has spent several days in Philadelphia meeting with former associates of Elihu Hoopes including black community organizers who knew him in the late 1950s and 1960s as one of a very small number of white citizens who gave money to their causes, as well as to the NAACP and Reverend Martin Luther King,

Jr.'s Southern Christian Leadership Conference; she has learned that, in some quarters, Eli Hoopes is considered a "hero"—that is, he'd behaved "heroically" in joining civil rights activists who'd picketed City Hall, protested Philadelphia police brutality and harassment, campaigned for better schools in South Philly, better health-care facilities, an end to discriminatory hiring in municipal government. He'd established a fund for university scholarships at Penn, earmarked for "disadvantaged youths." He'd given money to *Philadelphia Inquiry,* a local version of *Mother Jones* that appeared sporadically during the 1960s. (In one of the issues, which the former editor passed on to Margot Sharpe, there appeared a personal account by Elihu Hoopes titled "Hiding in the Seminary & the Afterlife"—a provocative memoirist piece in which Elihu Hoopes speaks of his experience at Union Theological Seminary and why he'd dropped out after two years: "I felt that I was living in a cocoon of privilege. My eyes were opened by a black Christian who told me of lynchings in the South—following World War II.")

As a way of being friendly and winning the amnesiac subject's trust, Margot has several times asked E.H. about his "activist" life and his "seminary" life; E.H. is likely to become overexcited talking of these past lives which he seems to know are "past"—yet has no idea how he knows this, and what has happened in the interim. He has a vague understanding that he has not seen, for instance, the black community organizer with whom Margot had spoken, for some time; yet, since he believes himself to be thirty-seven years old, and living still in Philadelphia, he is confused about why he hasn't seen the man—and whether the Philadelphia Civil Rights Coalition has disbanded. (Margot is hesitant to tell E.H. that the Coalition has not disbanded; she fears he would not understand why it isn't possible for him to reconnect with it.) E.H.'s memories of the seminary are both vivid and vague as in a film that goes in and out of focus. And his memory of his recent past is becoming strangely riddled with blank spaces. He is beginning to forget proper names—a symptom, Margot doesn't like to note, of the more general, inevitable amnesia of an aging brain.

So, Margot has learned that it is wisest to steer the amnesiac subject into activities and routines that don't arouse his emotions, or provoke his memory. This morning she leads him through the first of a battery of tests designed to measure "working memory." Initially E.H. performs well, like a bright twelve-year-old; these are complicated tests, tests of some ingenuity—(Margot designed them herself); yet as Margot works with E.H. she is less buoyant than usual.

She forgets to praise the amnesiac, who so yearns to be praised but will not recall what is missing if you don't praise him; tears gather in her eyes and threaten to spill down her cheeks. She is so unhappy!

At last E.H. asks what is wrong?

Nothing! Of course, nothing is wrong.

Margot proceeds with the testing like one with eyes riveted straight ahead. To glance to either side is the danger.

"I'M SORRY. I shouldn't be telling you this."

This should have been the strategy. In Margot's memory, something like this will have been the strategy.

But it happens, Elihu Hoopes is so gentlemanly, yet so tender and solicitous, Margot begins to weaken and confide in him, far more than she'd intended.

Margot thinks—*This man was training to be a minister. His soul is so much vaster than mine.*

Margot hears herself tell E.H., who is her amnesiac subject, that—that she is very unhappy . . . She trails off into silence wiping at her eyes.

At once E.H. tells her yes, he understands. He is sorry for her and wonders if he can help her.

No, Margot says. No one can help her.

But is she sure?—E.H. asks.

In the sequestered privacy and quiet of the testing-room they are speaking together quietly. The tests have been set aside—for the moment.

It would be a matter of great astonishment if anyone (outside the testing-room) could hear what they are saying.

Margot had no intention of telling anyone—certainly not E.H.—of the singular unhappiness of her life, which she believes to be entirely her own fault, a misery inflicted upon herself. Yet, Margot hears herself confessing, unforgivably—she is in love with someone who does not love her in return.

She is in love with a man who is married—a man who is thirty-two years older than she is.

She is *so ashamed*. She *can't believe such a thing has happened to her.*

Seeing the expression in E.H.'s face—surprise, concern, sympathy—Margot begins to laugh. It is all so—ridiculous!

Well, she will concede—she believes she is in love. Naïvely she has believed that the man is in love with *her*.

She has *made mistakes* in her relationship with this man. She has *acted stupidly, blindly*.

Yes, the man is a professional colleague. Yes, he is her senior in every way—her mentor, her dissertation advisor.

So many mistakes Margot Sharpe has made, in her ill-considered plunge into—would you call it *passion*? In his office at the university when they'd worked together late or when she'd remained late under the pretext of needing to confer with him. Seeing his eyes moving onto her, and feeling that sensation of faintness, helplessness, that is both exhilarating to her, and distressing. For never has Margot Sharpe been a naïve person, never has Margot Sharpe wished to believe that (male, sporadic) interest in her has been anything to take seriously, and to cultivate. On the contrary: she recalls as a girl with two older brothers overhearing how crudely, how coarsely boys speak of girls when they think no one else is listening, or no one who matters is listening. *A female is her body-parts. A female is to be ridiculed, to the degree that she is vulnerable to the male.*

And there were incidents from high school and college, not traumatic, not humiliating, only just mildly degrading and embarrassing—the sort of quasi-sexual experiences all girls and young women have—which have reinforced Margot's air of caution and detachment.

Milton Ferris, however, exerted from the start a powerful gravitational pull. Working in close quarters with the man as she was, it was not sufficient for Margot to avoid looking at him: simply being proximate to him, hearing his voice, his dry, droll, kindly, jocular, teasing, deep-baritone voice was distracting to her, overwhelming. And all that she'd succeeded in ignoring in the man's presence would rush upon her when she was alone. And all that he represents, as a scientist of great distinction. All that he *is*.

Of course, there were rumors about Milton Ferris. His relationships with female colleagues, associates. His "exploitations" of the naïve and trusting. Such rumors, Margot steadfastly ignored.

She'd been in love with him from the start. Maybe.

She is not in love with Milton Ferris! Certainly not.

Yet she'd indicated to the older man that yes, she was attracted to him. Or rather, she had not blocked his interest in her.

Once these signals were sent and received, once certain reflexes were triggered, there seemed to Margot no turning back. An irrevocable decision to accept her advisor's invitation to accompany him to a neuroscience conference in Atlanta—*Your way will be paid of course, Margot. Every expense.*

She had said yes. She had not said no but *yes.*

Yes is not to be undone. *Yes* would be the devastation of her career, if it were undone.

He'd laid his hand on her shoulder, then. Not a heavy hand, yet Margot understood—*He is making his claim.*

A sort of delirium had come over her. A young woman unaccustomed to the attentions of men, especially men of distinction—a young woman somewhat ill at ease in her skin—how could she resist? E.H. listens to Margot without judging her, of course. He is unusually quiet. Margot feels again a sensation of great affection for him, which brings tears to her eyes. She is thinking—when was the last time she'd cried? At her father's funeral?—at the burial in the cemetery?—she feels dread at the possibility of remembering too vividly.

Margot is very indiscreet, to speak Milton Ferris's name. Yet she hears herself ask E.H. if he remembers "Milton Ferris"—of course, Margot knows that he does not. But E.H. nods sagely, to encourage her. They are facing each other across a table, leaning toward each other so intensely, Margot feels the strain in her back.

E.H.'s hand fumbles for hers, to comfort.

Margot's hand does not ease away . . .

Margot tells E.H. that Milton Ferris has been her Ph.D. advisor, her mentor, since she'd come to the university ten years before. He has helped her as a scientist—incalculably. He has arranged for her to be invited to give papers at conferences. He has been instrumental in her dissertation being published by the University of Pennsylvania Press and her having been hired at the university—the first woman appointment in cognitive neuropsychology.

In the past eleven months, however, their relationship has changed. Considerably.

And now, Milton Ferris is touring China for six weeks. There'd been a vague suggestion that Margot Sharpe would accompany him, as a younger colleague involved in original research on amnesia, but somehow that suggestion faded, and when Margot summoned all her strength to ask Ferris about it, whether she was coming with him, whether she should make travel arrangements, he'd told her evasively that his plans had changed.

What do you mean, she'd asked.

What do you mean, your *plans have changed.*

She hadn't raised her voice. She hadn't wept. She'd felt—well, yes she'd felt a kind of sick horror, bile at the back of the mouth. She'd tasted *shame.*

She is telling E.H., she'd managed to salvage some dignity.

She is assuring E.H., who looks with such pity at her, that she didn't embarrass herself any further.

Still, she has been waiting for the man to call her. One final time, they should speak. They should meet.

They have made love for the final time, she supposes. That she must accept.

They will meet—somewhere. They will have a drink together. Drinks.

Sweet fiery sensation of whiskey. Milton Ferris's favored drink, for which Margot Sharpe has acquired a belated taste.

Telling E.H., her face wet with tears, that she can't exactly remember how it ended between her and Ferris. Her memories seem to her muddied, splotched. As if she has been running through mud. Her body splotched with mud. Face splotched with mud.

The taste of bile at the back of her mouth. But she has not been sick to her stomach, she has not *vomited.*

She isn't a weak woman, she tells E.H. She isn't a woman who depends upon others, a woman who pleas with others, begs. She *is not.*

She tells E.H. that Milton Ferris is in China, and has not communicated with her since his departure. A brief call on the evening before he'd left and this last conversation did not go well.

She tells E.H. that Milton Ferris is not alone in China. She thinks he is not alone.

(Yet his wife is not accompanying him—Margot knows.)

A mistake, a terrible mistake, I was so grateful for his attention, I behaved desperately and stupidly.

Margot tells E.H.: there is no shame like the shame of rejection.

Margot tells E.H.: she has thought of killing herself—to alleviate the shame.

Margot tells E.H.: at the outset of the project on amnesia, Milton Ferris designed all the tests and experiments, and carefully oversaw their execution. Initially, he came to the Institute and worked with E.H. personally—"Do you remember him, Eli? 'Milton Ferris'—white-haired, with a wiry white beard—he's a distinguished neuroscientist, he has been nominated for a Nobel Prize . . ."

E.H. has no idea who "Milton Ferris" is but of course he nods encouragingly. He has been gripping Margot's hands in his and listening to her halting and not very coherent words with an expression of deep sympathy.

Such sympathy does not judge. Margot is deeply grateful, that she *be not judged.*

Such emotion! Her brain feels like suet, disintegrating.

The shameful fact is, Margot adores Milton Ferris.

Margot is in thrall to Milton Ferris.

Even now, when the man has broken off with her—whatever ill-defined, nebulous and exclusively clandestine relationship they'd had—(of which others in the lab certainly know, or suspect)—the shameful fact is, Margot has not broken off with *him.*

Milton Ferris is the most brilliant scientist she has ever met—she is sure. Milton Ferris is the most brilliant person who has ever truly cared for *her.*

She is frightened by the prospect of losing him.

She is terrified by the prospect of losing him.

She is the Chaste Daughter. She has never resisted Milton Ferris and it is not possible for her to imagine resisting Milton Ferris.

She is so ashamed! She is thrilled, and she is ashamed.

Even now speaking of it, for the first time in her life baring her soul and to a stranger, even amid shame she is thrilled. For simply to confess this clandestine love, this humiliating love, is to acknowledge that yes, there was "love"—and it was "sexual love"—(to a degree: Margot's experience of sex in their relationship has been uncertain)—and of this Margot Sharpe is proud. Even now.

E.H. listens, avidly. E.H. does not judge for he is kindly, patient—he is all that Milton Ferris is not.

Her error, Margot says, is that she has made Milton Ferris the center of her life. She has not behaved professionally. If she tells this story from a woman's perspective she will say *he took advantage of my weakness, I am his subordinate and he knew his power over me.*

Yet certain facts remain: she abased herself before the man.

She might have eased away from his first advances, which were not aggressive or coercive—(she must acknowledge)—but rather sweetly playful, oblique. A touch of his hand on her wrist, an offer to drive her through pelting rain to her rented apartment overlooking the deep ravine. An offer to walk with her, enormous black umbrella opened above them as in a cartoon by Magritte, to the rear door of her apartment where—(she recalls with stunning vividness, her heart nearly stopping)—she fumbles for her key as he stands close beside her and she feels his breath on her face.

His pronunciation of her name: "MAR-go SHARPE."

Always he has seemed somewhat bemused by her. She has wondered if, in his life, which has spanned nearly seven decades, he has been intimately involved with so many women, has gazed intently into the eyes of so many who have adored him even as they have slightly feared him—if, to Milton Ferris, "Margot Sharpe" is entirely real.

This past year. Not continuous, discontinuous. Days in succession when she neither saw Ferris nor heard from him. For the edict was, she must never call *him*.

She knows: she has not once resisted him in any essential way—only in the most trivial "daughterly" ways. She has never opposed him in the lab. If he is mistaken about something, she remains silent. She allows others to speak, and to risk antagonizing the great man. So bound to Milton Ferris, she cannot imagine a life without him.

"He has done so much for me, Eli! He has established my career. He has guided me, looked out for me. I wouldn't be an assistant professor at the university except for Milton Ferris—of course. I wouldn't know you—I wouldn't have had the opportunity to work with 'E.H.'—without Milton Ferris. 'The biology of memory'—I owe him everything."

Ferris has directed Margot Sharpe as one might gently push, with a foot, a light, floating vessel—at once the little boat moves in the water, and momentum will carry it far.

Yet, it is a fact that Milton Ferris has appropriated a number of ideas from the lab that are not his own. Margot Sharpe's ideas, and Margot Sharpe's experimental work with E.H., lengthy batteries of tests recorded by Margot and a graduate student associate here at the Institute—"Olfactory compensation for memory deficit." Margot Sharpe is listed as an author, of course—a co-author, with Milton Ferris.

As if Margot Sharpe were Ferris's assistant. Possibly, Ferris's graduate student.

She tells herself—*But it is only fair, in his eyes. Without him, I couldn't have written the paper—couldn't have done the work.*

Margot tells E.H. how at the start Milton Ferris was truly the principal investigator in the lab. Milton Ferris wrote up the first-draft reports. Milton Ferris was involved in every stage including providing graphs, figures, footnotes. Carefully he looked through his associates' reports, checked their data. Weeks were involved in the preparation of a single paper. Each member of the lab was listed as a co-author; "Milton Ferris" was named last, as the PI.

Then by degrees it happened that Milton Ferris came less frequently to the Institute to work with the team. He was "away"—he was "traveling." He was in New York City consulting with a TV producer preparing a documentary on the human brain. He was in Washington consulting with the president's special advisory committee on bioethics.

Alvin Kaplan, Ferris's most trusted associate at the time, would write the first draft of an article. With corrections, the draft would be rewritten by Margot Sharpe. There might be a third draft, and a fourth, and a fifth—by Kaplan and Sharpe. To a degree others in the lab were involved.

Now it has come to be that Milton Ferris's appearance at the Institute is something of a rarity, like the visit of a royal person. And it is rare too that Ferris is involved in preparing articles on E.H.—though (as he insists) he continues to read everything that is written by his young associates. He provides detailed critiques, he subtracts and he adds, and returns the drafts to their authors with queries, suggestions, directives for revision. It is only by Ferris's decree that an article is declared "finished" and ready to be submitted for publication at one or another professional journal where Ferris is likely to know the editors very well. It is only by Milton Ferris's decree that anything comes out of his lab—you would not dare try to publish without his approval.

Over the years it has developed that experiments involving E.H. are designed by his young colleagues, and not by Milton Ferris. All data, all evidence, are gathered and collated by the colleagues—of course.

Yet, no matter who designed the experiments, who spends many hours recording experiments with E.H., and no matter who has written the article, "Milton Ferris" continues to be listed in the position of prominence at the end of the list of co-authors.

And sometimes it happens, a paper on E.H. appears in a prominent journal with just one author—"Milton Ferris."

Once, Alvin Kaplan tossed a copy of the *Journal of American Experimental Psychology* onto Margot Sharpe's desk at the university and turned away without a word and when Margot opened the journal she discovered an article titled "Constructive Memory, Memory Distortions, and Confabulation in the Memory-Impaired" by Milton Ferris—an article originally written by Kaplan and Sharpe based upon experiments designed by Kaplan and Sharpe and executed by the lab team.

Within the lab, Margot does not speak of such things.

She has never been close with anyone in the memory lab. The young woman who'd been an older graduate student when Margot first arrived has long since departed—without Milton Ferris's blessing, she managed to secure a position with tenure at Purdue University which is (as Ferris laughingly said) "somewhere west of here."

The Chaste Daughter does not betray the Father. Even when the Father has betrayed her, the Chaste Daughter does not betray.

Until this moment Margot has not quite realized the depth of her shame, and the helplessness of her shame. Until this moment Margot has not comprehended that she might have a professional complaint.

He is stealing from us. He is sucking our blood.

He is a thief, he must be exposed.

No words! The Chaste Daughter has no words.

If Margot Sharpe brought up such subjects with her mentor, if Margot Sharpe inquired about just one of the articles Ferris has published under fraudulent pretenses, he would be incredulous. He would deny whatever she was suggesting, in the most decisive terms. He would cease to love her, at once.

He doesn't love me now—does he?

Someday, he will love me—will he?

The displeasure of the Father is a terrible thing. Ferris would be furious with her.

In an instant, all that existed between them—so assiduously cultivated by Margot Sharpe, with the care of a madman constructing an elaborate ship inside a bottle, over a period of years—would be smashed.

He would see her as a traitor, the betraying Daughter. Worse, he would see Margot Sharpe as a threat to his scientific reputation, and he would expel her from his lab.

Ferris is a man of moods. On a number of occasions, with virtually no provocation, he has been critical of his adoring young female colleague—he has been disapproving, sarcastic—(how swiftly bemusement can turn to sarcasm!)—for no evident reason. At the slightest provocation, sensing the most subtle opposition or questioning of his authority, he becomes enraged. (Margot wonders if this is why Alvin Kaplan left the university. Needing to get free of his powerful mentor whom he too adores and resents.) Ferris would deny her charges, if they are charges—he would so confront her, Margot Sharpe would back down in confusion.

My word against his. But I have no word against Milton Ferris.

All this while E.H. has been gripping Margot's hands tightly in his. Margot's slender fingers, E.H.'s larger, stronger fingers. They are close together, like conspirators. Margot feels a sensation of giddiness, faintness. For here is a man who respects her, someone who is her true friend—as Milton Ferris could never be her friend.

Of course—what had she been thinking? Milton Ferris could never be her friend but only her mentor.

He is not her lover, though Margot Sharpe is his lover.

Ferris is someone who has had, surreptitiously, somewhat distractedly, sexual relations with Margot Sharpe: "sexual relations" being such a crude and reductive term, indicating virtually nothing of the emotional experience which was, on her side if not on his, cataclysmic.

With a choked little laugh Margot tells E.H.: she wasn't serious a few minutes ago, she would certainly not *kill herself.* Not ever.

She would certainly not kill herself for a man. And not for that man.

And now, E.H. surprises Margot Sharpe. He has been listening to her intently, and he is fiercely sympathetic as she has never seen him—

"Someone should kill him."

Margot stares at E.H.'s stern face. The amnesiac is not smiling now. Margot isn't sure that she has heard correctly.

"If that—that man—lied to you—and stole from you—and took advantage of you—and made you feel so bad—someone should kill him."

E.H. speaks almost calmly. It is clear to Margot that E.H. has no idea who "Milton Ferris" is—only that this is a person who has made her distraught, and thus must be punished.

"No, Eli! Of course not—*no*."

Margot is shocked. Such a remark isn't characteristic of mild-mannered kindly Elihu Hoopes!

"Eli, please. I shouldn't have told you this . . . *No*."

Her close proximity, her tears, her utter lack of discretion and control may have triggered in the amnesiac an upsetting memory. His feeling for her is the result of a dislodged memory that predates his illness, when he'd been a sexually vigorous man in the prime of life—Margot thinks.

E.H. persists: "Tell me who he is. Where he is. I will find him."

"Eli, I don't think so. I don't think this is a good idea."

"Tell me. I will kill him for you."

She is astonished. She is beginning to be frightened.

Such conviction in Elihu Hoopes. Such certitude!

The amnesiac's narrowed eyes. No childlike sweetness in those eyes, now.

Margot wonders—*Has E.H. killed? In his past life?*

And no one knows? And E.H. himself only dimly remembers?

Out of an amnesiac's past emerge islands of memory, unpredictably.

Islands of memory. A beautiful expression, she thinks it is Milton Ferris who first employed it.

Margot is feeling very exhausted. Margot has never spoken at such length, in such a way, exposing her soul to another. Though Milton Ferris is her lover, or has been her lover, Margot has never spoken openly to Milton Ferris about virtually anything. She shuts her eyes seeing something floating in the dark—islands, in an inland lake. Small islands that float in reflected light. The lake itself is enormous, its circumference is not visible. The water is rough, rippling. Yet creased with light from an (invisible) sun, or moon. Connective tissue among the islands is the earth, the lake-bed, but it is invisible to the eye. If you don't know the connective tissue is there beneath the shimmering surface you could not guess at it.

E.H. is holding Margot, to comfort her. Never before has anyone held Margot Sharpe in such a way.

Never before have Margot Sharpe and Elihu Hoopes touched so intimately. Never before have they been alone together for such a sustained duration of time. Though her heart is beating rapidly in the knowledge that what she has done, what she is doing, is very wrong Margot presses her face against the man's chest, against the soft cashmere wool beneath which, at a distance of just a few inches, the amnesiac's heart beats warmly.

Margot thinks—*He is a beautiful man. A beautiful soul. Here is the one I love, not the other.*

WHAT SHE HAS revealed, what she has done. The shame of it!

Professionally, she would be disgraced. Will be, if anyone knows.

Almost, she feels a compulsion to confess. But to whom?

"Milton. Forgive me. I've said terrible things about us to a stranger . . ."

(The humiliating fact is, even now Margot Sharpe hopes that her married lover will return to her. And if he will not "return" to her exactly—for indeed he has never been *with her*—she will settle for their former relationship in which, when he wishes, he contacts her; and she is forbidden to contact him.)

Her eyes are reddened. Watery and stricken, in the white-skinned face.

In cold water in the women's restroom she washes the face—of course, she recognizes it as "hers."

The most extreme amnesia would be prosopagnosia—the inability to recognize one's own face in a mirror.

Except prosopagnosia isn't amnesia, strictly speaking. It is a defect of perception, not of memory.

Returning to the testing-room, and there is E.H. seated at a window with shoulders slightly hunched, rapidly sketching with a stick of charcoal in his sketchbook. When Margot enters the room, E.H. looks up startled and quickly closes the book.

"Hel-*lo!*"

She sees how completely the amnesiac's smile transforms his face, like a skintight mask.

MARGOT DOWNS A shot of whiskey. Quickly, so that her hand doesn't shake.

Like fire, the liquid in her throat. A burning sensation in her chest, in the region of her heart.

I have abased myself before two men. My shame can go no further. Someone should kill him. Yes!

Yet she is smiling. Her mouth has twisted into a strange loose smile as of mockery, or despair.

Another shot of whiskey, enough to get her through the night.

FIRE IN HIS brain!—slow-smoldering at first then bursting into flame.

He is sick for a long time then. He is told.

What he is, is what others tell him. What he "is" has vanished like rising fading smoke.

Except: feverishly drawing in a sketchbook provided to him—(by his aunt who is his father's younger sister, recognizes her face but can't recall her name)—figures of drowning children, young girls, and a boy with affrighted hair (like little snakes lifting from his head) and a long brooding face. Animal-faced, with hooved feet. *What is this? Who is this, Eli?*—he is asked.

Can't reply, can only shake his head vehemently.

You know who this is. This is Elihu Hoopes, who died.

HERE IS A surprise: E.H. on the tennis court!

Margot Sharpe has several times observed the amnesiac playing tennis on a court attached to the Institute. He will play with staff members, most of them much younger than he, and he will nearly always defeat them despite poor vision in one eye.

"Great serve, Eli!"

"Jesus, Eli! How'd you do *that*!"

At such times E.H. is suffused with happiness, and with certainty. He is a canny tennis player—he has been playing tennis (Margot has learned) since childhood. He'd been a champion in his prep school league and as an Amherst undergraduate he'd had a national ranking.

By instinct his strong-muscled legs carry him deftly about the court. By instinct his strong right hand swings the racket. His backhands are dynamite. His serves are terrifically fast. Unconsciously he compensates for his diminished vision. Only between sets when E.H. has to pause, to think, to reflect—you can see the confusion in his face as in the face of one who has been rudely wakened from a dream.

Where is this? Who is my opponent?

What is the score?

THE BLUNDER. MARGOT has arranged to play tennis with E.H. In emulation of E.H. she is wearing proper, pristine white: T-shirt, shorts, tennis shoes.

They are smiling at each other across the net. Gentlemanly E.H. expects Margot to serve first but Margot calls to E.H., "Please begin. Please serve first."

She is a "promising" tennis player. She has been told.

In high school in Orion Falls, Michigan, Margot Sharpe was rarely better than average in any sport. Her high grades, her precocious seriousness, protected her like body armor from the sneers of her classmates.

As her quick sharp brilliant intelligence shielded her from the sexual sneers of her classmates, or rather from an acknowledgment of these sneers.

E.H. serves rapidly, unhesitatingly. Margot fails to return the first serve.

And of course, Margot fails to return the second serve that flies past her like a missile.

E.H. is laughing at her, not unkindly. (Margot knows: he has forgotten her name by now, and who she is, but she is certain that he has not forgotten *her.* Since their embrace the previous week, he has certainly not forgotten *her.*) When Margot serves, E.H. does not slam the ball back at her but relents and allows a volley of sorts, in a way that might be called gentlemanly and bemused. And when she begins to play with more assurance, if often wildly, E.H. steps up the intensity of the game as if by instinct. His fierce concentration on the ball, his deft movements about the court, the ease of his backhand—E.H. is so practiced a player, he doesn't have to think. He forces Margot to stumble backward, nearly falling as she flails at the ball; he forces Margot to rush forward, nearly falling into the net. E.H.'s tennis skills, internalized decades before, are as deep-imprinted in his brain as running, bicycling, swimming, driving a vehicle are deep-imprinted; but it has been observed that, if E.H. practices serves, though strictly speaking he will not be able to "remember" the practice sessions, his playing will improve.

Non-declarative memory—Margot thinks. She has written on *non-declarative memory in amnesia* and has ideas for further experiments with E.H.

She is beginning to sweat, unbecomingly. Rivulets of oily sweat run down her back, her sides. Her dark hair, pulled back into a ponytail, is loosening and erupts in wispy tendrils around her heated face. She is distracted recalling how tenderly Elihu Hoopes held her not long before, how sympathetically he'd listened to her halting words, how his heart beat against the side of her face . . .

They had not kissed. Margot had felt the man's sexual arousal, and her own, and had eased away from him deeply embarrassed.

If anyone had seen! One of the Institute staff!

Far worse, one of her lab colleagues who would report back to the university!

Worst of all, if Milton Ferris learned of her behavior . . .

Margot is distracted by such thoughts circling her head like gnats attracted to her damp face and hair.

"Point!"—E.H. calls, triumphant.

There is something hurtful in the man's belligerence on the court, that is not evident elsewhere.

Margot decides to laugh at herself, too. Calls out gaily to the white-clad male figure on the other side of the net, crouching, gripping his racket in both hands, gaze fixed coolly upon her—"You're a savage tennis player, Eli! Just as everyone says—you take no prisoners."

Take no prisoners. Margot's heart pumps in chagrin, why has she said something so foolish?

Like one who hasn't quite heard another's words, or doesn't quite understand another's joke, E.H. laughs thinly in response. He is still standing in a slight crouch, knees bent and feet apart. Margot sees him now staring at her as an individual, not as an opponent. He is trying to determine—*Who is this person? What is her connection to me?*

When Margot serves, E.H. makes no effort to slam the ball back over the net but returns it in mimicry of Margot's serve: the ball seems to drift over the net like a balloon. A volley then, as if in slow motion. And finally E.H. fails to return the ball at all—he stands blinking after it as it rolls out of bounds at the side of the court.

"Is something wrong, Eli?"—Margot calls out anxiously.

In his dazzling white T-shirt, white shorts, white tennis shoes E.H. stands in a fugue of confusion. As if a haze has settled upon him. She has broken the spell, Margot thinks. Foolishly speaking to him, distracting him, Margot has caused the amnesiac to lose his concentration on the game because he has been forced to consider *her.*

And who is she, this panting anxious-eyed woman facing him across the net, whom he has never seen before?

MARGOT SHARPE DOESN'T enter this incident in her log. In her lab notebook for the day there is no indication of a tennis game with the amnesiac subject, not even in code.

Margot hopes that no one on the Institute staff noticed. Or if noticing, had a second thought about it.

Thinking—*It will not happen again. Must not.*

MARGOT DRINKS A shot glass of whiskey.

Oh!—the kick in her chest, as the flamey liquid eases down.

Delicious burning sensation in her throat. Slithering flames of a sexual fire. *I love this.*

CHAPTER FOUR

Eli, what a beautiful necktie! You are always so well dressed."

Each day he is brought to the Institute for testing Elihu Hoopes dresses with the care of one who anticipates good news.

Over a period of more than three decades this will be! And Margot Sharpe will have been a witness through these years.

E.H. is usually fresh-shaven, and his hair that thins and recedes over the years is neatly combed, and trimmed—a haircut every three weeks. His fingernails are clean and neatly filed and so, Margot has assumed, his toenails are as well.

To assure that he remains well groomed, in public at least, E.H. assiduously keeps a calendar. It is a large calendar hung on a wall beside his bed on which he marks dates for haircuts, dental and medical appointments, "test-days" at the Institute; when he goes to bed each night, carefully he crosses out the date.

In this way moving forward, a day at a time.

(And if the amnesiac chooses to look back at previous months, solemn weeks of X'd-out dates, the experience replicates the experience of any stranger to a life, curious about that life now *past tense.*)

E.H.'s clothes are equally calibrated. With Post-its in widely varying hues he keeps a record of the clothes he wears so that he doesn't too frequently repeat them. *How handsome you look today, Eli! What a beautiful necktie!* Though E.H. doesn't know it perhaps he can sense that the Institute is his only "public" place now.

Shoes, of which he has many pairs, E.H. rotates on the floor of his walk-in cedar closet. At the Institute he alternates between sporty wear, casual wear, and (occasionally) dressy wear.

And he likes to be taken shopping, always to the same men's stores in Gladwyne where "Elihu Hoopes" is known by name, and his guardian-aunt, Mrs. Lucinda Mateson, is known. Mrs. Mateson has to be vigilant to prevent her nephew from eagerly purchasing shirts, sport coats, footwear identical to what he already owns.

It is from Mrs. Mateson that Margot learns these intimate facts, fascinating to her. Any information about Elihu Hoopes is fascinating to her.

Before his illness, Mrs. Mateson tells Margot Sharpe, Eli wasn't so fussy about his appearance—"He had so much more to think about, you see."

Margot asks Mrs. Mateson what Eli had to think about and Mrs. Mateson says, bemused, "What would a man like my nephew Eli Hoopes have had to *think about*? You would have to ask him."

A stupid question on Margot's part. Sometimes her brain feels like her hands in oven mitts.

Or, Margot is playing a role, not unlike the role (she suspects) the amnesiac subject often plays.

The dumber we are, the less threatening. No risk in being kind to us. Telling us your secrets, we won't remember anyway.

To Margot's (disguised) disappointment, another time E.H.

declines to have tea with his aunt and Margot in Mrs. Mateson's drawing room. Courteously he has excused himself—he disappears upstairs clutching his sketchbook.

So frustrating! It is like a variant of the experiment known as *The Cruel Handshake* except in this case, Margot Sharpe is the unwitting subject, and Eli Hoopes the perpetrator.

For each time Margot drives E.H. home, though they have chatted companionably on the eighteen-mile drive, mostly about subjects that drift into E.H.'s mind from out of his pre-amnesiac past—(E.H. has riveting stories of civil rights rallies and marches, in Philadelphia and in the South, to which Margot listens fascinated; he is very entertaining reciting the whole of the film he calls *Battleship Potemkin,* with an impassioned outcry of "Brothers!" at a melodramatic moment)—as soon as he sees where Margot has brought him, to the dignified old English Tudor house at 466 Parkside, Gladwyne, he loses the thread of their conversation first in wonderment, and then in his eagerness to get inside.

(Does E.H. think that it's strange, he is being brought "home" to his aunt's house, and not to Rittenhouse Square? He never speaks of this. And so Margot has to wonder if he "knows"—in some intuitive way—how his life has been altered.)

Yet, E.H. is always courteous, and invites Margot inside to meet his aunt Lucinda—though Margot and Mrs. Mateson have been introduced to each other numerous times.

"Hello, my dear! Very nice to meet you."

"Hello, Mrs. Mateson. Very nice to meet *you*."

For the amnesiac's sake the women give no indication that they have ever met. How easy it is, Margot thinks, to slip into such a role—one humors the afflicted, if one hopes to shield them from distress.

And how easy, as a strategy for one's life—to humor others.

Margot is not ever sure that she is not, in some unexamined way, humoring herself as well.

Mrs. Mateson is a woman of some "presence"—Margot has seen that at once. She is the younger sister of Eli's now-deceased father, Byron Hoopes, of whom Margot knows only that Byron Hoopes was a highly successful businessman, and a supporter of such conservative politicians as Taft, Dewey, Goldwater, and Nixon; he'd liked to "tease and infuriate" his activist son, Mrs. Mateson said, by reminding him that the Reverend Martin Luther King, Jr., was a Republican, and not a Democrat.

(Is this true? Margot herself is surprised. Poor Eli!)

Lucinda Mateson is in her late fifties, perhaps: not old, though old-seeming, and thin in the way of someone who has lost weight recently, whose skin is slightly loose, flaccid. Her face is powdered, her cheeks discreetly rouged, her thinning-blond hair has been brushed back and fastened at the nape of her neck with a tortoiseshell comb. She speaks in a way Margot can't help but associate, perhaps unfairly, with wealth: a hoarse, husky, whispery voice to which Margot must stoop (like a servant?) to hear.

From a remark of Eli's, Margot has gathered that his aunt had married a very wealthy, older man when she'd been quite young. She has the petulant air of a faded beauty. Even on a weekday evening at home she wears expensive-looking clothes—dresses with long skirts, cashmere sweater sets, fine-woolen trousers in cool weather, linen in warm weather—that fit her loosely. She never fails to invite Margot to stay for "tea"—as if "tea" were a custom in the household and not rather a makeshift snack-meal precipitated by a stranger's arrival. Each time Lucinda Mateson tries to coax E.H. into having tea with them he lingers in the drawing room for only a few minutes before muttering *Well—sorry!* with an apologetic grin and slipping away.

Lanky, long-legged on the stairs, like a teenager escaping his elders. Margot wonders if, at such moments, E.H. has forgotten that he is supposed to be thirty-seven years old.

She supposes that, once E.H. is alone, he looks through his sketchbook and the little notebook he keeps in his pocket to see what he has recorded that day—to see what has happened to him, and around him, that day.

Margot too is not always certain what has happened to her, and around her, until she checks her logbook for the day. Often she is surprised. Sometimes, she is touched. The rapport she feels with Eli Hoopes seems to deepen upon reflection.

In her throaty voice Mrs. Mateson is declaring:

"Miss Sharpe, you're very kind to drive Eli home. Everyone at the Institute we've met has been so very kind to us. The family will never give up hope, you know, that—well, not a 'cure'—but some sort of—'restoration'—of poor Eli's memory—might be possible . . . Dr. Ferris has said Eli is a special case, and experiments are being done to find a way to help him . . . Of course, it has been a long time he has had his 'injury': at least eight years." Mrs. Mateson speaks wistfully and yet with an air of subtle reproach. Margot wonders if she should tell the woman that it has been ten years since her nephew's illness, and not eight? Tactfully, she says nothing.

Margot feels a stab of guilt: the Hoopes family continues to believe that research into E.H.'s amnesia is clinically directed, and for E.H.'s benefit.

Margot tells Mrs. Mateson that Eli Hoopes is indeed receiving the very best neurological care in the world at the Institute at Darven Park.

At the same time, as she has told Mrs. Mateson in the past, she tells her how crucial it is that Eli's identity be kept confidential.

"Everyone would want to work with him. All sorts of unqualified people would apply. His life would become too public—it could become a media circus. That can't be allowed to happen."

" 'Media circus'—what is that?"

"Too much exposure. Newspapers, radio, TV—wanting interviews with Elihu Hoopes."

Mrs. Mateson shivers with distaste. Certainly, the Hoopes family would not want *that.*

The drawing room in which they are having tea is fussily furnished with heavy, stolid Victorian relics: faded cushioned sofas and chairs, lamps with fringed shades, Oriental carpets, crimson velvet drapes covering much of the high, leaded windows. There is an enormous, beautifully proportioned grand piano, a Steinway, in a bay window; on the piano are Czerny lesson books, very likely decades old. There is even a crystal chandelier with bare, transparent bulbs in mimicry of candles. And on the walls stiff but idealized portraits of individuals presumably relatives and ancestors of the household, since the portraits' value otherwise, as works of art, is minimal. Margot has the idea that, if she were to draw her finger across any smooth surface in the drawing room, it would come away filmed with dust.

The teacups and saucers Mrs. Mateson has set are lightly coated with a film of dust also. Very beautiful, exquisite pieces of Wedgwood china which Margot examines with admiration.

"Thank you, dear! Is it—Margaret?—Mar*got.* These are all family things of course. My family, and my dear husband's family—Mateson. This residence is my parents' former home, however—it has belonged to Hoopses for nearly two hundred years. I moved back, after my husband died in 1961. And of course poor Eli has lived with me since—whenever it was he got sick."

Margot listens fascinated as the woman speaks in her throaty, whispery voice about herself, and her family—the name "Hoopes" is frequently enunciated, with an innocent sort of pleasure and vanity. Mrs. Mateson explains that it wasn't any longer possible for her nephew to live alone in his Rittenhouse Square place and so what better residence for him than this house in which his grandparents had lived for decades and which Eli had so often visited—"Eli has absolutely no problem remembering this house. Most of the upstairs rooms are shut up, in any case. And we never use the living room, or my father's old study. Eli is very good with spatial things—which direction to take for 'downtown'—how to get back home, walks in the park—he never gets lost. He can drive a car, you know—he still has his license—but the doctors don't think it's a good idea, and Eli has had to agree. If there was an accident, even if Eli was blameless the insurance company would probably not pay—they can be scoundrels, you know! New things confuse and upset him terribly but almost anything he'd done often, before he was ill, he can recall without seeming to think about it—except his work at Hoopes and Associates. They tried to take him back, but—evidently—it didn't work out."

Mrs. Mateson speaks with an air of oddly cheerful resignation. She insists upon pouring tea for Margot, and offers her cookies scattered on a silver tray. She laughs often, as if to herself. Margot is fascinated by the older woman's *composure*—this confidence in oneself, not shared by most people Margot knows or has known in Orion Falls, Michigan, and not natural to Margot herself, is impressive.

In Orion Falls, Margot recalls, women like Lucinda Mateson, widowed, living alone, usually stricken with some sort of female illness, just-diagnosed, in the midst of treatment, or post-treatment and skeletal—(Margot rarely allows herself to think of Orion Falls for just these reasons)—are likely to be *apologetic,* not *composed.*

By contrast Lucinda Mateson seems quite healthy or, at any rate, unperturbed by health problems. She is a widow only in name—not in person. Margot thinks: if a widow has money, a widow has not exactly lost a husband.

She is grateful for Lucinda Mateson in E.H.'s life. For what would E.H.'s life be without this generous kinswoman . . .

With a show of pleasure Margot drinks the lukewarm tea. Nibbles at chocolate chip cookies that taste like baked lard laced with tiny bits of tar. She smiles to think that there is nowhere else she would rather be than in this drawing room, in this house.

As Mrs. Mateson speaks to her Margot listens for sounds of footsteps overhead or on the stairs. Thinking—*Eli will come downstairs to say good-bye. He will want to see me before I leave.*

Or, better yet—*Eli will not want me to leave. He will take my hand, he will insist that I stay longer. For dinner . . .*

With an indulgent smile, as if she can read Margot's naïve thoughts, Mrs. Mateson says reprovingly, "Eli will often disappoint."

Disappoint? Margot stares blankly.

"Yes! It was said of him, 'Eli will break your heart if you're foolish enough to give it to him.' "

Mrs. Mateson tells Margot (whose face is burning, slightly) that even as a boy her nephew was a "problem" to his elders. He was "idealistic—but terribly stubborn." He lacked a sense of courtesy and restraint—"You see it in young people of the 1960s, and now it's just swept the land—a *coarsening.* Eli lacked charity and patience for those who didn't think as he did, or as fast as he did. He wasn't sensitive to those in the family who were more conservative than he was—that's to say, everyone! He particularly infuriated his father, my brother Byron. He certainly precipitated Byron's first heart attack. Just wearing his hair to his shoulders, and a red headband around his forehead—unforgivable! 'Hell no, we won't go'—but where was Eli *going*? Not to fight in Vietnam—hardly! Eli behaved like a Quaker—a 'radical'—but he wasn't a religious person. He enrolled in Union Theological Seminary though he didn't believe in God! Some of us thought he'd enrolled there just to provoke fights with his teachers. Of course, that didn't last. Finally Eli accepted his position in the family business, when he was almost thirty, and he did well financially, but his heart wasn't in it—'Making money is the death of the soul.'" Mrs. Mateson pauses, pressing a hand against her soft sloping chest. "He should have married, he'd been engaged at least twice—lovely young women—from very good families here in Philadelphia—but something always disappointed him. The last time, the date was set at the Unitarian Church of Philadelphia, a beautiful old church near the Free Library, but by that time—this was October 1964—the old Eli was lost to us . . . Oh, we'd been so exasperated with him for years! He wasn't nice—kind—at all. I mean, to girls and women. He was very handsome, you know—you can't judge from his appearance now. He broke hearts—and I don't mean just young women." Mrs. Mateson laughs breathlessly as if she has said something daring. She glances at Margot with a puckish expression as if to say *I hope you aren't one of those pathetic women who throw themselves at my nephew.*

"Eli was involved in civil rights activism in Philadelphia in the 1950s—much earlier than many people. He gave money to the NAACP and to the Southern Christian Leadership Conference—that is, to Reverend Martin Luther King, Jr., who was one of his heroes. He terrified his parents with his reckless behavior—not just that he marched with Negroes and white activists here but also in the South, in terrible places like Alabama and Mississippi. Some of his co-marchers were murdered—'Freedom Riders' they called themselves. They were all beaten, including Eli—it turned out later, they'd made out their wills before they went south! Imagine, making out your will as a young person, and going off to march knowing you might get lynched. Eli was always getting roughed-up and beaten. His cameras were smashed—he said by 'rabid' racists. He was arrested and thrown in jail in some terrible place in Alabama. We don't even think of Alabama as a part of the United States, why would a 'Freedom Rider' go *there*? Eli would call home—'I'm not dead yet!' It was a tonic to him, all that excitement. We were always worried he'd come back married to one of those activists—Jewish, or Negro . . . But he had to come home finally, he had to take his place at Hoopes, Inc. He always knew that. He wasn't totally irresponsible. He refused to live in Gladwyne—he preferred Rittenhouse Square, in central Philadelphia, in a beautiful old building on the north side of the park—owned by the family, in fact. He gave money to activist causes. He gave money to Negro churches. He subsidized that scruffy radical newspaper—*Philadelphia Inquiry*. He endowed scholarships for 'minority' students at Penn and Drexel. He'd been shocked and depressed by the assassination of John Kennedy—(thank God he doesn't know that his beloved Reverend King has been assassinated, too! Of course, Eli 'knows'—but he wouldn't remember, since it was 1969 it happened—I think). Eli was always careless with his life—hiked and camped by himself in the Adirondacks even as a boy. He'd swim by himself, canoe by himself in bad weather—d'you know, Lake George is like an inland sea, it is *very wide*. He'd terrify his poor mother, out in a canoe alone, in a thunderstorm. Long after the rest of the family returned home in early September, Eli would stay at the lake. This awful thing that happened to him, this 'infection'—'brain fever'—wouldn't have happened except he'd been at Lake George alone. Eli was always damned *stubborn*."

Margot is disconcerted by Mrs. Mateson's way of speaking of E.H. as *was*. Chilling to think that his aunt considers his life over.

"Eli seemed to be living several lives at once. If you knew him in one of his lives, you wouldn't know him in another. My son Jonathan said he was sure he'd seen Eli once—in the city—on a street near the university with some 'crazed-looking scruffy people'—Eli with his hair all shaggy and wild and the head-band around his forehead like a 'hippie'—and as Jonathan drove past, very slowly since the street was partially blocked, these people—including his own cousin Eli Hoopes!—began pounding on the hood of his car, yelling obscenities and even spitting on his windshield. And now, sometimes—that's exactly how Eli seems to behave with all of us. Like he has never seen us before, and wants to pound his fists against us, without any care how our hearts are broken for him."

"But Eli is never violent, is he? He has never been reported—in any way . . ."

"No, *no*. Eli is never 'violent.' Of course not. I mean just—it's the way he looks at us. Or doesn't look at us. You would have to have known my poor nephew beforehand, to know."

Margot has been noticing on the older woman's hands a number of jeweled rings. Indeed she is fascinated by the rings, as Mrs. Mateson continues to speak pettishly.

Margot thinks *If I could marry into the Hoopes family! I would take care of Eli for the rest of his life.*

"I would invite you to stay for dinner, Miss—is it Sharpton?—except we just don't 'have dinners' anymore. My housekeeper who'd been with me for twenty years has returned to the Philippines and I haven't yet been able to replace her. Eli rarely gets hungry unless I remind him, and when he does eat, he doesn't want to sit down with me but to take a tray upstairs to watch TV. (Those damned news programs! They make him all excited and upset and a few minutes later he doesn't know why, and can't explain to me what has made him so angry.) Sometimes we have 'TV dinners' on trays—I'm embarrassed to say, our favorite is Birds Eye Frozen Chicken à la King—and watch old movies together—'classics.' We've seen *Wuthering Heights* and *Rebecca* so many times, Eli knows all of Laurence Olivier's dialogue. He's very amusing reciting the words exactly in unison with Olivier. And *Potemkin*—that's a Russian Communist film—a silent film from a hundred years ago—not anything I'd care to see more than once—but Eli has memorized it and is never bored by it. But mostly I've gotten into the habit of nibbling little meals through the day and never have much appetite in the evening. Since Harold died I've lost eighteen pounds." Mrs. Mateson speaks with regret, wistfully.

Margot thinks—*Oh but you could invite me anyway, Mrs. Mateson! We could watch TV together upstairs with Eli.*

Margot tells Mrs. Mateson that Eli has to be reminded to eat at the Institute, also.

How strange it is, that some amnesiacs forget to eat, even as some amnesiacs forget that they have just eaten: the danger for one is malnutrition, for the other, obesity.

Margot does not tell Mrs. Mateson that one of her most successful experiments in *Project E.H.* has been testing E.H.'s capacity for hunger. The amnesiac is presented with a complete meal and told that he is "hungry"—he will eat this meal and, within an hour afterward, if he is presented with another, identical meal, and told that he has not eaten for many hours, E.H. will eat this meal also, or most of it, in a manner that would appear to the objective observer to be "normal."

Conversely, if E.H. is told over a period of hours that he has just eaten he will give no evidence of being "hungry" at all—politely, he will even decline offers of "more food"!

Margot is overseeing similar experiments, executed by her cadre of graduate students, testing the amnesiac's thirst, and his capacity to endure pain; with her most reliable postdoc, Margot is planning a battery of tests to measure E.H.'s capacity for sleep and dreaming.

Some of these findings have been reported in Margot's recent article in the prestigious publication *Science* titled "Memory Deficit and 'Appetite': The Case of 'E.H' "; another, in the *Journal of Experimental Neuropsychology* titled "Social Determinants of 'Appetite': The Case of 'E.H.' "—but Margot decides against mentioning this to Mrs. Mateson, for it might seem boastful. She says, carefully:

"Much of being human depends upon our memories, you see. Some things you might think are instinctive like appetite—including also 'sexual appetite'—are not, entirely."

Seeing the older woman's expression of disbelief tinged with distaste Margot regrets having said quite so much.

"Isn't it strange!" Mrs. Mateson says, with a shudder. "You'd think that a person would eat when he feels hungry. I just don't understand how Eli can go for so long—as long as twelve hours—without getting 'hungry'—or so he claims. But then, when he begins to eat, he will eat and eat and eat—I have to watch him or he would make himself sick." Mrs. Mateson pauses, frowning. "And the same is true with drinking— Poor Eli must not be allowed to *drink*."

Margot assures Mrs. Mateson that there is no alcohol allowed at the Institute. And smoking is confined to restricted areas.

Still with an air of disapproval Mrs. Mateson says, "Well—we had beagles once, and those sweet dogs will eat and eat until they make themselves sick. And goldfish will eat until they explode. Nature doesn't seem to have been designed with much common sense."

Margot considers saying with professorial authority that nature has not been "designed" at all. But this might be offensive, and in its way it is a boastful statement, also.

Margot says, with an attempt at humor, "There isn't much place for 'common sense' in nature, as in humankind."

Margot describes to Mrs. Mateson how at the Institute E.H. always has the identical lunch: tuna salad on whole grain bread with lettuce and tomato and potato chips on the side.

Yet, when lunch orders are taken, E.H. always studies the menu carefully. Each time he appears to be choosing a tuna fish sandwich *for the first time*. And he will deliberate over the choice of bread, invariably choosing whole grain—*for the first time*.

Margot has presented this information with a smile, meant to be a warm confiding smile. But Mrs. Mateson frowns.

"Yes. Poor Eli is like that, of course—where once he was the most unpredictable of young men, now he is the most predictable. Oh, God."

Margot is stricken with remorse. She'd meant to make Mrs. Mateson smile fondly; she has been hoping that they might smile fondly together, united in their affection for the absent, eccentric Eli. Instead, she has made the woman feel sad. What thoughtless remarks has she been making!

Still, she wants to ask Mrs. Mateson more about the women in

E.H.'s life. Two engagements? She'd heard of just one. What has become of the women?

Are they still in love with him? Or—have they abandoned him, like everyone else except you?

Even more Margot wants to ask Mrs. Mateson about the disturbing drawings in E.H.'s sketchbook, of what appears to be a drowned child in a shallow stream.

It has been—how long, now?—ten years? Countless weeks when Margot has worked with the amnesiac E.H. over the course of these years, each session recorded in her logbook, rarely less than two or three times a week. And during these weeks, E.H. has executed this sketch hundreds of times.

Thousands of times?

Sometimes the sketch is done in pencil, sometimes in charcoal. Sometimes the figure is small on the page, sometimes it takes up the entire page. Margot is reminded of those (terrifying, to a child) drawings of Alice in Wonderland by the Victorian illustrator John Tenniel, tiny Alice, giant Alice, Alice trapped in a room in which she has become so large, her head is crushed against the ceiling and she must shove her arm out a tiny window . . .

The image itself is virtually identical each time: a streambed, rippling water, a (naked) girl of about eleven lying beneath the surface of the water with hair flowing about her head, eyes opened wide and sightless and skin deathly pale.

The girl is always positioned with her upper body in the left half of the page. Her hair streams into darkness in the left-hand margin and her pale, naked feet dissolve into shadow in the right-hand margin.

The girl's nakedness is not vividly rendered but rather shadowy, suggestive. Between the girl's legs, a deeper shadow.

Each time Margot has seen the sketch she has been shocked—it isn't an image to which one grows accustomed. If she asks, with a pretense of casual interest, *Eli? What's this?*—E.H. will frown and shut up his sketchbook.

E.H.'s other drawings and sketches are obsessively repeated as well. Most are set at the lake which she supposes to be Lake George.

There are many lake scenes—at twilight, and by moonlight; there are landscapes of pine forests with the tree-topped mountains of the Adirondacks in the background; there are rivers, streams; deep-shadowed interiors of forests; marshlands; fields and meadows. There are sailboats on the lake, canoes and rowboats tied to docks. There is a large, lakeside house made of logs, that must be the Hoopes family summer place; there are (deliberately smudged or indistinct) portraits of individuals, and there are figures (adult) seen at a distance. There is a small propeller plane, a "Beechcraft single-prop" (as E.H. has identified it to Margot) both on the ground and precariously aloft; in some drawings, you can see a child in the front cockpit, and an older man behind him at the controls of the plane. Many of these recur more frequently than the ghostly drowned girl but none is so intensely rendered.

Margot has fantasized an experiment: she will (surreptitiously) take E.H.'s sketchbook from him while he's engaged in a test at the Institute, and she will photograph a sketch of the drowned girl; she will make a negative of this sketch, and from the negative she will make a print and a slide, but it will be the reverse of E.H.'s image: the girl's head will be positioned at the upper right, her naked feet at the lower left. Margot will show it to the amnesiac subject with no explanation and see what his reaction will be . . .

For the best results, the experimenter should include other images. The drowned girl should be one of a sequence.

Eli, do you recognize this?

Eli, just tell us what you think this is. The first words that come to you.

Mrs. Mateson is telling Margot that her nephew doesn't mean to be rude—"He will have forgotten you are here, you know. He doesn't forget me, of course—he knows his 'Aunt Lucinda' from before his illness when he was—when he was himself."

When he was alive. Margot wonders if this is what Mrs. Mateson meant to say.

"Mrs. Mateson, your nephew isn't at all rude. He's the most gentlemanly person I've ever met. He's kindly, considerate, thoughtful, observant—he *listens.* Almost no one else truly *listens.*"

Mrs. Mateson thanks Margot for these extravagant words, touching Margot's wrist lightly. "Margot, you're so sweet. I wish Eli had friends like you, now—the others have all abandoned him. Even his brothers and sister have abandoned him."

"Have they! That's very sad."

"It is very, very sad. Very selfish of them, but they say it just makes them upset, to see Eli the way he is now. 'Like a zombie'—they say. Even the girl—the woman—the nicer of his fiancées Eli was going to marry . . . Fortunately, I will always take care of Eli, as his mother would have wished. I'm not a young woman but I'm young enough to care for him for a long time—I hope! I love Eli like a son—and I have my own sons, in fact." Mrs. Mateson laughs, mysteriously. "But now I have a spare son, who will never leave me."

Margot laughs, uncertainly. She liked Mrs. Mateson touching her wrist as in a seemingly spontaneous gesture of complicity.

Margot accepts from Mrs. Mateson a second cup of Earl Grey tea in the exquisite Wedgwood teacup, and another slightly stale cookie. There is an appetite generated sheerly by nerves, Margot thinks; a sort of anxious mouth-hunger.

Mrs. Mateson nibbles at the cookies, too. "Will you have more, dear? I'm sure that there are more in the kitchen—on the cupboard counter."

Margot declines with thanks, before wondering if this remark of Mrs. Mateson's is a hint of some kind: she might volunteer to go into the kitchen for the cookies, and see more of the house. She has been wishing that Lucinda Mateson would offer to take her on a tour of the elegant old Hoopes house. Especially, she wants to see E.H.'s quarters on the second floor.

Eli, hello! It's Margot—Dr. Sharpe. Yes, I'm here . . . visiting with your aunt.

From Parkside Avenue the Hoopes house is a striking English Tudor in a neighborhood of small mansions, most of them stone and brick. It is set back in a deep, wide lot of elm trees, plane trees, oaks and evergreens.

Close up, the house is weatherworn and stained and smells of wet, rotted wood: a house that time has bypassed. Straggly overgrown shrubs block much of the first-floor windows, casting the downstairs rooms in a perpetual twilight.

Nothing can be altered in this house, Margot realizes. Or Eli, poor Eli, would become disoriented and lost.

Dreading the moment when she will be expected to leave—when she will be *expelled* from Eli's household—Margot inquires about the portraits in the drawing room, which she has been admiring. Like the matron-overseer of a small museum Mrs. Mateson is delighted to identify the subjects—indeed, they are Hoopes ancestors, all male—the oldest, the patriarch, is Erasmus Hoopes who was a prominent Quaker Abolitionist in the years preceding the Civil War and whose fate was to be "martyred" in a scuffle with antiwar demonstrators hostile to Negroes in 1864; Erasmus's eldest son is Benjamin who with his younger brothers established Hoopes Emporium in the 1870s, on Broad Street, Philadelphia, one of the first and "very grand" department stores in the United States. Margot listens with great interest: how different Elihu Hoopes's family background is from her own! And all of this family history, the amnesiac can recall. He will have lost very little of his ancestral identity.

"Very interesting, Mrs. Mateson—all the portraits are male. Weren't there any distinguished women in your family?"—Margot asks such a risky question in a light, nonconfrontational voice; almost, a flirtatious voice. But Mrs. Mateson only frowns, and then smiles, as if Margot has said something obscurely witty, or meant to be witty. In such circumstances the polite response is not to indicate that one has heard.

On the fireplace mantel a porcelain clock chimes—it is 6:00 P.M. "Well!"—Mrs. Mateson sighs. As if to signal *Teatime is over.*

Margot searches for her heavy shoulder bag, which she has left on a sofa. How reluctant she is to leave this house, with Eli Hoopes upstairs! How reluctant to return to her car, to a headachy drive back to her house with no company but her own.

Sometimes when she is alone Margot talks to E.H. Since she knows E.H.'s response to most remarks, it is not entirely as if she is *alone.*

"Mrs. Mateson, I'm so sorry to ask—but—was there a death in your family—the death of a young girl—at Lake George—sometime before Eli was sick?" Margot hears herself uttering these words impulsively. She is appalled at her audacity but cannot now stop.

"It might have been long ago—when Eli was a child himself."

Mrs. Mateson stares at her as if uncomprehending. Margot

immediately regrets her rude question. Quickly she says, "I—I mean—Eli seems to be haunted by the figure of—what looks like a drowned child . . ." When Mrs. Mateson doesn't reply, but continues to stare, now with an expression of just perceptible indignation, Margot can only say, awkwardly, "Eli has sketched this scene many times. He seems quite—fascinated by it . . . And so, I was wondering—if . . ."

If the drowned girl is anyone you know.

"I can't ask Eli about the drawing, or the girl. It seems to upset him too much. And I can't risk losing his trust."

"And I'm afraid that I can't help you, Doctor."

With an expression of polite perplexity, and very subtle distaste, Mrs. Mateson shakes her head. As one might dismiss a servant.

In the exigency of the moment Margot isn't able to determine if the older woman is telling her *no,* she knows nothing about any drowned girl; or *no,* Mrs. Mateson is not going to help her learn anything about any drowned girl.

In the awkward silence Margot can only repeat that she hasn't wanted to upset Eli. "He's very protective of his art, and I'm honored that he shows his work to me, at times. I would never betray his confidence."

And then suddenly, when Margot has been thinking she will have no choice but to leave, Mrs. Mateson begins to speak as if to deflect Margot's question with a flood of words, in a tone of intimacy.

"Eli always used to brood on—things. He took after his father that way—my older brother. 'Fear and trembling'—whatever that was. With Eli, no one outside the family could have guessed his true nature. He was as sociable as—well, Bing Crosby, in some song-and-dance movie—when it pleased him. And then so solitary and stubborn, when it pleased him. The men in our family have had a fixation on that place—Lake George. I would not call it a 'morbid' fixation—of course, Lake George is very beautiful. The old house, that was built back in 1926, is very beautiful—if you like Adirondack log-cabin architecture. It's a place that grows on you—I've been told. Sometimes it's like—(this was a remark my brother Byron made)—there's a cemetery there, and our ancestors are buried there, and not here in Gladwyne . . . Well, Eli should never have spent so much time alone there as an adult, it's no wonder he got sick. Shouldn't have left his poor fiancée to become all emotional and hysterical. And when he got sick, he delayed medical care. He'd hike in the mountains and tramp for days in the woods—I can't imagine what a person does with himself, all alone like that. He said he was taking pictures and painting but do you need to be alone, to do these things? And he'd throw away most of what he did in disgust. I think that 'perfectionism' is a kind of spite—you can't acknowledge that your talent is what it is, God-given, and not something more. And all those years, Eli kept returning to Lake George after Labor Day. He and his fiancée poor Amber were going to be married in October of 1964—I remember that clearly!—but for some reason Eli went off to stay at the lake by himself. No one knew what Eli and his fiancée quarreled about, or if they'd quarreled about anything. Eli was the kind of gentlemanly person, he'd have arranged it to seem that Amber had broken off with him, not the other way—as if anyone would be taken in by that. Her name was—is—Amber McPherson."

Amber McPherson. The very name is romantic, mysterious.

Margot asks what has become of "Amber McPherson"?

Mrs. Mateson smiles, oddly. It is a sad smile, yet a smile that suggests an obscure sort of satisfaction.

"Really, my dear, I don't know. Our families are not in close contact."

Margot feels a pang of satisfaction also, that Amber McPherson had not married Eli Hoopes, and is not married to him now.

Then, Margot feels a flush of shame. Only an individual with a stunted soul rejoices in the unhappiness of others.

She is a very good scientist, she has no reason to be envious of anyone else. Certainly not a "fiancée" who'd been jilted by a man now severely amnesiac.

She should want Eli Hoopes to be happy, at least. If he'd been married before his illness, his life would be completely different now; he would have a wife, he would probably have grown children, he would be cared for and loved by someone other than this woman.

To be loved by Elihu Hoopes, Margot Sharpe would have had to meet him before his illness—after that date, for the afflicted one, love is no longer possible.

Mrs. Mateson says, with a sigh, like one who is both exasperated and admiring, "Maybe Eli was always going to be the way he is—I mean, maybe he was fated for a solitary life—a 'tragic' life. He is not unlike his Quaker ancestors, after all: how difficult they must have been to live with! 'A martyr for a just cause'—easier than living a normal life, with a family and responsibilities. Miss Sharpton, you would not believe it now but no one—absolutely no one—had more friends than Eli Hoopes, in school, in college, and the years after—but it was all too easy for him. When women adore a man, what is a man to do but succumb to—being adored? There was some madness in him that drove him away from us and into the seminary, then drove him out again. He was 'searching for God'—he said. Oh, dear Eli! Sometimes I think—there are those cruel persons in the Hoopes family who have said—'Eli found God all right, at Lake George. Now he can live with God.' "

Mrs. Mateson has been speaking with a restrained sort of emotion, like one who must carry herself with caution. Now she leans close to Margot, as if fearing she might be overheard: "Please be frank with me, dear: has his neurological condition improved? Can it improve? The 'experiments' you and your colleagues have been doing with him all these years—has his memory been strengthened at all, do you think? Can he ever be—'normal'—or almost 'normal'—again?"

But he is missing a part of his brain! What you ask is impossible.

Margot considers how to reply. She is not a clinician, she does not interact with patients and their families, and so she has had little experience in the craft, or the art, of seeming to say one thing while saying quite another, in medical terms. It is a violation of Margot Sharpe's personal integrity to *lie;* yet, surely there are occasions when *lying,* or a kind of professional subterfuge, is required.

And so Margot says yes, in some ways Eli's memory has been "strengthened." It is not untrue that E.H. can perform certain tasks without needing to consciously recall them, and it has been demonstrated that, if he practices his tennis serves, for instance, he can improve his performance on the tennis court though he will not be able to recall the practice sessions. By practicing piano, he can play more adeptly—but he insists upon playing those compositions which he has already learned, the memory of which lies deeply imprinted in a part of his (uninjured) brain, and summoned to his fingertips without conscious effort.

Margot has noted and recorded these instances, and has recently designed a radical new experiment to further explore the phenomenon of non-declarative memory in amnesia.

"But can Eli ever be 'normal,' dear? Or is that too much to ask?"

"We can never tell definitively, Mrs. Mateson. Something new is being discovered about the brain every day. And soon, we'll be able to photograph the brain, as we can't do yet."

Margot speaks carefully, soothingly. It is Professor Sharpe's public manner, at a podium, politely answering a question put to her from the audience.

"'Photograph the brain!'" Mrs. Mateson seems struck by this possibility. "Do you mean—like an X-ray?"

"Something like an X-ray, though not exactly."

"And what of the soul, then? Will we be able to see the 'soul'?" Mrs. Mateson speaks with a brave sort of wistfulness.

Margot is stunned. How to answer this naïve question!

She wants to take hold of the older woman's delicate hands. She wants to console Mrs. Mateson, and in this way console herself.

Carefully she says, "Mrs. Mateson, maybe—one day."

The ceramic clock on the mantel is chiming again—delicately, unmistakably. Teatime is over.

AT HER CAR, at the curb, Margot pauses to look back at the Hoopes mansion. She is feeling mildly dazed, both tired and excited—exhilarated. She will replay her lengthy, rambling conversation with Lucinda Mateson countless times, and she will realize belatedly that the woman never quite answered her question about a drowned girl—a "death in the family."

It is painful to her, though hardly surprising, that Eli Hoopes did not come downstairs to say good-bye to her.

Of course he'd almost immediately forgotten her existence.

Car key in her hand. (When did she take out her car key? She has no recollection of doing so.)

No choice but to leave . . .

Next week, she will arrange to drive E.H. home at least one evening. If it can be arranged without suspicion.

Milton would not approve, probably. Her lab colleagues would disapprove.

What on earth is Margot doing with E.H.? Is she testing him somehow—secretly?

Margot hasn't fallen in love with the amnesiac—has she?

Margot shudders, hearing cruel laughter. She has been trying to envision a man's face at one of the upstairs windows of the Hoopes house: E.H. gazing out at her. But she sees no one—of course.

The part-timbered facade of the old house is broad, unyielding. No one at any of the windows. On the slate roof is a faint shimmer of green, moss is growing there in patches. In the putty-colored stucco are faint jagged cracks like arrested lightning.

CHAPTER FIVE

To reply to your question which I will refrain from dismissing as an ignorant and provocative question, in fact it is a question much asked if indeed ignorant and provocative and with maddening frequency and in admission of a basic incomprehension of what science is and does—No. We did not exploit the amnesiac subject E.H. in more than thirty years of our association with him.

The amnesiac lived in the present tense, and in the present tense we shared with him over the years, E.H. was happy, and hopeful. He loved to be tested and didn't tire for hours. He was a superior subject in our testing-lab, as obviously he'd been superior as a child and adolescent, winning the praise of his teachers and high grades. Tests of the kind we administer are often the only opportunities of intellectual engagement available to the brain-damaged and so, as it was carefully explained to E.H., our work with him would benefit countless individuals unknown to him—as to us: victims of stroke, Alzheimer's, dementia, brain tumors and lesions. For the brain-damaged individual who has once been a highly functioning citizen, and is now incapacitated, being a part of such an endeavor is deeply satisfying, and so it was with "Elihu Hoopes"—whose name can now be revealed.

Yes. The world is much emptier without him—"Elihu Hoopes."

Even E.H.'s "failed performances" were valuable to us—to science. All that E.H. could not do, that a normal person could do, has been illuminating to us. It was the hypothesis of our principal investigator Milton Ferris that the amnesiac had suffered memory loss as a consequence of damage to a part of the brain called the hippocampus—in those early days, there were no MRIs to scan the brain.

Basing our hypotheses on memory work in other neuropsychology and neuroscience labs, some of which conducted experiments inducing lesions in primate brains, we came to a more or less firm conviction that E.H.'s hippocampus had been devastated by encephalitis but we had no way of knowing this, or whether other, adjoining areas of the brain had been affected, and to what extent—we would not know until E.H.'s brain was at last scanned by an MRI in 1993.

Often I am asked that question—indeed, it is one of the foolish, provocative questions of the kind scientists are asked by ignorant interviewers though I will respond more courteously than most of my—virtually all of my—male—colleagues would respond: No. E.H. did not "exhibit sexual proclivities"—not so far as we know. (Recall, we saw E.H. only under clinical conditions, and for a relatively small part of his time. We had no idea apart from anecdotal information casually and infrequently provided by his guardian Mrs. Lucinda Mateson how he "behaved" at home.) It was our hypothesis, borne out by the MRI, that there was encephalitic damage to E.H.'s amygdala—a part of the brain related to emotional and sexual activities.

Perhaps as a consequence of this deficit, E.H. behaved like a gentleman of another, bygone era. He did not raise his voice. He was never quarrelsome. He was courtly, courteous. His speech was never suggestive or rude. When he was older, he came to refer to women as "ladies"—female medical workers he described as "lady nurses." We came to believe that he was emulating older male relatives, as he became older himself.

And here is the crucial fact: without Project E.H., *the afflicted man would have been marooned in his solitary life from the age of thirty-seven to his death.*

And so, my final answer is no: we did not "exploit" Elihu Hoopes.

And I, Margot Sharpe, do not feel any regret, any remorse, any guilt for having worked with this remarkable individual for thirty-one years. I feel instead immense gratitude.

And whatever other emotions I may feel for Elihu Hoopes will remain forever private.

"I am not a jealous person. I am 'investigating.' "

She behaves riskily! Finds herself doing things she would not ever have anticipated doing as Professor Margot Sharpe who is a methodical and conventional scientist and (indeed) a methodical and conventional person.

Except in this instance: seeking out the ex-fiancée of Elihu Hoopes.

The woman whom he'd left with no explanation. The woman who must have felt herself abandoned, rejected. Not knowing if their engagement had been broken off—since Eli Hoopes had not informed her.

There is something thrilling in this. A low, dirty thrill—the kind abhorred by Professor Sharpe.

A woman who has loved, and has been abased. And by Elihu Hoopes.

From what Margot has learned, Elihu Hoopes simply drove

alone to the Adirondacks. He might have told his fiancée that he was going—or his sister told her—but he did not invite her to accompany him, and he made no effort to keep in phone contact with her.

And so: how did "Amber McPherson" endure the embarrassment?—shame? A public sort of humiliation, a woman rejected by a man, treated so rudely by a man, how did the fiancée endure, how did she survive, what is the "narrative" this woman tells herself now after a decade, Professor Sharpe is eager to know.

On university stationery the professor types a letter to Amber McPherson, now "Mrs. Prescott Adams" residing at 28 Balmoral Drive, Bryn Mawr, Pennsylvania. Receiving no reply diligently the professor writes again a week later, and a third time another week later on university stationery introducing herself as a neuropsychologist who has been working with Elihu Hoopes for several years at the University Neurological Institute at Darven Park: would it be possible for Mrs. Adams to speak with her?

I will happily drive to your house in Bryn Mawr. Our interview would not take more than an hour.

Deliberating whether to sign these letters Professor Margot Sharpe or rather, Professor M. J. Sharpe.

Deciding yes, she had better sign "Margot"—there is no advantage to surprising Amber McPherson in a way that might seem unpleasant, deceptive. Not a good strategy if Professor Sharpe wants to win the woman's confidence.

Still, in her precisely worded letter Margot has not informed Amber McPherson that she isn't a clinician but a research scientist. She may be called "Doctor" in some circumstances but she is not "Doctor of Medicine." She has not informed Amber McPherson that Elihu Hoopes is not her patient but her research subject. But Margot does not correct Amber McPherson's assumption that this is so though she feels—oh, just slightly!—a stab of guilt.

"Dr. Sharpe, how is Eli? Is he—improved at all? I—I've felt so—so terrible— I hope that his family doesn't think that I abandoned him . . ."

Amber McPherson is literally wringing her hands—her beautiful beringed hands. Amber McPherson speaks in a faint, breathless voice. It is the very voice of exquisite "femininity" of the 1950s which Margot recalls from her girlhood as she recalls, with some reluctance, a mild and annoying envy of such blond beauty, poise.

Margot indicates with a sympathetic nod of her head *no.* Amber McPherson can't know that Margot knows how Eli Hoopes had abandoned *her;* and no one would harshly judge a fiancée who'd been herself abandoned.

"It's so strange to realize that Eli is still—alive . . . And all these years have passed . . . Is he well? I mean—as 'well' as can be expected?"

Margot indicates with a sympathetic nod of her head *yes.* Eli Hoopes is as well as can be expected.

"It was like becoming—being—a widow. Except Eli and I were never married."

This too, a striking remark, a remark to evoke a pang of sympathy but also envy in Margot Sharpe, provokes Margot Sharpe to incline her head *yes. Oh yes.*

It is something of a giddy triumph for Margot, who rarely ventures out of the carefully constructed routines of her professional life, and who begins to feel physical, visceral anxiety if she hasn't started serious work by midmorning of any day, to have driven, one weekday afternoon, to the leafy suburb of Bryn Mawr, Pennsylvania, and to the immense granite house at 28 Balmoral Drive.

The house, and the prestigious residential neighborhood,

remind Margot of Mrs. Mateson's English Tudor home in Gladwyne. *His world, that he tried in vain to leave.*

The former Amber McPherson, now Mrs. Prescott Adams, speaks haltingly but bravely. Clearly she has prepared for this visit. On a glass-topped table are packets of snapshots and photographs she has gathered together for Margot to see, if she wishes. So many! Margot feels a sensation of vertigo.

It is startling to Margot at such times to perceive how others have lived their lives entwined with the intimate lives of others. How is this possible? Is it still possible, for her?

Amber McPherson is a gracious woman, just slightly overweight, beautiful still in a wan, fading-blond way. Her pale blond hair is stylishly bouffant, her clothes are expensive—woolen slacks, cashmere sweater. Clearly she has been reluctant to meet with Margot Sharpe whom she calls "Dr. Sharpe" in a way that might be defined as mildly deferential; she is the wife of a wealthy man, Margot surmises, and very likely the daughter of a wealthy family. As she speaks, swiping at her eyes, her expensive rings sparkle and wink as if to undercut the gravity of her sorrow.

"I'm so sorry! I am truly, truly sorry. I know that I behaved badly—selfishly. I know that people expected me to marry Eli—some, in my own family—and take care of him—there was always the expectation that he would 'recover'—'get well'—but I knew that could not be—and I didn't have the strength, or—courage. The fact was, Eli didn't love me. He'd more or less left me, at the time of his illness. No one knew, only a few knew, close friends of his, possibly his sister—he'd wanted to marry me for family reasons, his and mine—but when it came to it, he'd have broken off the engagement, he wouldn't have gone through with the wedding. And if he had—if we'd had a child, or children—he would have left the marriage, eventually. I knew this. I know this.

I never stopped loving Eli, but—it was not a love that could come to anything but heartbreak even before he got sick. And so—"

And so, Margot thinks, the fiancée of Eli Hoopes became matronly Mrs. Prescott Adams of Balmoral Drive, Bryn Mawr: wife of another man, mother of beautiful and beloved children, a fate not freely chosen but one that happened to her, like weather, subsequent to the defection of Eli Hoopes in the summer of 1964.

"It's been a long time since I've talked with anyone about—Eli. Though sometimes I say his name aloud—'Eli.' Did you say, Doctor, that he's 'doing as well as can be expected'—?" The question is plaintive, the wanly beautiful face tensed in apprehension.

Margot assures the anxious woman: Eli Hoopes's condition has not "worsened."

Mrs. Adams has welcomed Margot Sharpe into her house—she has answered the doorbell herself, though Margot sees that there is a housekeeper or a maid in the background. Surprised at the sight of Margot—(was she expecting someone who looked older, more authoritarian? More "clinical"?)—nonetheless Mrs. Adams has ushered her into an elegant room that might be described as a "library"—(floor-to-ceiling cherrywood bookshelves, massive very masculine mahogany desk, Oriental carpet, exquisite molded ceiling)—adjacent to an ornately furnished living room the size of a ballroom; nervously she has offered Margot coffee, tea, or fruit juice which Margot has politely declined; she has been showing Margot photographs of her old lost life as a younger woman who'd unwisely fallen in love with Elihu Hoopes. (Margot has determined that Amber McPherson is at least ten years younger than Eli Hoopes, a fact that discomforts her. Margot has wanted to think that, younger than Eli Hoopes by fourteen years, she occupies a unique significance in the amnesiac's romantic/erotic life.)

On a mantel is a Chinese vase filled with flowers. Fresh-cut, surely very expensive flowers. (For an ordinary weekday at the Adams's home? For *her*?) A beautifully arranged bouquet in which the predominant flowers are gardenias, carnations, and day lilies the heady scent of which pervades the room.

"Dr. Sharpe, I know that I have behaved badly—unconscionably. I tried to remain in Eli's life after his illness but—it was just so painful. At first I visited him every day—but that didn't work out well. I visited him with his sister Rosalyn—we were close friends then. Eli 'remembered' me of course but it was as if a stranger was 'remembering' me—pretending to be Eli Hoopes. Eli was impersonating himself—awkwardly. Almost it seemed mockingly. He would stiffen when I tried to touch him, or kiss him—forced himself to respond 'naturally.' He made jokes, he seemed to be always trying to entertain visitors—he wasn't comfortable with just one visitor at a time. I could recognize this 'Eli' but it was like a shrinkage of his soul. He'd had a side to him that could be sarcastic and petty, and say things to wound, but now this was the only Eli we saw. I suppose he was driving us away . . .

"It was such a tragedy! How small his life had become, how repetitive and routine . . . how depressing for others who'd known him well to see. Eli had always been so concerned with what he called 'social justice'—he could be hypercritical of others close to him—like his family—(and like me)—who weren't committed as he was to such ideals. He did well in his family's business but scorned his work as contemptible—'money-grubbing.' We all thought that he shouldn't have dropped out of the seminary—he'd have made a wonderful minister. Not a conventional minister with a congregation but someone like the Berrigans who were willing to go to prison for their beliefs. (How Eli would have admired the Berrigans! But they came too late for him.) Though

I guess the difference between the Berrigans and other activists is that the Berrigans were Catholic priests and so not encumbered by wives and families . . ."

Amber McPherson has begun to speak vehemently now. Inside the stolid-bodied middle-aged woman is a girl who has been hurt, her love flung back into her beautiful face, and has never understood why.

"Eli was always the center of attention. He was always a natural leader. He hadn't much awareness of or interest in other people, except people he could help—like the poor, and Negroes. He needed to be *revered*—I think that was Eli's secret. Of course, it was what made Eli special, too. A person like myself, people like his family—sister, brothers, cousins—he hadn't much patience with us for being who we were."

Waxy-white gardenias—the scent is strong. Margot inhales the fragrance with something like an inward swoon.

Margot assures Amber McPherson, she understands. Of course.

Margot is trying not to feel an intense jealousy for this woman whom Eli Hoopes once chose as a lover, at least as a potential wife, at a time in his life before he was incapacitated and diminished. At such a time, Margot has to concede, he'd have hardly chosen *her*.

She is not a sexual being at all, is she. Set beside this woman with an opulent body, sweetly vulnerable lined face.

"Well, Doctor, maybe they've told you—the Hoopeses—I stopped seeing Eli after about ten months. I just could not bear it. As soon as he was out of the hospital and his condition was 'stabilized'—when it was apparent he would never be himself again. I guess I had something like a breakdown of my own—I was very depressed. I was plucking out my hair, and stopped eating . . . Frankly, I didn't at all care if I lived or died. Even now I dream about that terrible time. It was relayed to me that Eli asked after me often—he did remember me—or some notion of 'Amber'—and he'd become convinced that I'd died—that I'd had a fever, and died of encephalitis . . ."

Amber McPherson's distressed voice trails off. She has been picking at the soft skin about a thumbnail as if to draw blood.

Margot thinks—*She wanted to die, for him. For love.*

And this, too, provokes jealousy in Margot Sharpe. Envy.

After a respectful interval Margot asks in what ways had Eli Hoopes changed, after his illness? What were the most significant changes? Could Amber describe?

"In what ways had he changed, Doctor?"

Amber McPherson stares at Margot Sharpe as if Margot Sharpe has uttered a particularly foolish question.

"In what *ways*? Every way."

"But you said that he did know you? He recognized, remembered you . . ."

"Oh yes. Eli 'knew' us. His relatives, his friends. Yet, at the same time it was as if he didn't know us at all—we were strangers to him. He tried to behave as if he knew us—as an actor might. But it was as if every cell in Eli's body had changed . . . He didn't even look like himself."

Margot has been looking through some of the photographs Amber has spread onto a table. Fascinating to her, this evidence of her amnesiac subject's earlier life! It is true to a degree that the middle-aged Eli Hoopes no longer quite looks like this young, very fit, vigorous man with thick tufted dark hair, of the 1950s and 1960s; yet a greater change has taken place in Amber McPherson.

Margot studies Polaroids of the slender young woman with

shoulder-length pale-blond hair and her tall handsome male companion, as Amber nervously chatters. If she were a clinical psychologist, Margot thinks, she would have a difficult time attending to a patient who spoke so effusively; far rather would one prefer a reticent patient who spoke tersely, but significantly. Where there is outspokenness, there is no selection; the psychologist must make the selection herself.

"We were very happy together—I mean, it seemed that we were. At least—I think that I was . . . When something like this happens, when you are rejected, you look back trying to make sense of—whatever it was that happened. But it's the other person, in this case Eli, who knows what happened—not me."

Polaroids, snapshots, photographs of the couple posed together on a lavishly green lawn, in a sumptuous garden, on a riverbank; on a tennis court, each grasping a racket and each dressed in impeccable dazzling white; in a long, heavy-looking canoe, on a hiking trail amid tall pines, on a white-sand beach (in the Caribbean?). In some of the pictures Eli Hoopes is darkly tanned, and wears a sailing cap; in some, his hair has grown long, hippie-length nearly, and he wears a red headband. Both Eli and Amber are wearing shorts, or they are wearing stylish sporty clothes, or they are wearing "dressy" evening clothes. Eli has his arm around Amber's shoulders, drawing her to him; Amber teeters on high-heeled sandals, perceptibly off balance. They are smiling happily at the camera, and they are demonstrably "in love"—or so the evidence suggests.

In certain of the photos Eli is gazing off into the distance with a slight, vexed frown, in a way Margot has noticed him do at the Institute. Amid the intensity of testing, the amnesiac subject has a way of fading from view. You glance up at him and he's gone—like that.

Eli? Mr. Hoopes? Hello . . .

In most of the photos he is standing beside the blond fiancée in a way to suggest protectiveness.

"Yes, you can see—so many pictures . . . What it all adds up to, I'm not sure." Amber McPherson laughs, sadly.

But Amber McPherson is proud of these photos, nonetheless. Margot supposes that there is nothing in her present life as Mrs. Prescott Adams that so compels her attention, her guilt and her regret.

"How beautiful you are in these pictures!"—Margot exclaims naïvely. She is fortunate not to have blundered *were.*

Margot sees that, when she was younger, in her twenties, Amber McPherson braided her hair; most strikingly, in several snapshots, Amber has braided a single strand of hair, that falls over the left side of her face beguilingly. It must have been a style of the era—a black influence. Instead of tight, cornrowed hair, a single narrow braid falling from forehead to shoulder. Margot wonders if it was to beguile Eli Hoopes, this appropriation of sexy black hair fashion. Margot wonders if Eli suggested it, and if he did, if Eli found the single narrow braid of pale blond hair sexually alluring.

There are a number of snapshots presumably set at Lake George—path along a rocky shore, figures in a canoe, vast expanse of water reflecting a gray-tinged sky. At the end of a dock, the white-clad couple poses beside a white-sailed sailboat. Margot asks if Amber McPherson had spent much time at the Hoopeses' Lake George house? If she knew much about his boyhood summers there? The setting seems to mean a good deal to Eli.

Amber McPherson wipes at her eyes. Yes, she'd spent some time there, in the summer. The lodge at Lake George was—is—a large, family house with many rooms, many people coming and going—the Hoopeses and their relatives and friends. She'd been Eli's guest at least a dozen times. Eli had a very special close attachment to Lake George. He hadn't felt much sentiment for his family home in Gladwyne where he'd grown up, but the beautiful lodge at Lake George, built of treated pine logs and fieldstone, with its several porches and numerous outbuildings, was special to him—"Eli said, he was always 'there' in his dreams. Even when the setting wasn't distinct, Eli knew he was at the lake."

"Had anything ever happened to him, at the lake?"

" 'Happened to him'—? I suppose yes, many things—over the years. He'd been brought to Bolton Landing—that's the name of the little town—since he was a baby."

"Do you think—do you recall—if anything particular might have happened to him there? Or—any family event, incident? A death, a drowning . . ."

Reluctantly Amber McPherson says yes, she does remember—something.

Not clear what it was. A death in the Hoopes family, she thinks.

"Eli never spoke of it but his sister Rosalyn told me, an older girl cousin had gone missing in the woods, and her body was found in a shallow creek—or maybe wasn't found . . . Rosalyn had been very young at the time. Or maybe she hadn't even been born, and had only heard stories, later."

"Eli never spoke of it?"

"No."

Amber McPherson frowns. She has not been comfortable with this line of questioning, Margot thinks, because attention is being drawn away from her and Eli, and in another direction. The record of the photographs is all the history she wishes to summon—it is her cherished personal history with Eli Hoopes. Beyond this, an earlier history doesn't interest her at all.

Every woman wants to think—*His emotional history begins with me.*

Amber McPherson says, with an air of accusation, "Eli was reckless with his life. We all thought he'd be killed—or terribly injured—in a civil rights protest. We almost thought he was expecting to be, himself. But—something else happened to Eli instead, catastrophic in a different way." Her voice isn't breathless now but grave, brooding. "Some of us who loved Eli thought it would have been better for him if he'd—died . . ."

A sun-dappled snapshot of the smiling young couple in T-shirts and shorts, leaning against a porch railing and in the background a shimmering lake—presumably Lake George.

Margot sees, on the back of the snapshot, the hastily scrawled date—*July 1963.*

He'd had only another year of his life as Eli Hoopes, at this time. The dark-tanned handsome youngish man in the picture, face partly obscured by sunglasses, arm around the shoulders of the smiling blond fiancée, has no foreknowledge of this catastrophe, which is why he smiles with such confidence.

Margot hears, belatedly, Amber McPherson's shocking remark. Margot hears, but doesn't want to judge. *Better if he'd died.*

This is not true. Margot wants to protest, it is *not true.*

The rejected fiancée is still in love with Eli Hoopes. With the man she'd known. That is her secret.

Amber is saying, anxiously: "You must think I'm a terrible person, Doctor. To say such things. But if you'd known Eli . . ."

"Of course. I understand."

Margot is grateful for Amber McPherson's generosity, and is not here to judge. Even as she is faintly appalled—*Better for him if he'd died? Better for you and for his family, perhaps. But not for Eli—and not for me.*

"Thank you, Mrs. Adams. You've been very kind, and very helpful."

"Have I, Doctor? I'm not sure how . . ."

"It's always helpful to meet with people who've known a patient *before*."

Half-consciously Margot has used the word *patient*. In this way she has allowed Amber McPherson to think that indeed, Margot Sharpe is Eli Hoopes's "doctor."

Is this deceptive? Is this unethical? Would her colleagues be surprised, and questioning of her motives? Margot doesn't want to think.

Amber McPherson can't leave Margot Sharpe with a memory of her blunt, despairing words, and so the last several minutes of the visit are taken up with Amber's assurance to Margot that her life as a wife and a mother is "very rich, full"—her work as co-chair of the Bryn Mawr Historical Society is "very challenging, and rewarding." To offset the photos of her younger self with Eli Hoopes she shows Margot photos of her several children—"Todd, Emily, and Stuart. Aren't they beautiful!" She laughs, showing her pearly, perfect teeth for the first time.

Margot agrees, yes the children are beautiful. Studying the features of the eldest, the boy Todd, Margot would like to imagine that she can discern a ghostly glimmer of Eli Hoopes—but no, there is none.

Departing the house, led to the massive front door, Margot sees in the foyer a seven-foot grandfather clock, made of an old, polished, exquisite wood. Behind the stenciled glass, a gravely-moving brass pendulum like an exposed heart.

Amber McPherson is so gracious by both instinct and training, she can't allow her "doctor"-visitor to leave without murmuring to Margot, with apparent sincerity, and a sudden startling embrace, that she hopes they will see each other again—"Sometime soon."

Margot returns to her car mildly dazed. Margot drives away feeling the soft imprint of the other woman's body against her own, and smelling still the rich, intoxicating odor of gardenias. She is halfway home before she realizes that Amber McPherson didn't ask her to "say hello" to Elihu Hoopes for her.

She thinks he is dead. Whoever lives now is not him.

He has fallen, he has been thrown onto his back. So hard, the wind is knocked out of him.

Rough fingers grip his ankle and drag him in the dirt. He is panting, whimpering. (Where are his brothers? Why don't they come to help him?) High-pitched jeering laughter as a cushion from one of the porch chairs is pressed against his face, hard.

Can't draw breath to scream. Can't draw breath. The cushion is pressed harder, his assailant is leaning his weight on the cushion, on Eli's face.

Later it will be said—Oh Axel doesn't mean to hurt, he just teases too hard.

Later it will be said—Eli is such a timid boy. He has got to be encouraged to play with the others, and to swim. He has got to learn to swim this summer.

Beneath the porch where he is hiding he sees the girls' legs, their slender bodies in shorts and halter tops. One of them is his cousin Gretchen.

Gretchen cups her hands to her lips and calls—Eli? Where are you? E-li . . .

*He will hear her voice—*Eli? E-li . . . *—like an echo inside his head.*

Eli? Oh, E-li . . .

TRYING TO EXPLAIN. It is an effort like that of Sisyphus rolling his boulder up the hill again, again, again.

At first he has thought that the young woman is a relative of his, for she looks familiar. Then, he has thought that the young woman is a girl he'd known in grade school. Or, later in high school.

She is not his fiancée. Not the blond fiancée, or the other.

She appears to be one of the medical staff. Though not a doctor, for she isn't wearing a white lab coat, and there is no plastic ID on the lapel of her black jacket.

She has introduced herself to him, and he has clasped her hand. He remembers the warmth of the hand-clasp but he has forgotten her name.

"I have some trouble with my memory, I think."

"Do you, Eli? What trouble?"

"I just—it's—I don't know . . . It's like a fog or a swamp, and if I walk into it, it just—dissolves . . ." He laughs, embarrassed. He would like the young woman to know that it is not at all characteristic of Eli Hoopes to dwell upon his health. Not at all characteristic of Eli Hoopes to speak much about himself as if there are not myriad other, far more crucial subjects about which to speak.

"I think it has been like this for a while—this memory 'deficit.' "

"How long do you think it has been, Eli?"

"Well—six months, at least. It seems that I may have had an accident and hit my head—or, someone hit my head deliberately—and then when I was hospitalized I got an infection, and my brain was 'on fire' . . ."

"About six months ago?"

"It could be longer. I'm not sure." E.H. laughs dryly, but his eyes are pained. "I think that must be why I'm in this hospital.

Or—is this a clinic? I see people in lab coats and I see nurses but I don't see any beds—maybe I'm an outpatient?"

"Yes, you are an 'outpatient.' Which means you arrived here this morning and you'll be going home in a few hours. You are only brought here, Mr. Hoopes—you are not *hospitalized*."

"Well, that's good news! For a while there, I'd begun to think not only was I *hospitalized*, I was *dead*."

Margot Sharpe laughs, weakly. She is socially conditioned to respond to remarks meant to elicit laughter; it is very difficult to resist.

Margot would like to tell E.H. that he isn't "ill"—rather, he has a "chronic neurological condition." But she doesn't want to perplex him further, since he seems less affable and relaxed than usual. He has just finished a battery of tests that are repetitions of tests he'd taken several years ago, so that their scores might be compared, and a graph of changes plotted; of course, E.H. doesn't recall these tests, nor does his performance today suggest that he has incorporated any residual memory of the tests. A quick glance at the previous scores indicates to Margot that, uncannily, E.H. has performed almost identically today as he had in past years.

"Is it like that with you, too—'Mar-g'ret'?"

(Margot is touched, E.H. has remembered her name—almost.)

"That I'm an 'outpatient'?"

" 'I'm Nobody! / Who are you? / Are you — Nobody— Too?' "

E.H. recites these lines with a chilling sort of merriment. Margot believes that this is poetry, and possibly it is poetry by Emily Dickinson . . .

"I'm not exactly an 'outpatient,' Eli. I'm a professor at the university."

Pointless to refer to the "university," since E.H. has not the faintest idea which "university" this might be, no more than he knows that they are at the Institute at Darven Park.

"You are a 'normal' person, eh Professor?"

" 'Normal'—I suppose so."

"Yet not 'average'—eh?"

Margot smiles, considering. This is flirtatious banter that leaves her breathless. E.H. often stands close to her, as if inhaling her scent—(she is sure that this is an acquired, unconscious way of his to help identify her); in turn, Margot can't help but inhale his scent, discernible beneath the more abrasive clinical odors as a distinctly masculine aroma, astringent, possibly cologne, shaving cream, hair oil, good soap . . . And E.H. wears the very best leather belts, shoes; supple Italian calfskin, as Margot has learned from E.H.'s aunt Lucinda who is (Margot wants to think) her friend.

Alone among outpatients at the Institute, at least those whom Margot sees in Neuropsychology, Eli Hoopes dresses with care and taste; today, he is wearing a mauve cashmere sweater over a white cotton shirt, dark corduroy trousers, "loafers." On his left wrist, a handsome watch. (Not a digital watch of course. E.H. is appalled by the "ugly look" of digital watches and clocks, and it is a kindness to him to shield him from such.) His graying hair has been recently trimmed. His teeth look unusually white. He is—how old?—Margot can't seem to calculate for such a calculation would involve her own age as well, of which she doesn't want to think.

Soon! It will come about, soon.

What I have been waiting for.

Effort is required to recall that E.H. is a subject of scientific inquiry, and not quite an equal.

"Everyone has memory problems, Eli."

"Do we! Or I mean—*you.*" E.H. laughs, obscurely.

This is a strange remark. It's as if E.H. knows about an incident in Margot Sharpe's life of the other day—a disagreeable incident involving memory.

Margot isn't sure she wants to share the incident with E.H., for it may cause the man to judge her harshly. It is clear from E.H.'s manner that, for all his good-natured joking, and air of naïveté, he has a strong moral sense; perhaps even, given his Quaker and activist background, deeply imprinted in his memory below the more recent layers of ruins, a puritanical righteousness. Even if E.H. will forget what Margot tells him she is afraid that some residue of memory, some smudge of memory, will remain, and color his feelings for her. Badly she wants the man to approve of her.

Carefully she says, "Eventually, if we all live long enough, Eli, we will have deficits in short-term memory, but we may remember our earliest childhood until the very end of our lives. That's a good thing, I think."

"But why is it a 'good thing,' Professor? Do you think that all our childhood memories are 'happy'?"

Margot is taken aback, for E.H. has spoken just slightly sharply.

And why does he call her "Professor"?—he knows her name.

Seeing the look in her face, of which Margot herself is unaware, E.H. says, relenting, "Of course—I think it is a 'good thing.' We want to think so, of our earliest memories."

E.H. speaks with a measure of stoicism like one at the edge of a precipice.

He has fumbled for Margot's hand, and clasps it firmly in his as if to secure her in place.

Margot thinks—*His hand remembers another hand. My hand can become that hand.*

Amber McPherson's hand? She doesn't think so.

Amber McPherson could not have been a strong enough presence in Eli Hoopes's life. No wonder he'd abandoned that young woman!

"Dear Eli! I am always happy when I'm with *you*."

Prudently then, quick before anyone can see, Margot eases her hand from E.H.'s hand.

HERE IS WHAT happened. It is so unfair!

Margot knows herself cruelly and stupidly judged—*mis*-judged.

She will not tell E.H. She has not wished to tell anyone—though, apart from E.H., there is really no one in Margot Sharpe's life she might tell.

Returning home from the university, and in the twilit kitchen of her house listening appalled to a rambling and accusatory phone message from her older brother Ned—*Margot God damn why the hell haven't you called back, called you and left God-damn messages five, six times since Monday, aren't you fucking* there?—so shocked by her brother's furious voice she isn't sure exactly what he has said, and quickly deletes the message.

Discovers then that there have been previous messages from Ned, and from other relatives—*Margot, where are you? We've been waiting for you—your mother is waiting for you—is something wrong? Has something gone wrong? Please call back, we are having a terrible time here your poor mother has tried to call you too, and you never call back—Margot?*

Trembling badly Margot doesn't call her brother Ned—(whom she has always feared and disliked, he is such a bully)—but instead calls her aunt Edie, her mother's younger sister who is Margot's favorite aunt, and she is hoping that Edie won't pick up the phone so that she can leave a message but Edie picks up the phone on practically the first ring—"Margot! Thank God."

Upset to hear that her mother is not "doing so well"—her mother has been asking where Margot is, she has been expecting Margot to visit her in the hospital—"Margot, you'd said you'd try to come last week. You told us, and we were expecting you."

Margot is astonished as well as upset—tries to explain that she certainly has not promised anyone in Orion Falls that she was coming home last week or anytime soon—hasn't received any calls from them at all or if she had it was weeks ago, and Mom was "doing well" then—after the surgery. It is *utterly untrue whatever Ned has been saying, accusing. Utterly untrue and unfair.*

Margot's voice is shaking, her eyes have filled with tears of alarm and indignation.

"I—told him? Told *you*? That isn't possible, Aunt Edie, there must be some terrible miscommunication, I couldn't have told anyone there that I could fly back home right now because I'm too busy—I am far too busy to take even a few days off for a personal matter—maybe I didn't explain to you that I'm now the director of a very important project at the University Neurological Institute at Darven Park—it's something of an emergency situation here also, we are working with a severely brain-damaged individual and my—my presence is—is mandated . . ."

Margot repeats, denies she'd promised a visit. Can't recall any such promise nor even any conversation with her brother Ned—in months. Vaguely she recalls—yes, but very vaguely—a conversation with her aunt about her mother's tests, and her mother's diagnosis, and her mother's surgery, and her mother's schedule of chemotherapy and radiation—she remembers being told that Mom was "doing well"—"as well as can be expected at this point"—but she does not remember subsequent conversations, and she certainly does not remember promising she will return home anytime soon—"That is just not possible, Aunt Edie. Please explain to Mom, will you? Please."

Such an unpleasant exchange! Margot is astonished that her aunt doesn't relent, doesn't concede she is mistaken, or that anyone there is mistaken—clearly, the Sharpes have closed rank against her, and have turned against her. The exchange is particularly painful since Margot knows that she is correct: she did not make any such promise to anyone in Orion Falls, not even half-consciously, for she would remember if she had, and she *does not remember.*

The conversation is painful also because Margot Sharpe isn't a girl any longer, she isn't an adolescent to be lectured, scolded and willfully misunderstood; she is an adult woman of nearly forty, a professional woman who has become accustomed to being agreed-with, placated; she is not often challenged any longer, for she has become professor of neuropsychology at the university, and she has been named (by the distinguished Milton Ferris himself) principal investigator of *Project E.H.*—one of the great research projects in neuroscience history. Margot Sharpe is respected at both the university and the Institute. Her undergraduate and graduate students, her laboratory assistants, her departmental colleagues, the Institute staff are all respectful of her, and admiring of her, and so it is stunning—it is outrageous—that her own relatives, back in Orion Falls, Michigan, have so little idea of her accomplishments, and so little respect for her. Almost, Margot can't speak coherently, unfairly pressed to defend herself. "Whatever you're accusing me of, you are paraphrasing Ned's stupid accusations, Aunt Edie—there is just too much happening at Darven Park right now, I can't take time out. I wish I could—of course—but you say that Mom is in the hospital, and not in a hospice—you've said—so it isn't an emergency situation, in fact. Mom will understand, just explain.

You know how serious I am about my work—I don't take it lightly. There is Christmas break . . ."

"You haven't been back since Christmas two years ago. And you don't call or write."

"Actually, I *do.* I do call Mom, and I do write."

"Margot, what are you saying? That simply isn't true. Your mother is heartbroken, and we are all bewildered. We all helped with your college expenses, you must remember—don't you?"

"You're paraphrasing Ned. You and Ned—you are saying the identical untrue stupid things. You are accusing me of something I did not do, I *don't have to listen to any of this, I am hanging up.*" Margot is breathless, half-sobbing in hurt, indignation, resentment. They have always been jealous of her success, they'd never wanted her to go to the University of Michigan originally, it's an old, bitter issue between Margot and the Sharpes.

And so Margot does hang up, slamming the receiver down. Vastly relieved when no one calls back.

NOR WILL MARGOT tell E.H. of another, yet more shocking and unexpected call, which she receives months later in the first week of January 1984.

Margot, I need to talk to you confidentially.

The subject is related to Project E.H.

It is the Psychology Department chair who has called Margot. She is being asked to meet with him "confidentially."

Calmly Professor Sharpe enters the chairman's inner office, and sits facing the man across his desk. Like Milton Ferris, the chairman is a distinguished scientist; but he is not a close associate of Margot Sharpe, since his field isn't neuropsychology but clinical psychology.

Margot is very frightened. Margot thinks—*Someone has*

reported me, driving E.H. home. Someone has reported my spending time with E.H. alone. Someone who is jealous, and who hates me.

Through a panicked buzzing in her ears Margot can barely hear the chairman tell her, in a lowered voice, the most astonishing and unexpected news: several persons have made formal written complaints sent by certified mail to him as the departmental chair, to the dean of the faculty, and to the chancellor of the university not concerning Professor Sharpe's unconscionable behavior with her amnesiac subject but—Professor Milton Ferris's "protracted and repeated scientific misconduct as the principal investigator of the memory laboratory."

The chair asks Margot if she has anything to say, in strictest confidence, about Milton Ferris in this regard.

"Please speak openly. I know it's something of a shock, but—I suppose we might have seen this coming . . ."

Margot is stunned. Her heart has been beating so rapidly, she'd been so certain that she was herself under attack, she isn't sure that she has heard any of this correctly.

She has to grasp the arms of the chair in which she is seated, to keep from slumping to the floor. She can feel the blood drain out of her face.

"Would you like a glass of water? I'm really sorry to have so—upset you . . ."

Harry Mills is not a friend of Margot Sharpe, nor is he a detractor. Like others in the department he may have expressed some slighting criticism, over the years, of the lavishly funded high-profile *Project E.H.*; he may have expressed criticism of his renowned colleague Milton Ferris of whom it has been said—not meanly but simply accurately—that the great man has not so much as glimpsed an undergraduate student in the past twenty years, and that his doctoral dissertation advisees become his lackeys and slaves, and are allowed to take as long as eight years to complete their degrees in order to linger in the community as a ready source of free labor for the professor. It has been noted that Ferris's amnesiac lab has become the "crown jewel" in the department, unfairly eclipsing interest in the work of other, equally deserving researchers; and that Milton Ferris uses his influence to place his protégés in coveted academic positions and in elite academic journals, like a Renaissance prince bestowing favors. It is also said of Milton Ferris that for the past fifteen years he has been the "leading contender" in his field for a Nobel Prize—presumably for his pioneering work in memory.

Mills asks Margot another time if she is all right? If she would like a glass of water? Or a tissue . . .

(Has Margot begun to cry? Her cheeks sting with a kind of acid moisture.)

Margot shakes her head slowly. Margot's heart beats slow and hard now. She is not going to faint though she has never been so surprised in her adult life.

Managing to say, politely, that yes, she is all right. She does not need a glass of water.

Mills is apologetic. Clearly, he had not expected so extreme a reaction from Margot Sharpe.

"I'd assumed, Margot, without justification I see now, that you would know about these charges—since they've been made by former associates in the lab known to you." Mills pauses: Has he made a blunder? The identities of the accusers should remain confidential, surely? Quickly Mills continues, before Margot can respond, saying that he'd been hearing rumors for years about Milton's "unorthodox" research methods—"And since you've worked so closely with him, you would be in a position to know."

"No. I am not in a position to know."

Margot pauses, and repeats: "No. I have no idea . . ."

Though Mills will not reveal the identities of the individuals who have filed charges against Milton Ferris, he allows Margot to know that they are former postdocs who'd worked with Ferris within the past twelve to fifteen years; since their years in Ferris's lab they have gone on to professorships, and most of them have tenure.

Margot thinks—*Kaplan? Can it be?*

The privileged son betraying the father. That is not possible.

Gravely the chair asks Margot to speak "openly and at length" on the subject. Whatever she says will be kept confidential, she is assured; at no point, unless she initiates such disclosure, will her testimony be made available to anyone including Ferris; her name will not be listed on any document, unless she gives permission.

"Harry—is this being recorded? Our conversation?"

"Of course not, Margot! I wouldn't record anything unless you authorized it."

Mills is looking offended, hurt. Margot thinks, as Milton Ferris might have thought—*But can I believe you? How can I believe anything you say?*

"If you'd like to discuss this some other time, Margot, of course that would be fine. But—remember—our conversation must be kept confidential." Mills pauses, delicately. "Of course, Milton Ferris should not be told."

"Not yet, you mean. Milton should not be told—yet."

"That's right. Unless the accusations are borne out by evidence, Milton will never be told. The investigation is private and confidential and even the identities of the investigating committee are not to be revealed."

"Do you know who they are?—the 'investigating committee'?"

"N-No . . ."

Mills had hesitated just perceptibly. Margot suspects that he is lying.

Or rather, not telling the full truth.

(Mills may mean that he knows who has been asked to serve on the committee but doesn't yet know who has agreed to serve. Technically then, he is not lying to his colleague Margot Sharpe.)

"What was the charge?—'protracted and repeated scientific misconduct'? What exactly does that mean?"

"It doesn't mean that Ferris has falsified data in his published work. No one is accusing him of that, at least not so far. The primary charges are that over a period of many years Ferris has 'appropriated' the work of younger colleagues in his lab including graduate students—he has published articles under his name that don't reflect work he has done, and he has routinely 'punished' individuals who'd questioned him in even the mildest of ways. 'A reign of terror'—one of the former postdocs has said of his years with Ferris. 'No one dared complain or challenge him, for fear of retribution.' "

You will wind up in Siberia. Or somewhere west of here like Purdue.

Margot is still feeling somewhat shaky, light-headed. She is still wondering if the departmental chair—in collusion with the dean of the faculty—is conspiring against *her.*

Could it be that the accusations against Milton Ferris are a ploy? Or—there will be accusations against Margot Sharpe, as well as accusations against her mentor Milton Ferris?

The way in which Harry Mills stares at her, the very set of the man's mouth as if he is resisting a sneer, is disconcerting to Margot. For a moment she loses the thread of their conversation and can't remember what the charges are.

There has been nothing inappropriate between Elihu Hoopes and me.

It's true, we have a special rapport—as others have (probably) observed. But there is nothing unethical in my relationship with the subject and I challenge anyone to prove that there is.

When she can speak clearly Margot says that she knows "absolutely nothing" about misconduct on Milton Ferris's part. She has never heard of such accusations until now, and is very upset and astonished by them.

"Milton Ferris never 'appropriated' anything of mine in the many years I assisted him. When I arrived here, I was immediately invited to work on *Project E.H.*—the opportunity of a lifetime. I didn't even realize at the time what an opportunity—what a privilege—this was. I was only twenty-three years old."

Margot speaks carefully, calmly. Margot speaks as clearly as if she believes the conversation is being recorded after all. Several times she reiterates that Milton Ferris never appropriated any of her work, nor did he appropriate the work of anyone else in the lab at the time—she is certain. "Along with Alvin Kaplan, I was helping oversee the lab from an early stage. We worked with the other associates closely. We collated data, we collaborated. Milton was always the 'principal investigator' in every sense of the term. He designed experiments, he helped execute experiments, he helped collect data—most of the time. Of course, Milton was sometimes traveling; he was often at conferences giving important papers, based on our project. But not once in eighteen years—(I think it has been eighteen years?)—did I ever witness Milton behaving in any way unethical or unprofessional—far from being guilty of scientific misconduct, Milton has been a model of the very highest *scientific conduct*."

Margot pauses, breathing quickly. Her pulses are racing. The pupils of her eyes feel dilated.

"Harry, I'm distressed by these charges. I'm—outraged! There must be some personal vendetta against Milton Ferris. I know there has been a good deal of professional jealousy. Especially since Milton is so often on public television—no one is so envied and resented as a successful 'popularizer.' You should be trying to protect the reputation of your outstanding colleague, not undermining it. If Milton were to know, there might be grounds for—for a lawsuit . . ."

Quickly Dr. Mills assures Margot that indeed he is trying to do just that—protect Milton Ferris's reputation. That's why he and the dean are initiating an inquiry, only just preliminary at the present time.

"But you must not tell Milton, you know. That would be a breach of ethics, Margot."

"Of course, I won't tell Milton! I would not dignify these charges by repeating them, especially to Milton. He would be crushed, and he would be furious. He would want to sue, I think—for criminal slander and libel."

Mills hasn't expected such a vehement response from Margot Sharpe. If he knows of Margot's relationship with her mentor, or knows something of it, he would also know that Margot Sharpe and Milton Ferris are no longer intimately involved with each other; Margot would have no reason to defend Ferris, and might even be expected to be vindictive toward him. But clearly she is not, and this makes a strong impression on the chairman.

"I think—I think I want to leave now. I don't want to discuss this any further."

Margot rises to leave the chair's office. She moves stiffly, like a much older woman. When she almost stumbles Mills leaps to his feet to assist her.

Returning to her office like a sleepwalker Margot thinks—*I will go to Milton. I will warn him! He will know how I love him. He will love me again.*

SHE DOESN'T CALL Milton Ferris.

She will not call Milton Ferris.

She cannot risk hearing the surprise in the man's voice. That unmistakable dip in tone; the lack of enthusiasm cloaked by a forced-affable greeting edged with guilt—*Oh yes, Margot. Hello . . .*

For it has been some time since Margot has spoken with Milton Ferris privately. A considerable time, since out of pride she has refused to call him, and longer still since Milton has called her.

Instead, that evening she calls Alvin Kaplan. A shot glass of whiskey for courage, and then—the call.

As soon as Kaplan hears her voice, he knows why Margot has called.

"Alvin, how could you! My God."

Their exchange is halting, painful. Like a guilty child Kaplan tries to pretend that he isn't one of those who've filed charges against Milton Ferris but Margot insists that he is: she is certain. Then, Kaplan is defensive—"God damn him, he was stealing from all of us, even graduate students! For Christ's sake, Margot, he was stealing from you—he took advantage of you from the start . . ."

As Kaplan speaks in an aggrieved voice Margot holds the receiver a few inches from her ear. She can't bear to hear this! She thinks *Of course they knew, I was in love with him. They all knew. They laughed at me, but they pitied me. They did not hate me.*

She points out to Kaplan that without Milton Ferris, neither of them would have a career.

"Margot, how can you make such a statement? That's ridiculous. You and I are first-rate scientists—I'm sorry to sound vain, but it's true for both of us. Certainly we would have studied and worked with other people. We might have gone to other universities, and we might not have wound up with E.H., but it's possible—it's quite probable—we might have done just as well professionally."

"You don't believe that, Alvin. How can you say that! Milton taught us everything we know."

"It's true that Milton taught us many things, Milton is, or was, a brilliant scientist. But he lost interest in research, that was obvious. He lost interest in *work*. And so he just appropriated our work, and passed it off as his own. He was sitting on a gold mine—with Eli Hoopes. Everything connected with our amnesiac has turned to gold—for Milton. E.H. is unique in neuroscience and Milton appropriated him. And we never dared challenge Milton. And those who did . . ."

"I don't know what you're talking about. I don't know anyone who 'challenged' Milton. Who is it? Who is filing charges against him?"

Kaplan names a former assistant professor at the university, now at the National Institutes of Health in Washington, D.C. Margot, who knows this individual fairly well, is astonished and disbelieving.

"I'll call him! He can't be serious."

"You *will not* call him, Margot! Please."

"What do you mean, 'please'? How can I stand by while Milton is being falsely accused of misconduct? He will be broken, humiliated. His reputation will be ruined. He's seventy years old . . ."

"Because he has behaved unethically for more than a decade.

Because he has ruined some scientists' reputations—their lives. Young women's lives."

"That's ridiculous! That is *not true.*"

"You've been blind. You haven't wanted to know." Kaplan pauses, then says, cruelly, "He hasn't treated the others the way he's treated you, Margot. He'd always favored *you*—the other women, he simply used. It's your vanity that is driving this—not your professional judgment."

Margot is struck dumb. Though Kaplan can't see, a fierce blush rises into her face that is part shame, and part exhilaration. *Always favored you*—she will remember this.

She says, stammering, "But—we can't hurt Milton. He may have behaved unconscionably—at times—but we have 'consciences'—we can't break an old man's heart."

Can't break an old man's heart. Words out of a TV melodrama of the kind Margot never watches. Yet, Margot is sincere; she is trembling, and tears run down her heated face.

Spitefully Kaplan says, "He named you head of the project. Of course you feel grateful to him and protective of him."

"He got you your job at Rockefeller! And he would have named you head of the project, except you wanted to move."

"I didn't 'want' to move—I was urged to move. By Milton."

"You were? But why?"

"So he could promote you, why else? He'd always favored *you.*"

Spiteful as any sibling. And Margot can sense the hurt, and the fury beneath the hurt.

"But the fact is, Alvin, you wouldn't have your position at Rockefeller, you wouldn't have brought all that grant money with you, if Milton hadn't pushed for you."

"That's an insult. That isn't worthy of you, Margot."

"None of this is *worthy of you,* Alvin."

But by degrees Kaplan has begun to weaken. He is suffused with guilt and shame, Margot knows. Betraying the man who'd made their careers and their lives possible! Betraying their common father.

Kaplan speaks of a half-dozen others who are intent upon exposing Milton Ferris out of disgust with his "unsullied" reputation, and with the power he continues to wield in the scientific community. Some of these are individuals whom Margot knows, though not well. (Yes, one of those is the former colleague now teaching at Purdue. Margot knew this!) Kaplan tells her of other instances of questionable professional behavior on Milton's part which include "taking advantage" of his female associates; on this delicate matter, Kaplan is diplomatic, and doesn't humiliate Margot by listing other women by name. He allows her to know, however, that it is something like a general knowledge, that Ferris is "known, notorious" for taking advantage of the naïveté of young women scientists, sexually, professionally. Kaplan concedes, "Of course, Milton is also a very nice person—he can be. He's gracious, he's charming, he has won every award and has received every grant he's ever applied for. He's chair of the membership committee at the National Academy. If he hears of this, and if we don't follow through with our charges so that he's at least removed from that powerful committee, he will veto us for as long as he lives."

"What do you mean, 'if he hears of this'? I haven't accused him of anything—I've defended him. I was just in Mills's office defending him, and I will put my statement in writing, you can be sure."

"You can't sabotage this investigation, Margot. You know very well that Milton Ferris should be made to retire."

"I've told you, that is *not true*. I will never testify that *that is true*."

In any case, Margot says hotly that she doesn't give a damn for being elected to the National Academy or any other professional organization. She is a *scientist,* not a *social climber.*

Kaplan says that's bullshit. Of course she cares, and she should care. *He* cares.

Margot reiterates: she can't betray Milton Ferris. She will not—ever—betray Milton Ferris.

"He's going to retire soon. There's no point in destroying him now."

After an exhausting hour or more on the phone, Kaplan relents. Or seems to relent. Margot thanks him, in a voice trembling with emotion. They hang up the phone, each edgy and excited.

Soon after, Margot hears from Harry Mills that proceedings against Milton Ferris have been "temporarily suspended." Her remarks will be stricken from the record if she wishes.

"Yes, strike everything. Including this conversation. Good night!"

In exhausted triumph Margot thinks—*I would never do such a thing to you, Milton. We loved each other so much.*

IT WAS MILTON Ferris who taught her to drink. Taught her to prefer his favorite whiskey—Johnnie Walker Black Label.

Flamey-hot going down, and all of her body suffused with flame so she stumbles into her darkened bedroom and falls half-dressed onto her bed. Drifting into the sweetest and most delicious sleep from which it is becoming ever harder to awaken.

CHAPTER SIX

Eli? Eli!

Standing on a plank bridge in a low-lying marshy place with feet just slightly apart and firmly on his heels to brace himself against a sudden gust of wind.

Standing on a plank bridge in this place that is new to him and wondrous in beauty. Thinking it must be at Lake George—but he isn't sure. He has not seen this particular place before—he is sure of this. He seems to know that he must brace himself, he grips the railing with both hands, tight.

This is a place new to him and wondrous in beauty yet he is fearful of turning to see, in the shallow stream flowing beneath the bridge, behind his back, the drowned girl.

. . . naked, about eleven years old, a child. Eyes open and sightless, shimmering in water. Rippling-water, that makes it seem that the girl's face is shuddering. Her slender white body, long white tremulous legs and bare feet. Splotches of sunshine, "water-skaters" magnified in shadow on the girl's face.

They would shake him hard, they would say to him *Eli you*

did not see. You did not see your cousin in the woods. You did not see Gretchen at all that day, you are mistaken.

They would shake him hard, and harder. They would say to him *For God's sake you are having a bad nightmare, Eli. You can't give in to nightmares, you will drive us all crazy.*

"Mr. Hoopes?"

He turns. He is startled to see that someone has come up quietly behind him or has been standing behind him for some time, and he'd had no idea.

"We should go back now, Mr. Hoopes. You have an appointment at one o'clock, remember."

"Yes! That is correct."

He speaks lightly. He smiles.

It is perplexing to him, the sudden appearance of the girl. She is not the girl he has been imagining—she is not the girl he has been *seeing.* She is much older, in her twenties. She is caramel-skinned, with dark tight-braided hair in a complex weave on her head. She wears a pale green cotton smock over dark green cotton slacks. On her feet are crepe-soled white shoes and on her left lapel a laminated white ID badge. Probably a medical worker. Nurse's aide or an attendant. He squints with his good eye to read her name—YOLANDA.

Confused. Tries to disguise his alarm. (He knows) there is something behind him at which he is forbidden to look, beyond the railing of the plank bridge, the shallow stream flowing beneath the bridge. Frightened of seeing what this is but Yolanda continues to smile at him in a way to suggest that nothing is wrong in the slightest. She knows him—"Mr. Hoopes." She is not surprised or dismayed, she is not horrified. *She does not know about the child in the stream.*

"You been havin a nice time walkin out here, Mr. Hoopes? Real nice here in't it? My favorite place, around here."

"Yes. Mine also."

His voice which is the voice of an adult male. Feels this voice—deep baritone in his throat—and realizes that he is not a child, himself: he is not five years old. Much older, his body hangs on him like an oversized coat.

And whatever has happened, happened at some other time. And in some other place.

"Mr. Hoopes? You forgettin your—your drawin book . . ."

The caramel-skinned girl points to an artist's sketchbook that has been propped against the bridge railing with a look of having been distractedly put aside. The sketchbook is shut, there is no stick of charcoal or pencil in his hand but he has a pleasurable memory of having grasped something between his fingers—indeed, there is a charcoal stick in a pocket of his jacket. Evidently he has been sketching the rich marshland on the farther side of the bridge where redwing blackbirds and starlings have flocked.

"Thank you! I wouldn't want to leave this behind."

"That's right, Mr. Hoopes. Last time you left that book, I had a hard time finding it."

"'Yo-landa'—do you like to walk here, too? Do you live nearby?"

"No, Mr. Hoopes! Don't live anywhere near this place."

The girl laughs, showing small white teeth. Her accent is soft, pillowy. She is "from the islands"—he guesses, by her accent, Dominican Republic.

"Am I late, Yolanda? I hope not."

"No, Mr. Hoopes! That's why I'm here—to make sure you are not late."

"Am I late sometimes? Is that why you follow me around?"

The girl laughs, as if Elihu Hoopes has tickled her. "Mr. Hoopes, I don't 'follow you around'—I walk with you."

"So I don't get lost."

"For sure, you won't get lost."

"I hope they pay you sufficiently, to keep people like me from getting lost."

It is a query—*People like me.* Elihu Hoopes hopes to determine by the young woman's response whether there are indeed *people like me* or whether he is *one of a kind.*

To be *one of a kind* is a terrible fate. He is afraid that is what he is.

But Yolanda is walking ahead, and it isn't clear if she is really listening to him. Speaking with strangers is like volleying a tennis ball: if you can keep the volley going there is a connection, an urgent and exciting connection, but once the connection is broken—you are flailing, lost.

He has forgotten the plank bridge, the stream beneath the bridge, the shadowy shimmering rippling water at which he wasn't supposed to look—he has forgotten the warning against looking. Turning his head.

But he has turned his head, and there is nothing. What has so frightened him? He feels his heartbeat begin to slow, for the danger is past.

He rubs his hands together, chill perspiration of palm to palm.

Now he sees: they are on a wood chip path. He is not in the Adirondacks or any wild place but in what appears to be a parkland of some kind. Ahead, partially visible through a stand of trees, is a building of pale-glimmering glass.

A place of affluence, his heart sinks. Affluence is artifice, that deflates the soul.

Behind him is a marshy area fecund with reeds and cattails,

glittering with strips of water like the shards of a broken mirror. Monarch butterflies, redwing blackbirds. And on the rippling surface of the water a continual skittish play of water-insects like firing neurons.

Behind him and passing into forgetfulness, the plank bridge and the shallow stream.

Trails are marked here but they are all wood chip trails that probably just loop back upon themselves in a quarter mile as in a maze. He is disappointed, he isn't at Lake George—obviously, he is nowhere near Lake George—but in this place of fastidiously maintained trails, granite benches named for deceased donors, beds of colorful autumn flowers—zinnias, marigolds, asters.

The marshland is a natural place, he supposes. Someone had the idea of creating parkland to abut it. Affluence flows into nature and alters it, in its image.

Strange how he seems to know the direction in which they are headed, though he has never been here before. When the wood chip trail branches, both the caramel-skinned girl and Elihu Hoopes take the left branch without thinking.

The girl whose name he has forgotten—(he knows that it is a beautiful exotic name)—strides ahead on the path. Splotched sunshine falls like coins about their heads. He feels an urge to reach out to her, to touch her—the slender shoulder in the pale green smock, the hair at the back of her head that is so tightly braided. But he knows—*You can't. You must not. Not ever again.*

He is not aroused. Not sexually aroused. But he yearns to touch her, he is so lonely.

Must not. Not ever again.

As if she can read his anxious thoughts the girl turns to him, smiling. "Mr. Hoopes, you going to tell me the birds again? Seems like, I get them all mixed-up."

They are standing at the edge of a large pond bordered by willow trees. On the pond are waterfowl—mallards, geese, majestic white swans. And at the shore, smaller birds pecking excitedly at grain that someone has scattered for them.

He points to the ducks—"blue-winged teals"—"mallards"—"American wigeons." He points to the geese—"Canada geese"—"snow geese." He points to the swans—"whistling swans." The smaller birds are "cardinals"—"slate-colored juncos"—"vesper sparrows"—"song sparrows"—"field sparrows." The names of the birds come to him unbidden, as through a magical action of his finger's pointing and the birds themselves, provoking the girl to laugh in delight as if he has performed a remarkable trick.

"Except," Elihu Hoopes says, "the birds don't know their names. Only we know their names, because we have given them their names."

The caramel-skinned girl laughs uncertainly. She regards Elihu Hoopes with the wary reverence with which she would regard any middle-aged male patient at the Institute whose malady is hidden inside his head.

"And what kinda cloud is that, Mr. Hoopes?"

His gaze swings upward. The sky is somehow surprising, unexpected—steep canyons of cloud that look as if you could fall into them, without end. And beyond, the soft pale blue of rainwashed glass.

"Mostly cirrocumulus—'mackerel sky.' At the horizon, stratocumulus—rain clouds."

These names, too, come to Elihu Hoopes unbidden. He can sense that the girl has asked these questions of him before since his answers don't greatly surprise her; nor will she recall them, for essentially they do not interest her.

He wants to tell the beautiful caramel-skinned girl *I tell you these things because I love you. Whoever you are.*

He smiles, in secret. How surprised the girl would be, if she knew!

"Mr. Hoopes, you are a—teacher? Professor?"

"Sorry, no."

"Lawyer?"

"No. Don't think so."

"Somethin in business, then."

"'Somethin in business, then.' Yes."

Though when he tries to recall the work he'd done, desk-work, office-work, telephone, columns of numerals, calculations—when he tries to recall his father speaking urgently to him on matters of Hoopes, Inc.—something in his brain seizes. Like ice cracking. Can't bring himself to recall whatever it is, or was. All that is finished.

"This is a beautiful park the Institute has here, in't it, Mr. Hoopes?"

"Is it?"

"You saying it is *not*?"

"Too tame for me, Yolanda."

He sees (again) that the girl's name is Yolanda. Yet he is careful to pronounce the name casually, as if he has known it all along.

He has come to be hypersensitive to the expectations of others and has come to know by the most subtle, near-invisible alterations of another's facial muscles if what he says is plausible and reasonable or if it is senseless and irrational and will alert the listener that *something is wrong with this person.*

But Yolanda laughs as if Elihu Hoopes has said something scandalous.

"*Too tame?* How d'you like a place then, Mr. Hoopes—*wild*?"

"Yes, Yolanda. Wild."

Elihu speaks wistfully. Yolanda looks pained. He realizes that she has been enunciating *Mr. Hoopes* carefully: he has to wonder if the name *Hoopes* has associations for her, if she is from Philadelphia and has encountered the name previously, in quasi-exalted circumstances; or, more likely, if it is just a name to her, a curious name, as *Elihu Hoopes* seems to be a curious individual, one of those *not quite right in the head.*

Glancing down at himself: neatly pressed khakis, linen shirt, oxblood loafers. It seems that Eli is not wearing any sort of hospital attire, and so he is not a "patient."

Yet: he might be an "out-patient."

(Though he doesn't feel physically "unwell." His sense of pain—tactile, internal—seems blunted, numbed. As if parts of his body have gone to sleep.)

He would like to ask Yolanda where they are, and why—but can't summon the right, lightly bantering words.

"We goin up there right now, not a minute late, Mr. Hoopes"—Yolanda assures him, as if she can read his thoughts.

Leaving the private park now. Following a graveled walk to the rear entrance of the pale-glimmering building that is, he quickly counts, eight storeys high.

Hospital? Medical center?

Compulsion for quick counting of things that can be reduced to numerals but a compulsion that has little practical use for any numeral that comes into his head—(he knows, he understands this but not why)—very soon drifts out of his head, and is gone.

Averting his gaze so he can't count God-damned cars in the parking lot but the method is: how many cars in each row, how many rows, multiply.

"H'lo there, Mr. Hoopes! You havin a good walk?"

"H'lo, Eli. Yolanda takin good care of you, is she?"

Smiling strangers appear out of nowhere. Two women, a man also in uniform: pale green smocks or jackets, dark green trousers and crepe-soled white shoes. They seem to know him and to like and respect him—this is a positive thing. He makes no effort to read their ID badges for (he senses) he should know their names.

It is a positive thing to be liked and respected for it is not probable then that you will be hurt.

He'd been beaten, once. More than once. He can shut his eyes and recall the astonishment of being hit, punched, kicked, screamed at—*Nigger lover! Fucking Jew!* So quickly you are knocked to the ground and once you are on the ground, you are helpless. Try to protect your head, try to protect your face, stomach. He can recall the terror of believing that he would die, and a curious stillness within the terror, as if a part of him, his soul perhaps, had curled up tight in self-protectiveness, and had passed into oblivion.

Like islands emerging in a dark marshland, these memories. But he doesn't clutch at them, he has learned to let such memories rise, and fall back again into oblivion, for he has learned not to exhaust himself in an effort futile beyond all calculation. What drifts into his mind, will drift into his mind without this effort. And no matter the effort, it will disperse again and drift away.

He isn't sure if he remembers pain, or if he is remembering someone else's pain. A body kicked and dragged along the pavement, screams and grunts, the soft-sickening sound of a body being kicked by a booted foot but (possibly) not his body.

"H'lo, Eli! Great day isn't it"—another smiling stranger passing by. This one in a white lab coat, has to be a doctor.

"Great day, yes—if you're alive."

Strange that he seems to know the way to the bank of elevators though he has no idea where he is being taken. Stepping inside, and the caramel-skinned girl presses one of the buttons, and Eli sees, but in the next instant has forgotten. On one of the floors someone steps into the elevator and touches his shoulder, and he turns. Smiling face like a mask that sometimes slips if he turns his head too quickly and whoever this is might see his panicked eyes.

"Eli? How are you?"

"Very well, thanks. And you?"

"Very well."

The caramel-skinned girl leads him out of the elevator at the fourth floor. He will remember that: numeral four.

Four is yellow, usually. Not a bright yellow like his grandfather's little plane but a more subdued yellow.

And so: if he can remember *yellow,* he can remember *four.*

"Come with me! You're just in time."

Walking now with an energetic youthful man. Friendly and assured, talking to Elihu Hoopes as if he knows him. Whoever was with him in the elevator is gone now. Would turn his head to look yearningly for her but knows it is futile, she has been swept away.

Someone he loves. Has loved. Gone.

Through swinging doors—NEUROPSYCHOLOGY LAB.

White walls, stone-colored tile floor, fluorescent lighting—he has never been here before but there is something familiar about the place, and in this way comforting.

Now there are two individuals—two men—both in white lab coats—walking with him. One on his right and one on his left. The panicked thought comes to him—*They are neurologist and neurosurgeon. They will drill a hole into my skull, I will smell the dry smoke.*

Here in *Neuropsychology* he seems to be "Eli" more than he is "Mr. Hoopes." His senses quicken, he is approaching the heart of the mystery.

Strange to him that another time he turns into a room, through an opened doorway, as if instinctively, though he has never been in this place before.

If he shuts his right eye, sometimes half his vision falls away. And when he opens his right eye, everything is restored except—(sometimes)—there is another person with him, whom he has not seen before, who has appeared out of nowhere. And it is imperative, he knows, not to acknowledge any surprise or confusion.

In a sunlit room several persons are seated. Are they waiting for him? But why, waiting for *him*?—this makes him anxious. One of them is a woman who stares at him with an expression of commingled anticipation and dread, who rises quickly to greet him, in a bright voice crying, "Eli! Oh, Eli."

She seems dazed by the sight of him, anxious. Clumsily she tries to embrace him, or to step into his arms—but he stands very still, stiff and unmoving. "Eli, how are you? It's Rosalyn . . ."

Rosalyn is Eli's younger sister. But this woman is not Rosalyn.

"You know me, Eli—don't you? Hello . . ." The woman's voice trails off plaintively.

It is discomforting, how close the woman stands to Eli Hoopes. She grips his arms, staring at him pleadingly. Her eyes shimmer with tears of alarm and reproach.

"Eli, please say something. We've been told this would be a good time to see you . . ."

Detaches himself from the impetuous woman, politely.

"Hel-*lo*. So good to see you."

Hears his voice flat and mechanical as a programmed voice. He is not very convincing, he is afraid: it is difficult to pretend you are happy to see someone when you have no feeling for the person and have no idea who she is.

Like playing tennis with a sprained ankle. Barely, it can be done, but only with a herculean effort of will. Sweat oozing onto your forehead, the pain is so extreme.

"Oh, but it's good to see *you,* Eli!—you are looking better-rested than last time . . . Have you been sketching? Will you show us what you've done?"

The woman's voice is anxious and pressing. The woman is imploring him, with a bold sort of desperation. How can he respond? What is his reply? He has stopped dead in his tracks just inside the room, as if in a trance, arms at his sides. Close by, two men have risen to their feet, smiling at him uncertainly, with that same expression of commingled anticipation and dread.

My sister's name but she is not my sister.

My brothers' faces but not my brothers.

"Don't you recognize me, Eli? Your sister Rosalyn—Rosie. Oh, please!"

" 'Rosalyn.' 'Rosie.' " Eli utters the names softly, provisionally.

It is true, the woman's strained face does seem familiar to him in the unnerving way of déjà vu. It is an older, thicker, far less beautiful face than the face of his young sister, as he recalls it; he cannot bring himself to acknowledge it. Her eyes that are close-set and reproachful with tears are not Rosalyn's eyes. Her lipsticked mouth is unbecomingly smeared, from her effort at kissing him, brushing her lips against his cheek.

"You must recognize me, Eli. I'm wearing my hair the way I used to—before you got sick. And this sweater, I'm sure you remember this sweater . . ."

Eli does. Eli does remember the sweater. He remembers the soft purple wool, the wooden buttons.

The hair, he does not remember. The face, he does not remember.

He is feeling boxed in, they are so crudely manipulative. Establishing clues (like the sweater with the wooden buttons) and openly drawing attention to the clues to confound him—*How can we be tricking you, if we acknowledge we are tricking you?*

"Please say hello to me, Eli! Just say it—'Hello, Rosie.' "

" 'Hello Rosie.' "

"Doesn't it mean anything, I am your sister and I love you?"

" 'I am your sister and I love you.' "

Eli repeats these extraordinary words, which he has no way of decoding, since he understands that the woman who speaks them is not his sister, but it is not clear if the woman understands that she is not his sister, or is herself confused and mistaken.

"Don't you have any feeling for *me*?"

" 'Don't you have any feeling for *me*.' "

Wanting suddenly to placate everyone. Whoever the woman is, whoever the men who have approached him smiling (warily, guardedly—these are not smiles of happy recognition)—whose faces also seem familiar to him in the disreputable way of déjà vu.

Cannily sensing that he has made a blunder, he has allowed the imposters to know that he knows they are imposters, this might be dangerous. In his old, lost life he often inflamed the dislike of others through his self-sufficiency and intransigence, now he is in a weakened position and must proceed with caution.

Robust in greeting—"Hel-*lo!*"

He knows that his brothers are named "Averill" and "Harry" and that they are older than he: Averill is two years older than Eli, Harry is five years older than Eli. And so it is a challenge to Eli to consider which of the imposters is supposed to be which brother for it isn't altogether clear—(not that he wishes to stare at them, he does not)—which is the elder, which the younger.

Surprises them with his sudden energy and enthusiasm. Shaking their hands—"Averill!"—"Harry!" Blindly he grips the hand of the one brother, and blindly the hand of the other. If he has erred, he is daring them to correct him.

The other imposter, the sister, is close beside them. Each is speaking—trying to speak. Eli is very silent, at the center of the commotion.

Such a confrontation is like paddling a canoe, he is thinking. A long canoe, fashioned of precisely fitted strips of wood. Heavy, beautiful. But dangerous, for a canoe can overturn in rough weather.

Paddling a canoe across choppy waters, and each of them has a paddle. But they are not coordinated. Only Eli Hoopes is a skilled canoeist, the others are awkward, blundering. They are imposters, and are becoming defensive.

"Eli, you know who we are—I think you do."

"If we leave here today, Eli, we are not coming back. This is the last time."

The last time. But Eli knows, there have been no previous times, for he would recall these devious people, and he does not.

Eli says, with a faint stammer, "But—I do 'know' you. I've told you. 'Averill'—'Harry.' And 'Rosie.' "

The elder of the brothers, the one disguised as Harry, says sulkily, "Yes, you know us. But you are pretending you don't."

"I am *not pretending.* I am trying very hard to convince you that I am *not pretending.*"

The other, disguised as Averill, says, "This is such bullshit."

The woman, disguised as Rosalyn, says with a hurt little cry, "But—Eli isn't well! His memory has been damaged."

"He knows us, look at him. He's always been an arrogant bastard."

Yet, the imposters are uncertain. Does Eli Hoopes recognize them, and is denying them; or, has Eli Hoopes truly failed to recognize them, and is hoping to deceive them into believing that he has recognized them?

By this time Eli sees that a scene has been arranged. He and the imposter sister and brothers have been urged to sit down, to "talk"—"relate." The setting appears to be a lounge of some kind, in a hospital or a clinic; it is not a "natural" setting, Eli thinks; certainly not in a private home. He is sitting, and the others—"Rosalyn"—"Averill"—"Harry"—are seated facing him. A few feet away, a camera operated by a young person is aimed at them.

The issue is: these individuals, these strangers, Eli Hoopes doesn't know.

He will try to placate them, for he doesn't want trouble. (He is gripping his sketchbook. He knows that he must not let it out of his hands, for it will be taken from him.) But the fact is, he doesn't know these people. Though they speak to him with a goading sort of intimacy, as one might speak to a brother suspected of mysterious deceit, he can't speak this way in turn to them. He just can't.

Instructions are—*Please ignore the camera. Try not to look at the camera but at one another as in a natural conversation.*

But it is not a natural conversation. There is the God-damned camera, there are strangers in the room observing, this is not a natural setting.

"Eli, look at us! You refuse to look at us . . ."

"You recognize our voices, don't you?"

"It's hopeless, he doesn't know us . . ."

"Of course he 'knows' us—he just doesn't 'remember.' "

"He knows us! For Christ's sake."

"But why then would he pretend that he didn't?"

"Jesus! Ask him."

He listens to them with mounting outrage: how dare they talk about him as if he weren't present? As if he were some sort of subhuman creature?

"God damn you! Fuck you!"—astonishing them by rushing at them suddenly, with threatening fists.

The imposter-brothers shrink from him. The imposter-sister collides with a chair and nearly falls, in terror to escape his wrath.

He is shouting at them. He is braying, bawling.

They are predator animals, and he is their prey. Except—the prey has turned against the predator.

One of the imposter-brothers tries to placate him, by touching his arm. He strikes the astonished man in the face, with his fist; so hard, there is a satisfying *crack* of bone.

He winces with pain, and the imposter-brother staggers backward clutching his face, crashing into a table.

"Eli! Mr. Hoopes! No."

Now there is confusion, commotion. Observer-strangers appear, aghast.

They are circling him. They have penned him in. (The imposter-brothers and the imposter-sister have departed; within seconds, he has forgotten them.) He is sucking at the knuckles of his right hand, that feel as if the bones had been fractured. He wonders who has hurt him—or rather, whom he has hurt. His heart is beating hard, but it is a good sensation.

"Eli? Come with us . . ."

"Mr. Hoopes, we are your friends. You know us."

This is not true. He has no friends. But he is shrewd enough to know that one must feign friendship, in order to survive. Thus, he allows himself to be penned in a corner. He allows himself to be *pacified* in the eyes of strangers.

Fumbling for something in his pocket—a little notebook. Leafs through it, by instinct. He has little need to read, he has memorized:

"'There is no journey, and there is no path. There is no wisdom, there is emptiness. There is no emptiness.'" Pauses to add, "This is the wisdom of the Buddha. But there is no wisdom, and there is no Buddha." Laughing with inexplicable good humor.

THE LITTLE BOAT. Shuts his eyes tight. Remembering his parents saying good-bye to him. He was in a small boat, though it was not a boat he recognized from among the boats owned by the family, kept at their boathouse at Lake George. Alone in the boat, which was strange and unexpected for never in his life had he been alone in any boat. And the little boat was being pushed off from shore, and his parents were waving good-bye to him. His mother—so young! And his father—so young! Was this a mistake, they were sending him away too soon? He was crying to them, for he did not want to be sent away in the boat by himself; the horror was, the boat had no oars. The horror was, the back of the boat was awash in dark, dirty water. He was very shaky in the boat, sitting with his knees to his chest, hugging his knees. With a terrifying solemnity and inevitability the boat moved farther out into the stream, a swift current was bearing it away, for this was not Lake George after all but a river, and a wide river whose farther bank he could barely see. His parents walked along the shore quickly, at first keeping parallel with him, then falling back as the current accelerated.

Already, the water was too deep for him to step into, to wade back to shore. He was frightened of trying to swim.

Eli, good-bye!

Eli darling! Good-bye.

THE LOVERS' QUARREL. "Mr. Hoopes—Eli—hello! How are you this morning?"

"Very good. How are *you*?"

"Very good, Eli. Do you remember me?"

"Yes. I remember *you*."

(Is this true? Elihu Hoopes isn't sure, but he is a gentleman, and knows what must be said.)

"My name is"—pausing discreetly as if to encourage Elihu Hoopes to supply her name even as, with a smile, to alleviate any discomfort the amnesiac subject might feel, and to suggest the bond of intimacy and friendliness between them, seemingly of long standing, she provides the name herself—"Margot Sharpe."

"Yes! Mar-go Sharpe, hel-*lo*."

Shaking her hand. Closing her slender fingers in his. Leans close, to inhale the scent of her glossy black hair, threaded very lightly with silver.

Is she a doctor? Associated with this hospital or clinic? Though not wearing a white lab coat, and there is not a laminated ID badge on her lapel.

He has never seen this woman before, he believes. There is a sort of pale glare in her face, he can't see her distinctly. *We are something to each other. We are linked, in some way.*

He has forgotten her name, and so she tells him another time: "Margot Sharpe."

"Yes. 'Mar-go Sharpe.' "

"Though I think I resemble a grade school classmate of yours—'Margo Madden'?—or 'Margaret . . .' "

She laughs, and Elihu Hoopes laughs with her, though he is utterly perplexed.

"By saying that you resemble 'Mar-go Madden'—or 'Margaret'—you are not actually saying, you know, that you *are not* her. For if you are my old classmate, you would also resemble her. Is that correct, dear?"

"Yes, Mr. Hoopes. That is correct. But in fact, I am not your old classmate from Gladwyne Day School, and I don't know anything about her. My name is—"

"Excuse me, I know your name perfectly well: 'Mar-go Sharpe.' "

It is an obscure sort of sexual flirtation, Eli thinks. He is both perplexed and intrigued. Here is a woman not previously known to him—(he is sure)—who seems to know him, and whom in a way he seems to know, though he has never seen her before, and is sure she has never before seen him; even if she has access to his (medical?) files, how could she possibly know about the little Madden girl whom Eli Hoopes hasn't seen in—how long?—it might be a quarter-century.

More seriously, the woman introduces herself as a neuropsychologist at the university, who has been working with him for several years.

Neuropsychologist! Several years! He is stunned by this. He does not believe this.

He laughs, dismissively. "I don't think so, Professor."

"You don't remember me, Eli?"

"No. Maybe. I have trouble with my memory . . ."

"How long have you had trouble with your memory, Eli?"

He dislikes and distrusts this female professor. *Neuropsychologist*—what does that mean? He has had too much of *neuro-*. He would like to think of something other than *neuro-*.

"I'm not sure. I told you—I have problems with my memory, sometimes. Could be—six weeks."

"Six weeks?"

"Six months. Maybe that's a closer estimate."

"And did something precipitate your problem?"

"I think that I was ill. I had a fever, an infection. I think that I was hurt in a plane crash, but I'm not sure when this was. I think—I think I can remember being brought by ambulance to the hospital here, from Lake George. But I don't remember when."

"How old were you when you became ill, do you recall?"

"Thirty-seven."

"And how old are you now, Mr. Hoopes?"

"How old? Why, thirty-seven. It hasn't been that long—I've told you, six weeks." He laughs irritably, beginning to feel impatient.

He sees now, the woman is regarding him with an expression of intense sympathy, curiosity. She is white-skinned, as if unhealthy, her hair worn in a style slightly too young for her age—straight-cut bangs to her eyebrows, glossy black like Asian hair. She appears to be in her early forties, older than he; she wears a black long-sleeved jersey and black trousers, or leotards. (Like a dancer? *Is* she a dancer?) Her mouth is red, her eyebrows darkly defined. He finds her a sexually attractive woman. An inquisitive woman, a kindly woman, a strong-willed woman. A woman of whom you might say after the most fleeting of glances—*Professional woman, unmarried. Hard on herself and on others. Respected by colleagues and subordinates, grudgingly.*

She has asked him a question about his age, and he has answered her. He is certain that he's thirty-seven years old, for he can't be younger, or he wouldn't yet have succumbed to the mysterious fever that left him dehydrated, staggering and delirious, scarcely able to telephone for help; this occurred when he was thirty-seven. And he can't be older—he would know, if he were older.

Bemused he asks his interrogator, whose name he has forgotten, "How old do you think I am?" A slight, insolent emphasis on *you*.

The woman with the straight-cut glossy-black hair regards him for a moment in silence. Her eyes are beautiful eyes but there is something too intense in them. The irises are so dark, there is virtually no distinction between pupil and iris. In a faltering voice the woman says, "I don't think that I can guess, Mr. Hoopes—Eli. We are all as old or as young as we feel."

He laughs, mystified. Why are they having this strange conversation?—an unsettling mixture of the banal and the inexplicable. Is there someone else in the room, observing? (Is that a camera-eye turned upon them? But why would anyone be filming *him*?)

"And where do you live now, Mr. Hoopes?"

"Where do I—*live now*?"

It is a profound question, like a sledgehammer to the head. He is quite stunned by it. Where does he *live now;* or, if he lives now, *where does he live*?

The examiner sees that she has upset Elihu Hoopes, and regrets her question. Another time she touches his wrist with her forefingers, lightly. She seems to be signaling him—*I will take care of you. I will comfort you. I am your special friend, please trust me, Eli!*

But Eli surprises her by saying coldly, "I live in Philadelphia. I live at Forty-Four Rittenhouse Square. I've lived there since 1959, and I have always lived there alone. And I think I will be going home now, if you don't mind."

"But, Eli—Mr. Hoopes—we've only just begun . . ."

"No. We're finished."

He has risen to his feet, he looms above her. He has surprised and frightened her now! Almost, he could close his hands around her slender white throat—not to strangle, not even to inflict pain, but to allow the woman to know that he, Elihu Hoopes, is not a man to be trifled with. If he is an *outpatient,* he is still a man in the prime of his life.

"But, Mr. Hoopes—wait . . ."

"Am I 'committed' to this place? Am I 'detained'?"

"Certainly not, Eli . . ."

"Am I arrested?"

"Of course not!"

"Then, good-bye."

"Please wait—"

He does not wait. He does not have to wait. He is not committed to this place, he is not arrested. He cannot be legally apprehended and detained without a formal arrest, and there is no one here to make the arrest. No one here knows about his young cousin Gretchen and how he might have saved her but had not saved her, how he'd failed her and allowed her to die a terrible death. All that has been erased and forgotten.

He hears the woman's voice behind him, pleading—"Eli! Mr. Hoopes! Please come back . . ."

"Go to hell, all of you. *Fuck you.*"

He pushes through a swinging door. He does not glance back. He is suffused with a happiness so deep and so profound it leaves him trembling.

BY THE TIME he has left the Neuropsychology Department, and taken the elevator to the first floor, his resolve has begun to diminish. He has no idea where he is. The jigsaw puzzle-piece in his skull is missing, keenly he can feel it. Strangers surround him, oblivious of him. Some are in the uniforms of medical staff, some are in civilian clothing. Some wear white lab coats over dress trousers, shirts and ties—these are physicians. He sees, on a sign outside the gleaming new building, that it is the UNIVERSITY NEUROLOGICAL INSTITUTE AT DARVEN PARK—he recalls that Darven Park is a suburb of Philadelphia, and it is approximately twenty miles from Gladwyne, where his parents and grandparents live, or had lived. And he himself now lives in—is it Rittenhouse Square, in central Philadelphia? But why is he here in a medical center in Darven Park, who has brought him here? Has he driven himself? But he can't recall having driven to this place, and he has no idea which car, which vehicle, he might have driven.

Tries to recall—he'd left the building through a revolving door that seemed to suck him into it, and flung him outside. He knows that he should look for his vehicle in the parking lot, but—he can't bear the prospect of searching through the immense parking lot for it, as in one of those protracted and excruciating dreams that exhaust the dreamer even as they come to nothing.

No car keys in his pocket. And he is missing something else—what?

Something he is accustomed to carrying with him, that is too large for a pocket.

His fingers twitch. He is feeling uneasy.

A sensation as of small ants streaming over his lower body.

Finds himself on a graveled path leading away from the building and into a landscaped park. Here is a large pond beautifully bordered by weeping willow trees and sycamores; on the rippling surface of the water are swans, mallards, Canada geese and snow geese.

There is a temptation to think—(but he will not give in to this temptation!)—that he has (somehow) found his way to Lake George, and to another time. Making his way along a trail, beginning to walk at a quickened pace, now there is no one to observe him. And now in a marshy area, following a raised plank trail to a plank bridge where he stands at the railing, staring into the marshland. Is this a wild place, is this offshore at Bolton Landing? There is a shallow stream that passes beneath the bridge. But so slowly, you can't determine the direction of the current. He is relieved, for perhaps it has not happened yet.

His cousin Gretchen is still alive. He has not heard the adults whispering, and he has not heard his aunt scream. He has not been sent hurriedly away.

Water-insects, playing on the surface of the marshy water. He is fascinated by their faint shadows cast upon the creek-bed a few inches below.

If he could sketch these! He would feel so much better, if he could. But his fingers twitch emptily.

No charcoal stick or pencil. No sketch pad.

Everywhere there is life in this fecund place. Monarch butterflies, dragonflies. Redwing blackbirds, starlings, crows. Tall reeds and cattails. Even the lifeless trees exude a strange stark beauty. Yet he is feeling anxious. Something is wrong, or will be wrong. He grips the railing with both hands as if expecting a sudden gust of wind. But there is no wind, it is very still, calm. Is this a sign of something wrong—it is so very calm? A warm day, overcast and gray. Here is the horror: color has been draining slowly out of everything he sees—the monarch butterflies have become ghost-moths.

A sensation of utter despair overcomes him, rising from his legs like paralysis. As in a biblical curse he has been turned to stone.

Imagining the Future. He cannot.

Margot Sharpe asks, why? Why can't the amnesiac imagine the future? Is it because he has lost the past?

THE EXAMINATION. "MR. Hoopes, are you comfortable in that seat?"

He is being tested in a way that makes his heart race. It is not a sensation he likes, and yet he seems to crave it.

There is a senior examiner, and there are three younger assistants who may be graduate students, as well as another young assistant who is filming the examination. He has been told their names, which he has not remembered.

The senior examiner, an attractive, fiercely-pale-skinned woman with glossy, graying black hair, is showing him a sequence of photographs which he is to identify. She is, to Eli, a striking presence, of an indeterminate age, though not *young;* a mature woman, in black, very small-boned, intense. Her voice is softly modulated and yet steely, resolved. She has spread out photographs on a table: very young girls, children younger than ten, and among them a cloudy-haired girl with widened eyes—his younger sister Rosalyn, aged about five. Of course, Eli identifies her at once. "This would be about 1930."

Among photographs of girls, most of them strangers, Eli pulls out other photographs of Rosalyn, at older ages: eleven, fifteen, eighteen. He never hesitates, he recognizes Rosalyn at once. His beautiful sister whom he'd loved, and has not seen in a while, he thinks.

"That's our summer place at Lake George. Our dock."

Oh, God. Eli is feeling stricken to the heart.

The examiners are taking note. His success is being recorded. He is made to feel triumphant.

Mr. Hoopes they call him. Except the glossy-black-haired woman who is their coordinator sometimes calls him *Eli.*

Out of another folder are photographs of young boys. Again,

most of the children are strangers to Eli, but among the photographs are several of Eli's brother Averill and his brother Harold—Harry.

Again, he identifies them at once. Approximate ages eight, eleven, thirteen, seventeen. The deep back lawn of their parents' house in Gladwyne. Graduation at the Academy—a teenaged Averill in cap and gown, grinning at the camera. Christmas at their grandparents' house on Parkside Avenue, a tall, beautifully trimmed evergreen tree in the background and the brothers—Averill, Harry, and Elihu in the foreground.

He feels another blow to the heart. His brothers, and *him.*

How long ago it seems! He and his brothers have become estranged politically, and in other, more personal ways.

"And these?"

The examiner has spread out a dozen miscellaneous photographs on the table. These are family snapshots of adults and children in mostly casual unpremeditated poses. At first, they all appear to be strangers; then, Eli discovers family members—mother, father, grandparents, aunts and uncles. When were these pictures taken? Decades ago? Other photographs are of strangers, Eli is certain—but why is he being shown these? He can't remember.

He identifies as many faces as he can. This time he is feeling less triumphant.

"Is something wrong, Mr. Hoopes? Would you like to rest, before we continue?"

"Nothing is wrong! I'm feeling just—just . . ."

Depleted. Emptied out. Eviscerated. Not-here.

The examination continues. More and more the photographs are of strangers, at first teasingly reminiscent of Hoopes relatives and family friends, then total strangers; Eli frowns at them, trying to see why he is being shown these faces. So many minutes have passed, he has lost all sense of the logic of the procedure; vaguely he seems to recall, though this might have been one of his bad dreams, visual perception tests following brain surgery in those days when he (or someone who resembled Elihu Hoopes) had been unable to speak coherently, walk without staggering, or make the most elementary motions with his hands.

Please don't be upset, Eli. Please don't cry.

We are here to help you. And we will help you.

"None of these, Eli? Are you sure?"

Faces of adult men, strangers. He is sure.

Some of these men are alone, smiling or staring into the camera. Others are with women, children. Families.

He feels a tinge of envy indistinguishable from rage.

"My family is gone."

"Eli, what? What did you say?"

Shakes his head irritably. Had not meant to speak out loud.

The camera is recording every syllable.

The white-skinned woman with glossy-black bangs to her forehead and almond-shaped eyes—the woman who is a doctor of some sort, or a psychologist—has spread out a new set of photographs on the table for the amnesiac subject to identify.

These are photographs of "famous" people, mixed with photographs of seemingly "unknown" people. Eli Hoopes rapidly and bemusedly identifies the "famous"—Dwight Eisenhower, Carmen Miranda, Edgar Allan Poe, Richard Nixon, Booker T. Washington, Herman Melville, Abbott and Costello, Marlon Brando, Elizabeth Taylor, Lyndon Johnson, Reverend Martin Luther King, Jr., Jacqueline Kennedy, Edward R. Murrow, Ernest Hemingway, Joe Louis, "Gorgeous" George, the Lone Ranger and Tonto, Tom and Jerry, Mickey and Minnie Mouse; others, whose facial features are quirky and distinct enough to belong to individuals with public reputations, he can't identify. Yet thinking—*This is a trick. I know these people, and they know me.*

"No one in this set, Eli? You're sure?"

"Yes! I'm sure."

He pushes the photographs away, irritably. He sees how his examiners are regarding him. The female supervisor, the young assistants. It is chilling to think that they are examining his brain; in a way, they are dissecting his brain. No entry into the brain except by such labyrinthine indirections—until Eli Hoopes dies, and his brain can be autopsied.

A special set of photographs is particularly uncanny, unsettling. Exactly why, Eli can't say. He stares at strangers' faces that appear to his eye somehow *unnatural.*

"And why is that, Eli? Can you explain?"

No. Can't explain.

"Look closely. Maybe you will see why."

He looks closely. Thinks—*They are mirror-reversed.*

But—how would Eli Hoopes know this, if the faces are the faces of strangers?

(He is beginning to perspire. A rivulet of sweat down the side of his face.)

(Obviously, the examination contains tricks. It is an experiment, and he is the experimental subject, or dupe. He is being shown photographs of relatives again—is that it? Family members and relatives who have grown older, beyond the scope of the amnesiac's memory.)

"Him! Looks like my brother Harold."

"Your brother Harold? Are you saying that this is your brother, or that he 'looks like your brother'?"

"Both."

But Eli isn't so sure. In fact, he isn't sure at all.

"No. I think that's my uncle Nils Mateson. And this woman—my aunt Lucinda."

Again, Eli isn't sure. He pushes the photographs away, feeling sick.

"Would you like to stop for a while, Eli? We can take a break for ten minutes if you like."

So many faces! It is the most profound riddle, why a human being must have a *face;* and why human identity is so bound up with *face.* Eli wonders at the injustice of it. Why don't human beings more uniformly resemble one another, like many animals; what is the evolutionary advantage in such specificity of identity? If human beings more narrowly resembled one another, the distinctions between individual personalities and character would be less. A certain sort of desperate yearning and anguish might fade.

He has forgotten her name. The glossy-black-haired woman with the kindly eyes.

Except for her, Eli Hoopes would be lost.

She is showing him another set of photographs, taken from another folder. The subjects appear to be adult men, strangers. All are middle-aged Caucasians. They strike the eye as well-educated, well-dressed, attractive men; most are smiling toward the camera, not aggressively but in a friendly way, causing the corners of their eyes to crease. It is curious that their dark russet-brown hair is sharply receding from their foreheads and that their ears are rather long, and similarly shaped. Eli studies these photographs as if they were a particular riddle. He says, with a shrug, "They graduated from the same university. They belonged to the same fraternity."

"Anything more?"

"They're—related. Maybe they don't know it."

"Look closely, Eli."

Of course it's a trick. But what is the trick?

Then he sees: the subject in each of the photographs is the same individual, pictured in differing settings, and in differing degrees of darkness. He is a stranger to Eli Hoopes yet Eli wonders uneasily if this is someone in the Philadelphia area perhaps who knows him.

Seeing that Eli is staring at the photographs with a look of irritation, the glossy-black-haired woman says, "That's you, Eli. These photographs were taken within the past two years."

Eli laughs, stunned. Then, Eli is very quiet.

Eli stares at the photographs for a long moment, looking from one to another. *Himself?—him?* He feels a sensation of sick, physical loss.

" 'Elihu Hoopes'—this person?"

"Yes, Eli. You."

THE LOST ONE. She sees him, on the plank bridge.

He has fled into the marshy area behind the Institute, along a plank walk. He is standing on a plank bridge staring into the marsh as if transfixed.

She doesn't want to frighten him. Softly she calls, "Mr. Hoopes?"

He turns. He appears distraught, and yet relieved.

He knows me. He is not frightened of me.

"Eli! I was wondering where you'd gone to."

He is frightened. But he knows to disguise fear, by instinct.

A slender, black-haired woman whom he has never seen before is smiling at him. Lightly she touches his wrist, as if she knows him.

She is someone with authority, he can see. A beautiful woman with white skin, warm kindly eyes.

"Hel-*lo!*"

NURSING. "MR. HOOPES?—Eli? Have you hurt yourself?"

"Hurt—who? Where?"

"This looks like a bruise . . ."

"Looks like a *baby bat.*"

He is in a jovial mood. Not Margot's favorite mood.

Laughs, and pulls down his shirtsleeve. (His shirt is a beautiful shirt, fine pale-lavender Egyptian cotton with a monogram *EMH.* Elihu Michael Hoopes.) Margot has noticed odd-shaped dark-wine-colored bruises on the amnesiac's arms. When he wears shorts, on the tennis court, she has noticed that his muscled legs are often bruised as well.

The medical staff at the Institute has assured her that Eli Hoopes is examined at regular intervals. Because Hoopes suffers from a severe memory deficit, his health must be monitored by others. And he is in good health, they tell her—at least, "reasonably" good health. Margot has demanded to see his medical chart, though she is not a blood relative and she is not his legal guardian; this required some arguing on her part, and a confrontation with the Institute staff. But in the end Margot has persevered, for, as she repeatedly informs the medical staff, she is the principal investigator of *Project E.H.*—"The person who needs to be kept informed at all times of this man's medical condition."

The fact is, Elihu Hoopes is fifty-six years old and beginning to suffer from hypertension and arthritic pains in both legs. Since a bad case of bronchitis several years before, he has become susceptible to respiratory infections.

Most frequently he cuts himself shaving, and he shaves each morning without fail.

The thin cuts bleed. E.H.'s blood coagulates slowly. Then, he cuts himself again. His arms, shins, thighs are bruised, mysteriously—he can't remember why. Seeing Margot's look of distress he laughs—"Looks like somebody is 'accident-prone,' eh Doctor? Maybe if the poor bastard fell on his head, he'd get right there."

He boasts of not feeling much pain. An abscessed tooth, he'd scarcely noticed until at a routine dental examination the abscess was discovered, and emergency root canal work prescribed. Bruises on arms, legs, thighs—E.H. laughs, it means so little to him. When Dr. Flint, E.H.'s neurologist, checks with E.H.'s legal guardian Mrs. Lucinda Mateson, Mrs. Mateson tells him curtly that her nephew Elihu has "no medical problems" and is in "very good health."

At the Institute, Elihu Hoopes is scheduled for regular, routine physical examinations. At least, this is what Margot has been told.

Margot insists upon rolling up E.H.'s shirtsleeve, to examine the baby-bat-shaped bruise more carefully.

And there are other bruises. Dark-wine-colored, in the man's fairly pale flesh. "Does this hurt? *This?*" She strokes the bruised areas, that remind her of her grandfather's arms, when she was a little girl. A similar pattern of bruises in the flesh, that seemed to come out of nowhere and faded within a few days.

How tenderly she'd felt for her grandfather, and how frightened for him! Even as her grandfather seemed scarcely to feel the pain of his bruises, and laughed at his "little nurse" . . . But Margot cuts off this memory, it is not helpful at the present time.

Margot brings a tube of *Arnica montana* to apply to E.H.'s bruises, massaging the oily liquid into his skin. E.H. is both touched and embarrassed by Margot's attention. He grasps her hand with his. Twines his fingers through hers. Tight.

"Doctor! I love you."

HE IS LEARNING to trace a geometrical figure by way of a mirror.

She has devised an ingenious experiment in which the amnesiac subject "learns" a skill through repetition: watching his hand in a mirror as it grips a pen; learning to direct the pen into the shape of an octagon, by way of the mirror.

At first, E.H. is frustrated and exasperated—"God damn! I just can't do this."

"Please take your time, Eli. We have all the time in the world."

"Do we!"

Margot takes note: the stricken man doesn't ask *why*.

Why am I doing this. Why do you torment me.

Is this my life, my only life? Is this how I know that I exist—in my effort to please you whom I don't know and from whom I can expect nothing?

But E.H. is a "good sport." You can see that E.H. has been an athlete at one time in his life: an athlete *does not give up*.

And so, gamely, E.H. tries, tries and fails; tries again, and partly succeeds; tries, tries and tries until at last he has managed to outline an octagon flawlessly, in one single, fluid motion, by watching his hand in a mirror. He does this again, and again; takes a break of twenty minutes, during which time he forgets what he has been doing, but, under Margot's supervision, when he outlines the octagon another time, he does surprisingly well; and after a few attempts, his performance improves quickly.

E.H. laughs, perplexed. "This is strange, Doctor. I seem to know how to draw this damned thing in the mirror. Is there some trick here?"

Margot tells him there is no trick. Margot tells him that she is not a "doctor"—she is a neuropsychologist.

Margot is very pleased with the results. Margot will retest E.H. the following week, and the week following that. Margot will discover that the amnesiac subject can "remember" a complex skill though he has consciously "forgotten" it.

E.H. is made to feel proud of himself, though he isn't sure why. Outlining an octagon by watching his hand in a mirror? Is his examiner serious?

Wanting to laugh, he who'd once been a stockbroker in Philadelphia, in his family's firm. He who'd once graduated summa cum laude from Amherst . . .

Margot Sharpe will publish her findings in an article in the *Journal of Experimental Neuropsychology* titled, "Alternative Memory Circuits in Amnesia."

The headline leaps at her, astonishing—

Milton Ferris, 73—

(Her initial, terrified thought is that her mentor has died, and this is his obituary; and she had not known)—

Nobel Prize Recipient, Physiology/Medicine.

Milton Ferris has won a Nobel Prize! Above the single-column headline on the front page of the *Philadelphia Inquirer* is a photograph of the scientist as a handsome, ebullient-looking middle-aged man with flowing white hair and short-trimmed white beard, taken at least twenty years earlier.

So astonished is Margot, her eyes mist over as she reads, and rereads, the article. It is surprising—well, perhaps not so surprising—that Milton Ferris is being honored by the Nobel committee for work he'd completed before the age of forty-five.

He is sharing the prize of more than six hundred thousand dollars with two other neuropsychologists at UC-Berkeley with whom he'd done research into sensory perception, reasoning, memory, and problem-solving in the human brain in the 1950s.

By the third time Margot has read the remarkable article, with its continuation on an inner page, she is feeling less overwhelmed. Still, there is the aftermath of her initial shock, when she'd thought that her lover had died.

When her father had died, and the news had come to Margot belatedly—(that is, Margot had not listened to her phone messages for a day and a half)—she'd felt a similar sensation of shock, dismay. She'd had to grope for a chair, to sit down as her head seemed to sway on her shoulders. She'd thought—*But now there is no meaning in my life. Now I am alone.*

Soon after, she'd forgotten this observation. As she will forget her shock at seeing Milton Ferris's youthful photograph on the front page of the newspaper, and a similar conviction that her life as a woman and as a daughter is over.

When she has recovered, Margot staggers to a phone. Margot calls her former lover, whom she has never ceased loving; she dials the number without hesitation though she has not called Milton in years. A recorded voice answers, rather curtly, coolly; not Milton's voice, but a mechanical voice. Margot leaves a stammered message of congratulations.

I am so happy for you, Milton!

No one deserves this more than you . . .

She would say more, but her throat shuts up. She is crying, a raw wracking ache cleaving her in two.

She does not say—*We could have been so happy together, Milton. We could have worked together, and loved each other.*

I could have loved enough for two.

Then, in her excited mood, she can't resist calling Dr. Mills.

Guardedly, Mills answers his phone. He recognizes Margot's voice at once. He tells her that since news of Ferris's prize had gone out over Reuters very early that morning, and was picked up by the Associated Press, the department has been flooded with calls.

Margot says, "Aren't you glad that you didn't persecute Milton? Aren't you relieved, it has turned out as it has?" Margot speaks excitedly, aggressively. She is not altogether aware of how she sounds, her heart beats so quickly.

"Yes, Margot. We are all very 'relieved' it has turned out as it did."

"Did Milton ever know about it? The 'charges'?"

"No. I don't think so." Mills pauses, pointedly. "Unless you told him, Margot, he probably doesn't know."

"Then he doesn't know. I didn't tell him."

"Thank you for that, Margot. At least."

"Thank *you*."

Margot slams down the receiver, hotly. She has no idea why she is so excited, why her pulses are racing.

She will celebrate Milton's prize alone, since there is no one with whom she can celebrate. A shot glass of whiskey, or two.

Don't feel sorry for me, I am not sorry that I loved you.

I am not sorry that you used me, and discarded me.

I am in love with someone else now.

I am in love now with the love of my life, and he will never betray me.

CHAPTER SEVEN

The Lovers. He is saying he remembers what it was like to be married. He is saying he remembers what it was like to be married to *her*.

"You were my dear wife, I think? Before I got sick."

Clever Margot Sharpe has restyled her hair: she has brushed the shiny dark silver-threaded hair straight back from her forehead, and she has braided a single, narrow strand like a pigtail, that falls along the left side of her face, to below her chin. At the university, and at the Institute, this tight-braided pigtail has drawn the attention of admiring eyes—or so Margot would like to think.

E.H. is one of these. E.H. has been staring at Margot, and at the braid, since he has first seen her that morning.

"Pretty!"—E.H. has tugged at the braid. He is being playful, or—maybe not.

Margot feels her face heat with a sudden stab of pleasure. It has been some time since anyone has touched her with such a playful sort of intimacy. It has been a very long time since anyone has tugged her hair.

"Are we going to our special place, dear?"

"Yes, Eli. Yes, we are."

Margot has discovered that if she brings the amnesiac subject outside the Institute and walks with him in the quasi-wilderness parkland adjacent to the Institute, E.H. will begin to speak more seriously to her, in a quieter voice. His usual bright bantering manner subsides and his eyes rove about her hungrily.

"My dear wife! It was wrong of me to leave you, and I was punished for leaving you. One of them struck my head with a baseball bat—I could feel the bone crack. 'Nigger lover'—"

Margot has discovered that E.H. will become emotional at such times, and will reach for her hand. He will clasp it firmly, and draw it against his side.

Margot has discovered that the walks into the "green sanctuary" behind the Institute are thrilling to her. These walks with E.H. are like floating islands of light amid the shadowy interiors of her routine life.

Margot has not said to E.H. that yes, she was once his wife. She has not said that she is his wife now. But Margot has not dissuaded E.H. from thinking that they were once husband and wife.

E.H. speaks gently, urgently. It is hard to Margot not to think that the amnesiac is thinking out loud.

"I'm trying to remember what it was like to be 'married.' I think it would be a safe, warm feeling—like now. There would be someone beside you, always. You would sleep with her, and she would be beside you, and hold your hand. And hold you if you were feeling lonely and frightened. I think I remember that." E.H. speaks like a man drifting into a dream open-eyed and trusting. He clasps Margot's hand, harder. "Always she would be with you—a 'wife.' But I lost my wife through my carelessness. I failed her, and she died of a raging fever. The fever was intended for *me.* Is that why you are here with me, Doctor?"

Margot is hurt, that E.H. has forgotten *she is his wife.*

As she has corrected him countless times, so Margot corrects E.H. again: "Eli, I'm not a medical doctor. I have an academic Ph.D. In theory I'm a 'doctor' but not the kind you mean. I'm a professor—a research neuropsychologist at the university—and I am attached to the University Neurological Institute at Darven Park, which is where we are now."

"Are we!"

"We're going for a walk in the parkland behind the Institute, as we often do. We call this 'ambulatory testing.' " Margot laughs, for this is a thought that pleases her.

"Whatever you say, Doctor. You're the doctor."

They laugh together, giddily. Margot feels laughter fizzing inside her throat like champagne.

Except, Margot doesn't want anyone from the Institute who knows them to observe them. Margot is cautious not to allow E.H. to clasp her hand in his until they are some distance from the Institute, in the quiet interior of the pinewoods and the marsh that buzzes with its rich fecund life well into autumn.

Margot's pulses quicken with feeling, and with the risk of the illicit. Though she is not being deceptive, she believes. She is not misleading E.H., for in her heart, and truly, Margot Sharpe loves Elihu Hoopes; and if they were not literally married, that is but an accident—"An accident that might be remedied one day."

They are leaving the graveled path, and are walking now on the wood chip path. They are on the raised boardwalk through marshy land, hand in hand approaching the little plank bridge at which E.H. always insists upon stopping. Here, he will stare avidly into the marsh; he will open his sketchbook, and begin to draw. And Margot will observe him, noting his intensity, and his obliviousness of her. Until at last he will have forgotten her, she knows.

When she sees that he is feeling lost, and is looking helplessly about, Margot will touch his wrist lightly, and identify herself to him. And E.H. will stare at her in amazement. He does not recognize her, yet Margot is certain that a part of his brain registers familiarity; she has been studying the phenomenon in the amnesiac subject, who can identify very few items in a visual test, for instance, yet unfailingly indicates those items as "familiar" which he has seen before, amid others that are totally new to him.

Margot is always devising tests for E.H. It has come to seem a way of appropriating him, loving him. As he clasps her hand, and squeezes her fingers tenderly, and talks to her in his slow meandering way, Margot's brain never ceases creating tests and experiments to further define this remarkable man; though she is listening closely to him, as well. If she is recording the amnesiac's speech it is not for the purposes of the lab, but for her own, intimate purposes, to be replayed privately. None of the intimate speech of E.H. will find its way into a professional paper. (Margot vows.)

She has had very few lovers. She has had few male friends who might have been lovers, if Margot had encouraged them. (If Margot had not intimidated them with her intelligence and ambition.)

E.H.'s words are precious to her. No one has ever spoken to Margot Sharpe as E.H. does.

Not Milton Ferris, certainly. For Milton spoke mostly of himself, and, at times grudgingly, even bitterly, of his "complicated" emotions for her, Margot Sharpe; for Milton Ferris is one of those men who is frightened by vulnerable feelings of his own, and resents emotional dependence upon others. Milton did not ever speak of the things of which E.H. speaks so readily, of such exquisite intimacy and trust.

"Were you my dear wife, Doctor? You look like her, I think. Before you got old—*older*."

"What do you mean—'*older*'?" Margot laughs, hurt. "I am not so *old* as you, dear Eli."

"Of course, of course—I know. We are 'old'—'*older*'—in the same way."

With no provocation the brain-damaged subject will say the oddest things. Whatever part of E.H.'s brain was devastated by fever, some part of the area that monitors inhibition was affected as well. Where most of the time E.H. is courtly and gentlemanly, at times he behaves with an impish irreverence, like Groucho Marx among the somber-minded. (Groucho is one of E.H.'s favorites: E.H. can imitate the comic brilliantly, wriggling his eyebrows and [invisible] mustache, repeating outrageous Groucho dialogue.)

In fact, Margot is fourteen years younger than Elihu Hoopes, who is now nearly sixty. But, in E.H.'s memory, he is frozen at the age of thirty-seven; Margot assumes that, when he sees himself in the mirror, he somehow "sees" the younger man.

As, when Margot Sharpe glances into a mirror, narrowing her eyes, she "sees" a still-young woman whose severely chic straight-cut black hair isn't threaded with silver; nor does she see the pale creases in her white skin, at the corners of her eyes and mouth. *A principle of perception: we see what we are primed to see, not what is there. We can look at anything but we can "see" only what we allow to be seen.*

Margot's vanity is stung by E.H.'s careless remark. Though she would have described herself as totally lacking in female sexual vanity, yet she feels hurt and even alarm.

Old! She will not allow herself to be *old* before she is prepared.

"I love to hold your hand, Eli. Your hand is strong and—masculine . . ."

Her own hand, soft and *feminine.*

She is determined to make E.H. feel comforted and safe in her company. Since the first hour of their meeting she has been conditioning him to trust her.

It is not so difficult to "condition" another. Especially if the other has no idea what you are doing.

"You remember, your mother held your hand, too, Eli, when you were a little boy. There have been many—many of us—who've loved you . . . You should not ever feel alone."

"Doctor, I love you."

Is it wrong of Margot Sharpe to encourage the amnesiac subject in this way? She doesn't want to think—(she doesn't allow herself to think)—that her behavior, in private with E.H., might be considered by some (narrow-minded, jealous) observers a type of scientific misconduct; for E.H. is suggestible and impressionable as a young child in her presence. (With other examiners, particularly male examiners, E.H. can be curt and dismissive. He is not nearly so universally obliging and naïve as he'd been at the outset of *Project E.H.*)

E.H. has paused in their walk. Still holding Margot's hand, and twining his fingers in hers so tightly that Margot nearly winces with pain, he recites:

"Ah love, let us be true
To one another! For the world, which seems
To lie before us like a land of dreams,
So various, so beautiful, so new,
Hath really neither joy, nor love, nor light,
Nor certitude, nor peace, nor help for pain;

And we are here as on a darkling plain
Swept with confused alarms of struggle and flight,
Where ignorant armies clash by night."

Margot is riveted by this recitation. E.H.'s voice is low, intimate, tremulous. It is not uncommon for E.H. to recite poetry but it is uncommon for E.H. to recite poetry in so impassioned a way. It is the first time anyone has ever recited a love poem to *her*.

Not knowing what to say foolishly Margot cries, "Oh, Eli! That's beautiful. Is it—Shakespeare?" even as she supposes it can't be Shakespeare, for the language is modern.

E.H. shrugs. Not Shakespeare.

(Has Margot disappointed him? She feels his fingers loosen their grip.)

"Maybe I wrote it myself. Would you be impressed?"

"Yes. I would be impressed." Margot laughs, for obviously E.H. is joking. But the tone of his joke is—melancholy? Ironic? Or simply playful?

Margot feels that she has missed something. She has blundered in some way. She thinks, not for the first time, that she is not equal to Elihu Hoopes. His soul is more expansive than hers—if one can believe in "soul."

As they walk on, fingers less tightly twined, E.H. reverts to one of his favorite subjects—"game theory." No longer is his voice tender and impassioned, now he speaks briskly, somewhat derisively. He has his fixed and irremediable thoughts on the subject and if Margot tries to ask him a question, he is likely to ignore her. In graduate seminars in the Psychology Department Margot learned a little of game theory—but only superficially, for game theory is fundamentally mathematics, and not relevant to Margot's subfield of psychology. Nor is it clear when E.H. lapses onto this favorite topic whether he is himself a strong advocate, or a skeptic; or whether he has his own "theory" with which he hopes to counter others.

Margot assumes that E.H. was disappointed in her weak reaction to the love poem—(if indeed it was a love poem)—but she has no way of reverting to it, for by now E.H. will have forgotten he'd recited it, and all she can clearly recall of the lines is the raw appeal—"Ah love, let us be true to one another!"

She will be true to Elihu Hoopes. Even if no one, including Elihu himself, will know.

Immersed in the knots and snarls of game theory, E.H. laughs frequently, baring damp gums. He has lapsed into his mode of quasi-public banter, calculated to keep others at a distance; but Margot believes that she is special to E.H., and he should not wish to behave this way with *her*.

They have made their way into the interior of the wooded parkland. It is quiet here, secluded-seeming. As politely as she can Margot suggests that E.H. stop for a while here and do some sketches—"You've brought your sketchbook, Eli—see?"

E.H. has carried his sketchbook under his arm, and in his pockets are drawing pencils and stubs of charcoal, but he has forgotten these, and is delighted when Margot reminds him.

For the next half hour E.H. works eagerly in his sketchbook with both pencils and charcoal. Margot has found a place to sit close by, but not so close that she distracts the artist.

Margot takes notes in her own notebook which she carries with her everywhere in her shoulder bag. This is not Margot Sharpe's lab book but a private book. She will date the entry, and she will note the place. All that she can recall of E.H.'s remarks she will record. (She will make an effort to locate the poem and will discover that it is a nineteenth-century poem by Matthew Arnold titled "Dover Beach." She will surmise that Elihu Hoopes memorized the poem at Amherst, in one of his several literature courses. She will not speculate in her notebook that the poem was recited particularly to *her*.)

If there is something crucial that Margot feels she should record, that suggests the intimacy between her and the amnesiac subject, she finds a way to record it without being overtly explicit. Sometimes, she will abbreviate crucial words; she will use a kind of code.

Yet, she feels a defiant sort of pride in what she records that might be construed as "intimate" between her and E.H., even as she feels unease—for what if the notebook is discovered by someone at the Institute or worse yet, at the university? What if a rival discovers it? What if—(so Margot persecutes herself, absurdly)—she dies unexpectedly, and her departmental chair appropriates all of her papers, her data, her notebooks, her secret, undisclosed self?

What if, one day, Margot Sharpe is exposed as having behaved in a way some might condemn as unethical, even immoral; what if she is condemned for scientific misconduct, with her own amnesiac subject, posthumously?

Yet—she can't break off her feelings for E.H. No one else in her compressed circle of a life means so much to her.

Watching E.H. she murmurs aloud—" 'Ah love, let us be true to one another!' " The rest of the poem, the melancholy beauty of the language, is lost to her.

But E.H. is touched by these words which he doesn't recall having uttered within the hour; he is drawn to touch Margot's cheek, tenderly—"My dear love, let us be true to one another—*yes*."

E.H. returns then to his work. But soon, E.H. becomes distracted, distressed. He has been sketching too intensely perhaps and now his fingers ache; he flexes them, and stretches his arms. Abruptly he shuts the sketchbook and rests it against the plank railing. What is he thinking? Margot wonders. What has surfaced in his mind, like an emerging light? *Is* thought a kind of light, a leaping of neurons? Electrical currents? Where does thought abide, and out of what wordless region does thought arise? She feels a powerful love for this brave man who stands alone, as on the brink of an abyss. She observes him as he grips the plank railing of the bridge as if to brace himself against the wind—but there is no wind. He peers out into the marshland, frowning. Margot supposes that, if she were to approach him, daring to interrupt his solitude, she would see that his facial expression is intense, anxious; she would see that he is no one she knows.

By this time Margot has drifted out of the amnesiac's peripheral vision. It is a sad, yet sweet, swooning sensation as she feels herself drifting out of his consciousness. How like a moon, in a lunar eclipse! Yet, though Margot is effaced, she does not cease to exist. Rather, she is in a suspended state, until the man sees her.

"Mr. Hoopes? Eli? Hello."

E.H. turns. He is startled by her, perhaps for a moment he is mystified and even frightened but soon he is smiling eagerly and hopefully.

"Hel-*lo*."

SHE HAS BROUGHT a present for him.

She has brought a present for him which must remain *our secret*.

When they are far from the Institute, and on the plank bridge, and Margot is satisfied that no one is in sight, she removes from her shoulder bag two small items of jewelry: two rings.

Wedding bands, in silver. Not expensive but tasteful, beautiful. A Celtic pattern, the silversmith told her.

"For you, dear Eli. And for me."

She has measured E.H.'s finger, and so has purchased a ring that fits perfectly, as her own matching ring fits perfectly. She slips the ring on E.H.'s finger, the third finger of his left hand; and Eli takes the other ring from her, to slip on the third finger of Margot's left hand.

E.H. kisses the palm of Margot's hand. He is quivering with emotion, and with desire. Margot kisses both the palm and the back of E.H.'s hand; the knuckles are covered in fair brown hairs.

"Doctor, you are so beautiful! I love you! Are we married now?"

"Yes, Eli. We are married now."

She pulls at his hand, that has gripped her hand so tightly. She kisses his mouth, that kisses her greedily in return. The man has been pulling, tugging roughly, at her clothing. He has been making a pained, whimpering sound. He is very aroused. Margot feels a thrill of desire deep in the pit of her belly, a small flame about to flare into the most intense pleasure. Blindly Margot leads the man deeper into the woods, though the ground is marshy underfoot. She finds a place for them to lower themselves, clumsily but eagerly; below a gigantic white oak amid a patch of splotched sunshine.

For a long time then they lose themselves. Margot hears herself cry out, a hoarse guttural cry, scarcely recognizable as human. The man's cry is softer, a hissing sigh. She will hear that sound, that faint hissing of breath, like the hissing escape of a soul. A shadow passes over Margot's brain, her brain is cleaved, obliterated. She cannot speak. Her face is wet with tears. Her lower body is ablaze with sexual sensation, her legs are weak, fainting. She must straighten E.H.'s disheveled clothing, and her own. She must tamp down his hair, and her own. Their hands scramble at each other's body like ravenous creatures. When they emerge from their secret place they are breathless, as if they've been running for their lives. Laughter catches in their throats like sobs.

Oh what have we done. What has happened to us.

It is no one's fault, it will not happen again.

Of course it will happen again—and again, again . . .

E.H. is rapt with love for her whose name he has forgotten. How terrible it must be for the man, Margot thinks, to love someone for whom he has no name.

"Wait. Wait please. Come back. *Please.*"

"No, Eli. We can't."

"But why not? You are my wife, aren't you?"

"Only in secret, Eli. No one must know."

"Really! Is that it." E.H. is suddenly resigned, stoic. He does not resist when Margot works the wedding band off his finger and slips it, with her own, into a zippered pocket in her shoulder bag.

"No, Eli. We must go back now."

"Yes. 'Must go back now.' "

Margot has straightened his clothing, and combed his lank, thinning hair. She jokes that Eli's hair was once much longer—"You were a hippie, darling. You wore a red headband. But you were reckless with your life." She has kissed the myriad bruises on his arms and chest. She has brought a tube of *Arnica montana,* to massage into the bruises.

Her own hair she has brushed with a small brush out of her bag. The single, tight-braided plait falls against her eye and stings. There are nettles on her clothing and yes, damn!—in her hair. It will require many brushings and fine-tooth combings to rid herself of the nettles.

Quickly Margot leads E.H. back to the plank bridge, and to the wood chip path. Quickly, for it is suddenly late afternoon, and the staff at the Institute will begin to wonder where they are. (Margot has been telling them that she is testing E.H. on another floor, in a rehab learning lab suitable for her purposes. But she has been vague about this place, and is hoping no one will question her about it.)

"Eli, hurry! We must get back."

"Back—where? Are we living in Philadelphia now? In Rittenhouse Square?"

"No, Eli. Not in Rittenhouse Square."

"Were we married there? Is that our home together?"

E.H. is becoming confused, distressed. Margot loves the man fiercely but she is fearful of their secret being revealed. She thinks—*I will take him home with me, one day. We will be truly married and what I have done now will be redeemed.*

Alone in the elevator ascending to the fourth floor Margot dares to kiss E.H. a final time, gently pushing her tongue into his mouth, and when he embraces her tightly, she pushes him from her. "No. We can't, Eli. They will discover us, and take you from me." Seeing the look of dismay and confusion in the man's face she relents; she dares to take both his hands in hers and brings them together against her midriff and her breasts, in a swooning sensation.

It is nearly the fourth floor. Within a few seconds, the door will open.

"Are you my dear wife, Doctor? I love you."

"Eli, I love *you*."

LOVEMAKING WITHOUT WORDS. Without speech, memory.

And afterward, she must never forget to remove their rings.

What passes between us will not be recorded. It will be lost to all memory.

YET, IT HAPPENS that Margot Sharpe can't resist confiding in one individual.

"I think—at last—I am in love . . ."

For she must tell *him*. That he will not continue to think that he should feel guilty about his treatment of her, and wish to avoid her as he has been doing.

"Are you, Margot! This is very good news."

His voice suggests surprise. And not such clear relief in the surprise as Margot might have anticipated.

"Is he anyone I know? At the university? Not in the department—I hope?"

They laugh together. Their history together includes much talk of the department that is amusing, exasperating, and semi-scandalous.

During the brief interlude they were lovers Milton Ferris quite enjoyed astonishing the much younger Margot Sharpe with tales of his older, distinguished colleagues. Tales from the perspective of Milton Ferris when he'd been young himself, a junior faculty member. The Father indoctrinating the Chaste Daughter into the history of their shared terrain, of which the Chaste Daughter has been mostly ignorant.

"Well, Margot! Will you be—getting married?"

(She has seen Milton glance surreptitiously at her left hand. But there is no ring on the third finger of that hand.)

"We are looking to that, yes. Soon, I hope."

"Soon? How soon? Will I still be here to help you celebrate?"

Margot stares at Milton, smiling uncertainly. *Still be here?*—for a moment she thinks that Milton is referring to his age—his mortality. Then, she realizes he means something far less extreme, and must disguise her look of alarm.

"I'm afraid not, Milton. I think you're leaving too soon . . ."

Bathed in post–Nobel Prize celebrity, Milton Ferris has retired from the university with much acclaim. He has given interviews in which he speaks of having "passed on" his famous memory lab to younger colleagues; sometimes he names Margot Sharpe as his "successor" at the university, which is deeply gratifying to her, and fills her with a kind of exalted anxiety. At Milton's Festschrift it was joked—affectionately, if with a mild edge—that Milton Ferris is the Genghis Khan of neuropsychology, populating the science world with his DNA—his descendants.

It is the twilight of the great scientist's career. Though Milton has accepted a part-time position at the National Institutes of Health in Washington, D.C., and there is a rumor that he will soon be appointed by the president to serve on a prestigious national science committee. A rumor too that he will divide his time between a town house in Georgetown, D.C., and an oceanfront condominium in Boca Raton, Florida, where his aging, ailing, longtime wife is living close by the Ferrises' married daughter and her family.

Margot Sharpe finds it painful to think of Milton Ferris as "retired." She does not accept that this is the "twilight" of her mentor's career. Though young scientists who would once have worked with Milton Ferris now work with Margot Sharpe who is understood to be Milton Ferris's "daughter."

How guilty she feels, sometimes! She has no idea why.

She'd defended Milton against the erroneous charges of scientific misconduct, but perhaps she had not been adamant enough. She had not summoned the courage to tell *him*.

How furious he would have been! How deeply, irrevocably wounded. *I could not do that to him, even if I no longer loved him.*

Margot has never known if Milton knows about the alleged charges brought against him by former students and associates whom he'd trusted, and whom he'd helped with their careers; Margot supposes, given the web of relationships and intimacies in Milton Ferris's life, that he must know, or suspect—something. By this time, in the aftermath of the Nobel Prize, which bathes its recipients in something like armor, someone surely must have told him—some loyal former student wishing to curry favor with the great Milton Ferris and strike a blow against rivals; and yet Margot Sharpe, who has been so close to Milton, and so fiercely loyal to him, could not bring herself to tell him. And Alvin Kaplan, one of those who'd loved him, and had betrayed him, certainly could not have told him.

In the end, evidently there wasn't enough substance to the charges. Not only Margot Sharpe but another former (female) student of Ferris's, now a distinguished psychologist at Harvard, refused to acknowledge any wrongdoing on Ferris's part, and threatened to "go public" with her own countercharges if the investigation continued. Margot knows who this person is, and is both impressed and troubled by the woman's loyalty; she tortures herself with the probability that Milton must have had an affair with this woman too, just a year or two before his affair with Margot, but she doesn't care to know details.

Nor does she want Milton Ferris to know details of her new love.

Her passionate, doomed and deranged love for Elihu Hoopes.

For all love is a derangement of the senses, else it is not love but only sentiment.

Margot smiles. There is a faint buzzing in her ears. As Milton Ferris regards her quizzically.

(He has aged, she sees. A slight tremor in his left hand, and a near-imperceptible quiver of his eyelids. Telltale bruises of the elderly visible on his hands, symptoms of blood-thinning medication.)

(Oh but he has not aged, much. She is relieved to see!)

"He is—he isn't?—a scientist?"

"No. Not a scientist."

Margot speaks quietly. The Chaste Daughter is soft-voiced.

"Really! You surprise me, Margot."

Is that good, or rather not-so-good? Margot sees her elderly mentor frown. His hair is thinning-white, lifting in airy waves above his pink scalp; his teeth are impossibly white, ceramic-perfect.

The broad forehead crinkles in disapproval. The genial banter has ceased. Margot is forced to think yes, she has disappointed Milton Ferris, she has failed him, for clearly something has gone terribly wrong in the life of a (female) scientist if she must content herself with a civilian companion, and not another scientist.

Margot thinks—*God damn you, I am not going to apologize for loving E.H.!*

"I hope you will be happy, Margot. You are a woman of great intelligence and integrity—you are a lovely woman whom I lacked the imagination to make happy, I think. I am so sorry about that."

Gravely Milton Ferris speaks, like one about to give a blessing, then reconsidering. His words can't possibly be sincere, and yet—Milton looks so very penitent, almost you might believe him.

Margot has heard rumors that Milton Ferris has had health problems; on the very eve of the Nobel announcement, he'd been scheduled for an MRI at the University Hospital. His old ebullience has subsided into a kind of benevolent glow; even his wiry white beard seems to have thinned, and his fleshy chin and raddled neck are exposed beneath. And the tremor in his hand—Margot will not see.

I loved you, you know.

I will always love you.

Does Milton Ferris understand this? Very likely, he who has

published crucial work on meta-linguistic psychology will have no difficulty understanding Margot Sharpe.

It is time to leave—is it? Margot feels a pang of dismay.

Quickly before Milton departs, Margot congratulates him another time on the Nobel Prize—as others have, countless times. A deafening chorus. Almost there must be something terrifying in such congratulations, that sweep away all distinctions other than that of the great, grand prize; as if the scientist's other, important and influential work had never been, and the prize itself something of a posthumous acknowledgment, since for some reason known only to the Nobel science committee, Milton Ferris received the award for "original, groundbreaking research" he'd done at least thirty years before in collaboration with other scientists, now elderly.

"Well, dear Margot! One day, maybe—for your remarkable work on E.H.—*you*."

It is a sweetly gallant wish. The quiver in both eyelids gives Milton Ferris a sly, foxy look.

At parting they are suddenly shy. (Is anyone watching? They are in a quasi-public place.) But Margot knows that if she shrinks away foolishly, she will regret it; and Milton seems to feel the same way, for he clasps one of her hands in both his hands, and leans forward to brush his surprisingly chilly lips against her cheek.

"Good-bye, dear Margot! And congratulations on—whatever this is, that has come into your life so deservedly."

DOES HE KNOW, of course not. Could he guess, not ever.

"E.H."—*his* amnesiac subject!

Though Milton Ferris cannot know that Margot Sharpe is in love with Elihu Hoopes, he knows that Margot Sharpe is still in love with him.

Margot smiles, considering. She regrets nothing, for what is there to regret? *Her* life lies before her.

Sipping whiskey until her eyelids droop, and it is time to sleep.

SEXUAL NATURE OF the Amnesiac Subject E.H. Of myriad proposals that were made to Milton Ferris by research psychologists at rival institutions, the one that most offended Margot Sharpe was from a clinical psychologist at a distinguished Ivy League university requesting the opportunity to test and measure the brain-damaged subject's "sex-drive," "sex-fantasies," and "sex-potency." When the proposal was read to the lab by a bemused Ferris, Margot Sharpe, thirty years old at the time, was particularly upset—"That would be a terrible exploitation of Elihu Hoopes! He trusts us, and his family trusts us. He is a human being, not a research animal."

Milton Ferris had been surprised by his young colleague's vehemence, for Margot Sharpe was usually, in his presence, very quiet and unassuming. But he'd been impressed with her integrity and her passion. (As he would later tell her, in the brief interlude when they were lovers.)

At the time he'd laughed heartily at the young scientist's indignation. All of the lab had laughed. *He* wasn't going to invite a rival to examine *our amnesiac*—no fear of that.

Now that Milton Ferris has retired from the university and Margot Sharpe has become principal investigator of *Project E.H.*, and "E.H." has become ever more famous in neuropsychological quarters, Margot is deluged with proposals as offensive as that proposal, or worse. She fears what would happen to E.H. if she were not there to protect him; she fears that his elderly aunt Lucinda, like his other Hoopes relatives, could have no idea of the intricacies and (possible) duplicities of the highly competitive world of research science, and might unwittingly give permission to the wrong people. She is sure that, without her constant vigilance, the identity of "Elihu Hoopes" would be known to the world by now, and unwanted, unscrupulous sensation-seekers would be flocking to the Institute at Darven Park or worse yet, to the austere old English Tudor house in Gladwyne, Pennsylvania. And the amnesiac subject, with his short-term memory of less than seventy seconds, would not remember any outrage perpetrated upon him, unless he recorded it in his notebook or sketchbook.

Once, in a weak moment with Milton Ferris, when Margot was feeling emotional, and Ferris was feeling protective and paternal, Margot confided in the older scientist that she sometimes worried that there was something fundamentally immoral in what they were doing—experimenting upon a brain-damaged human being who could have no clear sense of what was happening to him, and whose "consent" was questionable.

"Even, at times, it worries me—it makes me anxious—about animal research. Primates have such—personalities . . . If you get to know them."

"Dear Margot. Don't get to know them."

Her white-bearded satyr-lover kissed her mouth, laughing somewhat crudely. If there is such a thing as a bemused and condescending kiss, that was it.

Yet, Margot recalls the kiss with a pang of happiness.

How simple life was to her then. She was Milton Ferris's brilliant and promising young colleague, and had not yet taken his place.

She is oversensitive, her colleagues tell her. And she is overprotective of E.H.

(Some of them laugh at her behind her back, she knows. Even her young colleagues, lab assistants, and dissertation advisees. Others smile to her face.)

The fact is, Professor Sharpe is fiercely principled, unyielding. As she grows older, and renowned in the rapidly-growing field of memory research, she becomes less tolerant of others' limitations. She is furious at others' ambition which is invariably "crude"—"shameless"—ambition. In the way of her mentor Milton Ferris she speaks contemptuously of "lazy science"—"bad science"—"quasi-science." In her department she is one of three top-earning professors; she is lavished with grants, for every research foundation wants to fund memory/brain-damage research and the mysterious "E.H." is the most famous of amnesiac subjects. Margot Sharpe publishes articles in prominent journals as frequently as Milton Ferris once did. She has become noted for her astute, fair-minded, incisive reviews, that draw upon a history of psychology; she is at once a working scientist, and a historian of neuropsychology. In a citation for an award from the American Association of Experimental Psychologists it is said of Margot Sharpe that she exhibits, in reviews as well as articles, a "breathtaking knowledge of the literature of the field, where most scientists are but dimly aware of the history of their (professions)."

She has become, in middle age, something of a legendary figure herself: perennially youthful, even girlish in appearance and manner; with glossy-black hair falling straight to her shoulders or elegantly gathered at the nape of her neck, straight-cut bangs to her eyebrows. No matter that her hair is threaded with silver, or that there are pale creases at the corners of her eyes, Margot Sharpe dresses like a schoolgirl-ballerina in tight black jersey tops and jackets, black trousers or leggings, flat black shoes. She is disarming, disingenuous. She is quick, agile, graceful on her feet—lithe as a dancer. (*Is* she a dancer? it is wondered.) At professional gatherings, she is immediately recognizable; she has heard awed whispers in her wake—*That's Margot Sharpe. God, she looks young!*

In her early forties Margot has accumulated an elite circle of former students who have achieved tenure and reputations in their competitive field and who constitute a third generation of sorts, their grandparent the Nobel laureate Milton Ferris and their parent Margot Sharpe. If required, Margot is as protective of her young as any actual parent might be.

She is unfailingly protective of E.H. Just to suggest an experiment that might "upset" her subject is to risk Margot Sharpe's ire. She is credited with having said, wittily: "Eli Hoopes is the only gentleman in neuroscience."

It is also said that, of ten proposals from colleagues to work with E.H., Margot Sharpe rejects, on the average, ten.

Notorious as Margot is for rejecting virtually all proposals from colleagues outside her department, she has been more diplomatic with her university colleagues. These proposals, from research scientists like Professor Karl Peirce, a neurophysiologist with a particular interest in the hippocampus and the amygdala, parts of the brain it has long been assumed were damaged by E.H.'s encephalitis, Margot can't reasonably reject; her strategy is to postpone making a decision, and then to postpone meeting with the researcher, and then to postpone, as long as possible, the researcher's meeting with the subject.

"Margot Sharpe doesn't own E.H., for Christ's sake! She isn't his guardian."

Her (senior, male) colleagues murmur together. They complain of her both in jest and bitterly.

Indirectly she knows of the collective dislike of Margot Sharpe, commingled with grudging admiration for her work and for her tenacity. What do they say, in derision? *Sharpe is married to her work—she's his wife.*

SO VERY TIRED! A hole has been bored into his skull, a piece of bone has been removed like a jigsaw puzzle-piece, and the delicate dura has been pierced. Can't recall why this terrible surgery was performed on his brain but knows it is irreversible.

A man's brain has been touched by strangers. Lights have been shined into the recesses of his soul. He has been turned inside out like a rubber glove, and tossed aside.

Shuts his eyes tight. The girl's body has only just been discovered—his cousin Gretchen. (But you must never say her name again, aloud. No one must hear.) He'd been hiding beneath the plank porch where he'd crawled to escape their eyes. And now his father staring at him with a look of commingled shame and contempt.

You saw nothing, Eli. You've been dreaming.

Go back to bed, son. There is nothing here for you.

"Mr. Hoopes? Are you feeling strong enough to get up? If you could swing your legs around here . . ."

He is being helped to his feet. He has been strapped flat on his back inside a sleek metal coffin and now he is being helped to his feet.

His knees are weak, his head feels as if air has been pumped into it—ever more air, ever more pressure.

Don't look. You didn't see.

There is nothing to see.

MARGOT NEVER THINKS, when she is apart from Elihu Hoopes, of how utterly lonely she is in her life, and *alone.*

It is fierce, such loneliness. A freezing wind, a very dry wind, that sucks at the marrow of the bone. Yet, enveloped in the busyness of her life, like one propelled along an endless stretch of white-water rapids, Margot rarely realizes it. When she is interviewed she will say in her bright happy voice *The life of a scientist is a continual adventure. Continual discoveries. Even our failures are adventures.*

She will say *Do I regret not having a personal life?*—laughing happily she will say *But this is my personal life! My career, my work, my science, my life.*

STUBBORNLY HE CONTINUES to believe that he is thirty-seven years old.

Though seeing in the mirror—(for how can he not?)—a much older man.

"How do you account for that, Mr. Hoopes?"

" 'Account for'—what?"

"The face in the mirror is not the face of a thirty-seven-year-old man—do you think?"

Margot Sharpe is not asking these questions. She is overseeing the interview of the amnesiac subject E.H. by one of her young colleagues. She would not phrase the questions quite so bluntly as the young man is doing but she does not interfere; it is a principle of Margot Sharpe's not to criticize her younger colleagues and associates (to their faces) quite so readily as Milton Ferris had done.

In the end, many had resented Milton Ferris. *The great man* is the one who is resented for his very *greatness.*

Margot Sharpe thinks of herself as a good, perhaps a very good, but not a great scientist. Hers is the modesty of resignation: she does not compete with greatness. She has been very lucky in having inherited the "gold mine"—(to use Alvin Kaplan's expression)—E.H. Her only hope is that greatness will in some way envelop her, and protect her.

Reluctantly E.H. is peering into a mirror. It is not really a natural thing to do—to scrutinize one's own face before witnesses. If done, it is likely to be in utter privacy, as a most intimate act.

Margot thinks, with sympathy—*He doesn't look at his face if he can avoid it. It is no longer "his" face.*

With an air of bravado E.H. addresses the young professor: "What's the problem, Doctor? That's my 'reflection'—not that it is exactly *me*."

"You see your face as familiar, then—there is no surprise to you, seeing your face."

This is very awkwardly phrased. It is neither a question nor a statement. Yet Margot does not interfere, just yet.

The young man says, "You see your reflection as *familiar*, then? Though in some way, as you say, it isn't 'exactly you.' "

"Is your reflection 'you,' Doctor?"

The young man is caught off guard and can't think of a ready reply. He glances at Margot Sharpe, with a small frown.

"My reflection is the reflection of—my appearance. Of course, it is not *me*."

"Same with me, then." E.H. laughs, stroking his jaw. "Some kind of funny conversation we are having, Doctor, in't it?" (E.H. has taken to joking in an odd, seemingly semi-illiterate accent. Margot has been noting *in't it* for *isn't it?* recently. She wonders where this is coming from.)

After a moment E.H. says, as if placating the frowning young man, "Something about the mirrors in this place—eh?"

"Mirrors? Here at the Institute?"

"Yes. 'In-sti-tute.' "

E.H. shrugs, still with an air of bravado. Sidelong he glances at Margot Sharpe as if he hopes this female observer will support him.

(Though E.H. has forgotten Margot Sharpe, in the sense in which he no longer knows her name, or why exactly she is observing him, he seems to recall that there is something consoling and comforting about her; Margot is grateful for this.)

"There are 'funny' mirrors here. Like undersea, in a cave. Nobody is his actual self here. That's why they are testing me—to see if they have fooled me." E.H. smiles, disdainfully. "Sometimes I let them think yes, sure. Other times, I tell them it's all bullshit."

"Mr. Hoopes, who is 'they'?"

" 'They' are the doctors who operated on you, too."

"And what sort of operation do you think I've had?"

"Lobotomy. With an ice pick."

Seeing the startled look in the young man's face, E.H. bursts into derisive laughter.

(VERY INTERESTING, MARGOT thinks. How did E.H. know that some of the earliest lobotomies in the United States, in the late 1940s and early 1950s, were in fact performed with common ice picks, crudely and expeditiously? If he'd been reading about the history of psychosurgery recently, he could not retain the knowledge; if he knew this obscure fact, he must have read of it, or heard of it, before his illness. And with the unimpaired part of his brain he "remembered" it—but why, Margot wonders. Why would Eli Hoopes remember such a thing?)

IT IS A crucial test, the amnesiac subject and the "mirror-self."

Clearly the subject both sees and does-not-see his reflection in the mirror; or, he sees a reflection clearly enough, but detaches from it so that it is not "his."

In this way, Eli Hoopes remains thirty-seven years old as his contemporaries age beside him.

As Margot Sharpe ages beside him.

Stubbornly too E.H. refuses to envision the future.

Shown a calendar by one of Margot's associates, and asked to speculate what he will most likely be doing on a specific date in a week, twelve days, a month, E.H. will "disengage" visibly.

For instance, E.H. is often brought to the Institute on Wednesdays for a full day of tests. But if he is asked what he will (probably) be doing on the first Wednesday of the next month he will seem to be shielding his eyes, avoiding the calendar. Grudgingly and vaguely he says, "What needs to be done, I guess."

"Can you be more specific, Eli?"

"I will do what—it happens to me, I will do. Or will be done to me."

Margot enters in her notebook *Subject is passive-tense. What is done to him, not what he does. Why?*

"Please try to be more specific, Eli."

The examiner prods him but E.H. is blank-minded. How can one be *more specific* about something that has not yet happened?

"Or—tell us what would you like to do on this day?"

E.H. gives the impression of struggling viscerally with a thought as if threading a length of twine through the labyrinth of his brain.

"I—I think that—I will—w-will . . ."

Margot realizes, the word *will* is giving E.H. difficulty. Discreetly she intervenes. She sees that the examiner, a younger colleague in the Psychology Department, is becoming frustrated, confused. Margot urges E.H. to think of the "high probability" that, three weeks from today, for instance, he will be doing something quite safely routine and familiar: (probably) he will eat several meals, and he will write in his notebook and/or sketch in his sketchbook; he will certainly become sleepy at night, and go to bed at his usual hour—"I think it's eleven-thirty, after the late news? In your house in Gladwyne, on Parkside Avenue?"

"Y-Yes."

But E.H. seems tentative, disoriented. Margot wonders why this is.

In conversation (normal, unimpaired) individuals speak casually and constantly of what they intend to do; the future tense is elastic, and unexamined. Though the future doesn't exist in any way, yet it is spoken of as if it were an actual place, and there is no anxiety or concern about entering it. As one might speak casually of "Heaven" without believing in "Heaven" in the slightest. But to the amnesiac there is something about the future that is unthinkable—inconceivable.

They appear to be at an impasse. No matter how the question is phrased E.H. can't seem to reply. The normally articulate man has begun almost to stammer. Margot speculates that the amnesiac can't contemplate the future because the part of his brain that has been impaired is also a part of the brain that "plans"—there must be, in future contemplation, for the normal subject, some measure of recollection; one can't anticipate a future if one can't recall a past, for much in the routine of life is cyclical, repetitive. The only past E.H. can recall is now decades old, and he can't seem to summon it as a stimulus for thinking of the future.

A common brain circuit for both mental functions?—which has been impaired in E.H.

Margot is feeling very excited! Thrilled, like one who has been grasping at the wisp of a dream, and has managed at last to haul it into consciousness.

Of course, exploring this theory will require much time. Months of testing, careful experimentation with the amnesiac subject and with control subjects including individuals whose amnesia is less pervasive than E.H.'s. (Fortunately there are several of these in more or less permanent residence at the Institute in the dementia and Alzheimer's wing.)

Margot Sharpe will title her groundbreaking paper "Simulation of 'Future' Identity and Episodic Retrieval in Amnesia." She will send it to the most prestigious of newer publications, the *Journal of Neuropsychology and Neurophysiology*. In decades to follow, Professor Sharpe's article will be one of the most frequently cited in its field.

Expanded, it will be a key chapter in her most admired book, *The Biology of Memory*.

All this future achievement—this future success—Margot Sharpe can glimpse, as one might glimpse a mountain peak behind shifting clouds. For Margot Sharpe has no difficulty leaping ahead into her future—so long as she does not leap too far ahead.

Now, she wishes that she could stroke E.H.'s hand, to comfort him. For she sees that her dear friend who is trapped in the present tense is gripped with anxiety. The tendons in his neck have become taut.

Indeed, *will* is a strange, metaphysical word. How can anyone comprehend what he *will* be doing, when the time of such an action does not (yet) exist? It is an existential conundrum. No normal person would give it a second thought. As Freud may have observed, to give such a conundrum a second thought is to identify oneself as abnormal—neurotic.

In her gently authoritarian voice Margot Sharpe declares:

"Very good! Thank you all. Mr. Hoopes has been very patient with us and has had enough strain for now."

And quickly, before anyone else can volunteer, or the sly-cat-faced caramel-skinned nurse's aide steps forward, Margot declares that Elihu Hoopes needs some fresh air. She will take him outdoors on this windy late-autumn day, for a vigorous walk—"In his favorite place, the marshland."

"I LOVE YOU."

"And I love *you.*"

Between them there is a small desperate flame stoked of loneliness.

Always at such times Margot is struck by the *physicality* of the other. The man, who is the other.

It is not an idea, or a scientific theory—love, lovemaking. It is a *physical act,* or it is nothing.

She sees in Elihu Hoopes's face a raw, undisguised hunger. The face is no longer unlined and youthful but it is *his face.*

How is it possible for Margot to deny this hunger? It is not possible.

This is wrong—of course. This is a violation of ethics.

This is—classically!—"scientific misconduct."

She thinks, she will risk professional exposure, disgrace. She will risk it for him.

Excitement between them rises rapidly, vertiginously. Entering the interior of the parkland, in the thickest part of the woods, they seem to have lost language.

Margot clutches at the man who drives himself into her, hiding his heated face against her neck. They are partially clothed—this has happened so swiftly, and irrevocably. It is the *physicality* of the act that shocks her anew each time, for she is likely to feel some pain, physical discomfort and distress, the man is *so large, so forceful.*

Margot feels herself cleaved, somewhat brutally. Yet—there is tenderness in the man's embrace, his anxious kisses. It is this tenderness Margot craves, it is the very nourishment of her soul, of which she takes care not to think in her ordinary life.

Out of cleaving, a sensation of wholeness. Happiness. Knowing that she has made the man feel intense pleasure, and so he has not been alone, and she has not been alone, in this quick frantic coupling.

When she can think again, it is an unexpected thought that grips her—*Will I have his child? Is that the way this will be?*

In the aftermath of love she is naïve, disoriented. She is hardly a scientist, she is not thinking clearly. Feelings wash over her like currents of warm water.

She holds the perspiring man tight against her. He is holding her also, but her embrace is as fierce as his own, which is surprising to her who has never thought of herself as a very physical, still less sensual, person.

It is this new person I've become. But only here, only now.

Only with Eli.

By degrees, their quickened breaths subside. By degrees, exterior sounds intrude.

An airplane passing, high overhead. In the near distance, the ugly guttural sound of a chain saw.

"Dear Eli! I love you . . ."

". . . . darling, I love *you*."

He has forgotten her name, no doubt. Until he draws back to look at her, very likely he has forgotten her face.

She wonders too if he remembers that they have made love together in the past—not quite like this, but yes, like this. She wonders what he recalls, in his body.

Still: they have been together, they have been intimate. *She* will never forget.

His seed is inside me. That can't be altered.

Margot adjusts her clothing, combs her hair. She is careful to remove from her hair any leaf-fragments, any telltale twigs. She has been careful with her clothing, overall. It is wrong of her to think of any other man at such a time, she feels that it is crude, vulgar, distasteful, but she can't help but recall with a sense of satisfaction, a kind of reproachful satisfaction, that she'd never been so intimate with Milton Ferris as with this man.

By degrees she has forgotten how desperately she'd loved Milton Ferris, years ago. How long?—can it have been fifteen years, twenty years? She will not think of this now, it is a mistake to think of her lost love now. She has been so close to this man, she has scarcely needed to name him, or see him. The heartbeat of the other, so near! Her eyes fill with tears of the most intense happiness.

If I have ruined my life for Eli Hoopes, very well—it could not be helped.

If I bear his child—that will be enough.

Earnestly E.H. is asking, "Are you my dear wife? Did you come to take me home with you?"

Margot hears the wistfulness in E.H.'s voice, as if he knows the answer beforehand but must ask.

Margot hesitates before saying yes, she is his wife.

Margot says yes, she will drive him home that day, to Gladwyne. But she can't stay with him just yet.

Why not? E.H. asks. If you are my wife.

His voice rises, alarmed and petulant.

They must return now to the path—a wide, wood chip path. It is possible—it is even probable—that someone will see them on this path, in the more populous area of the park. E.H. doesn't know this, has not the slightest awareness of this. But Margot is keenly aware, and draws away from him, just perceptibly.

E.H. grips her arm at the elbow. He grips her shoulders, to force her to face him. "Why won't you come home with me, and stay with me, if you are my wife?"

Margot says, "I—I will come home with you, Eli. Soon. I promise."

" 'Soon'—? What's that mean?"

"In a—while. I'm not sure when."

"Weeks? Months? Years?"

"Weeks. Or—months."

E.H. is hurt, and E.H. is angry. They are walking on the wood chip path now, bypassing the pond. Several times E.H. has taken hold of Margot's arm at the elbow, and Margot must detach his fingers, not rudely, but firmly.

Margot is alarmed at E.H.'s agitated voice.

"Eli, please! Mr. Hoopes! We don't want strangers to overhear us."

"Then why are we here? Why am I here? I want to go home—I can drive us home."

"Yes, well—I can drive, Eli. I don't mind driving. I've made arrangements to drive you today. You don't remember—I guess—but you were brought here this morning, by that very nice young driver—he's a Dominican—hoping to go to medical school. But I am driving you back to your aunt's house."

"We're living in Rittenhouse Square. I don't want to live anywhere else."

"Eli, your living quarters with your aunt Lucinda are temporary. Just until—"

"What do you mean, 'temporary'? Why am I living with that old woman? I want to live with *you*. I have a right to live with my wife."

"But we aren't married yet, Eli. We will be married—soon—after the first of the year—in the Unitarian Church of Philadelphia . . ."

Eli Hoopes's face creases in suspicion. " 'Unitarian Church of

Philadelphia'—that was long ago. I don't know those people now. I don't believe you. I don't even know your name, Doctor."

Eli Hoopes's face is contorted with rage, and grief. Tears have filled his eyes. Margot is horrified, appalled. It is a relief—if but a mild relief—that two medical workers eating their lunches by the pond haven't noticed them, and don't appear to be, in any case, anyone who knows Elihu Hoopes or Margot Sharpe.

She takes the man's restless hand, she strokes it as you might stroke an agitated animal, to give comfort and to exert control.

She feels a sick, sinking thrill—Eli Hoopes will wrest his hand from her, and strike her with his fist.

In the lowered voice of tenderness, concern, intimacy she assures him—"Yes, you know my name: 'Margot.' I have come into your life to love you, and take care of you, dear Eli. You know—you've had some trouble with your memory? You've had neurosurgery?"

"I have?"

"You had a virulent infection—your brain swelled with encephalitis, and you had to have emergency surgery in Albany."

"Really! That would explain a lot, I guess. When the hell was this, Doctor?"

"In late summer 1964."

E.H. counts on his fingers—(Margot isn't sure what he is counting). "Was that—last year?"

"No. It was some years ago."

As usual at such perilous times E.H. becomes very still. The amnesiac isn't capable of mental time-travel; Margot envisions him as an individual who has opened a door in preparation to stepping through, but discovers that the door is a brick wall. The shock is both mental and visceral.

Gently Margot encourages him: "If you think for a moment,

Eli, you will remember getting sick. The infection—the fever. You had a fever of a hundred and three point one degrees Fahrenheit when you were sickest. You took your own temperature during those days you were sick at the lake, and kept a record."

Is this true? Margot can't quite remember.

True in some way, Margot thinks. She is sure of that.

E.H. tries to think. He casts his gaze aside, he frowns, grimaces . . . It is uncanny, Margot can almost feel the man *thinking.*

The effort of the damaged brain to reconnect—to recharge itself. Margot is touched by sympathy, and pity; and a kind of futile hope. But the circuit is broken, the neurons can't properly "fire." Such effort resembles the effort of a paraplegic trying to walk—the memory of walking, the will to walk, is not enough.

Poor Eli! Margot yearns to embrace him again but dares not in this public place.

Haltingly E.H. says, "I have some problem with my memory—I think. I forget things I used to know—I think that is the problem." But he seems doubtful, as if hoping he will be contradicted.

"How long do you think you've had this problem, Eli?"

"I think—maybe—six months?" E.H. speaks uncertainly, watching Margot closely. He is sensitive to something in her face for he quickly amends, "Maybe more like eighteen months. I think it must be that long, Doctor. Do you think so, too?"

Margot explains that she is not a doctor, but a neuropsychologist. Margot assures E.H. that she will be with him for the rest of the day.

"Darling Eli, please trust me. *I will never abandon you.*"

It is all that E.H. needs to hear. Though her statement is not literally true, Margot feels that it is true, in a deeper way. *I will never abandon you in my heart.*

E.H. seems placated, if guardedly. He is not so very surprised to see the Institute before them and to see that the path they are taking leads to an entrance.

As they enter the Institute E.H. invariably steps aside to allow Margot Sharpe to precede him through the revolving doors. He is gentlemanly, courtly; as he has left the parkland, and approached the luminous high-rise building with its myriad panes of vertical glass, he becomes somewhat formal, his expression neutral and his manner tinged with irony.

His clothing is not disheveled. His hair—(now thinning, silver-gray and somewhat dry)—is not disheveled. Margot wonders if there is any erotic memory in him—in his body. (There is certainly an "erotic memory" in a woman, Margot thinks.) But in E.H., this possibility is not at all evident. He will leave the outdoors without a backward glance; if you saw him, you would assume that this is a man who knows exactly where he is going. He stands tall, his posture is impressive in a man of his age.

In the elevator with Margot Sharpe and several others (strangers) he takes his little notebook out of a pocket and scribbles in it, earnestly. When the elevator door opens on the fourth floor, E.H. is prepared to step out though (Margot knows) if she'd asked him at which floor they would be getting out, he'd have had no idea.

With a sweetly playful little gesture of gallantry E.H. allows any woman in the elevator to precede him out. Margot has wondered on such occasions if he is mimicking an older male relative, or if he is recalling his own, former self.

In the lab with no protest he allows smiling Margot Sharpe to hand him over to younger associates of hers who have prepared a complicated battery of tests involving encoding, storing, and retrieval of information in the amnesiac subject. He seems happy to see these "strangers," and shakes their hands.

"Are you—medical students? 'Interns'?"

Margot remains close by, observing. Within seventy seconds Eli Hoopes will have forgotten her, in his concentration upon being tested. It is urgent for Eli Hoopes to be a good testing subject, to evoke praise and affection in these friendly young strangers.

Margot is taking notes for what will be two linked articles—"Memory Deficits and Déjà Vu in the Amnesiac Subject E.H." and "False Memory and Déjà Vu in Severe Retrograde and Partial Anterograde Amnesia."

AM I PREGNANT? I will have his child, if I am.

CHAPTER EIGHT

Margot Sharpe will become Elihu Hoopes's archivist. She is determined.

Margot Sharpe does not want E.H. to die—of course: she loves him. Yet, Margot Sharpe coolly considers the fact that E.H. will one day die, and she will outlive him—of course: she is younger.

After E.H.'s death hundreds of little notebooks of uniform size will be recovered among the amnesiac's possessions. Hundreds of sketchbooks as well.

(Will E.H. still be living with his aunt, at the time of his death? Or will he be living elsewhere? It is crucial, Margot thinks, that Lucinda Mateson provide for her disabled nephew, in the years to come. She will speak to Mrs. Mateson—soon.)

With a team of assistants Margot Sharpe will one day edit *The Notebooks of "E.H"—The Sketchbooks of "E.H."*—to be published in numerous volumes by the University of Pennsylvania Press.

Among the vast *Project E.H. Archives* will be audio and video interviews with the subject as well as audio and videorecordings of the subject's many tests. Thousands of tests, since 1965! CDs,

DVDs. The unique (posthumous) brain of Elihu Hoopes will be scanned in an MRI machine for ten hours; preserved, embedded in gelatin, frozen, cut into two thousand thin slices from back to front; these slices will be eventually digitalized and assembled into a three-dimensional image for continued study. How many Ph.D.s in neuropsychology and neuroscience will be spawned out of this treasure-trove, like bacteria out of a petri dish! As Milton Ferris foretold, *The most-studied amnesiac brain in the history of science—and it is ours!*

IT IS AN honor! Professor Sharpe has been assured.

News has come to her by way of her departmental chair. She is being awarded a major, prestigious award from a national science foundation. *Too soon!* she thinks. She is trying not to feel dismay, panic.

She recalls that Milton Ferris received this very award, but not until he was over fifty. It is premature for Margot Sharpe to be given the award.

"Margot? Is something wrong? This is very good news, you know. Good for you, for the department, for the university and the Institute. And for *Project E.H.*"

She thinks *But it is too soon, Milton will resent me.* She is feeling light-headed.

Later, she will wonder if Milton Ferris, one of the advisory trustees of the foundation, had a hand in giving her the award.

They will know that Milton Ferris was my lover. That Milton Ferris cast me off, and this is an acknowledgment of his guilt.

Haltingly Margot tries to explain that it is very good news of course—but it will have the deleterious effect of interesting more scientists and quasi-scientists in their work with E.H.; the Institute will be swamped with proposals, which will be turned over to Margot Sharpe to consider.

"We have to protect E.H. We can't let his identity become known. We can't let him become a—freak of some kind. I'm forced to turn down virtually every proposal that comes to me, hundreds a year . . ."

Margot has been stammering. Not knowing what she means to say.

Her colleagues at the university marvel at Margot Sharpe, and laugh at her—but kindly, with affection. How eccentric Margot is becoming, and she isn't even fifty years old yet!

What would be delightful news to another scientist seems to alarm and frighten her. What would be a public confirmation of the significance of her work seems to threaten her.

For Margot Sharpe is happiest at work. She is a good, devoted, reliable and responsible faculty member at the university, but her relationships with her colleagues and students are likely to be somewhat distracted. Her true life is in the lab, or at the Institute—testing the amnesiac subject E.H.

She has made a lifetime of E.H., has she! A career.

Grinding facts, data. Conflating results.

Composing theories. Designing new tests.

"—I'm very grateful of course. I'm very—honored."

Enduring congratulations. Enduring praise, flattery.

Her hand shaken. But not *her hand shaken by E.H. who is her only happiness.*

She is being told (now by the dean of the faculty) that she must, she absolutely must, accept this award. And she must accept it *in person.* She certainly cannot send a young colleague in her place!

Thinking *But what if I have no "person"—what will I do then?*

Often when others speak, even if it is her field of neuropsychology of which they speak, even if they are speaking specifically of "Margot Sharpe," she has begun to find it difficult to concentrate, and intrusive. She finds it difficult to follow the thread of others' words.

She is distracted by their brains inside their skulls inside their skins. Almost, she can observe the workings of brains, as in a brain-scan.

Energized by thought and by speech, brains are illuminated from within. There is a rapid, involuntary firing of neurons like electric shocks. To what purpose?

Beauty in such illumination, to no other purpose.

She has taken photos of brain cells, many times magnified. The most beautiful hues, shapes and textures. One day, she will pore over the ultra-thin slices of Elihu Hoopes's brain.

Oh my darling. I can't bear to live without you.

She will endure. She will live without him. At all times of the day and the night, when she is not with E.H., she must live without him.

Thinking how with E.H. she never—quite—loses the thread that connects them.

For with E.H., as with no other possible lover, the relationship between them is always shifting back to zero. Always, they are discovering each other for the first time.

"—I am very happy for us all. But the award ceremony comes at a difficult time, when I have so much work to do . . . We are bringing E.H. to the University Hospital, for an fMRI . . ."

Her voice is oddly hollow, nasal. She has left central Michigan so far behind, so many years ago, how is this possible!

Eli, I wish you were here. Wish we could be together.

I miss your hand gripping mine. Your love.

SHE HAS NO time for anything but work but—after all, and despite her protests—she is being interviewed. The Institute director has insisted on this interview for the *Philadelphia Inquirer,* she has been told.

As if Margot Sharpe is placated by being informed that her interviewer is a *science writer.*

Asked with a fatuous smile/smirk, "Professor Sharpe, as a scientist do you believe that we have 'souls'?"

A question meant to elicit controversy. Though the (female) journalist is smiling, hers is not a friendly smile.

And so carefully Professor Sharpe replies, "The concept 'soul' is fundamentally theological, not scientific. So I am really not able to answer." Carefully smiling, respectful.

"Maybe if I rephrase my question—"

"Well, I'm not sure that I understand your question. Are you asking do I believe *as a scientist* that we have souls; or, do I, *who happens to be a scientist,* believe that we have 'souls'?"

The interviewer laughs as if Professor Sharpe has meant to be witty and not withering.

"You can answer either, please! I'm sure that our readers will be intrigued."

"As a scientist, I scarcely believe that we are 'we.' "

"Excuse me, Professor Sharpe—what does that mean?"

"What does that *mean*? Exactly what the words say."

"That we are—'we'?"

"That we have unique and definable and unvarying identities. That, in a manner of speaking, 'we' exist."

"But if we are not ourselves, who are we?"

"*Who* are we? You might better say *what.*"

"*What* are we?"

"Exactly. Science has only just begun that exploration. Neuroscience is the way *in*—but only *the way in*."

The interviewer is perplexed. The interviewer is embarrassed. The interviewer would be insulted except that Professor Sharpe speaks so politely, so earnestly and so gently.

"ELI? MR. HOOPES? Is—something wrong?"

She has slipped the Celtic ring on the third finger of her right hand. She knows that E.H. will not see it, or, if he sees it, will not identify it, and yet—it gives her pleasure to be wearing it, at the university and at the Institute.

"If you'd rather not begin our tests right now, Eli—we can wait. Would you like to wait? Would you like to sit by the window here, and write in your notebook? Make some drawings? What would you like to do, Eli?"

He does not seem to care for her, this morning. He does not seem to "recognize" her.

His feeling for her, his sexual attraction for her—seems to have vanished. Is this possible?

He is not a youthful man any longer. He is "older"—an *older gentleman* as the medical staff calls him.

Margot is concerned. Margot is frightened. It has not ever occurred to her—not once in more than twenty years—(or if it has, she has forgotten)—that the wonderfully cooperative *amnesiac subject* might one day refuse to cooperate with researchers. Such a possibility had never occurred to Milton Ferris, she is sure.

His eyes on her, neutral. Courteous, yet cool.

He does not know her. He has never seen her before.

No rings on his fingers yet unconsciously he turns an (invisible) ring on the third finger of his left hand.

"Thank you, Doctor."

Doctor. Why does he call her that! She is not wearing a white lab coat or a stethoscope. By this time he should know the distinction between the research psychologists who are studying him and the medical staff at the Institute . . .

Except of course, Elihu Hoopes can't know.

Margot is undecided how to proceed. She might simply wait—an hour, a few minutes—and see what develops. Certainly, she is not going to give up and go home.

She has planned an important battery of tests for this week, and will be seeing E.H. three days in succession. She is working with several young associates and a colleague, an associate professor at the university, with whom she has designed these new tests based upon classical conditioning—"delay conditioning" and "trace conditioning." These are complicated tests involving much repetition and overlapping, as they are designed to measure subtle gradations in memory. It will not be helpful if the amnesiac subject isn't fully cooperative, or if he is distracted by a mood.

(Elihu Hoopes, distracted by a mood? Margot wonders what this could mean.)

Margot observes how one of the nurse's aides approaches E.H., with a bright smile. And she sees how E.H. responds. In his face a light like a smoldering fire that flares up at the sight of her.

"Mr. Hoopes, you wantin to take a little walk? Out where you like it, outside? I c'n take you, Mr. Hoopes."

Caramel-skinned girl, exotic and beautiful, very young. Oily black hair in tight cornrows plaited on her head.

Margot Sharpe sees, and looks away pained. Turning the Celtic ring on her finger.

THE TESTS. HAND-EYE coordination. Rapidity of reflexes.

In E.H., these are surprisingly good, for E.H. has been an

athlete for much of his life. But if he is instructed in a new skill, that in some way conflicts with an older skill, he will have difficulty mastering this skill even when it is a "simpler" skill than the original skill.

Margot is experimenting with intervals between repeated tests. She is discovering that motor-learning experiences seem to be consolidated in the amnesiac subject's non-declarative memory if there is an interval of between three and four hours; before this, the memory is incompletely consolidated. And if the interval is too long, the memory fades.

It isn't surprising that E.H.'s "mastery" of a skill is disrupted when he is required to learn a secondary motor skill within several hours; the second skill may be retained, but the first is lost.

However, the first skill can be more readily regained, if the subject is again instructed in it. Though the subject may remember nothing of the original instruction consciously, his eye-hand coordination improves at once, and he will demonstrate an ease with the procedure that suggests that, indeed, he is "remembering."

Margot Sharpe and her colleagues have the idea of returning to "intact priming" experiments performed with E.H. eight months before, and running them a second time; at another eight-month interval they will run them again. It is gratifying to discover that E.H. can perform virtually as well as a normal individual in recalling words cued with the first several letters of a word, so long as he is not asked to "remember" but only to say the first word that comes to mind—"Just speak, Eli! Don't think."

When E.H. is asked if he has ever performed one of these priming tests before, or a test in which he identifies a sequence of only partially drawn figures, his answer is invariably: "No! Not me."

Yet, given a pencil, E.H. completes the sketchy outlines of an octagon, a many-branched tree, a diamond, an orange divided into quarters, a church with a spire. As the test progresses the figures become less distinct, yet the amnesiac subject can complete most of them, like a sleepwalker making his slow, certain way with his eyes open; eventually, when no more than one-tenth of the outline is provided, that to the normal eye looks like nothing more than isolated, broken lines lacking coherence, the amnesiac subject can complete the figures with his pencil.

E.H. is startled to see a figure materialize beneath his fingertips. "Hey! It's a—what is it?—'rhomboid.' "

Margot teases him: "You've never done these tests before, Eli? Yet you are doing them so well—how do you explain it?"

"*You* explain it."

Eli is further flattered by being told that other subjects have failed to complete the drawings as he'd done.

E.H. smiles as if exulting in secret knowledge. As if thinking—*But of course I know how to do this, I have mastered it many times in the past.*

Margot knows that E.H. is simulating such knowledge. The amnesiac wishes to provide the examiner with the sort of socially-determined response that would seem plausible in a normal subject; in E.H., this response is a confabulation.

Margot has explored E.H.'s strategy of confabulating. The subject is infinitely fascinating to her as a (possible? probable?) foundation of all human belief, mythology. Margot will ask E.H. why he is wearing his watch on his right wrist instead of his left, and E.H. will say matter-of-factly, "Because—I always wear my watch on my right wrist." (In fact, one of Margot's assistants instructed E.H. to switch it to the other wrist earlier that day.)

Under the guise of an experiment Margot pushes the Celtic ring onto one of E.H.'s fingers. She tells him it is a "present from a friend." And an hour later when E.H. is asked about the ring he stares at it as if he has never seen it before. (Indeed, he has never seen it before.) He is likely to say, "This is an old family ring. This is a ring I always wear."

Another time, E.H. will say, "This is my wedding ring. My wife and I have identical rings."

"And—where is your wife now, Eli?"

"She would be in our apartment at Forty-Four Rittenhouse Square. She would be waiting for me."

Margot is intrigued by this reply in the subjunctive mood. *Would be.*

Yet, she's rather hurt by her lover's remark. As if he'd slapped her lightly with the back of his hand in rebuke.

"But—what is your wife's name, Eli?"

Her question is faint, faltering. E.H. bares his teeth in an obstinate smile.

"What d'you think it would be, Doctor? If she's my wife she is 'Mrs. Hoopes.' "

THOUGH E.H. IS the amnesiac subject of *Project E.H.*, from time to time Margot Sharpe and her colleagues work with other impaired individuals at the Institute as well. And they work with "normal" individuals, student volunteers at the university; these "normal" individuals are their control group.

"Semantic" knowledge, "episodic" knowledge. The one is factual, impersonal, and non-contextual; the other personal, autobiographical, and contextual.

In E.H., all "memory" acquired after his illness in July 1965 has vanished. That is, all declarative memory.

E.H.'s more general memory, consolidated before his illness, remains more or less intact, and is considerable; he was a highly educated and highly intelligent man. But his personal memory,

Margot thinks, has begun to seriously corrode. By the time the amnesiac subject is in his sixties, his recollection of his early, pre-amnesiac life has become unreliable, at times surreal. (E.H. will say, "Did that happen? Or did I dream that happened?") Tests administered to the amnesiac subject at two-year intervals, drawing upon childhood and boyhood memories, record this decline. But why is this happening? Why, when E.H.'s brain hasn't been further injured? It is Margot's theory that E.H.'s personal memory is fading or breaking up because he has no way of consolidating it, as normal individuals do; even if E.H. recalls an event or a person distinctly he can't consciously preserve the memory for retrieval, for he has no present-time memory.

Without fail E.H. can remember historic events: Pearl Harbor, Hiroshima, the surrender of Japan on September 2, 1945. The Kennedy-Nixon campaign and election of Kennedy. Cuban missile crisis. But the connective tissue between these events and his own, personal life seems to be decaying. When he speaks of such events it's as if they occurred without his consciousness. Wryly he says, "It's like a bad job of caulking. Falls apart."

In a separate category of tests administered by psychologists specializing in sleep, E.H.'s sleep patterns have been monitored. EEGs have recorded electrical activity produced by neurons in his brain. E.H.'s presumably "normal" sleep is often disturbed, Margot Sharpe has observed. (She has spent many hours beside E.H. in the sleep lab at the Institute, taking meticulous notes. These have been deeply satisfying hours—an unspeakable intimacy.) The sleeping amnesiac grinds his teeth, squirms and shudders and thrashes his limbs. He mutters incoherently—he curses in a voice Margot has never heard before, and which pierces her, thrillingly. When wakened by the examiner during REM sleep and asked what he is dreaming, E.H. will blink his eyes in confusion before saying, in a way that suggests the fluency of a familiar anecdote and not the more halting recollection of an actual dream—*When I was a boy and it was Christmas . . . When we were going to my grandparents' house . . . It was somewhere in the mountains, but there were horses . . . It was a happy time, but there was a big snowstorm . . .*

The sleep examiners record E.H.'s responses as accounts of dreams but Margot Sharpe believes that they are simply confabulated memories. The amnesiac can't remember his dream scant seconds after he has been wakened and so he invents a plausible-sounding dream, or draws upon an anecdote out of his past, in itself corroded by time. From the EEG monitor it appears that the amnesiac is dreaming as if normally but his dreams evaporate even more rapidly than the dreams of the "normal." Eager to placate his examiners, genial and gentlemanly Elihu Hoopes provides them with neatly described dreams. Margot has experimented with putting suggestions to E.H. before his sleep to see if his dreams might be influenced but there appears to be no more memory in his unconscious brain than in his conscious brain.

It is an exciting theory of Margot's that the amnesiac subject E.H. is haunted by obsessive memories which he can't fix in place or exorcise, since he lacks the present-time ability to evaluate them. Nor is it clear (to examiners, to him) whether these are actual memories, quasi-memories, or frankly false memories that have corroded his identification with the person he'd been before his illness. Thus, his obsessive drawing in the sketchbook—that is, in his current sketchbook. E.H. has run through numerous sketchbooks in the years Margot has worked with him.

In her amnesia logbook Margot will speculate:

How do we know who we were, *if we don't know who we* are?

How do we know who we are, *if we don't know who we* were?

Margot escorts E.H. from the sleep lab on the first floor of the Institute to the more familiar fourth floor. When they walk together in this public place, E.H. seems to take the lead—definitely, you would not guess from E.H.'s stride that he has not the slightest idea where he is or where he is going; but he is acutely sensitive to the motions of the woman beside him, and can anticipate her turns. When he sees the bank of elevators, he moves to them unhesitatingly. Margot notes how E.H. prepares to exit the elevator at the fourth floor as if instinctively; yet, if you ask E.H. which floor he is going to, E.H. will shrug irritably—"Who knows? Where it stops."

Or he will say more genially, "Doctor, you're the doctor. You have the answers."

MARGOT PLACES HER slender hand beside E.H.'s larger, big-knuckled hand.

"Look, Eli! We're wearing identical rings."

It is the end of the day. It is the happiest time in the day.

E.H. is delighted. E.H. examines the rings with care.

"Are you my dear wife, then? My dear wife is a doctor in the hospital here?"

"I am not a doctor, Eli. I am—yes, I am your wife—but it's a secret, and no one must know."

"But why? Why is it 'no one must know'?"

"Because we want to tell them at a later time, darling. Because it's our secret right now."

"But—why is it a secret? I don't understand."

"Because your family would not approve."

Margot can think of no other reply. She regrets having spoken recklessly, and she regrets, or halfway regrets, having slipped E.H.'s ring on his finger, and her matching ring on her finger.

E.H. shrugs disdainfully. His fingers twitch as if he'd like to hit someone.

"My family?—the 'Hoopeses'? They are all dead, and gone to Hell."

Margot is astonished. "But why, Eli? 'Gone to Hell'—why?"

"They were building a big department store there. The Emporium in Hell."

E.H. speaks in so solemn a manner, Margot understands suddenly that he is joking. She feels a wifely twinge of indignation.

"Oh, Eli! That is *not funny*."

AT LAST IN February 1993 E.H.'s brain is "mapped." The Institute has acquired an MRI scanner and E.H. is one of the first neurologically damaged patients to be subjected to it.

Margot Sharpe accompanies E.H. to the Radiology unit. She has been awaiting this occasion for years. She is excited about learning at last what is physically wrong with E.H.'s brain even as she is fearful for her lover: she is fearful of what the brain mapping will reveal. More than thirty minutes E.H. endures the arduous procedure as Margot waits outside the windowless chamber. Badly she would like to be with him, to hold his hand and comfort him as he lies strapped inside the machine like a corpse while noises loud as thunderclaps sound erratically in his ears.

In the chill of Radiology no one recognizes Margot Sharpe. No one seems to know who "E.H." is—how distinguished a patient this tall courtly silver-haired gentleman with the faint, perplexed smile.

Repeatedly E.H. has asked where is he being taken?—and repeatedly Margot has told him that he isn't leaving the Institute but going just to another floor to have his brain "scanned."

And each time E.H. has said, tapping his head: "Well! Let's hope they can find something in here to scan."

Afterward E.H. is escorted unsteadily from the chamber, blinking like a man utterly lost. He has been wearing earphones to shield him from the abrasive clanking noises. It occurs to Margot that her dear friend has been shielded from such extreme surprises for years—his life has been carefully monitored by her, as by Lucinda Mateson.

Margot comes quickly forward to take his arm. He has no idea who she is but he sees that she is very concerned for him, as a wife might be, and she isn't wearing a uniform like the others.

Excitedly he calls her "dear"—"darling." Excitedly he tells her that he has been traveling somewhere far away—"And I was traveling in time, too. God damn, I forgot my camera!"

Later, upstairs in Neuropsychology, E.H. complains of a headache and a "strangeness" in his head. And still later, when he has forgotten the MRI ordeal entirely, he jokes to Margot: "You know, Doctor—I think they 'sterilized' me today. I don't think I signed a waiver, so I can sue the bastards."

SO VERY TIRED! A hole has been bored into his skull, a piece of bone has been removed like a jigsaw puzzle-piece, and the delicate dura has been pierced. Can't recall why this terrible surgery was performed on his brain but knows it is irreversible.

A man's brain has been touched by strangers. Lights have been shined into the recesses of his soul. He has been turned inside out like a rubber glove, and tossed aside.

You saw nothing, Eli. You've been dreaming.

Go back to bed, Eli! There is nothing here.

"Mr. Hoopes? Are you feeling strong enough to get up? If you could swing your legs around here . . ."

He is being helped to his feet. He has lain flat on his back inside a sleek metal coffin and now he is being helped to his feet.

His knees are weak, his head feels as if air has been pumped into it—ever more air, ever more pressure.

Don't look. You didn't see.

There is nothing to see.

THE fMRI RESULTS are as Milton Ferris had hypothesized in 1965: the amnesiac's brain is severely impaired in the region of the hippocampus and the parahippocampal gyrus (including perirhinal and entorhinal cortices); also damaged, less severely, are the amygdala, and parts of the temporal lobes. Other regions of E.H.'s brain (cerebral cortex, parietal lobe, cerebellum) appear to be reasonably normal.

With what relief, like any wife, Margot Sharpe sees that the really crucial regions of E.H.'s brain might be said to be *normal.*

For years Margot has been basing her experiments with E.H. on the assumption of severe hippocampal damage; less clear was the extent of probable damage to the amygdala, the part of the brain believed to be associated with emotion and sexual sensation. Now, the extent of the damage is known. It is evident that, though at least half of the hippocampus remains intact in the amnesiac's brain, the pathways that should carry information to it are gone—no neural activity *comes into* it. This answers a question!—solves an ongoing mystery of the brain and memory.

Batteries of new tests—degrees of complexity in visual stimuli, auditory, olfactory, tactual, "subliminal" awareness; multiple tests involving interruptions, distractions, contradictions, delays and acceleration; degrees of recognition and identification, which can vary widely—all lay ahead, to be designed and implemented.

Decades of experiments with primate brains will be supplanted by work on the amnesiac E.H.—the *human subject.*

Margot Sharpe is so very excited, it's as if research into the mystery of E.H. has only begun.

She might be twenty-three years old again, just entering Milton Ferris's lab for the first time! Just extending her hand to be shaken by "Elihu Hoopes" for the first time.

She will learn to decode the fMRI scans. She will pore over E.H.'s scans as over exquisite and riddlesome works of art. She will virtually inhabit them, she will dream of them.

It is like taking Eli Hoopes into her body, as in lovemaking. Her alert, hungry brain takes in the man's ghostly brain, his very soul.

Eli, I love you more than ever. I will never abandon you.

SOON TO BECOME classics of neuropsychology are Margot Sharpe's papers of the 1990s: "Familiarity and Recollection in a Case of Severe Hippocampal Damage"—"Toward a Theory of Déjà Vu and Jamais Vu: Sensory Stimuli and Recollection in the Amnesiac 'E.H.' "—"Toward a Theory of the Function of the Amygdala"—"Toward a Theory of Cryptomnesia"—"Maze-Learning and Somatic Recognition in a Case of Severe Amnesia"—"Spatial Memory, Visual Perception, and the Hippocampus." For the first time in her career Margot Sharpe has agreed to work in collaboration with a colleague from outside her lab, a university neuroscientist who performs surgery on the brains of capuchin monkeys to replicate, in a series of experiments, the precise neurological injuries of E.H. based upon the fMRI scans—"Pattern Recognition, Maze Performance, and Somatic Memory in the Human and Primate Brain" (1994) is the first of their celebrated papers.

Particularly, Margot is fascinated by the phenomena of déjà vu/cryptomnesia and its reverse, jamais vu (the conviction that one has never seen something which in fact one has seen, perhaps often). She has researched the subject thoroughly and has written on it a number of times, in regard to E.H. who so often feels as if he has seen something before, which he can't remember; even as, more or less constantly, he is certain that he has never seen something before, when he has seen it.

Margot wonders: Are these curious mental phenomena associated with (buried) memories? Are the neurons which react to them closely adjacent in the brain to neurons that store such memories? Or, as some researchers have argued, are they merely the result of a random firing of neurons, a nervous excitability of the brain as without meaning or significance as heat lightning flashing in the sky?

Yet, Margot can't concede that there is no meaning in any of these phenomena. There is only the possibility of not knowing what the meaning is just yet.

That uncanny sensation of believing that we have experienced something before, yet are unable to remember when, or where.

That uncanny sensation of believing that we have not experienced something before, though knowing that we have.

"MR. HOOPES? WILL you describe what you see here?"

In a dim-lit testing-room E.H. is seated in his favored comfortable chair being shown images on a screen which Margot Sharpe and her associates have prepared. Partly, this is a test E.H. has had before, a sequence of "familiar"—"famous"—individuals whom he recognizes readily (if the images predate 1964). Thus, he can identify Abraham Lincoln, Franklin Delano Roosevelt, and Dwight D. Eisenhower, but is nonplussed by Jimmy Carter, George W. Bush, Sr., Bill Clinton; he has no difficulty identifying Judy Garland as Dorothy in *The Wizard of Oz* but has not the slightest idea who the principals of *Stars Wars* are. Joe Louis he recognizes immediately but not Muhammad Ali.

Jonas Salk but not Richard Brauer, the neurologist whose patient he has been for many years at the Institute.

Amid strangers whom E.H. could not be expected to know Margot has mixed in Hoopes family members, relatives, and acquaintances whom E.H. might be expected to know; if these pre-date 1964 he can identify them, if not, he's uncertain—"I'd say this is my uncle Emmet in some surreal decayed state. That's an elderly man."

And, "This one looks like my cousin Jonathan Mateson except something alarming has happened to him. I never saw Jonathan looking like *that*."

And, impulsively: "Is that—*me*? The way I'm going to look in twenty years?"

E.H. laughs, and Margot tries to laugh with him. In fact the image on the screen is Elihu Hoopes at the age of fifty, somewhat gaunt-cheeked, with a faint, familiar smile. This is a photograph taken of him at the Institute sixteen years earlier.

Then, E.H. sits very still, staring. On the screen is an unexpected and startling image. Amid the succession of black-and-white photographs is an impressionistic work of art: a charcoal sketch of a young girl of about eleven, naked, very pale, seemingly lifeless, lying beneath the surface of a shallow stream. The girl's heavy-lidded eyes are shut, her lips are slightly parted, and her dark hair is spread out around her head. The surface of the water is lightly rippling so that the girl's naked body is not clearly seen.

The drawing's tone is shadowy, indistinct. The point of view is overhead, as if one were somehow above the stream, at a height of about ten feet, looking down.

E.H. has ceased breathing. Margot does not dare look at him, just yet.

"Mr. Hoopes? Eli? Do you recognize this drawing?"

"N-No."

During a previous testing session Margot managed to appropriate the amnesiac's sketchbook without his noticing so that representative drawings could be photographed and reproduced as slides. In this case Margot had the idea of reversing the image, and it is this mirror-image of the original at which E.H. stares.

In this variant, the drowned girl lies with her head at the upper-right corner of the page, and her slender pale feet in the lower-left corner, instead of the reverse.

"Eli, you've never seen this drawing before?"

"No."

E.H.'s mood has changed. He was feeling ebullient, correctly identifying many of the preceding faces, but now he's restless, and has begun to breathe audibly.

"Could you describe the drawing, Eli?"

"Describe it? Why'd I want to do that?"

"Can you see it clearly?"

"I'm not blind in both eyes, Doctor."

"Where do you think the scene is set?"

"Where's it *set*? It's a charcoal drawing—it's set on a sheet of parchment paper."

"A charcoal drawing? How do you know?"

"Well, isn't it? I *know*."

As a slide, the photograph of the drawing isn't so clearly a charcoal drawing. Its smudged surface reproduces as merely shadowy.

"Could you describe the drawing, Eli? Just use the first words that come to mind."

E.H. shakes his head *no.* In the faint reflection from the screen his face looks stricken, creased.

"If you were telling a story about this drawing, Eli, what would you say? Just—improvise."

But E.H. shakes his head again, emphatically. When Margot lightly touches his wrist he shakes off her hand.

"Do you think that the drawing is skillfully executed, Eli? Could you identify the artist?"

"Artist? A poor man's Edvard Munch."

"Excuse me—?"

But E.H. refuses to repeat his remark. He has been sitting with his arms tightly folded across his chest, eyes narrowed and mouth twitching. Margot feels a thrill of unease, as one might feel in close proximity to a wild creature that might suddenly lash out in fear and rage.

"Well—we'll continue."

Margot has followed the drowned girl with less disturbing images which E.H. can identify without difficulty, though he is still agitated—familiar portrait of Albert Einstein, familiar silhouette of the Empire State Building. When the amnesiac is feeling less threatened Margot reverts to reproductions of E.H.'s drawings of neutral settings—woodland lake, mountains and marshlands, birch trees on a hillside. These scenes, which seem to Margot exquisitely drawn, have been reproduced as E.H. drew them, and not in reverse; these E.H. contemplates for some time, as if entranced.

"Do you recognize these, Eli?"

"Y-Yes. But I don't know why."

"Do you know where they're set?"

"Lake George."

"And how do you know that?"

"I—I know. Just know."

"And are these charcoal sketches?"

"Could be."

The next image is a large, sprawling log house overlooking a lake densely bordered by evergreens. The house has first- and second-floor decks, immense fieldstone chimneys, and a steep roof with a heraldic cock lightning-rod at one of the peaks. In the background is a dock that juts out into the lake, with boats tied to its posts; one of these is a sailboat. It is sunset, or sunrise?—the sun's rays seem to skid, like knife-blades, along the pocked surface of the dark water.

"Hey! That's our place on Lake George. That's our dock. And our boathouse." E.H. speaks with boyish excitement, and some apprehension. "That boy out in the canoe, could be me."

"And who is with you in the canoe, Eli?"

"I didn't say that that was me in the canoe, Doctor. I said it could be me."

"Did you go canoeing often at Lake George, when you were a boy?"

"Yes of course. My father taught me—assiduously."

Adding, vehemently: "I canoe at Lake George now, Doctor! I was just there last month, and I'll be going back in a few weeks. Soon as I get—whatever it is that's wrong with me—get well again . . ." E.H.'s voice trails off uncertainly.

"Do you still stay in your family house when you visit Lake George?"

"I told you, I was just there. I'll be going back in a few weeks, assuming there hasn't been a blizzard. The Hoopes family has owned that property since 1926. I've been going every year since

I was a baby—that's to say, thirty-seven years. Not much changes in Bolton Landing—that's the name of the town. We have a very loyal, reliable local man there—Alistair Laird. In fact, I should call Al—he needs to know when I'm coming up for the weekend, to get the place ready . . ."

Following this, E.H. is very still. A thought has come to him—Margot doesn't interrupt.

"I guess—people have died. People have gone away. The last time I was there—I was alone."

"You went hiking in the woods, then? Did you camp in the woods, the last time?"

E.H. shrugs, as if he can't remember, or, to deflect his examiner's question, as if it is too melancholy a memory to exhume.

The next drawing Margot shows is of a small single-prop airplane on a dirt airstrip. Unlike the other drawings which are dark, this drawing is bright with color—yellow. The airplane is bright-colored and slightly abstract as in a Chagall painting in which whimsy and foreboding are conjoined. For this drawing, as for only a few drawings, E.H. used pastel chalks with charcoal.

"Looks like my grandfather's Beechcraft. Before it crashed."

"Is anybody inside? Can you see?"

"My grandfather is the pilot. There's a little boy in the front seat—could be me."

"The little boy in the front seat is you, Eli?"

"Well, it could be. I can't see his face clearly."

"And was your grandfather's airplane such a bright yellow, Eli?"

"Until the crash, yes."

"And after the crash?"

"Well—there wasn't any plane, then. My grandfather never climbed into a plane again."

"Was he injured?"

"No. Or maybe, yes. His 'motor reflexes'—'hand-eye coordination' . . . He didn't trust himself to fly a plane again, and so the plane was never repaired."

E.H. is silent for a while. E.H. is brooding. In his eyes, a glimmer of tears.

"After the time of the crash—people died. After that summer, people went away. I don't know where."

Other slides intervene, of an impersonal nature. E.H. has no difficulty identifying Bugs Bunny, Louis Armstrong, Robert Frost; then the charcoal drawing of the girl in the shallow stream returns. Margot notes that E.H. draws in his breath sharply, and sits very still.

"Do you recognize this drawing, Eli?"

"N-No."

"Have you ever seen it before?"

"No." But E.H. speaks uncertainly.

"You're sure—you have never seen it before?"

"Not this 'picture'—no. Is it a charcoal drawing?"

"It is. Yes—a 'charcoal drawing.' "

E.H. laughs, harshly. "Not a very good drawing, I think."

"You don't think it is? Why not?"

" 'Why *not*?'—it just isn't. The artist, whoever he is, is—fearful of something."

"Fearful of—what?"

"Fearful of seeing what a drowned girl in a creek in the summer in the Adirondacks would actually look like. This is—let's say—romantic bullshit."

"But maybe the artist is trying to create an impression? A mood? An emotion?"

"That's what we mean by 'romantic bullshit.' An artist should be pitiless, and *see*."

Gently Margot lays her hand on Eli Hoopes's arm, which is trembling. "Please try to describe it, Eli. We are trying to test your visual and linguistic abilities—to see how you have progressed."

"'Progressed'—that sounds optimistic! If you are an American, as we are, it is imperative to be optimistic." E.H. laughs, harshly. He is willing himself to forget, Margot thinks. It is not just the amnesia, the failure of information to find its way into the injured hippocampus; there is a willfulness too, which no test could measure but which the practiced neuropsychologist can determine.

But Margot is not going to let E.H. forget so quickly.

"Could you improvise a story about the figure in the drawing?"

"I'm a stockbroker, not a storyteller, Doctor. Why'd I improvise anything?"

"Because I am asking you to, Eli."

Margot sees that E.H. is not looking at the screen. His eyes are shut, he is refusing to see. She feels him trembling like one on the cusp of convulsing with cold.

"If—if there were a story to the drawing, Eli—only just *if*—what would the story be?"

Margot is familiar with the literature of hypnosis. The extreme impressionability of the human mind where suggestion is concerned. Eli Hoopes isn't a "hypnotizable" subject, she has thought. He is strong-willed, even obstinate. Only if he wishes of his own volition to tell a story, will he speak.

In a halting voice he says: "They are looking for her, but can't find her. Where she is, no one knows."

"Did someone take her there?"

"Yes."

"Who was it, who took her?"

" . . . they didn't let us see her. I was hiding under a porch—the veranda. They didn't tell us where she was or what had happened to her. At first they were looking for her and we knew about the search but not why and when they found her, we weren't allowed to know. We *knew*—but we weren't allowed to know. If we asked they said, 'Gretchen is away.' My parents, and my grandparents. And Gretchen's parents. All the adults—'Gretchen is away.' And when we were back home they kept saying, 'Gretchen is away.' And one day when we were alone my brother Averill said, 'Y'know what happened to Gretchen, she died.' And I asked him, 'But where is she?' and he laughed at me and said, 'She's where dead people go, stupid. Where d'you think?' "

E.H. speaks softly, rubbing at his jaws. His face is contorted with a look of physical distress.

"Sometimes I think I might've killed—someone . . . My God-damn brother who bullied and teased me, my other brother who never lifted a finger to protect me, an older boy who spent summers at the lake near us, also from Philadelphia, his grandfather was Bishop McElroy . . ."

"Did these boys harm you? Tease you?"

"No! But they tried."

"Was Gretchen related to you, Eli? Was she a sister, a—cousin?"

But E.H. has sunk deeply into himself, refusing now to look at the screen. He is trembling and tears of sorrow or rage glisten on his cheeks.

"Would you like to stop, Eli? We can resume again in a while."

E.H. shrugs languidly. His eyes are heavy-lidded as if he were about to lapse into sleep.

Margot and the other examiners have noted that the amnesiac E.H. sometimes lapses into a light sleep in the midst of testing. (This phenomenon, a kind of narcolepsy, has been reported in other amnesiacs with whom *Project E.H.* has worked, whose amnesia is the result of strokes.) Margot supposes that E.H. may be insomniac. His sleep in the sleep lab isn't continuous or deep, so that he may not be getting a sufficient amount of REM sleep; she has no way of knowing. Since E.H. can't recall how well or how poorly he sleeps, as he can't recall any of his dreams, it is difficult to acquire any objective data about his sleep.

All that part of his life, away from the Institute—away from Margot Sharpe—is a mystery to her, dark like the farther side of the moon in a lunar eclipse.

E.H. appears both exhausted and agitated. He is too distracted to continue. Margot is sure that he hasn't ingested any liquids or food for some time, and is in danger of becoming dehydrated.

Margot brings E.H. a small container of apple juice which he takes from her with a polite, fleeting smile—"Thank you, Doctor."

Margot goes away, and takes notes in her log. She studies test results from the previous week. It is forty minutes before she resumes working with the subject, and is surprised to discover that E.H. is still restless and irascible, though he has no idea who she is. He smiles at her politely if warily, hand extended like a well-to-do landowner greeting a visitor to his property—"Well, hello! Hel-*lo*."

"Hello, Eli—Mr. Hoopes."

Margot can imagine Eli Hoopes, in different circumstances, welcoming her to the Hoopes estate at Lake George. She knows something of those old Adirondack properties—the log-cabin summer homes of multimillionaires—more resplendent even than the summer homes of the wealthy of the northern peninsula of Michigan.

"And you are—?"

"Margot Sharpe, Eli. We've met before, and we've done quite a bit of important work together. May we begin now?"

"What is my alternative?"—but E.H. speaks playfully, and not at all threateningly.

Margot takes care to begin with general, impersonal subjects that will cause him no distress, or so she hopes. A sequence of iconic photographs by Ansel Adams, Edward Weston, Imogen Cunningham, Cartier-Bresson—paintings by Monet, Goya, Picasso—woodcuts by Rockwell Kent. All of these E.H. identifies immediately though he hesitates over the woodcuts of Rockwell Kent—coincidentally, as Margot has not planned this, depictions of Adirondack scenes.

She has decided not to risk showing the drowned girl again. But she shows other sketches of E.H.'s—moonlit Lake George, mysteriously burning pine tree, two-passenger aircraft with one of its wings tilted to the ground looking small as a child's toy. Haltingly E.H. identifies these as Lake George scenes but doesn't seem to recognize them as artworks of his own.

"Damn you."

As Margot is about to replace the airplane with another image E.H. turns to her in sudden fury. The ordinarily gentle man grips her wrist and shakes her. And shakes her. He is glaring at her with such loathing, Margot is terrified that he will snap her wrist in his strong fingers.

"You—God damn you! What did you do with—'Eli Hoopes' . . ."

Margot tries to quiet E.H. They are alone together in the testing-lab and she is in dread of someone hearing his raised voice, and coming inside.

"Why, Eli—what is wrong?"

E.H. tells Margot that he has retained a lawyer—there are

many lawyers in the Hoopes family—and he is going to sue "you and this God-damned hospital for malpractice." They operated on his brain, he says, and inserted—something. "An electrode, a magnet—something! You damaged my brain, and now you're leading me around by what is damaged in me. *I am not an experimental animal to be so led.*"

It is an astonishing outburst. Margot is speechless.

But of course you are an experimental animal to be so led.

E.H. continues, in a fierce accusatory voice Margot has never heard before, "You! All of you! You flatter me as someone special when in truth I'm a freak. But I am not a freak whose sole purpose for existing is to advance your careers."

Margot tries to protest: Eli has misunderstood! It was a fever he'd suffered—encephalitis—he'd had emergency surgery at a hospital in Albany, to reduce swelling in his brain and save his life—but not neurosurgery. Medical intervention had saved his life, not injured him.

"Bullshit! I don't believe that. I want to see the medical reports. I want new doctors—I don't trust any of you. You have made me into"— E.H. looks coolly about for an object to express visually what he is trying to say, leans over to snatch a tangle of wadded tissues out of a trash basket—"like this. 'Throw-out.' "

Margot is so shocked, she can hardly reply.

So shocked, she feels tears gathering in her eyes.

And so—all along, the amnesiac subject has known? That he is irreparably damaged?

To look at E.H. in that instant is to look into the ruin of a human being. A human face, amid devastation. The spark of the individual who was once "Elihu Hoopes"—or might have been "Elihu Hoopes"—peers out at her, desolate.

Help me, please! Help me out of this if you have any human compassion.

Help me to die.

THE REMEDY IS simple: you walk away.

Quickly, but not so quickly as to seem as if you are fleeing, you walk away from the agitated amnesiac subject.

In a calm voice Margot calls for one of the nurse's aides who comes at a trot to oversee the agitated patient as Margot excuses herself and departs. No one on the nursing staff is ever surprised, still less astonished, by any outburst or aberrant behavior on the part of any patient; immediately the young woman speaks to E.H. in a voice of comfort, common sense, and constraint. But Margot has fled, Margot takes refuge in a women's lavatory on the floor.

"Not again. Never."

She has vowed: she will not show E.H. his charcoal sketch of the drowned girl in the stream, ever again.

After a discreet several minutes Margot returns to the lab, and sees through the plate-glass window that a much-calmer E.H. appears to be talking and laughing with the nurse's aide.

She brings the amnesiac subject a glass of orange juice. The sugar will revive him, for another several hours of tests; and he will be warmly disposed to Margot Sharpe, as to any attractive female figure who befriends him.

"Mr. Hoopes—Eli—hello!"

"Hello? Hel-*lo*."

MARGOT SHARPE HAS read all of the major literature on amnesia, brain damage, impaired and selective memory—of course. She has read such classics as Alexander Luria's *The Man with a Shattered World,* a painful quasi-memoir by a brain-damaged Russian veteran of World War I; she has read Luria's *The Mind of a Mnemonist,* the case study of a man whose memory seemed infinite who was also, in a different and more subtle way, mentally damaged. And of course she has read publications on memory and amnesia by Milton Ferris and his most distinguished former students.

One day—(not now, while she is still dependent upon her elders' judgment if she wishes to advance her career)—Margot hopes to compose a highly personal sort of prose piece modeled after Luria's "romance sciences," not purely, or exclusively, scientific, but speculative and even "poetic" as well: she will convert her journal into a more extensive exploration of E.H. than she is likely to know as a research scientist, by learning what she can of his private life; or, at least, of the emotional landmarks of E.H.'s private life.

She has written to a number of newspapers and publications in the Lake George area of the Adirondacks making inquiries about the death of a young girl in the 1930s and 1940s—"Possibly, someone associated with the Hoopes family of Philadelphia"—but with no results; either the publications have vanished, or whoever opens Margot Sharpe's letters feels no obligation to reply. She has spent hours trying to make phone contact with the Warren County Sheriff's Office and with other law enforcement officers in the area; she has called and written to the Warren County Courthouse Department of Records several times. Her telephone calls have been futile, her letters have gone mostly unanswered.

No substitute for driving to the Adirondacks one day—but the thought unaccountably fills her with loneliness and dread.

If Eli Hoopes could come with me! Just the two of us.

I WAS "BURNING up"—it was a fire that never went out but smoldered for days. The marrow of my bones melted, I could smell the odor like rancid milk.

I can smell it, still. I can feel the fire smoldering all around my body and inside my head. Trees were on fire. The way pine trees blaze. My grandfather's plane crash-landed, and burst into flame. That's why there are yellow barriers in the corridors here, to keep you from walking in the burnt places. That's why there is a stink of burnt things. But I am almost recovered now. My hair has grown back from where it was shaved. My parents are coming next week to take me home—I will be in "rehab" for a long time they say.

Gretchen was not found, I think. She is still in the woods at Lake George where I will look for her when I am able.

DISTURBING NEWS FOR Margot Sharpe.

She is being informed that news has come from Darven Park that their amnesiac subject has been "behaving uncharacteristically"—"at times, dangerously."

Margot Sharpe has news of her own. Private news, incendiary news, of which no one else knows. She is breathing quickly like one who has run up a steep flight of stairs. She is smiling inappropriately for she is scarcely listening to the alarmed voice of the departmental chair droning in her ears. She is thinking—*But what do I care for any of you, I am pregnant at last! I am pregnant with Elihu Hoopes's child.*

Her hand drops to her belly, which is still a flat hard belly that betrays no secrets. Her eyes lift innocently to the concerned eyes of the new departmental chair Hendrik Latta.

Latta, Mills. What has become of Mills? Margot had not liked or trusted Mills but she had known him and Margot does not know this Latta, younger than she. His field is social psychology for which neuroscientists have a (not-so-secret) contempt.

Professor Sharpe has been summoned to speak to this man. She has been summoned to come at a trot like a craven little dog but she has ignored the summons for several days. And now, she has come into the departmental office as if accidentally, to get the mail crammed into her box. "Oh hello! Did you want to speak with me?"—her voice is urgent and insincere. She is swathed in layers of black—black trousers, black silk shirt, black quilted jacket. No jewelry except on the third finger of her left hand a narrow silver ring that might be a wedding band which fits her finger loosely, and which she turns nervously.

Margot is frightened, but she is thrilled. Margot is numb with astonishment, but she is not surprised. Calmly Margot is thinking—*We will have our child. None of you can stop us. We will live somewhere in the country, in the Adirondacks perhaps. Where no one knows us, and no one will judge us. I will protect both the father and the child—I will protect them with my life.*

Through the din in her ears she hears Latta's voice. She must try to listen.

"Margot"—the inquisitive man is calling her "Margot" with a grating familiarity, as if he has the right—"we've heard disturbing reports from Darven Park. E.H. is becoming 'violent' at times—'uncontrollable.' He has lost his temper with aides and he has hurt you, he has bruised your wrists. Is this true?"

Quickly Margot tugs her cuffs over her wrists. Quickly Margot says scoffing, laughing—"No! This is not true."

The sound in her ears is so distracting, she isn't sure what she has said. She speaks again, louder: "I meant to say—no. It is *not true*."

Latta has invited Margot to sit down. But Margot will not sit down, to be trapped in the man's office. Gravely he says, "I've been hearing that your amnesiac E.H. isn't so cooperative as he used to be. That he has been having health problems . . ."

Margot wonders if her young lab colleagues have been spreading these rumors. She has been keeping them away from E.H. recently; she has been working with the subject herself. E.H.'s "moods" scarcely worry her—Margot knows that E.H. trusts *her.*

If it's the Institute staff that is spreading rumors about E.H., there is not much that Margot Sharpe can do. But if it's an individual or individuals in her lab, she can take measures.

"It's true, Eli has had respiratory infections this winter. He doesn't play tennis as impressively as he'd once done. And he isn't quite so childlike and cooperative as he'd once been. But he has aged, after all—he's sixty-five years old."

Sixty-five! Poor Eli.

In fact, E.H. has lately become sixty-six years old. But Margot can't bring herself to say *sixty-six.*

Margot dismisses rumors that E.H. is becoming temperamental or difficult. She points out that E.H. remains youthful, despite his age; he continues to dress with care, and to shave each morning; his enthusiasm for his old, favorite subjects—civil rights activism and the bigotry of most whites, Reverend Martin Luther King, Jr., economics and "game theory"—has not abated, nor has his ability to recite favorite poems, song lyrics, passages from speeches. He continues to record faithfully in his notebook and to sketch in his sketchbook—"E.H. is a remarkable artist. I think that over the years he has recaptured some of his original, lost talent." Margot speaks so persuasively, and so calmly, no one could guess how rapidly her heart is beating. Unconsciously she turns the ring around her finger.

Latta asks if E.H. shares his notebook and sketchbook with the memory lab and Margot says stiffly, as if this were a frankly stupid question she will nonetheless politely consider, "No. Not usually. But he will share them, sometimes, with *me*."

"And are you alone together often, with the subject?"

"No. Not 'often'—I don't think so."

"Someone is usually with you?"

"The Neuropsychology Department at the Institute is a very busy place, Hendrik!"—(There: she has called him *Hendrik*. It is a discreet concession Margot hopes will placate him).

But Hendrik Latta continues to regard Margot with a look of concern. "He hasn't hurt you, Margot?"

" 'Hurt me'? How?"

"Well—physically. By accident or—deliberately."

"Certainly not! Eli Hoopes is a gentleman."

"He hasn't threatened you?"

"How could Eli Hoopes threaten anyone? The poor man has virtually no conception of the future."

Margot laughs. Turning the ring around her finger.

It is a peculiar thing to have said, it is not very logical, but Margot isn't about to retract it.

"He hasn't"—(an awkward pause, as Latta considers how to phrase this query, what discreet words that will not alarm and inflame Margot Sharpe who is notoriously quick to take offense)—"in any way—suggested—behaved—touched you—sexually?"

"Absolutely not."

"I'm sorry, Margot. But I had to ask. I've been hearing . . ."

"Eli Hoopes is not a 'sexual' person—so we've observed. His brain damage seems to have precluded 'sexual' and 'emotional' attachments. And so, to answer all your questions, Hendrik—*no*."

Stiff-backed and unyielding Margot exits the office of the departmental chair without a backward glance.

WHAT DO YOU know, you fool you know nothing.

(Hides her wrists, in case her wrists are bruised. Hasn't examined her wrists and if she does, and finds bruises, she rubs *Arnica montana* oil into the skin. Once or twice he has squeezed her upper arm, and shaken her, in frustration at all that his poor broken brain cannot communicate, and bruises on that part of Margot's arms are hidden in any case for she never wears short sleeves.)

(She has vowed never to upset him again. It is cruel, though the results are significant, exciting.)

(She has vowed never to upset him again and yet—she must risk upsetting the subject, sometimes. There is no progress without such upsets, and such risks. One more time to show E.H. the charcoal sketch of the naked girl in the stream, and to ask him to identify her, and the setting.)

(For each time is the first time for the amnesiac subject. Each time is a unique time, and it is not repeatable. And for the research scientist each unique time substantiates the experiment in which meticulously recorded data is the ideal.)

PROFESSOR SHARPE WAS some kind of fanatic. I'd never worked with any scientist like her, and I'd gotten my Ph.D. at Harvard. She was totally devoted to her work—to recording E.H. "Unlocking the mysteries of memory"—she'd say. Virtually nothing could interrupt her, that we knew about—a call might come announcing that she'd won another award, or another grant—Margot would thank the caller politely, hang up and return to work. Sometimes she wouldn't even tell us what it was—we'd read about it later in the paper. She was the most modest—selfless—individual any of us had ever met, and not just in science. Everything that wasn't work was a distraction to her, and she demanded the same sort of devotion from her students and colleagues. That she was a woman in a man's field made no difference. She was as hard on her female associates as on her male associates. Possibly she made no distinction—she didn't notice. It wasn't always a pleasure to work with Margot Sharpe but it was a revelation, we've all been changed by her. I scarcely knew what it meant to be a scientist before I'd met Margot Sharpe and I think it's fair to say that I owe everything to her.

Yes, it's true—she was strangely attached to E.H.—as he was then called. Some observers said she was "morbidly" attached to him. But there was nothing more than professional interest, I'm sure. Margot Sharpe was totally professional, and made sure that everyone around her was as well. Poor Eli Hoopes was in his sixties living with an elderly aunt in a Philadelphia suburb at the time I began to work in Margot's lab—a driver brought him to the Institute most days. He had no idea what was going on—his surroundings were always a mystery to him, and he never recognized us from one hour to the next. Of course he never recognized Margot Sharpe—he called her "Doctor." He called me "Doctor"—he confused me with someone he'd known long ago in Philadelphia.

When the aunt died, there was some difficulty, and how Margot Sharpe resolved it, I'm not sure. I'd left the university by then, and established my own lab at Caltech. And all that I know, Margot Sharpe taught me. And Margot Sharpe would always say, all that she knew, she'd learned from Milton Ferris.

In generational terms, Ferris is my "grandfather." Margot Sharpe is my "mother"—the least maternal woman I've ever met.

SHE TELLS HIM—"I think that I am pregnant, Eli."

She tells him—"Eli darling, I think—I think that I am pregnant."

She tells him—"Dearest Eli, I hope you won't be upset, or shocked, but—I think—think that I am—might be . . ."

She tells him nothing. She cannot summon the words. Though they are alone together. Though E.H. is happy, and has been calling her his *dear wife.*

SHE IS NOT pregnant, of course. She has never been pregnant, and she will never become pregnant. Vaguely she thinks of herself as *in her late forties* but in fact she is fifty-three years old.

Fifty-three! It is so astonishing to her, who believes herself to be the Chaste Daughter still, that it is a fact rarely allowed into consciousness.

Also, Margot Sharpe is a very slender woman. Since adolescence she has been underweight, perhaps purposefully so; being underweight, she'd menstruated far less frequently than women of normal weight, for she has always instructed herself *To be female is to be weak, and to squander time. To be female is a second choice.* In which case, it wasn't likely that she could have become pregnant even years ago.

Still, Margot is distracted by thoughts of *being pregnant.*

Her breasts are small, and hard. Hardly the breasts of a pregnant woman. Yet, the nipples are "sensitive"—and in the early morning, waking in a wintry dawn to rain pelting against her window, and Eli Hoopes miles away and oblivious of her, she has frequently felt nauseated.

Margot knows of hysterical pregnancies of course. Margot knows of the delusions of the (semi)conscious mind. She knows of the extreme impressionability of human beings, how "hypnotizable" many individuals are. Her stomach is flat, in fact just slightly concave if she is lying on her back. Her pelvic bones feel to her distinct as (for instance) the wishbone on a Thanksgiving turkey carcass. And yet . . .

At last she makes an appointment with a gynecologist at the university medical school, to determine absolutely and unequivocally if she is/is not pregnant.

Dr. Liu is "her" gynecologist but Margot has not seen Dr. Liu in six years—an unconscionable amount of time, considering that Margot Sharpe is a scientist and should know better than to avoid physical examinations. Mammograms, Pap smears, cervical and rectal exams for cancer—how can a woman so intelligent be so negligent about her health!

"Pregnant? You are—inquiring?"

Dr. Liu scarcely hides her astonishment. For after all, Margot Sharpe is no longer of childbearing age—is she? (Dr. Liu knows without equivocation that her patient is fifty-three years old.) Margot feels her face heat in embarrassment, and defiance.

"Yes, Doctor. I—I need to know, today."

Dr. Liu performs a very simple test and the results are, as Margot has anticipated, *negative.*

But Dr. Liu is uncertain. Is this good news for Professor Sharpe, or is this not-good news for Professor Sharpe? Lying on the examination table with her slender legs spread, white tissue paper crinkling beneath her, Margot shuts her eyes to prevent tears leaking out onto her cheeks but tears leak out onto her cheeks nonetheless.

"You are not pregnant, Professor Sharpe. I hope that this is good news."

Not wanting to consider for a fleeting second any possible scenario in which this news might not be good news for her supine patient Dr. Liu goes on to say hurriedly that the results of the Pap smear will be received by her office on Monday, and if that test, too, is negative, Professor Sharpe will not receive a call—"Good news is no news."

Margot is scarcely listening. If Dr. Liu means to be amusing by scrambling the words of the cliché, Margot hasn't noticed. Her lips move numbly:

"Yes. Good news. Thank you, Doctor."

Her heart beats sharp with scorn. Like the brass pendulum in the exquisite old grandfather clock in Amber McPherson's gray stone house except this pendulum moves swiftly and cruelly.

Pregnant! What a joke you are, Professor.

DRINKS DOWN A shot. Her lanky spiky-haired companion drinks down a shot.

Nothing to say. So they don't speak.

Johnnie Walker Black Label Margot has kept on a high cupboard shelf of her small utilitarian kitchen slowly disappearing from the sticky-necked bottle, how many years. Her former lover brought the bottle to her originally, to drink with her. Her lover whose name is painful to acknowledge like a tiny sharp burr in the brain. *Can't think of him now, poor Milton who has had a stroke in Boca Raton where he has gone to die and his elderly wife will survive him after all.*

Naïvely once Margot imagined that—well, she'd imagined too much.

I am naming you executrix of my estate, dear Margot. I need you in my life.

But that never happened of course. So much of her life has never happened.

Another drink? Another drink.

Searing flame, going down. Delicious!

She is laughing, hiding her eyes. Badly wanting to tell her younger companion *Can you believe it, at my age imagining I might be pregnant. And the father an amnesiac who would not remember me let alone any child borne by us.*

Not the first time that "Hai-ku"—(as Margot Sharpe mispronounces the Korean name)—has brought the senior scientist home from her lab at the university working late and alone and dazed about the eyes as if drugged. He'd found her slumped on the floor in a corner of the fluorescent-lit room mistaking her for a pile of discarded clothes, or rags—Margot Sharpe, one of the most distinguished professors at the university!

Professor? Hey let me help you up.

OK—no need to call 911.

Probably, she'd forgotten to eat that day. Dehydrated, having forgotten to drink. Hai-ku supposes that Professor Sharpe is anorexic—has been anorexic much of her life—without being aware of her condition and if it were pointed out to her, by the most concerned of colleagues, she'd have angrily denied it.

As unaware of her condition, Hai-ku thinks, as the amnesiac subject E.H. is unaware of his.

Tonight is not the first night that Professor Sharpe has insisted that "Hai-ku" stay for a drink or two—or three—and whatever they can find to eat ravenously out of her refrigerator: plain low-fat yogurt, hard chunks of multigrain bread, discolored cheese rinds, bruised remains of a cantaloupe, covered bowls of stale rice, stuck-together pasta.

"Hai-ku" will remain with Margot Sharpe until he's reasonably certain that she is all right. Poor distraught woman won't accidentally or otherwise harm herself.

Hai-ku does not speculate what has upset the professor so much for it isn't in Hai-Ku's interests to know too much. He was aware—of course—of the professor's desperate attachment to Milton Ferris and knows that this ended long ago; he has been aware of the professor's desperate attachment to Elihu Hoopes and does not care to think how this must end sometime soon.

For sedative reasons. That alone is why Margot Sharpe drinks.

(Is this an open secret in the department? Margot Sharpe's solitary drinking? Hai-ku knows that everyone knows and yet no one would mention the fact to Hai-ku any more than Hai-ku who is Margot Sharpe's disciple would mention it to one of her colleagues.)

"Hai-ku" is no longer a young man. No longer a presence in the department, one of the promising young graduate students who'd come to the university to work with Milton Ferris.

Not the first time "Hai-ku" will remain with Margot Sharpe into the early hours of the morning.

Hai-ku will not remove his university hoodie worn over dirt-stiffened jeans, sweatshirt. Hai-ku will remove just Margot Sharpe's shoes, he will not dare to loosen her clothing, or to tug her messy sweat-dampened hair away from the nape of her neck, that her head might rest more comfortably against a gnarled-looking pillow.

The single, narrow braid trailing down the left side of Margot Sharpe's head. It has become a bizarre feature of the woman's appearance, inexplicable and beyond even caricature by her departmental associates.

Poor Margot Sharpe! Yet, why feel sorry for Margot Sharpe who has lived the life she has wished to live. So one would think.

Neither has spoken more than a few mumbled monosyllables to the other this evening.

Hai-ku has a boy's wizened face. He is shockingly old—(that is, Hai-ku is shocked)—forty-three. He is skinny with a ring of slack flesh around his waist. Shock-black hair spiky as a punk musician's, metal-rimmed glasses. Both his skin and his teeth are tea-colored. Milton Ferris's most trusted lab technician whom Margot Sharpe inherited grateful for the young Korean's knowledge and trustworthiness.

Another drink? No? But—why not?

Hai-ku tells the professor it is not a good idea, he thinks. This he tells the professor with gestures rather than words. Behind the metal-rimmed glasses, a fierce concerned gaze.

Everyone knows of brilliant young scientists-in-the-making who unaccountably fail to thrive. Fail to leave the department that has nurtured them. Failed to leave the home, the lab family.

Hai-ku the most reliable of lab techs has no instinct for ideas of his own. Leave him in a room with nothing, a notepad and pencil, at the end of the hour you will see that the notepad is still blank, the pencil unused if not untouched—so Milton Ferris complained of him, years before.

He'd begun an ambitious Ph.D. project in cognitive psychology in 1977, with Ferris. But years passed, and no dissertation emerged. The department would have dismissed him when Professor Ferris retired but Margot Sharpe cannily intervened and secured for the capable young man a succession of three-year contracts in effect making him her slave as he'd been Milton Ferris's slave for a decade, or more.

They will be a team, Margot Sharpe and Hai-ku, for a long time to come. Graduate students, postdocs, departmental colleagues will come and go in the now-famous "memory" lab but Hai-ku will remain faithful for Hai-ku has no life outside Professor Sharpe's lab.

As Margot Sharpe protects him, so he protects Margot Sharpe. No more willing slave than the senior tech of the neuropsychologist whose career he has helped advance, in a sense, from beneath.

The Ph.D. in cognitive psychology has long since been abandoned. Hope of a full-time job in psychology at a respected or even a second- or third-rate university has long since been abandoned.

(Is Hai-ku in love with Professor Sharpe?—some wonder.)

(Is Professor Sharpe in love with Hai-ku?—this is more doubtful.)

Hai-ku does not acknowledge that he is Margot Sharpe's "slave"—or anyone else's slave. Hai-ku is proud that his salary as a lab technician is the highest tech salary in the department, and that many of the professorial staff call upon him regularly for advice and assistance.

Hai-ku will be happy to serve as Margot Sharpe's assistant for as long as Margot Sharpe remains at the university, and Margot Sharpe is determined never to retire.

Hai-ku will never speak disrespectfully of his mistress. He will never speak of his mistress at all except admiringly, reverentially. And briefly.

In fact, Hai-ku rarely speaks. He has long learned to hide behind his "foreign-ness"—he has become a master of reticence.

Still, Hai-ku knows that, like Milton Ferris before her, Margot Sharpe could destroy him with a single telephone call to the departmental chair, a single stroke of a computer key. She is utterly dependent upon him until such time as she decides she doesn't need him, she will train someone else. Their understanding is that there is no (evident) understanding. Their bond is that there is no (evident) bond.

In the dim-lighted untidy bedroom heaped with books, journals, papers. In the narrow bed that looks as if it has not been changed in some time Margot Sharpe sobs and hiccups and lapses into an abrupt and dreamless sleep like a plug yanked from a wall socket.

At 2:10 A.M. of this very long day—(unknown to Hai-ku, this has been the day that Margot Sharpe learns without any qualification that *she is not pregnant*)—Hai-ku perceives that Margot Sharpe has dropped off to sleep at last. He removes the near-empty shot glass from her fingers, and sets it on the bedside table. He sees, without internal comment, that the inexpensive maple wood of the bedside table is stained with the pale rings of glasses and cups, like the pale rings of Jupiter.

It has been years—(since Milton Ferris, in fact)—since anyone but Hai-ku has seen the interior of the professor's two-storey brownstone on N. Reading Street, a half-mile from the Psychology Building. Years since anyone but Hai-ku has seen the interior of the professor's bedroom in which a single bed takes up most of the space.

On the walls are a half-dozen pencil and charcoal drawings on large sheets of stiff white paper. In the dimly lighted room the subjects of these drawings are obscured in shadow.

Hai-ku recognizes these drawings of course. But Hai-ku would never comment on them, still less ask Margot Sharpe what they are doing on the walls of her house.

"Professor? Excuse me . . ."

Hai-ku hesitates to take hold of the professor's limp chill hand to check the pulse at the thin wrist. He can see, and he can hear, the professor's damp rasping erratic breath. He sees the closed eyelids quiver.

In a matter-of-fact voice Hai-ku announces that he is leaving now—"I will say good night, Professor."

Hai-ku switches off lights in the rear of the house. In the kitchen Hai-ku puts the sticky-necked bottle of expensive whiskey away on a high shelf and carefully shuts the cupboard door.

Rinses glasses in the sink. Hai-ku is a very methodical person wishing that no fingerprints, no DNA samples should remain to incriminate him if something happens to Professor Sharpe in the night.

Hai-ku will leave the professor's house by stealth. Darkened windows, and the outside light above the door seems to have burnt out.

Hearing, as he prepares to shut and secure the door at 2:18 A.M., a faint but forceful voice lifting in the dark—"Hai-ku? Seven forty-five at the lab tomorrow—don't be late. The car will be here. We're due at Darven Park by eight-thirty."

CHAPTER NINE

The ritual. The knife. Why he grips the railing of the plank bridge. Why he must brace himself against the wind.

Recalling how rifles and shotguns are forbidden to children at Lake George, locked away in a cabinet. But there is another cabinet that is rarely locked—in this, knives are kept.

Hunting knives, fishing knives.

Waiting until the adults have gone to bed. Through the house the prevailing smell of woodsmoke, cigarette smoke.

Downstairs, a prevailing smell of whiskey.

The hunting knife is heavy in his hand. A child's hand, but an adult knife.

He raises it. Heavy sharp-bladed hunting knife.

Stabs and stabs and stabs at the figure on its back in the bed, drunk-dazed waking instantly, desperate to escape but tangled in bedclothes.

Hate you! You need to die.

No one knows but me how you need to die.

The father's face, contorted with horror, astonishment. Seeing that it is his own son who has come to him in the night, in stealth. His own son who must murder him.

In the small dank bedroom at the rear of the house behind the fireplace. Where Daddy sometimes slept, too drunk to make his way upstairs.

Bled to death, it will be determined. Dozens of stab wounds to the chest, neck. Belly, groin. Stabbing stabbing in an ecstasy of hatred.

No child of five could be suspected.

And afterward carefully washes the hunting knife. In the little bathroom beside the kitchen.

Heavy knife that belongs in the cabinet on a shelf with other knives carefully washed and dried and put away where he found it.

AGAIN, REPEATED: BAREFOOT and shivering descending the darkened stairs with childish care counting fifteen steps. As making his way upstairs he must count fifteen steps.

Opening the cabinet door—it isn't locked.

The knife he selects is not the largest or the heaviest knife. It is not a deer-gutting knife. It is not a fish-gutting knife. Yet, it is heavier than he expects, there is the worry it might slip through his fingers slick with blood.

No matter which of his father's knives he lifts it is heavier than he expects.

Barefoot and shivering through the darkened rooms. He is wearing flannel pajamas, the bottoms tug downward he's so skinny. Always a smell of woodsmoke in the house of logs.

The figure in the bedclothes is trapped, astonished. Too surprised to scream for help. Too deftly, rapidly stabbed to scream for help. The throat is stabbed, blood bubbles from the mouth and not screams. It is futile for the father to try to defend himself against the murderous son, his hands are slashed at once.

Sharp-bladed heavy knife lifted and brought down hard multiple times *stabbing stabbing stabbing.*

AND THEN, IN the morning nothing has changed.

The drunken man is not drunk now. The drunken man is Daddy, winking at him.

Today we're taking out the big canoe, Eli. Time you learned to paddle properly.

"MR. HOOPES?—ELI? Excuse me . . ."

Opens his eyes startled and wary. Very surprised to see that he isn't where he'd have believed he is but too canny to show it.

Young caramel-skinned girl, very black glossy hair in cornrows, beautiful eyes, beautiful body in dull-green smock, trousers. White nurse's shoes on her size-three feet. Tugging at his arm with laughter when he's slow to respond.

In a kind of terror he has been gripping the plank bridge railing. Heartbeat rapid and erratic though there seems to be nothing—no danger.

Not sure where he is but quickly realizes it isn't the lake. Not the Adirondacks.

He is disappointed. He is not frightened.

This is a wooded place, marshland. Wood chip trails, nothing that seems familiar. No hiking trail he knows. No white pines that he can see. A marshy soil, humid air. In the distance no mountains are visible.

"Mr. Hoopes?—we goin back now, OK?"

"Yes! Good."

"Don't want to be forgettin your nice drawings . . ."

"Yes, Eva. Thank you."

Smiling to disguise his confusion he has seen the girl's ID—EVA.

Exotic name. From the Caribbean he guesses.

She's a nurse, or a nurse's aide. He loves to hear her voice—doesn't matter what she says.

It is comforting, Eva is so short. Hardly five feet one or two.

Yet, her body is the body of a mature woman. Shapely hips, shapely breasts even in the dull-green loose-fitting uniform.

Nurse, or nurse's aide. Small-boned, short—but with well-developed muscles—shoulders, legs. Her shapely body at which he stares. And her smiling face, beautiful face, beautiful kindly eyes not judging him harshly.

What has he forgotten?—the sketchbook.

Quickly he snatches up the sketchbook. Of course, he must have been sketching—his fingers are smudged with charcoal. He will wait until he is somewhere alone before he examines the newest pages.

"That is good, Mr. Hoopes! Don't want to forget anything, OK?"

By Eva's manner he understands that she is someone who knows him well, and who likes him. Thus she is someone whom he knows well.

Gold and ruby studs in her perfect ears. Smooth skin, warm skin, beautiful line of the jaw, and beautiful mouth—a sweet fleshy mouth, accustomed to kisses.

On the third finger of her left hand, a thin silver band. Eva is married? Possibly, Eva is a young mother.

Feels a sense of loss so great, he almost stumbles.

"Eva help me, I am so terribly lonely . . ."

He laughs. Better to laugh than to sob.

"No reason to feel that way, Mr. Hoopes—you got all these folks interested in you, see? Some of them waitin in the testing-room, by the time we get there." Eva tells him how the doctors are paying more attention to him than anybody else she ever met or heard of, he should feel real good about that, and proud—"They been writin about you too, so you are 'famous.' They takin care of you real good."

Yet he is not walking so steadily this morning. Shooting pains in both legs but especially the right leg. Can it be *arthritis*?

Too young for damned *arthritis.* Only thirty-seven, in very fit condition. Just a few weeks ago he'd gone backpacking on the rock-strewn twelve-mile trail at White Cross Mountain, by himself.

Terror in being alone. He has not shrunk from such terror.

Islands of memory arise in his head jolted loose from the black muck below. Islands of light amid darkness. Lost in an open-eyed trance as the beautiful beguiling girl in the green uniform whose name he has (temporarily) forgotten leads him along a wood chip path in the direction of a place that appears to be known to her, familiar to her, thus must be known and familiar to him, and so he must not signal distress.

Calmly he thinks—*They will not abandon me. The family will come for me. They have forgiven me by now.*

The high-rise building is not entirely familiar but he is not surprised to be brought to the rear entrance, and to navigate the briskly revolving doors. Would be panicked if required to think but there is no thinking required as he turns toward the bank of elevators even as with a gentle nudge of her fingertips the nurse's aide leads him in that direction.

Upstairs, fourth floor. Again, he isn't surprised to exit the elevator when the door opens.

Strangers are awaiting him. Always there are smiling strangers, happy to see *him*.

It is true, he seems to be someone special. Exactly why, he isn't sure.

"Mr. Hoopes?—Eli? Hello!"

"Hel-*lo*."

Quickly he speaks. Quickly he smiles. Extends his hand to be shaken, and to vigorously shake.

These are doctors, he guesses. He is in a hospital of some kind—though he sees no hospital beds—though fortunately he isn't wearing a hospital uniform but rather his own clothes, and his shoes.

The doctors are greeting him warmly, he is known to them. As he greets them warmly in turn though he has no idea who the hell they are.

"Eli, hello! How are you?"

"Very good, thank you. How are *you*?"

In their eyes he sees himself reflected and he thinks—*They feel sorry for me.*

He thinks—*Maybe this is the afterlife. It would feel like this—the afterlife. No way to recognize it.*

Several smiling strangers of whom the evident eldest, and the one who has assumed authority, is a middle-aged woman with a striking white skin, intense eyes, urgent smile. She is not a beautiful woman and she is too old for him—in her late forties, at least—yet he finds himself strangely attracted to her. As she speaks in her soothing voice he is listening and yet not-listening. Hears her words even as he forgets them. Disconcerted by the proprietary air of a woman whom he has never seen before who stands slightly too close to him as if to provoke him to step away, and clasps his hand too tightly. He is disturbed that she calls him *Eli*—as if they are known to each other.

In his life there have been numerous women. Like water falling through his fingers when he was young and reckless.

Somehow, he'd failed to marry one of them. He had not loved enough. And where they'd loved him, he'd felt scorn for them and fled.

Fitting that Amber died of the same raging fever that almost killed him. At Lake George she'd died, he'd had to arrange for her body to be airlifted home to her family. He fears that like his cousin Gretchen she awaits him in the afterlife.

And other wraiths of the dead he has betrayed.

"MR. HOOPES? ELI . . ."

Strange how the white-skinned woman provokes in him a curious stir of longing, and yet of dread. A sex-yearning, that uncoils in his groin like a snake coming to life.

Usually it is (much) younger women to whom he feels attracted and this woman is certainly not young.

But her voice!—her voice is soothing, seductive.

Her voice is (he thinks) familiar . . .

And that single narrow tight-braided plait falling down the left side of her face redolent of—what? The Caribbean, the summer streets of South Philly?

As others listen intently (and respectfully) the white-skinned woman with the incongruously exotic braid addresses him. She is explaining—something technical, complicated. No point in listening, he won't remember anyway. At the same time, he finds himself (perversely) attracted to her.

"Mr. Hoopes?—Eli? Are you listening?"

"Yes, ma'am."

He is juvenile, defiant. He will have to run away and hide himself. *God damn you leave me alone*—wants to shove the woman from him, and flee.

But knows he must not succumb to this impulse, that would be an error.

Soul mate. Is that what this woman *is*?

But Eli Hoopes is too shrewd, too canny, too educated, too steeped in the devious, self-deluding ways of late capitalism to believe in anything so naïve as a *soul mate.*

Marxist principles. Nothing naïve or sentimental about killing your class enemies, dumping their bodies in a ravine. Erasing their histories, for the enemy deserves no history.

He is worried, too: with their brain-X-ray machines they will detect that he has had a stroke. The Alabama deputy sheriff's billy club must've cracked his skull, a hairline crack no one noticed at the time. And years later, at each hairline crack a "stroke" in the brain. There is nowhere to hide, trapped inside such a machine. Arms and legs strapped in place. A strap at his neck, to secure the neck.

They will shave his skull, and operate (again) on his brain. This time will be fatal. They will touch his very soul with their rubber-gloved fingers.

A soul is nerve-endings. When the nerve-endings fail to respond, the soul is no longer living.

The several strangers are being introduced to him as if he has not already met them and shaken their hands. Suffused with the sensation of—what is it: déjà vu. Not doctors presumably since they aren't wearing lab coats nor is the white-skinned woman with the sexy braid a doctor after all. Their chatter hurts his brain like shaken bits of glass.

"Probably you don't remember me, Eli—my name is 'Margot Sharpe.' "

"'Mar-*go*'—yes. How could I remember *you*."

God damn, he has misspoken. Corrects himself with an irritable chuckle: "'How could I not remember *you*.'"

Politely and gallantly he speaks. Despite the pain in his legs he is straight-backed. Though he finds the woman's manner grating he is nonetheless friendly to her—it is the old Hoopes diplomacy.

The woman who has identified herself as *Mar-go*—(whose last name he has forgotten)—expresses an interest in his charcoal drawings. He is flattered, but he is baffled—for how does *Mar-go* know that he has been sketching in his sketchbook unless she has been spying on him?

"Will you show us some of your drawings, Eli?"

He sees that yes, he has his sketchbook with him, secured under his arm. But he is reluctant to open the book to the prying eyes of strangers.

They are waiting for him to misstep, he thinks. All these years they have been seeking the murderer of his cousin Gretchen, and the murderer's identity is hidden in the charcoal sketches.

"No. I don't think so. My work isn't good enough for anyone's eyes except my own."

"But that isn't true! Your drawings—and your photographs—are excellent. Your work has been exhibited in the Philadelphia Museum of Art, Eli. That's how good it is."

This is true. This he recalls, with surprise.

How strange, the white-skinned woman knows about his single photography exhibit in the museum. He wonders if this means that she knows many other things about him, too.

It is easier often to kill than to dissuade. But it would not be easy to get the woman alone, and to squeeze her white-skinned throat between his fingers.

"Eli? Mr. Hoopes? We would like very much to see some of

your drawings. I've seen a few of them in the past, and they are so very well . . ."

Felt that way about white racists. Often it was said of white racists in the Movement.

Easier to kill than to dissuade.

He'd had his chances to kill the enemy over the years. As a boy, he'd failed ignominiously. Too weak to kill his father though the drunk man had been sleeping flat on his back. Too weak to kill the bishop's grandson. Jeering white racists, faces ugly with hatred. As an undergraduate at Amherst he'd read of the revolt of Nat Turner and he'd felt a swoon in his soul, the exhilaration of slashing the throats of slave owners but also white women, white children. White-skinned children, screaming as they were murdered by the blades of righteousness.

"Eli? May I?"

The smiling woman has made a gesture as if to take the sketchbook from his hands.

But he is too quick for her. Grips the sketchbook tight and refuses to surrender it. Sees the startled expression in her face.

She is the one who knows who drowned Gretchen. All these years she has been hunting you, waiting for you to misstep.

"No, Doctor. Don't touch! This is private property."

Seeing the expressions on their faces he has to laugh. As a dog might laugh, baring wet teeth and panting.

Taking out his little notebook instead, to confuse and entertain. In a grave voice intoning:

" 'There is no journey, and there is no path. There is no wisdom, there is emptiness. There is no emptiness.' " Pausing then to add, "This is the wisdom of the Buddha. But there is no wisdom, and there is no Buddha."

DEAR HUSBAND THERE was the hope that I would be—pregnant.

But I'm afraid now, dear Eli—that has turned out to be a mistake.

Yes, we were so happy! We were married, and living in—Rittenhouse Square.

Oh but Eli, don't look so sad! We will be happy again! I promise.

When the tests are finished we will move away—to the Adirondacks. We will live in your beautiful family home at Lake George.

I will drive you there to live with me. I will love you and take care of you all the days of your life—our life. I vow.

"MR. HOOPES? ELI? Hello . . ."

She observes him from the doorway. She is determined not to be upset. Jealousy the most shameful of emotions. Sexual jealousy, unspeakable.

Eva, the nurse's aide. Very pretty, petite. Self-assured for a mere nurse's aide in dull-green smock and trousers.

Well, yes—*very* pretty. Her eyes are outlined in black mascara, her lips are moistly pink, her pert little body beautifully shaped though small, her legs oddly short. From a distance, Eva might be twelve years old. Closer up, she could not be mistaken for any twelve-year-old.

Before Eva there was Yolanda, the caramel-skinned beauty from the Caribbean whom he has totally forgotten. Now there is Eva, another caramel-skinned beauty from the Caribbean.

Of course at the Institute there are always nurses, nurse's aides, attendants. These are likely to be young, good-natured, flirtatious and many of them are dark-skinned, yes and very attractive.

"Absurd. You can't be jealous. *Just stop.*"

Margot Sharpe slits her eyes at her reflection in a restroom mirror: why is her skin so *white*? And now in her hair that has always been shiny-black there are ever-widening cracks of silver, gray, even *white.*

Strange that she, who'd so often been the youngest person to give a paper at a scientific gathering, the youngest full professor in the Psychology Department, the youngest award recipient, is no longer *young* but *middle-aged;* no longer promising but *accomplished;* no longer envied but *revered.*

In her smooth white skin, tiny lines, hairline fractures. You can only see close-up.

Still, she is an attractive woman. Not a beauty when young, she has acquired a solemn sort of dignity, even an air of hauteur in middle age. She prepares her hair carefully, with the signature little braid trailing down the left side of her face; she dresses in her signature black clothes, and sometimes now shiny black shoes with a small heel, to provide height. She wears silk scarves and shawls that her dear friend E.H. has given her—(that she imagines E.H. would certainly have given her if he could). She is sure that, when E.H. sees her, and is not distracted by the presence of a shapely young woman like Eva, he feels for her something more than a perfunctory emotion.

"He loves me. He loves his 'wife.' That doesn't change."

It isn't unlike an ordinary marriage, Margot supposes. A middle-aged marriage.

Not a surprise that E.H. forgets Margot Sharpe if his attention shifts from her for more than a few minutes but it is hurtful to her, the alacrity with which he "neglects" her when Eva is present.

Eva, with her musical Caribbean accent. Eva of the beautiful thick-lashed eyes, shapely little body and springy step. Eva who is very young, and looks younger.

It is hurtful. It is embarrassing. When Margot Sharpe is speaking to E.H., and should have E.H.'s fullest attention, how easily

E.H. is distracted by figures in the background; how openly distracted by the nurse's aide Eva, his gaze shifting in her direction, that soft-melting look in the man's eyes until at last he simply ignores Margot Sharpe, turns away from Margot Sharpe in a pretense of having forgotten her, and calls out—"Hel-*lo!* Is this—'Eva'?" Peering at the laminated ID on the girl's breast.

Margot Sharpe thinks—*If we were married! How embarrassing.*

But they are not married, and between Margot Sharpe and Eli Hoopes, so far as anyone at the Institute knows, or should know, there is only the professional connection: she is principal investigator of *Project E.H.*, and he is *E.H.* Nothing could be simpler.

Margot is too embarrassed to joke about her amnesiac subject's wandering attention, though others have surely noticed. And it is hardly uncommon that older patients are attracted to the young women who tend to them—*No fool like an old fool.*

Doesn't he know, he is old enough to be that girl's grandfather!

Margot means to be reasonable. She isn't a mean person. She will not speak sharply to the nurse's aide but (perhaps) she will complain to the young woman's supervisor, and see if Eva can be shifted to another floor at the Institute. Yes, certainly Margot will arrange for this.

"You see, the girl is a serious distraction. She flirts with our subject—she can't seem to help herself. She's very young, and very charming—and our subject is in his sixties, and vulnerable. You really must transfer her. Thank you!"—so Margot rehearses.

For she is helpless to control E.H.'s attention when she is herself not his sole focus of attention. Only when they are alone together can Margot claim the man's total attention.

Indeed, Margot Sharpe has written on the phenomenon of "attention" in amnesia—"Multiple Memory Systems, Visual Perception, and 'Attention' in Retrograde and Anterograde Amnesia" is the title of a forthcoming article in the *Journal of Experimental Psychology,* that will be included in the appendix of *The Biology of Memory.*

Margot does not display her extreme unease, of course. Not in any public way. Margot knows how people will talk. As she has become something of a revered and even intimidating figure, Margot knows that people will talk about *her.*

She understands that the amnesiac subject, now in his mid-sixties but imagining himself thirty-seven, does not perceive the awkwardness of his behavior—how the look of *avid yearning* in his face betrays him even as he tries to smile, to banter and to laugh exchanging remarks with the girl as if their interest in each other is reciprocal.

Margot recalls how years earlier she herself had been the distraction, and Milton Ferris had been ignored. How E.H. had been attracted to *her,* clasping her hand, sniffing her hair!

Those years. She'd been the Chaste Daughter, so young.

He can't love me—can he? I am too old for him now.

She will take E.H. on a walk that afternoon. *She,* and no one else.

She will drive E.H. home to Gladwyne at the end of the day. *She,* and no one else.

By which time, Eva will be forgotten. And since Eva will be shifted to another floor at the Institute, Eva will be totally forgotten.

At last, it is time for the nurse's aide to leave. Backing away from E.H. with a cheerful murmur *'Bye now, Mr. Hoopes! You have a good day y'hear?*—as E.H. gazes with undisguised longing after her.

All this while—(though it has been less than two minutes, probably)—Margot has been waiting patiently, calmly.

Only when the girl is gone does E.H. turn back to Margot Sharpe with his usual expression of surprise and interest, and a quick winning smile. Not sure who she is, exactly—but reasonably sure that she is someone more important than a mere nurse's aide.

"Hel-*lo!*"

"CAN THERE BE a person without a shadow? Without a memory is like being without a shadow.

"I am that person. I think."

Cautiously he speaks aloud. His own voice has become strange to him, in his own ears.

So trusting! Like any husband long habituated to a wifely presence.

As in a dream there is *presence* but often not a *person*.

(Margot has wanted to explore that curious mental phenomenon in dreams—why, when we dream of someone or something familiar, the visual image frequently isn't accurate; though encoded in our brain cells, these memories aren't precisely transmitted. Where "is" the dream, in relation to such memories? "Where Do Dreams Reside?"—is her projected title.)

And so, when Margot drives E.H. home from the Institute, at the end of a day of testing, the amnesiac subject takes for granted that she is his "driver"—also, in some way, his "wife."

Though he can't remember "Margot Sharpe" yet by degrees over the years E.H. has become habituated to her aura, or her fragrance, which is always the same lilac-cologne. He will say "Are you my dear wife?" in a tender though uncertain voice, and Margot will reassure him, "Yes, Eli. Of course."

So long as Margot remains within E.H.'s field of consciousness, he will not forget her. Her name, perhaps—but not *her.*

Based upon tests with E.H., Margot Sharpe has written on the distinction between "(anterograde) recollection" and "familiarity"—a crucial distinction, though for the average observer it is a very subtle one. For the amnesiac to survive with his sanity intact, he must create a web of associations that, lacking specificity, are at least *familiar,* therefore comforting.

And so when they are driving together if Margot feels the need to exit the interstate, to leave E.H.'s presence for a few minutes (to use a restroom for instance) when she returns she will stroke E.H.'s arm in a way to suggest *familiarity.* Through his pre-amnesiac life, and particularly in his childhood, such touching would likely have been common, thus *familiar.* And quickly she will say to him, as a way of identifying herself, "Eli, dear! Darling! How is my sweet husband?"

Scarcely missing a beat E.H. will say, "Very good! And how is my sweet wife?"

It is touching. You could say, it is tragic.

How the amnesiac will learn to disguise amnesia so that (Margot thinks shrewdly) it isn't always evident that the amnesiac understands what he is doing by instinct.

E.H.'s happiness is Margot's (secret) happiness. Margot has no happiness that is not bound up (secretly) with his.

By having studied E.H.'s yearbooks of decades ago—Gladwyne Day School, Gladwyne Prep, Amherst College—shrewd Margot Sharpe is able to construct conversations with E.H. about "mutual" classmates at these schools. She will say, "Do you ever hear from—?" giving the name of a classmate or teammate of Eli Hoopes, of long ago.

And E.H. will speak with much pleasure about this person, vividly recalling him or her. So convincing is Margot in these exchanges in which E.H. does most of the talking it is easy for her to forget that her recollection is *totally invented.* That's to say, *a lie.*

Yet it's easy for Margot, a day or two later, a month later, to pick up the conversation with E.H. who is likely to say the same things again, with the same feeling, which Margot can now anticipate. ("Remember how surprised we all were, when Claude Gervais never came back from Christmas break?"—"Scottie was such a good friend of all of us, it's so strange that we never heard from her after graduation"—"Professor Edwards was so brilliant—but so sarcastic . . .") In these *faux*-recollections, Margot Sharpe presents herself as a friendly acquaintance of Eli Hoopes, not a close friend, or a girlfriend; a friend of Eli's friends, whom she names with unfailing accuracy.

In Gladwyne yearbooks, available in the school library, Margot has sought out Eli Hoopes's earliest classmates. She has contemplated photographs of Eli as a boy—surprisingly, not a very handsome boy, but recognizably Eli Hoopes. Until the age of ten or eleven Eli was a "small" boy; soon after he grew to become one of the taller boys in his class. Even when his skin was blemished, young Eli exuded a brash sort of confidence. He was a very good student, clearly—always on the honor roll; and he was an athlete—lacrosse, swim, tennis, track teams. Class vice president, class president.

English Club, Latin Club, Math Club, History Club, Drama Club, Choristers, "Hi-Lo." Margot is surprised and impressed by the block of small print listing Eli Hoopes's activities beneath his yearbook photos, so much larger than those of most of his classmates.

Also in the yearbooks she has located "Margaret Madden"—"Margie Madden"—who was in Eli Hoopes's class. A slight girl, not pretty, with dark, slanted eyes and hair severely parted on the left side of her head, and a small wistful mouth—*Yes I know that I am plain but I am very special so love me please! Love me.*

It is so, Margot discovers: this girl does resemble her, if one looks closely. The slanted eyes, and also faint shadows beneath the eyes; the set of the mouth; small nose, narrow chin. The smart girl, the watchful girl. However different the adult Margot Sharpe and the child Margaret Madden might appear to the ordinary gaze, to a sharp eye like Eli Hoopes's there is something essential about their faces that links them like sisters.

Face recognition is a marvel of the human brain, only partly understood. There is a region in the brain that "remembers" faces instantaneously; there are said to be "face cells" specialized for each face known to an individual, a concept Margot finds difficult to comprehend though neuroscience colleagues in her department have tried to explain the phenomenon to her.

Obviously, "face cells" in the amnesiac's brain are no longer forming. Memories are no longer consolidating. But "face cells" pertaining to faces seen long ago are still active.

Margot is pleased to see that, shy-seeming and diminutive as she was, Margaret Madden was nearly as active as Eli Hoopes: English Club, Latin Club, History Club, Girls' Choir, "Hi-Lo." Yet more surprising, little Margaret Madden was on the girls' volleyball team.

Margot smiles. She is proud of her lookalike sister of the late 1930s.

"Eli, do you ever hear about 'Margie Madden'? You remember—we went to school with her at Gladwyne."

Eli laughs as if Margot has said something very witty. Then, a cloud comes into his face. Warily he asks,

"You are Margie Madden—is that it?"

Margot shakes her head *no,* certainly she is not Margie Madden.

She laughs, protesting. Eli regards her doubtfully.

"Yes, I think that I resemble her—I mean, we used to resemble each other. We were often mistaken at school, especially by some of our teachers. But my name is 'Margot Sharpe.' "

" 'Mar-got Sharpe.' Yes."

But Eli continues to look doubtfully at Margot, as if undecided whether he should speak further. It is unusual for Eli to be so silent, when the subject is his school past.

"Eli, is something wrong? Why are you looking at me like that?"

Margot speaks gaily, for her heart is beating rapidly. *He knows—this is all a masquerade. He knows everything.*

But Eli only strokes Margot's arm, and squeezes her fingers. She clasps his hand in response, tightly.

No. He is my dear husband, he doubts nothing. He loves me.

"Well, 'Mar-go'—I'm trying to calculate how Margie Madden, who would be approximately thirty-seven years old, could be a classmate of yours at Gladwyne Day. You're a beautiful woman, my dear wife, but you are not—obviously—thirty-seven years old any longer." Seeing the look of hurt in Margot's face, Eli lifts her hand to kiss it playfully, yet urgently.

"Don't worry, dear wife—I love you just the same. Even if you are *not her.*"

THERE IS A carpet, or a strip of something, that I am walking on . . . and it is being rolled up behind me. So that there is only the strip I am walking on, and nothing in front of me or behind me. Sometimes, I am so very tired—but there is no place to rest.

LIKE A MARRIED couple, they lapse into bickering.

Almost, there is pleasure in such bickering. There is familiarity.

Securing an uncooperative husband into the passenger seat of her car. Always it is a challenge for Margot, for it is always new to her husband.

Laughing she pleads, "Eli, please! Don't be ridiculous, we do this every time we drive," and Eli says, "God damn, nobody needs a 'seat belt' for a car. In an airplane, yes. Not a car," and Margot says, "Well, there are new laws in Pennsylvania now. There are state laws all citizens have to obey."

Eli says, snorting in derision, "If you want to 'belt' yourself in, go ahead. But not me."

"Eli, please! Will you let me buckle this, as a favor to me?"

"No."

"You're smart enough, Eli, to figure this out: if the car is equipped with seat belts, they are meant to be used. And if they are meant to be used, it's a good idea to use them."

"Really! What sort of illogic is that?"

"But a seat belt is a safety feature, Eli. You must know that."

"Why must I 'know' that? If we have an accident, how will I escape? I'll be trapped in a flaming car."

"Well, the idea is—you are prevented from being thrown through the windshield."

"The idea is, I will be immolated in my 'seat belt.' In a flaming holocaust."

Eventually, Eli relents. It is a husbandly gesture, gallant and exasperated, to humor a foolishly worried wife.

AND THEN, SOMETIMES he is furious with her. Out of nowhere like a match recklessly struck, his anger flares.

This evening at dusk on the interstate headed for the Gladwyne exit and Eli has been telling Margot about how his camera was taken from him and smashed by a "rabid" sheriff's deputy in Birmingham, Alabama—a story Margot has heard many times before, and is fascinated to hear again, noting not so much similarities in the recollections but small, subtle divergences which only Margot Sharpe could detect—when abruptly Eli wonders where his camera is; and Margot assures him, his camera is "back home"—"Eli, all your things are back home where you left them. Safe 'back home.' "

Margot has found that the words *back home* are a comfort to the amnesiac. Though the amnesiac's conception of *back home* may be insubstantial as a dream.

And stroking the amnesiac's arm, and hand—that often helps.

Margot has become E.H.'s nurse. Badly wanting to be for him what Yolanda and Eva had been—a source of female solace, with all the sexual accommodation that it implies.

But Eli is impatient tonight, and throws off the nurse's hand. Eli is in a sudden fury demanding to know where his sketchbook is—his camera is gone, and now his sketchbook—where is it?

He tries to twist around in his seat, but the seat belt secures him. He is fussing, cursing, panting—Margot, at the wheel, tries to calm him—she will stop the car, she says, and find the sketchbook which (she is sure) is in the backseat as it usually is, with other items; but Eli continues to be excited and upset and she sees in his gaunt face, in the fleeting light of oncoming headlights, a look of such loathing for her, she almost loses control of the car. "Eli, please! I'm sure that your sketchbook is just behind you . . ."

Margot brakes the car to a stop on the shoulder of the interstate as traffic rushes by. Still cursing, Eli manages to unbuckle his seat belt and turn around furiously in his seat, groping for the sketchbook—which is propped up against the back of his seat as usual on such drives to Gladwyne.

But Eli isn't mollified by finding the sketchbook which he leafs through suspiciously, concerned that some of the pages have been torn out. Margot assures him that no one has interfered with his sketchbook—she allows no one at the Institute to touch it—but Eli is sure that drawings are missing, his work has been "sabotaged."

Margot offers to look through the sketchbook with Eli, to see that nothing has been touched, but Eli shoves her away in a fury. And then, before she can protect herself, in a paroxysm of rage he strikes her with his fists and closes his fingers around her throat as he berates her—"You! God damn you! I don't know you! I don't trust you! Who the hell are you—'Doctor'!"

Margot claws at Eli's fingers, but his fingers are too strong for her, and too frenzied. Fortunately the attack is over within seconds.

So swiftly over, Margot can tell herself, dazed—*This is not happening. This did not happen.*

It was fleeting, and not deliberate—a kind of accident, not to be recorded in Margot Sharpe's *Notes on Amnesia: Project E.H.*

Not a personal attack, in any case. A flailing-out, as a drowning man may flail out against his very rescuer. And Margot did not lose consciousness, not even for an instant. She is sure.

When Margot recovers, she is alone in the car. She is gasping for breath, wincing with pain. Her vision is blotched—(is there blood in her eyes?). A man's strong, phantom fingers are still closed on her throat, pitiless.

For some minutes Margot is too dazed to comprehend what has happened, and where she is.

On a shoulder of the interstate? Alone in her car? Traffic rushing by, as in a nightmare avalanche?

In the twilit sky at the horizon, the sun resembles a great broken yolk bleeding into a bank of clouds massed and gnarled as brains.

She is on the interstate south, to Gladwyne. She remembers.

"Eli? Oh God, Eli—where are you?"

She finds him fifty feet away, staggering at the edge of the highway like a drunken man, as if hoping to flee the car. Margot dares to touch his arm and he turns to her in a panicked crouch, eyes affrighted and glaring in oncoming headlights like the eyes of a wild beast.

He is panting, he is whimpering. Rude gusts of wind from passing vehicles fling dust and bits of dried leaves into his face.

He has no idea where he is. He is utterly, utterly lost.

He is mine.

Though Margot is badly shaken herself she knows that she must exert control. She must prevent the amnesiac from running from her—throwing himself into traffic, for instance. She soothes him with her voice, stroking and calming his agitated hands. Gently she calls him "Eli"—"My dear husband, Eli"—until at last the amnesiac is calmed, or in any case subdued, fatigued suddenly, but managing a faint, hopeful smile—"Hel-*lo,* my dear wife."

So long they have floated in the present tense. So long each has floated without a shadow.

Yet now one evening in October 1994 Margot is listening in astonishment as, seemingly for no reason, in the drawing room at 466 Parkside, Gladwyne, elderly Mrs. Lucinda Mateson begins to speak in a halting voice of the drowned girl in the Adirondack stream.

" . . . a terrible thing. Just—terrible . . . She was my niece—my brother Edgar's daughter Gretchen—eleven years old that summer . . . She'd been watching some of the younger children including Eli and his brothers and evidently 'someone came by'—and next thing anyone knew, Gretchen was gone. And none of the children ever saw her again."

Margot sits very still, not sure what she is hearing. She and Mrs. Mateson are seated together in the drawing room smelling of lilies while upstairs, in another part of the stately old house Margot has never seen, Eli Hoopes has hidden away and has forgotten them.

Margot has brought lilies, an armful of lilies, for Mrs. Mateson who is her friend. And Mrs. Mateson has served Margot Earl Grey tea as she always does on these occasions, and a scattering of cookies on a silver platter.

How sweetly overpowering, the scent of lilies! It is almost too much, Margot thinks. She feels drunk—drunken.

And Mrs. Mateson's eyes blur with tears as she confides in Margot, in a husky, lowered voice, of a family tragedy that happened more than six decades before.

"Our lives were darkened by it—'enshadowed.' It would turn out that my beautiful little niece had been talked into going into the woods with an older boy—also from Philadelphia, whose family had a place at Lake George, and who were friends of the Hoopeses. This boy—'Axel'—'Axel McElroy'—was seventeen, tall and very thin, stoop-shouldered, troubled, difficult—he liked to play with much younger children and he had a history of harassing them, especially girls. It was said in the papers that Axel was the grandson of Bishop McElroy—(you wouldn't know that name, probably, but the McElroys were prominent Philadelphians at the time)—but in fact he was the adopted son of a niece of the bishop's—there was no close connection at all. You know what the newspapers are like, and today TV is worse—making scandal out of what they can, if prominent families are involved. The bishop—an Anglican bishop—was just devastated by this tragedy, and retired soon afterward . . .

"Most of our family was at Lake George at the time, just after

Fourth of July of 1929. Eli was five years old. It was believed that he was the last person to see Gretchen, before she went away with Axel. He insisted he hadn't seen Gretchen all day though she'd been watching over him and his brothers—Gretchen and another older girl. Eli was very upset saying he hadn't seen her but later he said he saw her in a canoe 'going across the lake.' But Axel didn't take Gretchen across the lake . . . There was a search for Gretchen immediately. Everyone was mobilized except the youngest children. My father—Eli's grandfather—insisted upon flying his little prop plane over the lake, and over the islands in the lake, looking for Gretchen. He was a very strong-willed man. He took Eli with him in the plane at least once. My brother and his wife—Eli's parents—didn't want him to go with my father, but somehow—my father took him . . . Something went wrong and he had to crash-land on one of the islands. I think my grandfather and Eli were out all night. Along with the anxiety about Gretchen, and the search for her, this was too much! It was a nightmare time and how many hours it lasted, I don't know.

"Gretchen's body was found in the woods, in a stream, about two miles from the lake. She had been strangled and her head struck against rocks and then she'd been dragged to the shallow stream. There was blood on some rocks, which was where she'd died. He'd done things to her—to her body—that terrible boy, Axel. He'd done cruel things, we were never exactly told. At least, I was never told. Maybe some in the family knew. Men might've known. But women and girls weren't told, and we did not want to know.

"The boy Axel had been behaving very strangely during the search. He'd hidden away in his family's house on the lake and no one knew where he was. When they found him he was immediately arrested. There was blood beneath his fingernails and his arms and face were scratched. He *was not* the bishop's grandson, but everyone seemed to want to think that he was. As if it was a worse thing, that a grandson of an Anglican bishop had done such a thing to Gretchen, than someone else. Axel never exactly confessed—he insisted that he 'couldn't remember' anything that had happened and that Gretchen had been the one to take him into the woods to look for a 'baby fawn.' Later, he contradicted himself, and still later, he told another story. At one point he said that it was Gretchen who was 'kicking and clawing' at him and he'd had to 'hurt' her to make her stop.

"Among those who knew the McElroys it was said that the death of Gretchen Hoopes was the parents' fault—they should not have allowed this mentally disturbed boy to come into our midst, to mingle with young children. There were many terrible recriminations and accusations—for a long time. For decades.

"The younger children were never told what had happened to Gretchen. There were not adequate words to explain such a terrible thing to children, at that time. Or any other time. For dear God, what do you *say*.

"Eli had nightmares for years. He never talked about his cousin, or asked about her. His parents worried that he might have some kind of epileptic condition. He had spasms, convulsions. But when he was tested, he seemed to be normal. He often behaved 'normally'—he was a popular boy in grade school. But one day he 'confessed' to his brother Averill that *he was the one who'd hurt Gretchen,* and Averill told their parents. They asked Averill why on earth would Eli say such a thing when it wasn't true, could not be true, and Averill said that Eli often said 'crazy things' that weren't true, or were true in some way that was all twisted. Averill said that Eli told him 'I was the one who hurt Gretchen but nobody knows, and they haven't punished me'—and that he'd started laughing . . .

"By this time Axel McElroy was in a youth facility, a psychiatric hospital for the 'criminally insane' in upstate New York.

"As for my nephew Eli—he has seemed to be a 'normal' person much of the time. He made himself into quite a popular boy at school. He made himself into an athlete. He was afraid of water as a little boy yet he forced himself to learn to swim well, and to dive, and he became a canoeist at Lake George. At the same time, he was a moody boy at home, with his family. When his parents confronted him with what he'd said about 'hurting' Gretchen, he denied he'd ever said anything like that. It upset him terribly to hear Gretchen's name. Of course, we rarely spoke her name—'Gretchen' was not a name any of us spoke. It was all too painful, and too awful. Even now, sixty years later, I wouldn't dare speak of Eli's cousin to him. You probably have no idea, at the Institute, where Eli is on his good behavior and everybody makes a fuss over him, how quick-tempered he can be, how easily upset and agitated. Some of us thought that Eli enrolling in the seminary and participating in civil rights protests was some way of his of doing 'penance' for Gretchen—not that he had any reason to do 'penance' of course, but that he might have thought he had. Because he was the last person to have seen the girl alive, except for—well, except for her murderer . . .

"And so in a way, it might be just as well for Eli to be living as he does—with no memory, and nothing to make him unhappy."

"But, Mrs. Mateson," Margot protests, "Eli does remember the past, of course. It's the present he can't remember—you must know that."

Upstairs, Eli is watching TV news. The volume is high and sounds like distant quarreling. Eli's hearing has deteriorated but he refuses to wear a hearing aid for, as he says disdainfully, thirty-seven is too young for any damn hearing aid.

"Sometimes I think my nephew remembers what he wants to remember," Mrs. Mateson says obstinately. "As he sees and hears what he wants to."

Margot wants to protest. This is such a foolish, cruel thing to say of a brain-damaged man! Yet typical of the uninformed, to blame the afflicted.

While Mrs. Mateson continues to speak of the drowned girl of sixty years ago Margot thinks of Eli Hoopes's obsessive drawings of the girl. It isn't true, as Mrs. Mateson has said so carelessly, that Eli isn't haunted by the past; precisely because he has no present, and no future, he is the more haunted by the past.

Margot asks Mrs. Mateson if "Axel McElroy" is still alive, and Mrs. Mateson says, with a fastidious shiver, "How would I know? I should *hope not.*"

So many years, probably not. Yes, Margot is sure—probably not.

Margot has told Mrs. Mateson that her nephew has depicted a "drowned girl" countless times in his drawings, but Mrs. Mateson has never commented on this phenomenon before, and so Margot had supposed she'd had nothing to say about it. Yet, tonight, for no evident reason, she'd begun to speak in her slow, halting voice, with an expression on her face of distress.

Bringing Eli home from the Institute, as she does frequently now, Margot is always greeted courteously by Lucinda Mateson, if not warmly; though many years have passed, and Mrs. Mateson certainly trusts Margot Sharpe more than she did initially, it isn't clear if Mrs. Mateson understands what Margot's relationship is to her nephew, or that she feels for her anything more than courtesy. It is part of the ritual of their teatimes that Margot gives Mrs. Mateson a "progress report" on Eli Hoopes, but this is a report that rarely varies: "Eli is doing very well, Mrs. Mateson! He's very popular at the Institute, there is no one quite like him there."

Margot has never told Mrs. Mateson about Eli's lapses in behavior. She has never told anyone, and she never will. No more than a loyal wife would speak of her husband's irrational behavior toward her, so long as it is fleeting, and not significant. For always Margot consoles herself—*He loves me. He has no one but me.*

The previous week, when Eli lost control in Margot's car on the interstate, had been an extreme episode. The assault—the closing of Eli's fingers around her neck, his shouting at her—the fury and despair in his face—had been an aberration. An accidental sort of assault that would not likely happen again.

Eli had been fatigued from a long day of tests, Margot supposed. And frustration. For the tests were variants of somatosensory tests the amnesiac subject had been given years before at the Institute, repeated now with an MRI to track and record the neural activities in his brain—an extraordinary experiment, with very interesting results. And though the subject could not "remember" the repetitive tests, he became restive and obstinate just the same.

It is so, though Margot Sharpe doesn't want to acknowledge it, that the amnesiac subject E.H. isn't nearly so cooperative and good-natured as he'd been. Gradually, his personality has altered. Or rather, a secondary, "coarser" personality sometimes emerges, who is not the true Elihu Hoopes, and is likely to be contentious and contrarian. But Margot Sharpe can handle this Eli Hoopes.

After the incident on the interstate, when Eli fled Margot's car to stagger along the shoulder of the road, Margot brought him safely back, calming the frightened and bewildered man, walking with her arm around his waist as he leaned heavily on her.

Margot knew to comfort him by murmuring a line from one of his poems—" 'Ah love, let us be true to one another!' " Sometimes this provoked Eli to recite the entire poem; at other times it simply calmed him, as with a promise of home.

In the car he'd been sweetly docile. He'd allowed her to buckle him into his seat without protest. He had forgotten his alarm about his sketchbook—he'd forgotten the sketchbook, which Margot discreetly returned to the backseat. Soon, as Margot resumed driving, he'd slipped into a doze.

Next morning, Margot was surprised to see unsightly bruises around her neck, beneath her chin, darkened to the hue of ripe plums. But very easy to disguise the impress of the man's fingers beneath a black turtleneck sweater of a fine-textured material like cashmere. Over this, a black-and-white-striped silk scarf.

In the mirror, before she'd left home she had made herself look quite normal. Smiling at her reflection, like one with a precious secret.

Mrs. Mateson is speaking to her: "Margot? Will you have a little more tea?"

"Yes, thank you."

"Is it hot enough? Or—a little lukewarm, I'm afraid?"

"It's fine, Mrs. Mateson. Earl Grey is my favorite."

In fact, Margot hates Earl Grey tea. She hates caffeine, which affects her sensitive nerves and will prevent her sleeping that night. Very much would she prefer a glass of wine, or whiskey, but Mrs. Mateson never offers anything alcoholic.

Over the years, Margot has befriended Lucinda Mateson. She drives E.H. home frequently from the Institute—her explanation is, she is saving money from the grant; she is known for her frugality, in refusing to spend money lavishly as certain of her (male) colleagues in the department. She has, not entirely deliberately, and yet not altogether innocently, insinuated herself into the life of the widow who'd been in her fifties when Margot had first met her, and was now presumably in her late seventies. Now white-haired, and somewhat ethereal, Lucinda Mateson has become a beautiful older woman of the kind Margot most admires, one who appears to be poised and unself-pitying, and not obviously eager for company. Her skin is still freshly powdered, and on her sunken cheeks are faint spots of rouge—Margot thinks it's touching that Mrs. Mateson takes care with her appearance. Even when her visitor is only Margot Sharpe, she dresses tastefully and expensively; she wears shoes, and not house slippers; she wears stockings, and not socks. Her beautiful sparkling rings have grown loose on her thin fingers, like the watch around her wrist, threatening to slip off as Margot observes, fascinated.

(Margot has tried to ask Eli about his aunt but his knowledge of the woman with whom he has lived now for nearly thirty years is fractured and incomplete: Eli "knows" his aunt Lucinda only as she was before his illness. It is an interesting phenomenon, about which Margot Sharpe has written, that the amnesiac seems to incorporate post-amnesiac knowledge into what he knows of a subject, unconsciously; in regions of the brain adjacent to the damaged areas, neurons must be absorbing such information haphazardly. Eli Hoopes is never surprised by the elderly woman who greets him when he returns to the house, though in theory he believes Lucinda Mateson to be much younger; as the amnesiac subject is not [evidently] startled seeing his mirror reflection each morning, which has become that of an older, if not "elderly" man.)

Not from Eli but from Lucinda herself Margot has gathered that Mrs. Mateson was widowed young, in her mid-fifties, and never remarried; she'd been, of a generation of ambitious Hoopes siblings, the daughter, who'd attended only a year or two of college, had lived mostly for her family, and had lost an active interest in the world after her husband's death and her children's departure. Now, as she likes to tell Margot, her life revolves around church (St. Luke's Episcopal Church of Gladwyne), maintaining the house and property, and "taking care of my disabled nephew who would be lost without me."

Margot is fascinated by Lucinda Mateson, and wishes that Lucinda Mateson would like her better. Somehow they have become old acquaintances without ever having become friends.

It is true, Lucinda Mateson reminds Margot of her (deceased) mother, and of older Sharpe relatives. Margot feels a stab of guilt at such thoughts, and at once she is on the defensive—*I had no choice. I have my work. I can't shirk my work, I can't always be flying back to Michigan.*

Margot brings the elderly widow flowers. A big armful of flowers is a generous gesture, she thinks. And Eli is impressed, and leans over to sniff the flowers which are likely to be fragrant—lilacs, gardenias, and lilies are her favorites. "You are a dear, thoughtful wife—my companion in the netherworld." Sometimes, his eyes fill with tears. Sometimes, he laughs.

It isn't clear what Eli means by this. Often, out of nowhere, the amnesiac will make extraordinary pronouncements which Margot Sharpe can scarcely comprehend but which she will record in her notebook as soon as she has a chance.

For instance, Eli has recently said *The annihilation is not the terror. The journey is the terror.*

And Eli has recently said, with a wry self-deprecatory smile, *This is Elihu Hoopes, who died. Hel*-lo!

Wishing to insinuate herself into the life of the Mateson/Hoopes household, Margot Sharpe not only drives Eli Hoopes home from the Institute but often returns on other days to drive him elsewhere, as needed: dentist, barber, men's shops for clothes and shoes. (Lucinda Mateson accompanies them to the men's shops, for she doesn't trust either Eli or Margot to purchase the proper things for her nephew.)

She has volunteered to drive Lucinda Mateson to appointments as well—doctor, dentist, hairdresser, shopping—like any devoted daughter-companion. Mrs. Mateson has a housekeeper, it seems, but the woman doesn't live in, and doesn't appear to be, in Margot's opinion, reliable. (Margot fears a stranger taking advantage of elderly Mrs. Mateson, forging checks, stealing. Discovering who Eli is, and exploiting him.) Margot has often thought—wistfully—how practical it would be, how sensible and time-saving, if Mrs. Mateson were to invite Margot to live with her and Eli in this absurdly large house.

She is lonely. And I am lonely.

Except for Eli, we have no one.

In fact, there are adult children in Lucinda Mateson's life, and presumably grandchildren. But Mrs. Mateson's relations with her children are not altogether happy, Margot has gathered; there are complaints that Jonathan, Samuel, and Lorraine are "always too busy"—"always traveling at holidays"—"never around when I need them."

There is a particular bitterness regarding the eldest, Jonathan, who seems to have wanted to place Lucinda in an assisted-care facility—"what used to be called, when people didn't mince their words, an old folks' home." Jonathan has also pressed his mother to assign to him her power of attorney—"As if I would do such a thing!" Lucinda Mateson snorts in derision. "I may be a vain, selfish, impossible old woman, but I am not stupid. Not yet."

Years have passed since Margot first brought Eli Hoopes home and was invited by Eli to come inside and meet his aunt Lucinda. Years have passed, and yet time has hardly passed. The routine of the household remains more or less unchanged as in a waxworks diorama.

Eli disappears upstairs almost as soon as Margot enters the house, to his TV news and movies—(Eli loves to watch classics, which he has seen many times before and has memorized)—though now, Eli's legs are not so nimble on the stairs. Eli doesn't run upstairs but hauls himself up, grimacing with pain.

Both his knees are arthritic. At least one hip. Eli should have replacement surgery but—how to explain such a major undertaking to one who resists all talk of the future?

It is very difficult, in fact it is virtually impossible, to force Eli Hoopes to do anything he doesn't want to do. Root canal dental work, hearing aid, eye examinations, let alone a colonoscopy—he simply refuses. Margot has considered conspiring with his doctors at the Institute to sedate him one day, orally and then intravenously, in order to subject him to a colonoscopy—she has discovered that Eli's father died of colon cancer at the age of sixty-eight, and so far as she knows, Eli has never had a colonoscopy in his life.

(Would this be ethical? Arranging for the amnesiac to undergo a medical test without his consent, or even his knowledge? Margot has no clear idea but if it is necessary, to save Eli Hoopes's life, she will risk behaving unethically.)

As principal investigator of the neuropsychology laboratory undertaking *Project E.H.,* Margot Sharpe makes all decisions involving the testing of the amnesiac subject. Of course she is not one of his medical doctors. She is not his legal guardian, and there are limits to her jurisdiction. She can deny the requests of other scientists to study E.H., but she has no power over E.H.'s private life. Discreetly she has asked Mrs. Mateson if she has provided for Eli in her will, and has never received a direct answer.

It's awkward to ask an elderly woman such a question but Margot summons up the courage another time: "I've been wondering, Mrs. Mateson—have you provided for Eli in your will? For—some future time when . . ."

Mrs. Mateson replies snappishly, "Yes of course, Professor Sharpe. I've established a trust for Eli. Years ago, in fact. Long before you first began asking. His own siblings won't lift a finger for him, and so I will provide for him."

Margot is surprised to hear this, and relieved. She has many questions to ask but fears offending the older woman, who seems annoyed with her.

"Eli's sister has made a hopeless marriage, her husband is a philanderer who has burnt through her money and will probably divorce her to marry another rich, foolish woman. Eli's brothers have made some unwise decisions in Hoopes and Associates, and losses have been considerable. No one tells me these things—I make it my business to find out. (In fact, my accountant is my informant. Sam Muller has been my accountant for forty years and I trust him in all things.) Averill and Harry married women who spend money carelessly, they each have second and even third homes, and their children are hopelessly spoiled.

"No, only his aunt Lucinda will take care of poor Eli. I am the only one who loves my nephew." She speaks both pettishly and proudly.

Margot wants to protest—*No. Not you alone, Mrs. Mateson!*

Margot has been awaiting a proper time to make this suggestion, and believes that this is the time, when Lucinda Mateson has been speaking frankly, and serious issues regarding Eli's future have been raised for the first time. It is a bold suggestion—that Mrs. Mateson appoint Margot Sharpe executrix of the trust for Eli Hoopes so that she can oversee his care in all financial matters;

so that she can maintain the very best living conditions for him; and so that she might, if there are sufficient funds, establish graduate fellowships in E.H.'s name—"These would be administered by a board of trustees at the Institute. They would be restricted to young scientists who are doing research into amnesia and memory." Margot doesn't tell Mrs. Mateson that she has already endowed a fellowship in neuropsychology at the university, with her own money; temporarily, the fellowship is named for "E.H." One day, when Eli Hoopes's identity is no longer confidential, the fellowship will be named for him in full.

Elihu Hoopes Fellowship in Neuropsychology.

When Margot first discussed the endowment with her departmental chairman, Dr. Latta expressed surprise that Margot wasn't establishing the fellowship under her own name; but Margot said, with a wincing laugh, "Oh but who would care or know about 'Sharpe'? It's 'E.H.' who is significant."

Latta expressed surprise, too, at the amount of money Margot was giving, which he calculated to be a high percentage of her salary for the past dozen years; and again Margot said, "Oh but what else is my money for? I have almost no expenses beyond minimal living."

This statement had seemed to the departmental chair a stunningly pathetic statement, and yet there was Margot Sharpe smiling strangely as if she'd confessed something laudable.

Now, Lucinda Mateson is frowning, and she is not looking at Margot. Margot fears, with a heart of dread, that she has made a blunder—she has offended the thin-skinned woman, and will be expelled from the household. (Is it because Margot Sharpe isn't from a socially prominent family? The Hoopeses were once Quakers, reform-minded and liberal; in later years, with the exception of Eli Hoopes, they have become more politically conservative. Margot is stung. Margot feels the hurt of exclusion on class grounds!)

Badly Margot wants to plead: "But I will love your nephew as you love him. I will love him more, I will be his wife. *I am his wife*. I will take care of him as no one else can."

After a moment, as if she has heard this shameless plea very clearly, Lucinda Mateson relents, with a sigh. She sets down a teacup onto a table. With the grim practicality of a gambler she says:

"Well—thank you for your suggestion, Professor Sharpe. I will take note of this in my will—a codicil to my will. We will want to make official your special connection with Eli—no matter what my son Jonathan might wish. Though I intend to live for a long, long time yet—I promise!"

Mrs. Mateson laughs almost gaily; and Margot joins in, though she is not altogether sure what has been promised to her.

"On your part, Margot, do you promise that you will always protect Eli? You will never let anyone exploit him?—any of your science colleagues, or strangers? And you will never let the poor man eke out his days alone, in a cocoon of forgetfulness?"

"Mrs. Mateson, I promise!"

Margot is so deeply moved, she has begun to cry. She would embrace Lucinda Mateson but the older woman resists her with a sharp little laugh and sharp upraised elbows. "Oh no—no no *no*. No tears, dear Margot! Tears will not help Eli—and tears will not help you. Life is cruel once you are in its grasp, and life begins to squeeze like that hideous Greek sea serpent who squeezed the father and his sons to death—'Layo-koon.' That has not happened to you—yet—but it has begun with me, and with poor Eli too. *You* must be young and healthy for my nephew and me, and help us to endure."

These are astonishing words. Margot is so moved, she risks

another rebuff—clasps Lucinda Mateson's sparrow-bone hand in both her hands, and kisses the thin blue veins at the knuckles to the surprise and consternation of the older woman.

"Mrs. Mateson—I love Eli, and I love you. You are my only family. You are the only people in my life who mean anything to me."

STANDING ON THE plank bridge. Gripping the railing tight.

Though you can prepare for hurricane-force winds, you are never prepared

And you are never forgiven.

CHAPTER TEN

He was my entire life. There has been no life for me apart from "E.H."

This award you are giving me, I am accepting in his name only. It is a posthumous award. But I thank you.

"HELLO? PROFESSOR? I'M afraid there's bad news. Eli Hoopes won't be coming to Darven Park today."

Margot is so shocked, she fumbles to find a chair. What is it? What? Through a roaring in her ears she hears, not the terrible news that Eli Hoopes has died or collapsed but that Eli Hoopes's aunt and guardian Lucinda Mateson died the previous night, of a massive stroke, in the University Hospital in Philadelphia.

"Died? Mrs. Mateson has—*died*? I didn't know that—that—I had no idea that . . ."

Helplessly Margot protests. Her voice is weak, faltering. The first impulse is to deny the reported fact of any death, for death cannot be assimilated into life. All that Margot knows is that Eli Hoopes *has not died*.

Awaiting him at the Institute they'd known that something was wrong. For the first time in many years, the amnesiac subject was late: an hour, ninety minutes, three hours . . . Telephone calls to the Mateson residence went unanswered, even by a housekeeper; calls to the limousine service that provides transportation to Darven Park were routed to a dispatcher who could say only that their driver arrived at the Parkside address in Gladwyne at the usual early hour, waited for his passenger who failed to appear, went to the door and rang the bell, and no answer, and no evidence that anyone was home—nor had anyone called to cancel the engagement.

"We'll have to charge, ma'am. Whether Mr. Hoopes was taken to Darven Park, or not. Thing is, the driver showed up as requested—and has had to come back without a fare."

"Don't worry, you will be paid. You've always been paid out of our grant for all of your services, and you always will be!"—trembling with fury Margot hung up the phone.

And so, Margot understood that something was wrong, terribly wrong, though Margot had driven Eli Hoopes home the previous Friday and she'd visited with Lucinda Mateson and everything had seemed so promising: a codicil in Mrs. Mateson's will, pertaining to Margot Sharpe.

And Margot understood that she must disguise her concern, and her mounting anxiety; Margot knew that her young lab colleagues from the university and her colleagues at the Institute would be struck by her deathly-pale face, and her inability to sit still; like the wife of a New England ship's captain of a bygone era Margot positioned herself at a high window, gazing down into the Institute parking lot, awaiting the arrival of the sleek black Lincoln Town Car in which the amnesiac patient would be brought as usual to Darven Park . . . Margot never arrived later than 7:30 A.M., and E.H. never arrived later than 8:00 A.M.

Margot knew but could not bring herself to care, how these witnesses would pity her—*It was painfully obvious, Margot Sharpe was in love with "E.H." It was sad and touching, and we were embarrassed for her, but there was a kind of tacit agreement among us—we would protect her, we would never violate her privacy.*

"Years have passed, and yet time has hardly passed"—Margot will recall these foolish words afterward, when all has changed.

The routine of the Institute tests, the routine of driving E.H. back to his aunt's house. The routine of the strained and yet (to Margot) pleasurable teatimes with the elderly widow Lucinda Mateson in which always there was the possibility, as in a magical children's tale, of an interruption of great happiness—*Oh Eli! You've come to join us! How sweet of you dear Eli, please take a seat beside Margot, please help yourself to tea and cookies, we have been avidly awaiting you these many years.*

Not until nearly 2:00 P.M. did the explanatory call come at last, and a very blunt and perfunctory call it was, from a harried stranger who asked to speak to "'Professor Sharpe'—one of the doctors there."

In a heart-hammering daze Margot listens. Tries to listen. It is a stranger's voice in her ear—a man's voice—it is not Eli Hoopes's voice. (Margot has never heard her dear friend's voice on the phone, but would recognize it at once. She is wondering why Eli doesn't call her with this shocking news of his aunt.)

Margot feels her tongue grow numb. Lips numb, and chilled. Her extremities—toes, fingers. It is remarkable how quickly—(thinking as a neuroscientist now, with the detachment ascribed to those "out-of-the-body" experiences in which no reputable scientist believes)—the body reacts, that's to say the brain reacts through the body, as shock is absorbed into consciousness. Margot is breathless but tries to laugh, as her colleagues rally to comfort her—"Really, I'm fine! I'm all right! It isn't E.H. who has died but his elderly aunt—the poor dear woman was in her eighties. We will be seeing E.H. again soon, later this week at least . . ."

Repeated calls to the Mateson number go unanswered. Margot considers driving to Gladwyne, a desperate measure.

Of course, Margot wants to see E.H. as soon as possible, to comfort him, and to commiserate with him; she has no idea how the amnesiac will absorb the death of his aunt, but he is certain to miss her from his routine, domestic life—"He will know that someone integral to his life is gone. But will he be able to name what is missing?"

And there will be an absence in his life, Eli will feel keenly. More than ever, he will be emotionally dependent upon Margot.

Margot is eager to drive to Gladwyne to attend whatever sort of funeral the Hoopeses have arranged for Lucinda, but she is not one of the family, she is not invited, she is kept wholly out of contact with any of the Hoopeses. Years before she'd taken pains to establish a connection with Eli's sister Rosalyn who seemed like a sympathetic woman—but she has not spoken to Rosalyn for a long time. Averill and Harry she knows not at all—as she recalls, they'd rather snubbed her. And she knows Jonathan Mateson not at all.

Margot makes calls, leaves messages with housekeepers, assistants, secretaries. Hears herself say pleadingly—*But I am Elihu Hoopes's doctor! I was a close friend of Lucinda Mateson! You must have heard of me—"Margot Sharpe" of the University Neurological Institute at Darven Park.*

There must be a funeral for Lucinda Mateson but so far as Margot can discover it is a "private, family" ceremony at St. Luke's Episcopal Church in Gladwyne. Margot does learn that the deceased was eighty-two years old—older than she'd appeared.

Margot feels a stab of grief for Mrs. Mateson, as for herself, that she'd never succeeded in making Eli's aunt trust her, and like her—and now it is too late.

As days pass, and no one returns Margot's calls, she becomes ever more desperate. Her other responsibilities, at the university, are slighted. She herself fails to return calls left for her by colleagues. She is confounded: How will she see E.H. again? What has become of the amnesiac, could he even know that his aunt has died—that she has died *irrevocably*? Is the work of *Project E.H.* to end so abruptly? Thirty years of remarkable scientific research, and ending like this?

At last, after many abortive attempts, Margot succeeds in being put through to speak with Jonathan Mateson, Lucinda's eldest son; she recalls how dissatisfied Lucinda Mateson was with him, and thinks how ironic it is, the petulant-sounding Jonathan is now executor of his mother's estate. And at last, Jonathan Mateson has his mother's power of attorney.

"Yes? H'lo? Who is this—'Doctor Sharpe'? Not my mother's doctor, are you? Never heard of you."

As in a nightmare Margot learns that Jonathan Mateson has not only never heard of her, but has never heard of any "codicil" in his mother's will applying to any Dr. Sharpe, or with reference to his cousin Elihu Hoopes. Coolly Mateson tells her that with all that he has to do following his mother's death he has no time for, and less interest in, dealing with his cousin Elihu; he has no intention of arranging for his "brain-damaged" cousin to continue to live in his mother's house as he'd been living for such a long time—"Like some kind of psychiatric hospital my mother was running, out of her own pocket. Now, that's *fini*."

Margot is astonished to hear these blunt words. Margot is so astonished, she asks Jonathan Mateson to repeat what he has said.

"Doctor—whoever you are—this is not negotiable. You and I are not 'negotiating' anything. I have a date in probate court in Philadelphia, and clearing my mother's estate will not be easy. She has many heirs, and there are many claimants. There appears to be a trust to provide for Eli Hoopes, and I am the executor of that trust. We will find a place for him—an assisted-care residence. Or some kind of 'halfway house.' My cousin Eli Hoopes is *non compos mentis.* He is not able to enter into any legal contracts, nor can legal contracts be arranged that bind him, without the permission of the executor of the trust, who happens to be me."

Margot is somewhat confounded by Jonathan Mateson's brisk manner. She wants to ask what has happened to Eli, where is Eli at this moment, how has Eli reacted to his aunt's sudden death, but she dares not. She hears herself pleading, "But Mr. Mateson, surely there is enough money in the trust to allow Eli to live by himself somewhere, in a private place, with a full-time caregiver?"

"No, Doctor. Sorry."

"There is not enough money? But Mrs. Mateson had said—"

"I've explained, Doctor: I am the executor of the trust. It is just one of the tasks that I've inherited with my mother's death, and not the most crucial one. I've contacted Eli's brothers and we are going to find a suitable place for him, as soon as possible. The house on Parkside will be put on the market as soon as possible. And now—"

"But where is Eli, now?"

"Where is Eli, now? Who are you to be asking this?"

"I—I'm his doctor—'Margot Sharpe.' I've been his doctor—one of his doctors—since 1965 . . ."

"Since 1965! And a hell of a lot of good you've done him, eh? His memory is as bad as ever, or worse. Doctors! 'Neurophysiologists'! Why do you care about him now?"

Margot speaks in a faltering voice. "Because—Eli is my patient . . ."

"And what has this to do with my mother, who has just died? We are all in grief here, having lost our dear mother. What's my cousin Eli got to do with it?" Jonathan Mateson's voice exudes disdain, and a kind of bemusement beneath the disdain, as Margot pleads with him to allow her to speak with him in person, to appeal on Eli Hoopes's behalf. But Jonathan Mateson is too busy, and is about to hang up.

"If I could—somehow—buy the house? Your mother's house? On Parkside Avenue? So that Eli could continue to live there, where he is familiar with his surroundings . . ."

"Buy the house? Are you serious, Doctor? Do you know what it will cost?"

"I—I don't k-know . . . How much will you ask for it?"

Jonathan Mateson quotes a figure. Margot isn't sure that she has heard correctly, but doesn't dare ask him to repeat it.

"And property taxes are thirty-four thousand a year. Just property taxes, not maintenance."

Margot is stunned too by this figure, tossed at her as one might toss a pebble at an annoying dog.

"Thirty-four thousand a year—property tax? How is that possible?"

With a mortgage underwritten by the university, Margot has purchased her own small house in a residential neighborhood of small privately owned houses and rentals near the university. Her yearly property tax is four thousand, six hundred dollars.

With scarcely concealed impatience Jonathan Mateson tells Margot that Gladwyne is a "desirable" suburb of Philadelphia. And Parkside is the "most desirable" of streets. The buyer will very likely purchase the property to tear down the old house and build a new, modern house in its place—"And we are eager to sell, since no one in the family wants to live in it."

But I would live in it! I will care for Eli there.

Margot hears her faltering voice protest: Eli Hoopes knows his aunt's house intimately and is at home there. He will not ever know any other residence—"He will be utterly lost."

Jonathan Mateson says sagely that his cousin has been "utterly lost" for the past thirty years. His mother was a saint to take care of him, or a fool—"But that's over now."

Margot grips the phone tightly. In her other hand, a glass of Johnnie Walker Black Label whiskey. Very carefully she sips the whiskey, and very carefully with her shaky fingers she sets the glass on a table. No one must hear. No one must suspect.

She is safely in her home, where the thermostat is kept low, to save on fuel costs. At home, the blinds are drawn through much of the day. She wears heavy-knit sweaters and woolen socks; sometimes, if the air is chill enough to make her breath steam, she wears a knit cap on her head. On her walls are pencil and charcoal drawings by E.H. which, over the years, always discreetly and very carefully, Margot cut out of Eli's sketchbooks; some she has had framed but most are affixed to the wall with double-edged adhesive tape. The largest measure three feet by eighteen inches. The smallest are tablet-sized. These are replica drawings, Margot considers them, that replicate other drawings of E.H.'s—they are drawings E.H. would never miss.

To Margot's eye the drawings are exquisite and dreamlike and beautiful indeed like the drawings of Edvard Munch, especially those of the drowned girl with her dark hair lifting in the shallow sun-lit stream, and tiny, near-invisible shadows of water-skaters reflected on her pale body.

And he never saw his girl cousin, in death. He has imagined it all.

Margot wants to explain to Jonathan Mateson how crucial it is, that Eli Hoopes be cared for as he has been. He is not an ordinary person, his is an eloquent soul, the soul of an artist. Losing his aunt will be a terrible trauma for him, and equally traumatic will be losing his home. But she dares not presume to speak in too proprietary a way of the amnesiac subject. She says, "Mr. Mateson, your mother left a trust for your cousin so that he could be taken care of humanely. She would not have consented to have him moved to an 'assisted-care facility' or a 'halfway house'—he doesn't belong with mentally or physically ill persons, this would be devastating to him. I happen to know—Lucinda told me about it in detail, less than two weeks ago. *She promised that I would be Eli Hoopes's medical guardian.*"

" 'Medical guardian'? No-oo. Not a thing in her will about that, Doctor."

"Lucinda didn't have time to prepare the codicil! But she intended to . . ."

"There's no evidence of that, Doctor. And if you don't mind, I would prefer that you call my mother 'Mrs. Mateson'—not 'Lucinda.' You were not her friend, or I would have known of you."

"I was your mother's friend—for years! I drove Eli home from Darven Park to Gladwyne, your mother and I had tea together two, sometimes three times a week . . ."

There is an awkward silence. Margot is made to wonder if she has invented everything.

Out of her yearning, an entire world has been invented.

Coolly Jonathan Mateson says, "Well—there is no codicil. There is no amendment to the trust my mother established for Eli Hoopes in 1987."

Weakly Margot protests, "But Mr. Mateson—don't you owe

anything to your mother's wishes? How can you be so cruel to someone who has already suffered terribly? Eli Hoopes is your own relative—please rethink your decision to sell the house."

Margot worries that she has gone too far, and that Jonathan Mateson is about to hang up. The property is immensely valuable, surely it's folly to imagine that the Matesons and the Hoopeses would wish to maintain Eli Hoopes as he'd been for thirty years. *No one cares for him but me. And I have no power.*

"What business is it of yours what happens to Eli Hoopes, Doctor? Seems to me that *Project E.H.* has wrung the poor man dry—how much longer are you going to 'experiment' with him?"

Margot protests that *Project E.H.* has been funded by the National Institutes of Health and the National Science Endowment; it is one of the most crucial neuropsychological projects in history. Already many of the *Project*'s findings have been beneficial in the field of post-stroke therapy, for instance—how amnesia happens in the brain, and how the amnesiac might be treated. She tells him that Eli Hoopes has always been fully cooperative with researchers and that she, Margot Sharpe, as the principal investigator, closely overlooks all testing. "Eli's visits to the Institute are the high points of his life, you must know. Tests to the brain-damaged are immensely beneficial to them. Otherwise Eli would have seen virtually no one for years except his aunt Lucinda—he has few visitors. He'd have vegetated at home watching TV."

"Ridiculous! Eli has plenty of visitors—except he can't remember who we are, so what's the purpose of 'visiting' him? It's damned depressing. And he can read perfectly well, he can read his favorite books over and over again—he can watch his favorite movies—my mother said he was very happy seeing the same old classics again and again. And he could take photographs again, if he used his old camera. He could take a bus to the art museum—he knows his way around Philadelphia from before his injury. It's no good coddling him, and infantilizing him, as my mother did—that's the reason his condition never improved. In fact, Eli has a life that's enviable—someone always takes care of him. He doesn't worry about the future, and he doesn't worry about the past."

Margot protests, "Of course Eli 'worries' about the past. It is all he has to think about."

"All right, then—he 'worries' about the past. But he can't remember anything that happens to him now, so the 'past' is getting smaller in his life."

This is a nonsensical remark which Margot ignores.

"But without your mother, he will be so lonely . . ."

"In the facility we'll find for him he will have plenty of company. People like himself who are 'disabled'—have lost parts of their personalities, or bodies. He'll get along just fine."

"But Eli isn't mentally ill! He will be miserably out of place."

"He will make new friends. Just give him a chance."

"He won't be able to remember his new surroundings. He won't be able to remember new people he meets. He will just be—lost."

Margot's tone is so forlorn, it seems that Jonathan Mateson can't bring himself to hang up just yet. Desperately Margot continues, "I—I could bring your cousin home with me at least temporarily. I could make a home for him. I'm a professor at the university—I have a private house near campus. When I had to be away from home, I would hire someone to care for him—he would have twenty-four-hour care. If I were to receive the payment—oh, just a fraction of the payment—you would be making to this facility, it would be a good compromise—don't you think?"

Mateson is silent. Is he confounded, stunned? Is he insulted?

"Of course—it would all be clearly designated in a contract . . . I would meet with you and any of Eli's other relatives, and we could work out a plan . . ."

"Jesus, Doctor! Why'd you take on such a burden? I haven't seen Eli Hoopes in years, my mother has said he was 'gradually deteriorating' . . . I don't understand this at all."

"If it were a matter of, of—money—if you didn't want to pay me out of the trust—I could use the grant money—in any case, I could support us both on my university salary . . ."

Margot is speaking rapidly, helplessly. She is so warm now, she tugs off the heavy-knit sweater. A flush rises through her body, groin to face. Almost, she fears that Jonathan Mateson can see her: a woman of late middle age, untidy dark hair shot with white wires, the former girl's face contorted in an expression of yearning, hope, and shame.

Mateson is embarrassed for Margot Sharpe, it seems. He has heard the raw yearning in her voice.

He asks her again why she would take on the burden of caring for an afflicted man who is no relative of hers and Margot tells him stiffly:

"It is the right thing to do, Mr. Mateson. Eli needs—someone to care for him."

How close she has come to saying *Eli needs me.*

Madness, desperation, folly.

Jonathan Mateson seems to be weighing the situation. Perhaps he feels sorry for her, suddenly. He tells Margot that her suggestion is unorthodox, he doesn't really think it's a feasible solution to the problem of Eli Hoopes but he will think about it—"I'll discuss it with Eli's brothers and sister tomorrow. My impression is they're all pretty much fed up with coddling their 'brain-damaged' sibling. In the meantime, thank you for calling, Doctor—is it 'Sharpe'?"

"Yes. 'Sharpe.'"

Quietly as an indrawn breath, Margot breaks the phone connection. She finishes the glass of whiskey, sticky-fingered. And then so light-headed, she can manage only to stumble to her bed before collapsing on it.

THE RAVENOUS LOVER. In her sleep she feels him. The man's touch, his mouth, his body hot and aching with life, and with desire. Everywhere against her skin she feels him.

It is a terror to her, the feeling comes so strong. She has been a cowardly woman, terrified of such feeling, the sex-sensation, that annihilates her, and leaves her desperate, helpless. It is how she knows that she loves the man—this annihilation. It is a risk she will make for him, the risk of utter abnegation.

He is so much stronger than she. His arms close tight about her like the wings of a great bird, folding and clasping its prey.

The pen falls from her fingers to the floor. The notebook falls to the floor.

What has passed between us will not be recorded. It will be lost to all memory.

AXEL HIS NAME. Skinny stoop-shouldered boy twisting Eli's arm behind his back. Whimpering with pain and Axel McElroy laughed. And pressing the canvas cushion from one of the heavy wooden Adirondack chairs against his face. Dirty cushion Axel said smirking, people's asses on it. Terrified he'd be suffocated forced onto the ground and the canvas cushion against his face and Axel leaning on it, hard—it was a joke (he wanted to think it was a joke) but it continued too long so his skin was scraped, his nose bleeding and he was trying to scream but could not.

The bishop's grandson they said of him. Axel he'd hated, and was frightened of for Axel was like no one else they knew, his brothers too were fearful of the older boy for Axel would say and do anything but never so adults knew. Nasty gestures with his hands like pulling at himself—at his crotch. The girls looked away, disgusted. Eli had tried to make Axel go away but he was too small and too weak. Upper arm so skinny, Axel could close his fingers around it laughing. The girl cousins were laughing. His cousin Gretchen looked away. She was laughing at poor shamed Eli—was she? Would not ever forgive her. Wished she would die. In a canoe, he'd tip over the damn canoe and she would drown in the lake. Wanted to run from Axel but Axel'd catch his arm, grab his hair pretending he was going to "scalp" Eli. He was such a little boy, and a coward. The older cousins laughed at him if but tenderly feeling sorry for him. And Averill laughed at him, and Harry. Hiding beneath the porch and they had no idea where he'd gone. Through slats in the lattice he spied on them. Girls' bare legs, hair tied back in ponytails for swimming. His cousin Gretchen only eleven but tall for her age—"mature"—trusted with little children. Flat little breasts in a pink halter-top, elastic-ribbed pink swimsuit panties. Bright fair-brown hair shining in the sun, ponytail trailing down her back. Her pale legs, bare feet. Her family had just come to the lake, it was their first week that summer. "Eli? Eli?"—she'd called for him. And he had not crawled out.

Telling the other children not to play on the dock, she'd be right back. Maybe she'd been flattered by the older boy Axel McElroy the bishop's grandson who was seventeen and wore his hair in a pompadour like Elvis Presley.

He had not seen where she'd gone. Not in which direction she'd gone. Hiding beneath the porch embarrassed and ashamed and filled with hatred for them all not just Axel McElroy the bishop's grandson but all of them—Gretchen too.

And later he had more reason to be ashamed. No way to make it right. No words for how cowardly he was, more contemptible than anyone knew.

Shameful too, their father drank too much. When Gretchen was missing Byron Hoopes drank too much and could not keep up with the other adults searching in the woods. And there was Granddaddy's chrome-yellow Beechcraft single-prop. An airstrip had been cleared on the Hoopes property for Granddaddy's aircraft. Convinced that they would find the missing girl—they would find Gretchen where she'd wandered in the woods and they would bring her home in the little prop-plane. Except the plane lost altitude suddenly above the lake and Granddaddy had to "crash-land." And they did not find Gretchen.

They had not found her in the woods. Not then.

He had not seen her in death. He had abandoned her, he'd been angry with her and had not seen her ever again.

Prayed to God, to bring Gretchen back. But God was higher than the highest white pine and paid him no heed.

(Where is this place? Why is he here? He has a vague memory of his office at Hoopes & Associates—staring out the window at high-rise buildings in the near distance. Windows of winking glass. Behind these windows, who?)

The view from the window here is very different. Not downtown Philadelphia, but an older residential neighborhood. He is in a "hospital" or a "clinic"—he thinks. At this height he can see a short distance. The tree line is ragged. Badly he regrets the days of his youth, he'd felt the presence of God so easily. And he'd lost God out of carelessness and self-absorption and now it is too late, he is damned.

In his white skin he is damned.

Trying to raise the window. But it is not a window that one can raise. Frustrated and furious brings his head against the plate-glass pane. Forehead against the pane—hard enough to draw blood, and harder.

She is very frightened. Her throat is very dry.

In San Francisco she is addressing the AAEP (American Association of Experimental Psychology) in a ballroom so vast, the farther, facing wall is barely visible. In Chicago she is addressing the NICN (National Institute of Cognitive Neuroscientists), rows upon rows of uplifted faces blurred and indistinct as the faces in dreams. In Washington, D.C., the NIH (National Institutes of Health)—waves of applause lapping at her feet, rising swiftly to cover her mouth and engulf her. In Orlando, Florida—in Seattle, Washington—in Denver, Colorado—in Boston, New York City, Philadelphia—she feels the rush of blood in her ears, the rapid drumbeat of her heart, as she makes her way through a glare of lights to a podium and a figure darts beside her whose face she can't see gripping her elbow tightly to steady her—"This way, Professor. Watch that step."

She is giving a keynote address. She is accepting an award. She is reading a paper. She is participating in a symposium. She is answering questions posed to her by an interviewer even as a part of her mind yearns for *him*.

Like an experimental animal that has long been penned up and its spirit broken and once the door of the cage is opened, remains in its cage.

Those chimpanzees who'd been "liberated" by animal rights activists but remained in their cages, cowering.

(Milton Ferris had told them of these poor animals. Milton Ferris had smiled as he told the story for it was amusing to him.)

"Professor Sharpe?"

Margot glances up. They are looking at her expectantly. They are strangers with no idea of how far Professor Sharpe has drifted from them as in a little skiff on a wide, churning river.

Margot feels a sharp pain in her breast. She is determined not to betray her sorrow, however. She is determined not to betray the slightest glimmer of her true self in public.

She tells a story of how she'd introduced the amnesiac subject "E.H." to a distinguished neuroscientist from Columbia University who'd come to the Institute to interview him, and contrary to his usual habit of courtesy "E.H." refused to shake hands with the man and instead folded his arms tightly across his chest and backed away.

He'd said *Doctor, my regrets! There isn't enough of my poor brain to go around any longer. The doctors here have gobbled up the last dry morsels.*

Margot laughs, for her amnesiac subject was very witty, she thinks. Her eyes glisten with tears. Her listeners who are primarily neuropsychologists and neuroscientists laugh in awkward waves through the amphitheater not knowing whether they should laugh at all.

"A posthumous life. Like breathing undersea through a narrow straw—it can be done, if barely."

She talks to herself, in this posthumous life. Often she is wry, good-humored. And often, she is being interviewed.

Breathlessly she laughs, clenching her small fists in her lap in a way that no one can see. (Of course, observers see. Margot Sharpe has become such a curious, eccentric *female scientist,* legends must be spun about her. That ridiculous, touching, silly-exotic "sexy" braid dangling down the side of her face! And the lavish silk shawls, scarves trailing down her back.)

Such solemn words as she is being introduced to applause that rises like waves to engulf her.

Except Margot Sharpe is not laughing. The death-grin has clamped onto her lower face.

Extraordinary work in the biology of memory, Margot Sharpe's research of decades, model for young women scientists who look to women like Margot Sharpe for inspiration and guidance in their lives as in their work . . .

Such helium-inflated words signal a public occasion. Yes, it is so—when she lifts her eyes upward she sees lights, a stage. If she turns her head, she will see rows of graded seats, as in an amphitheater.

Searching in vain for—a particular face.

"Face recognition"—the earliest mental act of the infant.

For survival depends upon such recognition. It is the most elemental, the most primitive and the most profound of human acts.

Yes, there has been a lavish dinner beforehand at a wood-paneled dark-lighted steak house. Valiantly the guest of honor tried to eat but was unable. Lifting her fork to her mouth, and lowering it. Lifting her fork to her mouth, and lowering it. Lifting a glass of wine to her mouth, and lowering it. She sees—*They are observing, memorizing. These tales that will outlive me.*

She is called "Professor Sharpe" here. There is no one who knows her as "Margot." She is the oldest person at the dinner with the exception of a gleaming-bald-headed neuroscientist whose reputation was established as a young collaborator with the great B. F. Skinner at Harvard in the 1940s.

Pleading with her eyes to this older gentleman—*Please do not speak to me of Milton Ferris! Not even in commiseration.*

Of course conversation often—invariably—swings onto Milton Ferris, if/when Margot Sharpe is the subject.

The tales told of that couple! No neuroscientist of younger generations at Penn, MIT, Yale, Harvard, Princeton, UC–Berkeley, and the Salk Institute has failed to hear of how the preeminent womanizer Ferris "identified" Margot Sharpe on the very first day she walked into his memory lab as a mere graduate student—how Ferris realized at once what a brilliant scientist the twenty-three-year-old was, or would be; how Ferris initiated an affair with Margot Sharpe that endured for years that allowed him to exploit her both sexually and professionally; how Ferris clawed his way to a Nobel Prize for himself, but not for Margot Sharpe; this affair of decades ending abruptly when Ferris found another, younger woman neuroscientist to seduce. Or, a yet more lurid tale is told of how as a mere graduate student Margot Sharpe coolly initiated an affair with the great Milton Ferris, in order to advance her career; how Margot Sharpe later blackmailed the older scientist into establishing her as the head of the memory lab, though she was not able to inveigle him into sharing his Nobel Prize with her (which even certain of Margot Sharpe's detractors believe she deserves). Equally lurid tales swirl about Margot Sharpe's (emotional, sexual) involvement with the amnesiac subject "E.H." which prevailed for years—but these tales lack the particular resonance of the accounts of *Ferris-Sharpe,* a delicious (if largely uncorroborated) scandal in the field of neuroscience and neuropsychology.

At the same time, Margot Sharpe is routinely heralded as a model for young women scientists. She is a passionate *feminist;* or, rather, she is a passionate *anti-feminist.* Her former women students revere her, or rather, they are intimidated by her. They love her, or rather, they hate her—yet admit that there has never been anyone quote like Professor Sharpe in their lives, and that they hope (in some way) to emulate her.

Thank you, Professor, for changing my life.
And my life—thank you!

WHICH OCCASION IS this, and which city—Margot isn't certain.

She has become disoriented. Her throat is very dry.

The numbness in her tongue, lips, and extremities has never really faded. The numbness since the terrible telephone call, and the elderly widow's death.

And never to see E.H. since that call.

And never to see E.H. again.

Mrs. Mateson died of a massive stroke, Margot has been told. A series of small strokes, and then a massive stroke. A massive stroke is a bolt of lightning. Instantaneously the brain is immobilized, consciousness is extinguished. The door is slammed shut, all is darkness within.

She hears her name pronounced. It's the public name—*Professor Margot Sharpe.*

She has been lavishly introduced. Streams of words like colored confetti, to which she barely listens. For she is so very lonely, they have taken him from her.

She is on her feet. She is not walking steadily. Observers will note how she pauses, staring out into the audience as if looking for—who?

A rocking buzzing sensation in her ears—not a rush of blood, but applause.

Her topics are "Memory, Sensory Registers, and Retrograde Amnesia in a 66-Year-Old Amnesiac"—"New Memory Circuits in the Brain of an Amnesiac"—"Memory Deficit and Compensation in Amnesia"—"E.H.: Mapping the Brain of the Amnesiac." With the advent of fMRI imaging in the 1990s there is a riches of new material for research and even a traditionalist like Margot Sharpe collaborates now with neurophysicists.

She has been elected honorary president, North American Association of Women Scientists. At her keynote address in a drafty ballroom in a refrigerated high-rise hotel in Toronto with a view of steely-frozen Lake Ontario from her room on the fortieth floor she receives a standing ovation that jolts tears to her eyes.

"Margot Sharpe"—the name seems to echo, like a name out of a revered past.

"Margot Sharpe"—it is a melancholy name, a lonely name.

Waves of applause. That churning sensation of blood in the ears.

If they are indeed mocking Margot Sharpe, such mockery is indistinguishable from the highest praise and adulation. Another distinguished award—and a heavy brass medallion to go with it. (Damned medallion is too heavy to pack in her suitcase. Of necessity she leaves it in a wastebasket in her hotel room, discreetly wrapped in tissues.) Membership in the National Academy of Scientists—in which there are very few women.

Margot Sharpe is not the only scientist to be receiving an award at the May conference of the American Society of Arts and Sciences in Boston but hers is one of the major awards, second in her profession only to a Nobel Prize.

Very straight and very still she is sitting in the first row of seats in the vast amphitheater. Very straight and her head straight and high as if there were an iron rod affixed to her head, her neck, her spinal column. She is swallowing somewhat compulsively. Her mouth is so very dry. "Professor Sharpe?"—she has forgotten that this is an awards ceremony. For a moment she seems baffled by the source of the applause which seems to rain down upon her head from all directions.

Oh, the "award" is so heavy! A twelve-inch-high crystal plaque with MARGOT SHARPE engraved on it, given to her by an earnest young scientist, so much heavier than Margot expects that she nearly drops it as the audience stares in fascinated horror. Yet she smiles, it is a rictus of a smile, and with both hands hoists the plaque high so the award-givers can take their innocent pleasure in seeing it so exalted: a heroic *Winged Victory* made of pure crystal with a polished wood base.

At first she speaks earnestly if somewhat haltingly. Then, with more assurance. Almost, a kind of eloquence.

. . . as a young graduate student. In the pioneering "memory lab" of the great Milton Ferris . . .

Then, her voice begins to quaver. She can't seem to catch her breath, she is hyperventilating. It's as if she were shaking in a sudden gust of wind. Her face seems to crumple like a sheet of very white paper crumpled in a fist. Her words are faltering, lurching.

She has come here to acknowledge—*He is my life. Without E.H., my life would have been to no purpose.*

All that I have achieved as a scientist. All that I am known to you for. All, a consequence of E.H. in my life.

I am not exaggerating. I am speaking the frankest truth as a scientist and as a woman.

He was the one who has suffered—not me. As others did, I saw an opportunity. A scientist is one who sees—and seizes—an opportunity. My career is a consequence of a thirty-seven-year-old Philadelphian contracting encephalitis in July 1964. Our science is built upon such sacrifices and opportunities. Our science is cruel in its mimicry of life which is its subject.

Her notes lie on the podium, ignored. The audience is very still. Tears shine in her eyes. Her makeup is radiant, or feverish. Her skin is white-powdered as a geisha. Her eyes are feverish.

He was my entire life. There has been no life for me apart from "E.H." This award you are giving me, I am accepting in his name only. It is a posthumous award. But I thank you.

And yet, she does not end. A sort of madness has come over her, she continues to speak. Lifts her left hand, to show the staring audience a silver ring on her finger.

This ring my husband's gift to me as his ring was my gift to him. We were married for many years—privately. No one has known—until now . . .

Her voice trails off into silence. She has been leaning on the podium to steady herself, therefore leaning most of her weight on one leg, and now when she tries to straighten her back and stand straight, she finds that she is semi-stricken: a tight, pinched nerve runs the length of her right leg, from buttock to mid-knee. She feels faint, panicked. She seems to have lost her place in a prepared speech on the subject of thirty years of experimentation involving the amnesiac E.H., which originated in Milton Ferris's laboratory . . . Stepping from the podium she stumbles. Quickly someone comes to her, to steady her.

"Professor Sharpe!—watch this step."

It is a blur and a buzz and through it the stricken woman moves like a somnambulist who dares not wake. Scarcely is she aware that her tech assistant Hai-ku has stepped forward to intervene. *Excuse me. I am Professor Sharpe's assistant. I will take her to her hotel room.*

And when next morning she does wake, abruptly and with a taste of hot bile in her mouth, she sees that she is lying fully clothed on an unfamiliar bed, a quilt pulled up to her neck; she'd been able only to kick off her shoes. A lamp is burning, redundant now in daylight, and on a bedside table is a large, crystal figure turned on its side as in a drunken spill.

What is it? She has no idea. She is far too exhausted to sit up, to lift the plaque and read the engraved inscription.

DESPERATELY SHE'D BEGGED *But where have you put him? Please tell me.*

And the sister said carefully *All you need to know is that our brother Eli is in a safe environment.*

CHAPTER ELEVEN

There's a female voice buoyant as a balloon—"Eli, hello!"

Bounces back his own balloon-buoyant deep-baritone—"Hel-*lo*."

Quick exchange. Like tennis. Causes his eyelids to open, quick. (Has he been asleep? Only way he can tell is looking out the window: if there's detail, intricacy of forms clearly visible, evident textures—very likely not a dream.) Must be on guard in this place new and unknown to him.

"And what is your last name, Eli?"

"You're looking at the damn ID bracelet, ma'am, why're you asking? What's it say there—'Eli Custer'?"

"Please tell me your last name, Eli."

"*Last name* meaning it's the *last damn name* I will have, it's 'Hoopes.' As in 'jumping through.' "

She laughs. She is a stranger yet she seems to know him well and to appreciate his wit which is important.

If they like you, they will not hurt you.

They will not hurt you as badly as they could.

"And what is your date of birth, Eli?"

"'Date-of-birth': Four—eighteen—twenty-seven."

Before she can ask the next stupid question—"Want to know my Social Security number, ma'am?—120-28-1416. Telephone number at home—(215) 582-4491. Number at Hoopes and Associates—(215) 661-7937. Number of our house in Bolton Landing—(518) 301-9928."

Rapidly these numbers flow from his tongue. Laughs to see the expression in the stranger's face.

"Thanks, Eli—that's wonderful. I don't need to know these but I would like to know—today's date?"

He pauses. He is thinking. This is a trick question, he may have been asked before. If he answers too quickly, he will make a mistake. And so he pauses, and he thinks. His strategy is to reply as the other person expects him to reply but in this case he has no idea what the other person, a stranger whom he has never seen before, expects him to reply.

Fact is, "today" is just—*today*. At the same time each damn day is a new *today* with a new *date* at the top of the newspaper page.

On a nearby table, a newspaper. By the print font he can identify—*New York Times*. Very likely this is "his" *New York Times* for it is not neatly composed. Its pages are scattered like pages of print that have been voraciously devoured, then pushed aside and forgotten. If he'd known he would be quizzed on the God-damn date he'd have kept the newspaper closer but now it's too late, can't lean over to peer at the top of the page for the lady-nurse, he supposes that is what the woman is, in her pale green smock and matching trousers, is closely watching.

Squints at the window. White-glaring snow beyond, which is a clue.

Yet, no Christmas decorations on the walls of this place. No New Year's.

"Must be"—(calmly he is thinking, calculating, with his gentlemanly smile)—"January 1966. Because I've been sick for a while, I think. Since last July."

"You think that today might be a day in January 1966, Mr. Hoopes?"

"I *think* it *might be* but there's no absolute way of *knowing*—is there? For all that we *know,* we've been told. The great John Locke believed that each mind is a *tabula rasa*. And David Hume argued something very similar. All that we *know* has been directed to us from the outside world, where appearances are deceiving, which 'lies before us like a land of dreams.' And so, yes—today might be a day in February 1966 or it might be a day in"—(he laughs, he is very witty, he likes to entertain the nursing staff who laugh so readily at his jokes)—"February 1996 and most of us are dead, and gone to this 'better place.' "

DISTRESSED AND FRETTING. Why are they not allowing him to walk! On a gurney, he's being wheeled. Like an elderly stricken patient, wheeled. Quite a ruckus he has raised, having to change from his own clothes into hospital attire—"Ties in the back, Mr. Hoopes. Like this."

Repeatedly he asks where the hell they are taking him and repeatedly they tell him. And he asks, and they tell him.

At last one of the interns has the inspired idea to print on a card, in large caps:

OUTPATIENT SURGERY. COLONOSCOPY.
LESS THAN 1 HOUR

The excitable patient is given this card but soon, somehow he has lost this card.

Despite his protests he's being transported somewhere. On a rattling gurney, being wheeled. To the morgue?—is he being taken to the morgue? Protests he isn't dead yet.

Trying to sit up, trying to sit up, repeatedly trying to sit up, and repeatedly an attendant urges him back down.

Now trying to find a vein in his (left) arm. God damn, that hurts and he's angry.

Trying to find a vein in his (right) arm. God damn, that hurts and he's angry!

Trying to calm him. Assure him.

Just a pro-ce-dure. Not an operation. Like they do here all the time, Mr. H'ps.

Sorry Mr. H'ps. Just wait here OK?

And later checking back, with a tug at his wrist—You OK, Mr. H'ps?? Waitin out here?

Soon as he's alone he is on his feet. Grunting, muttering. No idea where the hell he is but needing to escape.

Chill air at his buttocks, limp rubbery balls and penis—God-damn smock he's wearing swings open. So embarrassing!

And his thigh muscles, atrophied. And his gut, a little hard round drum where he expects to see flat hard muscles.

Careless with the God-damn needle they put in his arm, a "line" in the crook of his arm.

Except his shoes have been taken from him, ridiculous slipper-socks on his bony feet. If he's anywhere in Philadelphia he can walk to Rittenhouse Square, no problem. From there, pack for the lake. Badly yearning for the lake. Solitude, sanity. Lapping of lake, calming heartbeat. It has been months—(he calculates)—since he has been at Lake George, last summer when he'd gotten stupidly sick and must be five, six months now at least.

At the end of the corridor is a high window, ceiling twelve feet above. Hammered tin, white. But not clean-white. The white of opacity, time.

At a window, standing. A high window, and the exterior of the glass is streaked with rain.

He is waiting for—what? Waiting.

If this is a jail it is a strange jail with such high ceilings and his legs unshackled. The needle has been pulled from the crook of his arm, blood splattered on the floor.

Nigger lover! Nigger lover! *Shuts his eyes, there are too many faces. The profound truth is, he has not loved enough—"niggers," "whites." Has he ever loved anyone . . .*

He wants another chance, he is thinking. Another chance at life.

Mr. H'ps! Where you goin! Look-it what you done to that IV line, ain' that hurtin you? Oh man.

Mr. Hoopes, please lie down here. You pulled out your needle Mr. Hoopes. We need to get this line started Mr. Hoopes.

His muscles resist. A kind of spasm of resistance. Shoves the nurses. Uses his knee. He is panting. He is cursing—Fuck fuck fuck you all. Fucking hands on me, I'll kill you. *No weak God-damned child any longer. This time he will defend himself.*

Mr. H'ps? H'lo?

He is fighting them, but they are stronger. Injected with toxic-hot liquid in the crook of his arm.

Damn needle is stinging, they found a new vein and a toxic-hot liquid is coursing into it. They will send an X-ray tube up into his gut, many yards of his tangled gut, through his rectum. A radioactive implant like the one in his brain when they sawed through his skull to excise the fever-fire.

Why are his jaws so poorly shaven. God damn his hand shakes. Not forty years old and in the prime of his life but sick-feeling in his gut, something terrible and irrevocable has happened. Waiting for her to come for him—his aunt.

Lucinda Mateson, his father's sister. Where is she? Why isn't he at home? Where is his home?

He is the one to find her. Like a crumpled doll fallen from her chair by the TV. He could recognize her without "seeing" her. Has not "seen" her in years. You recognize people by their voices. Their mannerisms. Knows at once, his fingers against the artery at her neck—no pulse. Dial 911. Call for an ambulance speaking calmly. I think that my aunt has suffered a stroke. The address is Four-Six-Six Parkside, Gladwyne.

Wandered outside and by the time the ambulance arrived he has forgotten he'd summoned the ambulance and why.

Leading him stumbling from the house and his things left behind. Can't remain there any longer by himself but why? He is protesting his aunt Lucinda will wonder where he is.

Eli, you will stay with me. Please Eli, you know me—Rosalyn. I am your sister Rosalyn. Eli?

Shocked that Rosalyn looks so much older than her age. A woman of no more than thirty-four yet face lined and anxious, has she been ill? Cancer? Why doesn't he know this?

She is weeping in his arms. Someone has died—who?

Oh Eli we will take care of you. Dear, dear Eli this is so—this is so very sad . . .

Then he realizes, the woman is an imposter. His sister has died, and an imposter has taken her place.

Pushes against her—Go away, go away to Hell where you belong.

And now here, at the high window. The needle ripped from his arm, and the damned wound bleeding.

And now, outside. Rear of the bright-lighted building. Rain, stinging rain, ice-pellets striking his face. The pavement is puddled, his stocking feet are wet, God-damned ridiculous, a man's dignity such a precarious thing, yet he can move swiftly—terror has made him cunning as a hunted animal.

Hides in doorways. Running, stumbling. His breath comes quick and shallow, there is something wrong with his lungs. Bacterial infection, can't draw a deep breath. Reasoning if he can recognize a street sign, a landmark—he can make his way home.

To Rittenhouse Square, that is his home. Fourteenth floor.

Or, Bolton Landing. It is Bolton Landing—Lake George—to which he really wants to flee, except he has misplaced his car key and has no idea where his car is, in any case. Or which car, which vehicle. Tries to remember but God damn has no idea.

And no money, his wallet is gone. And these paper socks, shredded now. Bony bare feet, has to laugh, rich white man, rich white family, what you deserve, slaveholders in your Hoopes blood predating the pious Philadelphia Quakers, long before Philadelphia and the Abolitionists, in the original slave colony Virginia. Would flee to the Adirondacks if he could find his wallet, his car, his car keys, if he could recognize one of these streets, or landmarks—but he isn't sure where he is, or even if this is Philadelphia. And when—which time in his life this is.

No journey, and no path. No wisdom, only emptiness. But there is no emptiness.

No wisdom, and no Buddha.

Waiting.

CHAPTER TWELVE

Eli, hello!"

"Hel-*lo*."

His eyes lift to hers, narrowed. He is slow to take her extended hand. And how like ice her fingers must feel, in his hand.

"You do remember me, Eli?"

So excited, she is trembling. Approaching his room on the second floor of the facility, ascending the stairs to the second-floor corridor, parking in the lot of the Homestead Care Center in White Oaks, Pennsylvania, and all the while thinking—*He is alive, still! Nothing else matters.*

Her heart is a bell wildly rung. She has not been in the presence of Eli Hoopes for seven months, three weeks, and six days. She has not spoken to him in all this time. She sees that he regards her with that look of intense concentration that is the amnesiac's characteristic expression—*Who are you, do I know you, what does it mean that you know me?*

Is this Eli Hoopes? The man appears older than sixty-eight. There is an IV line attached to the crook of his left arm, that is badly bruised. His cheeks are sunken, the skin beneath his eyes is bruised. A red wet glisten in his eyes like the fatigue that follows madness.

"Do you remember me, Eli? 'Margaret Madden'—'Margie.' "

She has brought him flowers—an armful of strongly fragrant gardenias, recklessly purchased at a florist in White Oaks.

He is very ill, they tell her. Months they have kept her from him, refused her permission to visit him, and now—she steps into the dimly lighted room trembling. Eli has finished an aggressive eight-week course of chemotherapy and will have a PET scan soon, to determine if the treatment has been effective in stopping the spread of his stage three (colon) cancer. His veins are exhausted, his platelets very low. He is severely anemic.

Barely she can see the figure in the bed, foreshortened. Her eyes are aswim with tears.

Eli is engaged with the *New York Times* crossword puzzle. He is using a pencil with some difficulty, with stiffened fingers. With the passage of time these puzzles, incorporating topical material, have become more difficult. When Margot first enters the room he doesn't glance up at her at once, no doubt expecting one of the nursing staff. Though he looks weak and unwell he has cranked up his bed and has managed to hoist himself into a sitting position; Margot sees how discarded newspaper pages have accumulated on the bed, and on the floor—one of E.H.'s signature habits. He has not changed, even in illness!

Eli is smiling now. A flush rises in his face, as of boyish hope.

"Yes—'Margie.' My dear, how could I forget *you*."

He pushes aside the newspaper page, sets aside the pencil. His fingers are squeezing hers now, harder. Margot leans over him and kisses his cheek which is surprisingly warm and has been haphazardly shaved by a hand not his own.

She is laughing. She is shaking, and she is laughing.

How easy this is, now that she has found him! But until she found him, how utterly impossible.

E.H. wipes at his eyes. His visitor is trying to prevent tears from running down her radiant powdered face.

"My dear Eli! Have you been missing me?"

"Have you been missing *me*?"

"Yes, I have. Very much."

"Then—where have you been?"

"Well, I've been looking for you."

"Where have you been looking for me?"

"Everywhere! You are not so easy to track."

Eli laughs, pleased. He is flattered by Margot's extravagant words—he has always been easy to flatter.

So many years of *conditioning.* It is the one strategy Margot Sharpe has never recorded in the notebook.

Eli smiles with his old eagerness. He knows this woman now—(does he?)—and he feels comfortable with her. (Though the woman is older than he by a considerable number of years, and hardly resembles a woman his age. He will be gallant about this and seem to ignore it.) Somehow it must have happened, he and his old classmate from grade school Margie Madden became emotionally involved; it's clear to him that the smiling woman loves him, and it is his responsibility to love *her.*

Eli Hoopes straightens his shoulders. Makes a swipe at his untidy, thinning hair. So strange, he is wearing a ridiculous hospital gown, that ties in the back! The effect of this visitor's arrival upon him is not unlike a transfusion. Margot feels the impact of the blood coursing through his body in her own smaller and tauter veins.

"My dear husband. I've looked so long for you, I thought they'd taken you from me forever."

"Well—I've had a setback here. You can see."

With a gesture Eli indicates the hospital room, the IV stand beside his bed and the line dripping vital liquids into a vein in his arm.

Margot is wearing the wrought silver Celtic wedding band. Out of her handbag she takes her husband's matching band, to slip onto his finger where it fits loosely.

"Did you think you'd lost this?"

"No. I'd assumed that you had it."

Margot tells him how she has searched for him—and how finally, his sister Rosalyn took pity on her and gave her this address. She does not tell him how furious she is with the Hoopeses, and with his criminally negligent cousin Jonathan Mateson, ostensibly the executor of a trust established for his benefit.

She does not tell him that she'd approached his sister Rosalyn not as "Margot Sharpe" but as "Margaret Madden"—"An old classmate of Eli's from Gladwyne Day" as she'd explained to the sister.

In her most persuasive voice she'd told Rosalyn Hoopes that she had encountered Eli a few years ago and he'd remembered her. She'd heard of his hospitalization and felt so sorry for him—"Adrift on his ice floe—'amnesia.' If I could help in any way . . ."

Ingenious!—so Margot gloats.

It must have been a measure of Rosalyn Hoopes's desperation, Margot thinks, and her guilt, that Rosalyn failed to recognize Margot Sharpe—"Professor Sharpe"—though she'd met Professor Sharpe at the Institute some years ago. Of course, a considerable period of time has passed since then: Margot is now unmistakably middle-aged, and has refashioned her hair so that she doesn't much resemble her former self. Brushed off her forehead, and no longer hiding her forehead, Margot's hair is an exquisite silvery-gray, finely threaded with white. She has gotten rid of the exotic braid trailing down the side of her face. And she now wears colors other than black—muted greens, blues, beiges. She has imagined that "Margaret Madden" prefers such colors, and not black. For she is not in mourning, quite yet: Eli Hoopes is living.

Since the abrupt termination of *Project E.H.* Margot has closed the famed memory laboratory at the university. Her notebooks are crammed with material that will require the remainder of her life to be fashioned into *The Biology of Memory: My Life with "E.H."* She will keep only one assistant, the loyal Hai-ku; she will teach just one graduate course, on the biology of memory. She has an endowed chair at the university that assures her a high-paying salary virtually for life (for she intends never to retire) and she has become (to her own bemusement) one of the legendary figures of the renowned Psychology Department—almost as legendary as her mentor Milton Ferris.

And so there is room in her life—there is more than room in her life—for another person, for whom she might care intimately, selflessly.

How bizarre, and yet how understandable—Eli Hoopes's sister had stared into Margot Sharpe's face, and had not seemed to recognize her. Is Margot guilty of deception, and does it matter? Has she behaved unethically, as (some might claim) she'd behaved unethically through her career? She feels not the slightest tinge of guilt. In fact she is quite pleased with herself, for this has been the most ingenious, if unheralded, experiment of her life.

Some of this she will acknowledge in *The Biology of Memory* but most of it she will not. Why should she? Whose business is it except hers? She has come to the conclusion that most of life is a masquerade, especially the sexual life. And what is love but the most powerful of masquerades.

For her visit to Eli Hoopes she is wearing muted pastel colors, her lilac cologne, silver barrettes in her silvery-white hair. And the Celtic wedding band on the third finger of her left hand.

Margot is stricken with alarm and pity for Eli Hoopes, who has suffered unspeakably through eight weeks of chemotherapy. Yet—he might have turned a corner, as it is said . . . Worse cancer-cases have survived, if with a very diminished life, and in a diminished body. She will want to set up an appointment with his oncologist and see his chart. At least, Eli will have forgotten the hours of toxins dripping into his veins; he will have forgotten the shock of the initial diagnosis.

It has been Margot Sharpe's hope, that Eli Hoopes might spend the remaining years—months?—of his life with her.

"If we were married, I could take him to the Adirondacks. It was a terrible mistake for us, not to get married."

Often, Margot speaks aloud. It is to the (invisible, judgmental) executor of the trust established by Lucinda Mateson to whom she pleads most frequently.

Homestead Care is a very modern facility providing assisted-care living, a nursing home, and a hospice. It is a beautiful, weathered-looking stone residence set back in a small park, formerly a convent belonging to the Sisters of the Sacred Heart of Mary, in the affluent Philadelphia suburb White Oaks. Here, Eli Hoopes has a private suite on the second floor and even a small balcony overlooking, at an angle, a pond meant to resemble a woodland pond, that has attracted a noisy contingent of mallards and geese; he shares a wing with individuals suffering from milder mental disabilities—not the most severe cases of dementia, senility, depression. In other wings are schizophrenics and paranoid madmen whose families pay lavishly to hide them away.

The nursing staff at Homestead seems very friendly, welcoming. A visitor to Eli Hoopes on the second floor is (it seems) something of a rarity.

Rosalyn Hoopes had said to Margot, all but stammering with eagerness, "Oh yes—'Margie'—Eli might remember you. His memory is strongest for people and things out of his deep past. If you went to grade school together he'll remember at least something about you and that will be encouraging to him. You would make him very happy, Margie, if you visited him. Yes!" *You would make me very happy* the sister seemed to be pleading.

Margot finds it easy to impersonate Margaret Madden—a kind of sister-self. Almost, Margot thinks she has met "Margie"—she has managed to unearth pictures of the woman as an adult; so far as she could gather Margaret Madden is no longer living. Margot has cultivated a way of smiling with one corner of her mouth, and turning her head toward Eli as if she were just slightly hard of hearing in her left ear; where Margot's voice is a neutral voice, readily adaptable to a lecture hall, Margaret's voice is sweet, sibilant, and soothing.

"We were in grade school together at Gladwyne but not such close friends as we were later—when you were at Amherst, and I was at Bryn Mawr."

"Yes. That is so."

"We went to different high schools. But we never forgot each other, and kept re-meeting . . ."

"Yes . . ."

"Of course—we were young when we first fell in love, and we made mistakes. Regrettable but not irremediable mistakes."

" 'Margaret Madden.' We loved each other—did we? I am so happy that you've come back to me. And you've brought me such beautiful flowers—I remember these, I think."

Eli speaks so sincerely, it is clear that he remembers—something.

Margot will have to ask an attendant to bring a vase for the gardenias which she has let fall onto a table. Their fragrance is so sweet—almost overpowering.

Since entering the hospital room she has felt as if she is entering a sacred space—a dimension of profound happiness. Of all the places in the world Margot Sharpe is in the right place at last.

"When you're feeling stronger, Eli, we will drive to Lake George. You have a key to the house, I hope?"

"Of course! Of course I have a key."

"And is there someone there, at the lake, who oversees your property? I can contact him, when we know more definitely when we will be there."

"Al Laird—Alistair. I think Al is still there, in Bolton Landing."

"You were there not long ago, I think? You were at your family house last July, when you got sick?"

But Eli is frowning now, not so certain. For some reason he squints at his fingers, whose nails are discolored and oddly split.

"Well. I think it might have been longer ago than last July. A few years, maybe. I think it has been."

"But the house is still there at the lake, of course. And we can stay there, and be alone together. Would that make you happy, Eli?"

"Of course—I'm very happy right now. I didn't realize how lonely I was. Are you my dear wife?"

"Yes."

"You will never abandon me, will you? Please?"

Eli speaks so wistfully, Margot comes to him with a little cry. She presses herself into his arms, taking care not to dislodge the IV needle attached to his left arm. She kisses Eli, and he kisses her in turn, eagerly, hungrily.

She slips her hands inside his loose-fitting hospital gown—how gaunt Eli has become, how prominent his ribs, and how scanty the white wiry hairs on his chest. He slips his hands beneath her peach-colored quilted jacket. "My dear wife, my darling"—he murmurs to her, in a transport of happiness.

She will curl up beside him on the hospital bed. It is very strange to her—it is vertiginous—to be lying down here, and so disarmed; how without defense, when we are *lying down*. She tries to recall what Rosalyn told her of Eli's illness—his "condition"—but a kind of buzzing intervenes. He is being treated for metastasized colon cancer—"aggressively." She thinks that that is what she has been told. In Lake George, that might present a problem—arranging for good medical care. Margot might drive Eli to Albany for radiation therapy, if that's prescribed.

Even if Eli is in remission he will have to have periodic examinations by an oncologist—blood work, PET scans. She will find the very best oncologist in Albany and she will pay for his treatment herself—Margot Sharpe has plenty of money.

Margot has noticed that there is no notebook in sight here in Eli's room, and there is no sketchbook. She has no idea what this means. She tells him excitedly of her plans: she intends to curate an exhibit of Elihu Hoopes's pencil and charcoal drawings. She will approach the Philadelphia Museum of Art, whose director will surely be interested—for not only are Eli Hoopes's drawings significant works of art, but the Hoopes family has long been one of the museum's prominent benefactors. There are hundreds—thousands—of these remarkable drawings, which Margot assumes are in storage somewhere. Of these, many are of unusual interest. She has already spoken to his sister Rosalyn who is "very supportive." (This is true though Rosalyn seemed unsure of the exact location of the sketchbooks.) She will begin work as soon as she can. Perhaps she can bring some of the major drawings with them to Lake George where she will write a preface to the exhibit brochure—"The Art of Recollection in Amnesia."

"Yes. As soon as I am feeling a little better. The doctor has told me next week sometime, probably I will be discharged."

"Really!"—Margot knows that this can't be true.

"I will have to have therapy. 'Physical therapy.' "

"Of course. I can drive you to the clinic, if you need transportation."

"*I* can drive. But thank you, dear."

Margot wonders what it means that Eli does not ask her more questions about this exhibit, or about his "thousands of remarkable drawings."

They lie together in Eli's bed, awkwardly but companionably. As Margot talks, Eli sleepily concurs. *Yes, yes!* Margot has never felt so suffused with happiness. There is a faint odor of something acidulous, chemical in poor Eli's breath. In his thin, scant hair. Yet she kisses him, she tells herself she does not mind.

After some time, however, she must disengage herself from her husband, to use a restroom at the end of the corridor. She moves as carefully as she can, not to wake him. She shuts the door when she leaves. And when she returns she is struck anew by the powerful scent of the gardenias—almost, the smell is too strong. It is as if the beautiful white flowers are sucking the oxygen from the room. In Margot's absence Eli has dragged a pillow up behind him and taken up the newspaper again, and the pencil, and is squinting at the crossword puzzle which is only half-completed. This is a good sign, is it?—Eli is restless enough to be doing the puzzle, and not sleep? Except the lighting is poor, why doesn't he simply turn on an overhead light? There is a switch beside his bed which he surely knows how to use.

As Margot approaches the bed Eli glances up at her in surprise and bewilderment—no doubt he expected one of the nursing staff since he can see that this is a hospital setting. What is painfully clear is that he has never seen Margot Sharpe before in his life.

Eli lowers the newspaper and tosses the pencil aside. At once his expression is eager, hopeful. His bloodshot eyes seem to lighten. It is the identical expression (Margot is certain) she saw in his face on the first morning they met long ago in 1965.

If the amnesiac notices that his visitor—(a slender, attractive silver-haired woman with a pale, lined face, alarmed eyes)—is crying he is too gentlemanly to acknowledge what he sees.

"Hello? Hel-*lo?*"

ACKNOWLEDGMENTS

Among the numerous valuable books and articles which have been useful in the preparation of this novel the most significant is Suzanne Corkin's *Permanent Present Tense: The Unforgettable Life of the Amnesiac Patient, H.M.* (2013). Also consulted were materials by Brenda Milner, Larry Squire, and Nicholas Turk-Browne.

Thanks also to Clare Tascio for reading this manuscript with particular thoroughness as Hertog Research Fellow at Hunter College, and thanks as well to Greg Johnson for his continued and cherished friendship, sharp eye and ear, and impeccable literary judgment.

And I am grateful as always to my "first reader"—my neuroscientist-husband Charlie Gross—whose close scrutiny of this novel from start to finish, and whose enthusiasm, support, and sympathy throughout, have been inestimable.